# THE PRIESTESS AND THE DRAGON

## DRAGON SAGA 1

## NICOLETTE ANDREWS

MAGPIE PUBLISHING

*This one goes to my Wattpad readers. Your love for this story has kept me going despite long delays between updates and my love of cliffhangers. Thank you, darlings.*

# 1

-----------

$S$ weat rolled down her neck, slid down her spine and pooled at the basin of her lower back. Suzume resisted the urge to itch a tickle near her nose, lest she smear the white paint that adorned her face. The high priestess chanted in a sonorous voice and the procession moved forward a half step. Suzume sighed and lowered her head. The bells hanging from the decorative pins in her hair jingled as she did so. The second to the high priestess whipped her head around, somehow hearing the insignificant sound beneath the high priestess' chanting. The second glared at Suzume, who returned the look with a half-smile and a tilt of her head, which jangled the bells further. The pinging sound felt like a declaration. *I did not choose this life and I will not obey your rules.*

The second pursed her lips as she glared at Suzume. She would not dare interrupt the ceremony to chastise Suzume. But if looks could kill, Suzume would be dead three times over. She would most likely get a tongue-lashing when they were alone again. If she had learned anything since coming to the temple, it was that the Maidens of the Mountain took their ceremonies seriously.

The procession moved forward another half step and the second turned back to the head priestess. Suzume sighed as she inched towards the temple. What she wouldn't give to rip this constricting robe and sash off. *I would trade all my father's—no, the emperor, as I must now call him—I would give up all his gold and the power of the Eight to be free of this robe!*

True, she was no stranger to fine garments. Indeed, she had often donned fine silks, she had been served by ladies from the noblest families and had men fall in love with her at least once a week. That was until her mother had ruined everything. You couldn't tell from the bitter chill rolling off the mountain peaks, but at the White Palace, the cherry blossoms would be blooming. She should be viewing the cherry blossoms with General Tsubaki, her onetime intended, and having courtiers slipping her poetic love notes. *He was the perfect match, powerful and old enough not to notice when I flirted with the younger lords.* She sighed again.

The second spun around, breaking rank, and said with a hiss, "Silence."

The young priestesses that were in three lines behind her giggled. The second glowered past Suzume towards them and the giggling died away, leaving only the sound of the high priestess, who continued to chant without breaking stride. When the second turned around, Suzume rolled her eyes. The procession moved another half step.

Suzume's thoughts returned to her own lamentable fate. When she had imagined her wedding day, it was not like this. Instead of marrying General Tsubaki as was her right and his honor, she was to become an unwilling bride of the mountain god. Which was a romanticized way of saying she had been exiled to a life of a priestess. As the emperor's trueborn daughter, she was born of divinity and as such she could not be simply married off. Her father insisted on adding insult to injury.

They approached a group of red torii arches. Before she passed beneath the first one, the wind picked up and jangled the bells in her hair, pushing against her as if trying to keep her from entering. She hesitated for a moment. She felt a tingle along her fingertips, a slight burn as if they had come too close to a flame. The second saw her dawdling and jerked her head to the side, indicating she should cross the barrier. *It's just a gateway.* She crossed the threshold, and as she did, a prickling sensation ran up and down her arms. She pressed against an invisible barrier, as if the archway wanted to keep her back. She stumbled through and nearly lost her balance. She overcorrected and heard the priestesses behind her laughing, thinking she had lost her balance.

When she looked to them to see if they experienced the same phenomenon, they passed through without resistance. At least the wind had dried the sweat that was surely streaking the white paint on her neck. She chanced a glance to her side; beyond the red columns of the arch the pathway had a sheer drop. And in the distance she could see the mountain range shrouded in clouds. The pathway leading up to the shrine was carved from the mountain, one side a flat mountain face with a few sporadic plants growing in the cracks. The shrine was wedged into a cave; four columns supported the front facade, and beyond the veranda, the latticework doors had been pulled open. She had come a long way from the White Palace to this desolate mountain temple. Suzume suppressed another sigh, lest the second's scowl grow deeper. *Let's get this over with*, she thought.

After what felt like hours, but was closer to a few minutes, they passed beneath the last of the red arches and the house of the God of the Mountain lay before them. The wood on the front had been carved with a scene depicting the mountain range. Above the mountains, the god sat upon a cloud, and with an outstretched hand he brought rain to the needy farmers down at the bottom.

The high priestess stopped the procession. She finished her chant with one last echoing note that bounced off the surrounding mountains, and the following silence was more defined. The wind howled ominously. Suzume's skin itched and burned. She fought the urge to rub her palms against her flesh to assuage her affliction; she wanted to maintain at least the illusion

3

of respectability. The head priestess and all the other shrine maidens bowed in unison. Suzume, distracted by her fevered skin, did not follow but instead stared into the inner sanctum of the god. A pedestal was the room's only adornment and upon the white pillow was an obsidian stone.

"Bow, you ungrateful girl," the high priestess scolded.

Suzume did so with reluctance. Her skin trembled and twitched like a horse trying to shake off a fly. She could not remove her eyes from the stone. It seemed familiar, as if she had seen it before. As she knelt, she lost sight of it. She lowered her head in feigned obedience. However, a sensation began to stir in her gut; she felt like she might retch. *I cannot do that, not now, not here.* She glanced up once more, trying to regain control of her body.

The high priestess approached the shrine while swinging a brass bowl attached to four chains, with a stick of incense in it. The white smoke swirled around her and trailed after her as she approached the pedestal.

The high priestess lit a few incense sticks that were in holders on either side of the pedestal. She knelt down with her head bowed low to the ground as the room filled with the pungent smoke. The smoke tickled Suzume's nose. She wiggled it back and forth, the churning feeling in her gut creeping up to the back of her throat. It felt as if there were an inferno burning inside her.

"God of the Mountain, bringer of the rain, great master who parted the lands from the sea, please accept this bride as yours." She clapped her hands together, finishing the prayer. She rose up onto the balls of her feet and turned to face the group without rising from a kneeling position. She motioned for Suzume to come forward.

She rose on shaking limbs. Only her mere stubbornness kept her moving. As she crossed the threshold, a sensation like a punch to the gut stopped her in her tracks. Whatever was inside her was coming out, now. She stopped, afraid to move for fear her very

4

skin would melt from her bones if she went too near. *Is this a part of the ceremony? If so, I refuse to be a part of it.*

The high priestess frowned and once more beckoned for her to come forward with a sharp impatient movement.

Suzume shook her head and set the bells jangling. They echoed across the room and seemed to reverberate tenfold, rattling around inside her skull.

"You cannot turn back now, you will anger the god," the second snarled, now standing beside her with a rough grip of Suzume's elbow.

The second forced Suzume forward; then Suzume's knees buckled beneath her. Her stomach heaved and she feared she would empty its contents in front of everyone. She grabbed her abdomen in a last effort to hold back, but something bubbled up from inside her, the burning receded from her arms and pooled in her stomach before traveling up and out of her mouth. Bright red light burst from her lips and shot out like a current that sparked and undulated as it made a direct trajectory for the pedestal and collided with the obsidian stone.

For a moment the stone vibrated, and then it began to rock back and forth on its stand. Finally it rolled and began to ricochet around the pedestal, colliding with the raised edges of the stand. Then the pedestal exploded in a shower of splintered wood. The force of the explosion threw the high priestess backwards. Suzume fell to the ground just in time to avoid a deadly piece of wood from piercing her heart.

Fragments of wood rained down on her as she covered her head with her hands. When the raining debris ceased, she looked up again. Smoke filled the chamber—she could not tell if it was just the incense or from whatever had caused the explosion. The burning sensation had left her body, but Suzume felt a new tingling warm sensation that flooded her skin like a warning bell. She could not get up, however; it felt as if an invisible hand held her down, nearly forcing the air from her body.

"High Priestess!" the second shouted somewhere in the smoke and debris. The other maidens were chattering in fear.

"I am here, and unharmed," the high priestess said. The smoke cleared and revealed her to be lying on the ground. She sat up and bits of wood fell off of her. She looked at Suzume, her eyes wide. "What did you do?" she asked.

Before Suzume had even the chance to answer, a hollow maniacal laughter filtered through the chamber. The head priestess' mouth dropped open as she turned her head back to where the pedestal had been. The smoke rolled away and a coiled serpentine body covered in opalescent scales dominated the room. The creature's muzzled face looked down upon Suzume, his long whiskers brushing against the bells on her hair pieces.

"God of the Mountain and bringer of the rain, I presume?" Suzume asked.

The creature smirked, revealing rows of dagger-sharp teeth. "You awoke me?" His voice echoed and filled the room with thunder.

Had she been a cautious woman, she would have listened to the underlying threat in the creature's stature and his words. But Suzume prided herself on the fact that she did not cower before anyone, even the God of the Mountain.

"And if I did?" she asked.

The beast exhaled; his breath, as cold as winter, froze her skin until that warm tingling sensation defrosted her.

"God of the Mountain," the high priestess gasped.

He turned his large head towards her and looked her up and down and said, "Your voice has been in my dreams."

Tears gathered in the old woman's eyes. "Thank you, lord, it is a great honor. I always hoped you heard my fervent prayers. I have dedicated my life to your service. Please tell us, why now have you—"

"Silence, you speak too much, human. I did not awaken to hear your prattling. You should stick to your prayers and songs, they are much easier upon the ears." He growled and the high priestess fell onto her knees and laid her face to the ground.

"My apologies—" she started to say, but he growled and she silenced herself.

The god turned back to Suzume. "I can sense little spiritual power in you, yet you have undone the seal," he said while regarding Suzume. He tilted his head to the side. The shrine maidens and high priestess had moved out of the way of the god's coiling body and were huddled outside the shrine.

She looked at them and back at the god. How had she unleashed him? As far as she could tell, it had been an accident, an involuntary action. Regardless of the how, she did not want to admit her ignorance in front of the other shrine maidens.

"It was simple, the seal was weak," Suzume lied.

He tilted his head and barked a thundering laugh that shook the building down to its foundation. He took a few steps back and then with a puff of smoke transformed. When the smoke cleared, a young man stood in his place. A naked young man. His sleek black hair hung loose about his shoulders in an almost obscene way.

Suzume admired his lean physique and let her eyes trace his body downward. Before she could get too far, however, the high priestess forced Suzume's head down so she could not admire the god's other masculine assets. Suzume sighed; if this is how she was expected to act for the rest of her life, then she was not going to like living here at all.

The god approached her and loomed over her. "You are my newest servant?"

She bristled at the servant distinction and was preparing to correct his misconception when the high priestess chose that moment to interrupt.

"She is your newest tribute, my lord, your pure bride."

He raked Suzume up and down and she met his gaze with an

out-jutted chin and only took a quick peek at his manhood. *Not bad,* she thought. He laughed again.

"I don't know how pure she is."

Suzume glared at him. How dare he insinuate she was anything but chaste! She had been attempting to get a sneak peek at his godly assets but nothing more than that. It didn't make her impure to be curious.

"My lord!" the priestess proclaimed. He turned to her and looked her up and down.

"You keep calling me that, but I am not your mountain god. I am a dragon, and before I was trapped inside that stone, I ruled this realm. And you"—he knelt before Suzume. Now she did avert her gaze; she did not need to be that familiar with his manhood —"shall help me exact my revenge."

## 2

---

The Dragon sat legs crossed, his posture erect and regal as he gazed down upon the shrine maidens. Though it was hard to believe, he was even more magnificent in the robes that had been procured for him. The head priestess bowed low before him; the tip of her nose brushed against the tatami mats. The Dragon regarded her as she blushed like a young virgin.

"I am thirsty. Bring me sake," he said.

The head priestess trembled like a leaf in the wind. "Yes, right away." She turned her head just enough to order the nearest shrine maiden to do the Dragon's bidding. "You heard the lord Dragon, get him some sake."

Two girls jumped up and tripped over the hems of their hakama pants in a rush to do the Dragon's bidding. Suzume laughed behind her hand. The head priestess and her second heard and shot daggers at her with their eyes. *They are jealous of my new position.*

The Dragon kept her close at his side, like a pet lapdog. She had only been out of his sight long enough for him to dress—at the head priestess' adamant behest—and now she sat beside him like the bride at a bizarre marital feast. In fact, she had not even been given the time to change and she still wore the ceremonial white robes, though now they were dusty and her makeup was smeared. Her skin continued to itch and it was taking all of her self-control to keep from scratching. At least her stomach no longer felt like it was in revolt.

The shrine maidens returned with the sake. One with a look of triumph on her face, the other's eyes downcast, making no attempt to hide her displeasure at being beat to the honor. *They do not even care that he is a charlatan. Are they so desperate to serve?* The girl handed the clay jar to the head priestess with trembling hands. The liquid inside sloshed back and forth.

The high priestess approached the Dragon with the bottom of the jug on the flat of her palm and the neck held in her other hand as if she were presenting him a sacred offering and said, "My lord, we have brought you what you requested."

"Ah, good." The Dragon snatched it from her without ceremony.

The high priestess bowed and scuttled backwards from the dais on which Suzume and the Dragon sat. *At least I am back in my proper place,* Suzume thought. She disregarded the fact that her current elevation in status was in part based on a lie. She did not know how she broke the seal or how she could help the Dragon with his revenge. However, she had to keep up the facade or else risk losing what little reputation she had managed thus far.

He brought the jug to his lips and took a long draught of the rice wine. Suzume sat mesmerized by the bobbing of his throat as he drank. A rivulet of milky liquid rolled down his chin and along his throat. He set the jar aside and then smacked his lips.

Suzume crinkled her nose, a charlatan and crude, *delightful.*

He leaned back and rested on his arm and regarded the two shrine maidens before him.

"Now tell me, when was this temple built?"

The high priestess replied to the reed mats and did not move from her deep bow as she replied, "My lord, in the year one hundred and three of the Taiyō reign."

He picked up the jug and swirled the contents. He furrowed his brow as he looked at the high priestess. She could see him coming to the same conclusion as her. She was not one for arithmetic, but that had been roughly five hundred years. He had been trapped inside that stone for that long. Nothing changed in his expression, but that same pressure she had felt in the shrine weighed on her chest, making it difficult to breathe.

Perhaps the high priestess felt it as well, because she gasped. "Forgive us, my lord, we did not know it was you who slumbered inside the holy object."

"There is no need to grovel, Chiyoko. I may not be your god of the mountain, but your songs eased my long slumber. Please rise and share my sake wine with me." He held out his hand to her, beckoning her towards him with the crook of his finger.

The head priestess raised her head and tears brimmed on her lashes. "My lord, I am not worthy." She placed her hands flat on the ground in front of her, nearly flattening herself on the floor.

Suzume sighed and rolled her eyes. It was all too dramatic. She reached for the sake. If they were going to continue to carry on in this manner, she too was going to need a drink. As she reached for the jug, the second's hand darted out and knocked Suzume's aside. They spilled the sake, which soaked into the tatami flooring. The air stank of alcohol. Suzume raised her own hand to slap the second for daring to strike her.

"You idiot girl, that was for the lord Dragon." The second glared at her. She had few wrinkles, despite being middle aged, but for the hard lines around her mouth as if she spent her entire life frowning.

Suzume lowered her arm, remembering her place once again. Suzume glared at the second and rubbed her hand. *You will pay for this, believe me. The Dragon has chosen me and I will see you punished.*

From the corner of her eye, Suzume noticed the Dragon

watching her. That same tingling sensation zinged over her skin. It was not painful, more like the sensation of a limb falling asleep, but her entire body felt that way, but also poised alert and focused on every move the Dragon made.

He turned back to the second. "You are Zakuro, I believe. What gives you the right to hit my bride?"

The second's head popped up, her eyes wide and terrified. She opened and closed her mouth, fumbling with a reply.

The Dragon reached over and grabbed Suzume by the nape of her neck and squeezed. Sparks bristled along her skin where he touched, but she was too busy gloating over the second to really notice. Suzume smirked at the second. *He has chosen me as his bride, and to think I could have settled for a general. Now I am the bride of a dragon!* Even if he was a fake, it still put her in a most advantageous position. It made her superior to these women. She was on her way back to where she had been before she was exiled. *I may be even better placed. I do not know anyone who married a dragon.* She could not keep the grin from her face. *I cannot wait to see the courtiers' looks when I return with him.*

"My lord," Zakuro said, having found her voice, "she is not in actuality your bride but a servant of the mountain god, and at your own admission, you are not him."

He smiled at Zakuro and tightened his grip upon Suzume's nape. Suzume gasped in pain. His touch felt like ice, and her body seemed to respond to it by burning; the sparks from before had been fanned into flames. The Dragon did not seem to notice. "Well, that is a shame since there is no mountain god. There never was."

The shrine maidens gasped and then nervous whispers filled the room.

"How can you say that when our sisterhood has protected this place for generations? Just because you were sealed in the holy object does not mean the mountain god does not exist!" Zakuro shouted. She rose up to her feet and pointed at the Dragon.

He released Suzume and she rubbed her neck where his nails had left half-moon indents on her pale skin. The Dragon leaned forward, his elbows resting on his knees, as his narrowed eyes focused on Zakuro. Suzume wanted to triumph over her mistake, but the pressure she'd felt before was building, closing her windpipe. She clutched at her chest; when she looked down at her hands, red sparks flew off her skin. *What is happening to me?*

"Because this is my mountain and my realm. I have been here since before you humans had the ability of speech. I have watched you crawl out of holes in the ground, build palaces and kill one another. I am the lord of this island!" When he spoke, thunder seemed to roll from his throat and a menacing aura hung about him. The shrine maidens recoiled and scurried to the back of the room, huddling together. One of the younger girls cried out.

Only the high priestess, Zakuro, and Suzume did not flinch. Suzume focused on breathing. This pressure was immense and she could only guess it came from the Dragon, and when he was not pleased, she felt it. The high priestess had her eyes closed as she muttered under her breath. Zakuro stood very still, staring at the Dragon as if in a trance.

After a few tense moments, she bowed her head. "Forgive me, my lord."

He sat back, seemingly appeased. The pressure receded and Suzume gasped for breath. He did not so much as flicker his gaze in her direction. The head priestess opened her eyes once more. Now Suzume was sure she could sense the Dragon's feelings as Suzume did, but she seemed to have more control than Suzume.

"Shall we entertain you, my lord?" the high priestess asked.

"Yes, that would please me. And bring more sake."

Three girls jumped to fetch more sake and another came to sit before Suzume and the Dragon. She was young and pretty, with eyes lowered demurely. "I would sing if it pleases, my lord Dragon," she said.

"It would," he replied. The Dragon smiled in a way Suzume

knew all too well. She glared at the young woman, who wanted to take Suzume's place.

The young priestess started to sing. The Dragon watched her, enthralled.

Suzume leaned close to his ear. "My lord, you are very powerful. I am surprised you were trapped for so long."

He turned towards her and storm clouds seemed to be gathering in his eyes. Suzume swore she saw lightning flash in his dark pupils. "Yes, as am I." His words sent a chill down her spine.

She had to keep his attention. She knew men—the moment the next pretty young thing fluttered their way, they were lost. She would not lose this opportunity.

"How did it happen?"

He had turned to face her entirely now and she had to fight a smile. She knew asking about his past would flatter him.

"A priestess tricked me."

She laughed; she thought it had been a joke. But the storm clouds gathering in his eyes turned them an icy blue. She had made a terrible mistake, but she had also gone too far now to back down and asked with an arched brow, "You were sealed by a mere human?"

The Dragon smiled and rested his elbow on his knee and regarded her. "You are testing my patience. Perhaps my bride has tired of her ceremonial feast and wishes to make our union an official one? Though I must warn you, dragons often kill their lovers in the heat of passion. The sensation and the taste of a woman has been known to drive them to madness."

*How dare he say such things to me and without any remorse!* A burning blush branded her neck and cheeks. She was fortunate the shrine maiden's singing drowned out their conversation. She hoped the white face paint was disguising her discomfort. No matter how he tried, she would not be cowed by this dragon. "Perhaps we should tempt the fates and see if it is true," Suzume replied.

He laughed a barking laugh and the moment was finished. Suzume thanked her quick tongue for saving her. Now his attention had returned to Zakuro and the high priestess as a shrine maiden brought him a new jug of sake.

"The woman who began your order, what was her name?" he asked

"The oldest recorded high priestess is Fujikawa Kazue, my lord," High Priestess Chiyoko replied.

The clay pot shattered in his hand and the shards fell onto the woven mats and the sake dribbled down over his fingers. A thin line of blood mixed with the milky liquid and pooled on the ground and stained the mats.

"Is that the woman, my lord, the one who defeated the Dragon and imprisoned him in a tiny stone?" Suzume asked and the silence that followed was deafening. She thought they had come to an understanding, a playful jesting, being equals. She could not have been more wrong. She could hear her blood pumping in her ears. The tingling sensation was back and it shouted a warning—run! Then the Dragon turned on Suzume. He pushed her back against the tatami mats and pressed his forearm to her throat.

"Do not pretend to know me, girl. You are my servant, and if I want your opinion or thoughts, I will ask for them. Is that understood?" His voice echoed in the chamber and the walls shook with the force of his anger.

Suzume wiggled beneath his grasp and struggled for air. The red sparks jumped off her skin, colliding with blue sparks that came off his flesh. She had pretended not to be afraid of him before, but now she did not give any such pretense.

"I am keeping you alive because you amuse me, but if you overstep your bounds again, I will not hesitate to kill you."

He eased off her windpipe and she rubbed her throat, glowering at him as he rose to his feet. Her skin was warm to the touch and all the hair along her arm stood on end.

"I wish to spend time in solitude," he announced before he strode out of the room.

Once he was gone, the high priestess and the second turned on Suzume.

"You idiot girl!" the high priestess shouted. "How dare you speak to our lord in such a way."

"You are fortunate he did not kill you," Zakuro added, though Suzume suspected it would not be a loss to her if she had perished.

"You would be glad to be rid of me, I am sure. You may think the cast-off daughter does not make for an ideal priestess, but you cannot deny the truth, I was the one to awaken the Dragon! I broke the seal and I have been here less than a fortnight while you have toiled and devoted your lives to a god that does not exist. I exposed the truth and it is me he has chosen as his bride." She lifted her chin in a show of regal superiority and then glided out of the room. The other shrine maidens watched her go, their expressions ranging from disgust to something akin to awe.

*Good,* she thought, *let them realize who I am. My father may have set me aside, but that does not change the fact that I am a princess, and as such I am better than them. It only makes sense that my spiritual powers would awaken the Dragon.*

Suzume closed the sliding door behind her and hurried down the hallway. Her mind raced. No matter how she tried to explain it, she could not convince herself. Never in her seventeen years of life had she ever shown the slightest indication of spiritual power. If she had, she would have been sent to the White Palace shrine to learn the ways of the royal priestesses. She might have one day been equal to that of the emperor. She would not have been sent to this remote temple, set aside to be forgotten.

A hand darted out from the darkness and grabbed Suzume by the wrist. She twirled in place and attempted to break free but could not. She was pulled forward and collided with a firm chest. He held her arms at her sides and breathed across her neck, and the small hairs at her nape stood on end along with the all too familiar crackle of energy that seemed to come along with being near him.

"Come to my chamber, my bride. It is our wedding night, after all."

# 3

The Dragon's hands burned Suzume's flesh and sparks erupted wherever his fingers brushed exposed skin. She was immobile, transfixed by his touch and the breath that caressed her skin. His lips brushed against the sensitive space behind her ear and his hands captured her wrists and pulled back her sleeves, revealing her forearms. Her heart beat faster. Despite what he may think, she was a virgin. Her father, the emperor, would have done more than banish her if her purity were not intact. Her value lay in her chastity. Though she was known to be flirtatious, she knew her place and what that entailed. Illicit affairs were not permitted.

*Does it matter now? I will never be a real bride. My father annulled the marriage contract to General Tsubaki.* Deep down, she had hoped she would one day return to the White Palace. Perhaps that had been naive of her to think that.

The Dragon pulled Suzume into a chamber. The sliding doors at the back faced out onto the mountain range, which glowed blue beneath the night sky. The Dragon trailed his hand along her hair and set the charms on the pins to jingling. Then, with a fluid movement, he withdrew the pins and her hair tumbled down and cascaded over her shoulders.

He turned her to face him. She felt exposed with her hair in a jumble and her makeup smeared. Before coming here, she would never have let someone see her this way. Her meetings with General Tsubaki had always been through a screen, and when her admirers had come at late hours, there was a fan covering her face. Where she rejected almost all other conventions, she liked that. It was a shield and a way to keep others from seeing the real her. That's how she preferred things. This Dragon had stripped her bare of all her masks in just a few simple movements.

He cupped her cheek and leaned in close. His lips ghosted over hers but did not touch them. She inhaled his breath and closed her eyes, waiting for the tender touch. She felt at once desire and fear for what could transpire here. The burning fire built in her gut, radiating to all her limbs. *I am his bride; did he not declare me so? This is an even more fortunate placement. I am above the emperor himself, as the bride of a dragon!* Her body betrayed her and she trembled beneath his touch.

He pulled away and she felt the loss of him and mourned it. She slowly opened her eyes and looked into the deep depths of his inhuman eyes, brown but ringed with blue. He hosted a crooked smile on his face.

"How did you release me?" he whispered.

His voice was coaxing, and lulled by his touch and the burning desire in her gut, she found her usual quick wit muddled and slow. She opened her mouth and words escaped her. She swallowed and then tried to coerce her dry tongue into working. "As I said before, the seal was weak. I sensed that and released you."

He tilted his head and his smile grew wider. "Then I owe you a debt of thanks, let me." His hand brushed along her collar and her trembles became shivers. The cold from his touch brushed against her skin, and if any frost thought to linger, the fever of her skin melted it. His hand slid along her collar and moved down to her chest, pushing aside the heavy fabric of her white kimono. She was short of breath and every inch of her trained on him, wondering what he would do next.

He pulled her close and snaked his hand around to her back. He pulled on the cords around her sash, which kept it in place. It pulled loose easily and with it the sash underneath came undone. She felt as if she too were losing control, unraveling as he pulled off each layer, a bit of her reservation sliding away with it. He undid the layers of sash that had belted her into the robe. They fell to the ground and pooled there. If his hand had not been on her waist, she would have joined them. Her knees felt like water.

He turned her around and unwound the outer layers of the robe. Her entire body was made of flame at this point; she was surprised she did not burn him to cinders, she felt so hot and malleable. Her heart beat erratically in her chest. He could do anything he wanted with her as far as she was concerned. It was the anticipation that was killing her.

His gazed burned upon her and she felt the need to disrupt the silence. "What you said before about killing lovers, you were teasing, were you not?" She hated how afraid and weak she sounded.

He stopped pulling off her layers of robes and turned her to face him. He cupped her hands in his face.

"I am serious, my bride, but since you have strong spiritual power, you will be able to shield yourself, so it does not matter."

Suzume's eyes grew wide. *Does he suspect? How could he? There's no way he could know.* The Dragon slid the second to last layer off her, leaving her in only a thin underlayer. A breeze from the open doors blew through her and she hugged her arms close to her body, afraid to let him near. She was cold suddenly; the fire had ebbed and the foggy intoxicated feeling had sharpened into suspicion. *What is wrong with me, I never let myself get carried away like this before.* When he leaned in to kiss her, she turned her head away, in case his kiss too could be deadly.

"Why so shy, my bride? This is our wedding night. Are you not meant to give yourself to me?" He grabbed her chin and forced her to look him in the eyes. Once more he had that infernal smirk. *He does know! He is testing me!* She would not let this go further, not if she were to keep her purity. Now that the haze of desire faded, she could see clearly. The Dragon thought to play a trick on her, take her purity, play with her as he will. Whatever it was, two could play at this game.

"I was thinking about what Zakuro said." She lowered her lashes in a perfect imitation of a demure woman. It had always been a favorite of General Tsubaki. Playing the shy maiden had practically won her the marriage contract. *Men love a weak woman.*

"Forget what that hag said," he replied. "You gave yourself to me with a pure heart and freed me from my prison; you are my bride."

He pulled her close again, but Suzume pushed him away and ran towards the open doors overlooking the valley below. This was also a long-practiced tactic. The chase had always stirred the general's desires while giving her the space to keep him at bay, and malleable as clay in her hands.

The wind that came blowing off the mountains had a bite to it. Wearing nothing more than a thin underlayer, her flesh prickled or maybe that was his touch on her shoulders that caused that. She never knew someone's hands could be so cold.

She ignored him for a moment, staring at the mountains. The clouds had rolled back and the snowcapped peaks looked iridescent under the full moon. She turned to the side, letting moonlight fall on her skin, lending it the same ethereal glow. Manipulating natural lighting to her advantage had become an art form at the White Palace.

"This is all so quick." She covered her mouth with her hands as if she was stifling a cry. She lowered her hand. "And I am afraid." Her voice wobbled as she spoke.

He squeezed her shoulder. "That is fine."

She pulled away from him, taking a few steps to the edge of

the veranda. She kept her head turned away to hide her smile. "I'm glad you understand," she said.

"The fear only makes it that much more exciting."

Suzume spun to face him in surprise, and as she did, he grabbed her hard and held her against his chest. She thrashed about, wriggling away enough to beat his chest with her fists.

"Let me go this instant!" she shouted.

He laughed that same mad laughter and a chill worked its way up her spine. She tried to summon the power she had felt in the shrine. Even the sparks of energy did not seem to deter him. She scrunched her face and tightened her muscles and balled her hands into fists in an effort to summon that same power that had broken him free. *If I can release him, perhaps I can seal him.*

His laughter turned from maniacal to amused as he pushed her away. She fell to the ground. She braced herself with her palms and glared up at him past the curtain of her dark hair, which had fallen forward.

"You look like a fool. Stop before you hurt yourself," he said.

Suzume glowered at him and kept her hands bunched at her sides. "Do not play with me, Dragon, or I will send you back from whence you came!" She pointed a finger at him.

"You must be a fool to think you can trick me." He placed his hands on his hips and regarded her with his head tilted to the side, just as he had in the shrine.

"You knew! Then what was the need of this?" She motioned to the discarded robes strewn about the room.

"I told you before, you entertain me. I wanted to see how far you would let the game go. I must admit I have never met a woman who could withstand my charm quite as well as you."

*How dare he threaten my purity in such a way!* "I suppose you consider that a compliment," Suzume said as she sat up and straightened her robe to conceal her exposed flesh. He stared at her collar and she decided she did not care what he saw. *Never let them see your true feelings.* That's what her mother always said. He might think he had the upper hand, but he was mistaken if he thought she was beaten. She sat up straighter, taking on a regal pose.

"It is what it is; you may interpret it however you like, Priestess." He smirked again and settled on the floor across from her. "Now tell me truly, how did you break the seal?"

She lifted her chin in a haughty dismissal.

"I am not adverse to eating you, though I am sure you will be dry and foul tasting."

"You're joking." Suzume raised a brow at him, but her heart beat faster in her chest. She had no doubt he would, given half the chance. She would need to be more careful in the future.

"You're right, I am sure you'd be delicious." He licked his lips. Her stomach flip-flopped and the tingling sensation danced across her skin. She refused to look away, however. Doing so would admit defeat, and that was not an option.

Pressure built behind her eyes and a heavy weight burdened her breathing. She locked gazes with the Dragon. Her breaths were short and painful as if with each breath she was taking water into her lungs. Sparks ignited along her skin; the slow burn she had felt in the temple returned and it coiled in her stomach and began radiating to her limbs.

Then it stopped. Like water being poured from a jar, the river of energy halted as if the jar was righted once again. As the pressure ebbed away, Suzume's breathing was freed and she panted to regain a regular rhythm once more.

"Interesting," he said. He stood up and paced around her in circles. "When you are sitting here, I cannot sense any spiritual energy about you. Yet, when I lower my own barriers and release my spiritual energy, your body goes into the defensive."

"Are you saying my power is only awakened when threatened?" *Is that what that feeling was?* It made sense that she only felt it when she was around him, he seemed to be a constant threat to her life. *Why have I never felt this before?*

"Possibly, it does not explain why you would have broken the seal. Tell me what happened at the shrine." He continued to pace about with his hands folded behind his back.

Suzume pondered the incident a moment before replying. She had no reason to answer his questions other than to sate her own desire to understand why these powers had manifested now. "We were in the middle of the ceremony and I walked into the temple. I felt like a wave came over me and was pressing the air from my body, and then a burning feeling built into my gut and in my limbs, and eventually it just came out and went straight towards the holy object."

He paced away from her and stood in the doorway. He looked out across the valley. The stars were out and they blanketed the blue-black sky, adding twinkling light. He stood very still, like a statue. From her vantage point she could see nothing but the twinkling of the night sky beyond him and he appeared to be a bird about to take flight and never return.

After several minutes of pensive silence Suzume said, "Do you know what happened to me? How did I break the seal?"

He turned around and regarded her as if just noticing her for the first time. "You are still here, then? You should return to your chamber; a young woman like yourself should not be out sneaking into a man's room."

She jumped to her feet. He acted as if their conversation had never happened. "You dragged me in here!"

He waved at her over his shoulder, dismissing her once more. She thought of several curses she would like to fling at him but decided she valued her life too much to risk awakening the darker side of his personality. Instead, she stormed out, slamming the sliding door after her.

When she was alone in her bedchamber once more, she found that sleep eluded her and she wondered what had caused this sudden awakening of her spiritual powers. Could it be as he suspected: a defense mechanism? Living in the White Palace, she had not had much opportunity to get into trouble. She was always surrounded by guards and ladies and lords of the court.

She sighed and rolled over. It was best not to think of what she had lost. Perhaps tomorrow would be a better day. She could only hope.

# 4

"I heard the Dragon took her to his chamber last night."

Suzume pushed herself up on one arm and scowled at the offending sound of twittering voices. She was no stranger to gossip, it was common fare at the White Palace. Gossip was a way to pass the time and it was also a way to control those around you. She was curious to hear what these shrine maidens thought of her.

A second girl gasped. "She must realize that she is not *really* his bride. It is just a title!"

"She's from the palace. Maybe they don't understand northern customs?" the first woman asked.

"I am shocked she would give her virtue so lightly."

"The way I heard it, she's had countless lovers. I don't think there was any virtue that remained for her to lose."

Suzume had enough. They were nothing but a couple of prattling idiots. She stood up and poked her head through the open window that looked unto a garden where the two women were conversing. They spotted her as she rested her head on her upturned palms, her elbows resting on the windowsill.

"I've had one thousand lovers. One for each night of the week, and they would shower me with treasures from countries you can only imagine, the finest silks, and poems were often written comparing my beauty to the changing of the seasons. That was until a warrior stole my heart and I forsook all other lovers for him. My father, the emperor, however, had already chosen for me one of his best generals: General Tsubaki. When the general learned about my lover, he challenged him to a death match. They fought and lost their lives to win my love. That is why the emperor banished me here, because his favorite general died." She smirked.

The two women cowered and lowered their gazes to the ground. The girl on the right wrung her hands together and the girl to the left fidgeted as she stole glances at her companion. *They're brave when they are talking behind my back. They would not last two minutes at the palace.*

"What, nothing more to say? I thought that would make for much better gossip than what you were saying."

"We did not mean any offense," the girl on the left said.

"Oh? I suppose I sound favorable having spread my legs for hundreds of men rather than thousands and being foolish enough to believe a dragon would be my husband?"

"No, that is to say..." The girl on the right raised her head to try to defend herself, but Suzume's glare had her staring back at her feet the moment she made eye contact.

"Get out of my sight before I call down the Dragon's wrath upon you," Suzume said. She sliced the air with the hand, miming what she would have the Dragon do to them. They both scattered like maple leaves in the wind.

Suzume slid down from the window and sighed. She gathered her knees up to her chest and stared at the blank wall across from her. She was used to gossip. She had grown up surrounded by it, but somehow Suzume had hoped this far from the White Palace, her reputation would not have preceded her. It seemed her mother's legacy was stronger than she expected. *It doesn't matter. I don't care what they think.*

Suzume got up and dressed in her everyday clothes: a pair of crimson hakama pants, a white haori tucked into them and cinched at the waist. The long billowing sleeves got in her way as she tied her hair back in a low tail with white ribbon. Learning to dress herself had been a challenge, she had always had lady's maids to do these things. And the clothes itched and rubbed against her skin, which was used to silk. There was no looking glass; such a luxury item would not be found here. She imagined she looked as every other priestess at the shrine did, dull. A part of her had hoped when the Dragon had claimed her that she would not have to go about her menial duties, but after last night, she doubted the Dragon would spare her from anything. If anything, he was likely to make her life worse.

After a quick breakfast, during which none of the other shrine maidens even so much as looked her in the eye, Suzume went to meet with Zakuro to get her morning assignments. It was an unfortunate side effect of being a shrine maiden. She was expected to clean and learn about what it took to serve the god of the mountain. *I don't even know why it is necessary when the god is a fake.* She sighed and then when she looked up again, the Dragon stood across the garden beneath a maple tree. His head was tilted back as he stared at the crimson leaves.

He wore a long white outer robe that hung down past his knees over a pair of billowing black pants, and his long hair had been tied up in a topknot. He looked like a proper courtier from a distance, the only thing that was missing was a hat. She had never seen a man without one before now. He would have caused a scandal at court, with his charming smiles and apparent disregard for social norms. From a distance, he appeared handsome. But Suzume knew beneath that pleasing outer veneer was a monster and a maniac.

He spotted her and waved her over. At first she considered

pretending not to see him and walking away, but he did not give her the chance. He crossed the garden, jumping over a small decorative pond before landing gracefully beside her.

"Good morning, my bride," he stage-whispered.

A few of the shrine maidens looked in their direction, but when Suzume scowled at them, they ducked their heads and went back to sweeping or carrying linens to be washed.

"I thought we had established that I was not your bride," she said with fake sweetness as she fluttered her eyelashes at him.

"Mmm," he said and cupped her cheek, running his thumb along her high cheekbone. Sparks rose where his hand touched her. "Isn't it fun to pretend, though?"

She scowled at him. The air crackled around her and she felt the burning pool of energy rumbling in her stomach. Now would be a good time to learn to master this power and burn him to a crisp.

The Dragon pulled away from her and laughed. "You are so predictable. I am glad I chose you."

"You did not choose me, my power unleashed you!" she countered.

"How do you know I did not give you that power?" he asked with a quirk of his lip.

She glowered at him and had no appropriate response. It seemed these newfound abilities only manifested around the Dragon; could it be nothing she could control but her body's reaction to his presence? She refused to give him credit; it would only go to his head.

"There you are!" Zakuro shouted and bustled over to the pair of them. When she saw Suzume with the Dragon, however, she faltered. She folded her hands in front of her and bowed low to the Dragon. "My lord Dragon."

He looked down at her with a narrowed gaze and the crackling sensation tinged the air and made Suzume's skin itch. Zakuro did not seem to notice. She did maintain her averted gaze as she spoke to Suzume. "The head priestess wishes to speak with you."

"We will be there in a moment," the Dragon replied for Suzume.

"I can speak on my own," Suzume snapped.

"Can you now? Since you were not able to answer my earlier question, I thought perhaps you had lost the power of speech."

She puffed up her chest and considered shouting at him, but Zakuro and the other shrine maidens were staring. She didn't want to reveal even a small weakness to them. She lifted her chin and turned away. "We will speak to the head priestess now," she said.

Zakuro bowed again and showed them the way to the high priestess' room. Zakuro kept a few steps ahead of them as if she were eager to put distance between herself and them.

When they arrived at the high priestess' rooms, Zakuro and Suzume knelt by the door. The Dragon stood over them, shaking his head. Zakuro slid the doors open. Inside, the head priestess sat at the far end of the room on a cushion upon the floor. Suzume entered and walked with her head bowed before taking a seat across from the head priestess. The Dragon, adversely, declined to sit and loomed above the two women.

"I am glad you came, Lord Dragon," the head priestess greeted him.

He nodded in response.

Then to Suzume she said, "I called you here to speak about what happened yesterday. I am writing a letter to the head of the temple at the White Palace, but I wanted to hear your side before I send it. "

Suzume's heart beat faster. She had been caught out in her lie! They would banish her for sure, or worse. She panicked; there was nowhere left for her but here. It would have been wise to confess the truth and hope for mercy from the head priestess, but she was too prideful to admit to a lie.

"What do you want to know? I am an open book," Suzume replied.

The Dragon snorted. "That is an understatement."

She shot him a glare, but he only smiled at her and extended his palm, indicating she should continue.

The high priestess glanced between the two of them and sighed. "I did not ask before, given the circumstances under which you were brought to us." She cleared her throat.

Suzume stared past her, pretending the words and the judgment behind them did not sting.

"Given recent developments, I think it bears investigation. Have you been tested for spiritual sensitivity?"

This, Suzume could answer honestly. "No. Because I am a descendant of the Eight, it was always assumed I had some spiritual powers. Though perhaps they underestimated just how much ability I had." Well, partly honestly; no one would have assumed Suzume, the fifth daughter of the emperor's second wife, would have anything remarkable about her. She had been lucky enough to have such a fortuitous marriage arrangement, but that was all in the past now.

"I suppose you are right," the high priestess said while scratching her chin.

Suzume sighed. She had accepted her lie so easily. *Then again they would not have taken me into the temple if they did not think I had some spiritual sensitivity.*

"Perhaps you can answer a question for me, Chiyoko?" the Dragon asked the head priestess. "How does a woman with previously no indication of spiritual power break a five-hundred-year-old seal? I know it could not have been weakened because the priestess who made it would not let such a thing happen. I suspect that is why she built this shrine. Your prayers should have kept me sealed for another five hundred years and beyond. Nothing but the fall of mankind would have weakened it, and even then perhaps it still would have held and locked me in eternal slumber."

Chiyoko, the high priestess, glanced between Suzume and the Dragon, her mouth working as if she were trying to give him a reasonable explanation, but she had none.

"I cannot say, my lord," she said.

He waved off her response. "I did not really expect you to. Instead, tell me, the first priestess of your order, did she have any descendants?"

She went to shake her head no but paused. She held up a wrinkled finger. "There is a myth that when High Priestess Fujikawa began our order, she was great with child, but there is no proof of this. It is probably superstition or allegory. She is often called the mother of our order; she is said to have traveled all around the empire, building shrines and temples wherever she went."

"Is there more to the legend?" the Dragon pressed.

Suzume squirmed under the force of his spiritual pressure, which seemed to be bearing down upon her. She laid her hands down flat on the reed flooring and tried to steady her labored breathing.

Chiyoko frowned and looked at Suzume, who struggled to breathe. The Dragon stood above her with an intense gaze that seemed it could burn her just with a look. The high priestess continued, though her voice too had become strained, "Some say High Priestess Fujikawa died bringing that child into the world..." She took a deep breath. Beads of sweat bloomed on her forehead and she wiped them away with the back of her hand. "Others say she lived and raised the child, who became a great spiritual leader. Other tales claim that she gave birth to the first emperor and that she is the mother of our empire, but these are all just legends without recorded evidence." She paused, inhaled and exhaled. "A fire one hundred years after her death burned the temple to the ground and the historical records were lost."

The Dragon paced about the room. Only Zakuro seemed unaffected by the release of his energy. Chiyoko was doing her best to maintain control, but her hands were pressed firmly onto the table in front of her.

"There must have been copies somewhere. Are there any great places of learning?" the Dragon said, oblivious to the priestess' suffering.

"Just the records at the White Palace, but—" The priestess stopped to catch her breath.

Meanwhile, Suzume panted and clutched at her neck; it felt like her throat had collapsed.

"What is wrong with the girl?" Zakuro asked.

The Dragon noticed Suzume lying on the ground, forced down by the weight of his spiritual energy. He pulled it back and she gasped a breath. The weight disappeared in an instant and she felt as if a ton of bricks had been taken off her chest.

"Your energy is pouring out of you unchecked. She is particularly in tune to your energy, my lord," Chiyoko remarked. Her hands trembled as she hid the effects the spiritual energy had on her.

"Yes, she is." He stared at Suzume, who perspired and glowered at him. Then he said to Suzume, "You will take me to the palace. I would investigate these claims about that woman's offspring and together we will find them and kill them."

Chiyoko gasped and Suzume sat up and swayed in place. "My lord, she is the daughter of the emperor. What if the legends are true and High Priestess Fujikawa is the mother of the emperor?"

"Then I shall kill her and her entire family," he replied in a calm voice that gave Suzume chills. He meant what he said, of that she had no doubt.

"What if she had no children, if she died without descendants? Will you hunt down her sisters' legacy or her brothers'?"

"There was a child, of that I am certain," he said, and the thunderclouds seemed to gather in his eyes once more. He kept his spiritual energy in check, but the sparks were racing up and down Suzume's back. Suzume stood up and a bright red aura hung around her like a shroud. She lifted her hand, staring at the energy that twirled around her fingers.

"How can you be so certain?" she challenged, and the red of her aura shot towards the Dragon.

He pushed it aside as he would a fly. "I know because it was mine."

# 5

The Dragon's proclamation was followed by silence. *Is this another trick?* She scrutinized his expression, searching for a hint. He crossed his arms over his chest and stared past Suzume at the wall behind the head priestess. His dark eyes were rimmed with blue—something Suzume had learned indicated his temper was rising. She clutched at her chest, waiting for the release of the pressure that would surely suffocate her. Though his anger made a lot more sense now, she would be pretty upset if her lover locked her away for five hundred years too.

"Are you saying...?" Chiyoko prompted.

The Dragon bared pointed teeth at the high priestess. "Yes, your beloved founder was pregnant with my child when she sealed me away for eternity! Though I suspect she was not aware of it at the time. I had only just realized myself."

Suzume shook her head. *Just like a man to think he knew more about a woman than she did.* "You must be joking! How could you know before she did?"

He turned towards Suzume; his face had transformed along with his teeth. The handsome young man was gone, replaced by a terrifying hybrid of human and dragon. His skin had a faint blue sheen, and scales overlapped the flesh along his cheeks, which were sharp and angular. His pupils were large and just the barest hint of his iris ringed the outside in an icy blue. His cheeks were sunken and his hands were tipped with claws.

"Do you question me, mortal? I could squish you like a bug. Do you know what I am? I can see each beat of your heart within your chest. I can see the river of energy of life that flows in your veins. I watched humans climb their way from being ignorant animals to the pestilence you are now upon the land. I know more about you than you know about yourself."

Suzume should have been cowed by his posturing; perhaps a smarter woman would have been. He had done nothing but flaunt his power from the moment he woke. She had seen his type before. Every season when the young lords came to make their petitions to the emperor, there was always one among them full of hot air and of his own greatness. She suspected the Dragon was the same. He had done nothing but make threats since his arrival; she had yet to see him make good on any of them. Suzume squared her shoulders and looked him dead in the eye.

"But you were defeated by a human," she said.

He smiled; it was a terrifying sight. His daggerlike teeth gleamed and the threat hinted at there made her stomach flop.

"You've outworn your value to me, Priestess," he said. His voice was deadly calm.

His spiritual energy poured out of him. Suzume saw it spiral out of him like a thick mist. It reached for her, grasping like tentacles; it prodded and poked the air around her but did not touch. It coalesced into a river of shimmery blue light that spun around her, creating a sphere of energy that covered her. Before the energy closed around her, she saw the high priestess fall over, grasping at her throat while Zakuro rushed to her side.

Inside the bubble of energy, Suzume felt her skin prickle. Small jolts ran up and down her skin as the red sparks leapt at the Dragon's energy, keeping it at bay. The pressure mounted, and though she felt it growing, it was not overwhelming as it had been before. Suzume's bright red energy flickered out of her from unseen pores, leaping like flames to create a secondary ring that enclosed her and shielded her from the Dragon's energy.

When she was fully encased in her own bubble, the building pressure ceased entirely and she stared up at the colliding of their energy. Fire and ice met, causing small explosions. Clouds of vapor and sparks blended together. *When I unleashed him, this is the energy that broke him free, and now it is protecting me.*

As a test, she imagined the energy reaching out as if she had her own tentacles of energy. But instead of a graceful probe, one section of her shield burst forth, burning a hole in the Dragon's energy. Smoke curled away and the Dragon stared down at her through the hole it had created.

He had transformed from the monstrous half dragon back to a man. His brow furrowed as he stared down at her. He examined her as if trying to puzzle out a mystery. She would like to know where these powers came from as well. The Dragon's energy receded, wrapping around him like a shimmering cloud of frost. Then when Suzume blinked, it disappeared. Her own energy flickered and faded like a candle snuffed out and her knees gave out beneath her as she collapsed to the floor. She felt drained, her arms were too weak to even lift, and holding up her head to watch the Dragon came with a great effort.

"How?" He shook his head. "We leave in an hour's time. Meet me at the gates."

He turned and stormed out of the room, slamming the sliding door on his way out. The force of it shook the building. Suzume considered shouting a parting insult, but decided to let things be. She was too tired to even speak. She looked down at her hands; they felt like a stranger's. *What just happened here?*

The high priestess had lost consciousness when the Dragon unleashed his powers on Suzume. Zakuro had her head resting in her lap. The high priestess moaned and Zakuro looked down on the elderly woman with a surprising amount of tenderness. *It's good to see she is not entirely heartless.* When the head priestess tried to sit up, Zakuro said, "Do not rise. You will hurt yourself."

The high priestess sighed but lay still with her eyes closed. Suzume's strength was returning and she looked to the door, wondering if now would be a good time to make a graceful exit.

"What shall we do about this?" Zakuro asked Chiyoko before scowling at Suzume as if accusing her for the Dragon's actions.

"We must do as the Dragon asks," said the high priestess. Her voice was thin as a reed.

"He threatened to kill the entire royal family," Suzume protested.

"Do not question the will of the gods," Zakuro snapped back.

Suzume glared at her. "You wouldn't be saying that if it was you he was threatening."

Zakuro glowered back.

"Enough," Chiyoko said. Despite her current fatigue, her voice commanded them both. The two women turned to the high priestess.

"Suzume, you must go with the Dragon. Whatever he asks, you must do."

*Why?* she wanted to ask, but she knew the answer without speaking. *Because he would kill her otherwise. For whatever reason, he had chosen her, and now it seemed she was stuck with him.*

"You are dismissed," the head priestess said with a lazy wave.

Her casual dismissal riled Suzume, but she took her cue to leave. She dipped a hasty bow before skittering out of the room.

―――――

When the door closed, Chiyoko sat up. Her old bones creaked and her head pounded with the beginnings of a headache. She rubbed her temple as Zakuro fussed over her. She waved away her concerns. Zakuro sat across from her, hands flat on her knees and intense dissatisfaction written on her features.

"You are displeased?" Chiyoko asked. She knew the answer, but she also knew Zakuro did not know her emotions were so transparent.

"Why send that girl along with him? She is likely to incite his anger again, and who knows what will happen if he is not in a holy place then." Zakuro jabbed a finger towards the door.

Chiyoko did not answer right away. She looked down at the beginnings of the letter she had been sending to her friend at the palace. It had been a long time since she had been in the presence of a Yokai like the Dragon, and the last time she had been a young woman. Few people had spiritual sensitivity and for this girl, with undiscovered powers, to come to this shrine was either a coincidence or by design. Only Chiyoko's family's long history with this shrine had kept her here. When her abilities were discovered, she had already learned about the shrine's secret and it was too late to send her away. Had life been different, she would have been trained at the Sun Temple at the White Palace. She had never expected someone with that level of spiritual sensitivity to show up at her shrine. *Who is this girl? She cannot be a mere disgraced princess. How could her powers have lain dormant until now?*

"Chiyoko!" Zakuro said.

She glanced up at Zakuro; her pinched mouth accentuated the lines around her eyes and mouth. She still remembered the young girl who had come to her shrine, without a family but desperate to please. She had not even a fraction of the raw power that Suzume did. But she was loyal and she would lead the shrine well when Chiyoko was gone. Only years of training allowed Zakuro to see the world of the Yokai. Because Zakuro had not lived with the knowledge of that other world, the Dragon and his threats scared Zakuro more than she would ever admit aloud. He had threatened the entire royal family—and it was no idle threat. He meant every word; if he could sate his desire for revenge by killing hundreds of innocents, he would do it. Yokai were different than humans; they had no sense of honor.

"We cannot stop him from going, and the girl can withstand his energy if she can learn to control her own. I only wish I had time to train her. But he will not wait. She will have to learn about her powers alone."

"Then why do we not seal him once more?" Zakuro suggested. "Surely it will be a small feat for the princess."

Chiyoko shook her head. "No. Fujikawa Kazue was a powerful priestess; Suzume does not have the strength to do what she did." *It really is a shame. Had I known, I would have been able to begin her training at least, but I did not suspect. Now I can only hope she survives.*

"Then what shall we do? We cannot let him run wild."

Chiyoko stared down at her letter once again. She had only to make her mark and send it out. She knew this was the right thing to do, but knowing that her entire life's work was coming to an end left her feeling empty. She had kept the temple's secrets so long, even now that the end was near she found it difficult to loosen her tongue and speak the truth. *I should tell Zakuro everything. I do not know how much time is left to me.* She folded her hands on the table. *Not yet but soon, when she is ready to take my place, I will tell her about Priestess Fujikawa's final wishes.*

The head priestess stood and walked over to the window. She could not stare at the paper a moment longer. Seeing it in black and white felt too final. She looked out into the garden beyond. A pair of shrine maidens who were meant to be sweeping the courtyard were chatting and giggling behind their hands. Another girl was peeking through the door that led to the Dragon's chamber. Their lives had been rocked when they found out the God of the Mountain was not real, what would they think when they learned the entire shrine was a lie? How would they react when they found out she had known from the start that there was no god and this shrine had been built with the intention of keeping the Dragon sealed, all to keep their founder's secret. These girls

40

carried on, oblivious to the fact that their entire order's purpose was preparing to leave and never come back. *I never thought I could come to care for a stone so much.*

She turned around, and Zakuro watched her, brows furrowed. *Shall we carry on, find a new god to worship, or do I risk them all to put him back?*

"I am writing to the head priestess at the White Palace. I will inform her of the Dragon's intentions," she said, answering Zakuro's question at last.

"And then what? Will she be able to seal him once more?"

*If only it were that easy. I would not let him leave.* Chiyoko folded her hands in front of her to disguise their shaking. The truth dangled from her lips. "Only Kazue's reincarnation could do that."

"Then our first priority should be to find her before the Dragon does."

Perhaps it was time to tell Zakuro everything. She hated to see the worry that creased her brow and to know she caused it.

"He has already found Kazue's reincarnation. She is the one who unleashed him."

# 6

The shrine maidens made short work of packing supplies for Suzume and the Dragon's journey. They seemed eager to be rid of her, or perhaps it was the Dragon they were happy to see the backside of. She waited for him at the gates, a pack on her back that felt heavy enough to drag her down to the ground. *Why can we not fly, or at least ride in a palanquin? Even when my father dumped me at this forsaken place he had the decency to send me in a proper conveyance.*

The Dragon came storming through the courtyard. Fallen leaves kicked up in his wake and swirled around his head. From the crackle of energy she felt tingling up and down her arms, she suspected the Dragon was still in a foul mood. *Oh good, this shall be a delightful trip, off to kill my entire family.* She crossed her arms over her chest as he approached.

"Where are we going?" she asked him.

He looked her up and down. "To my palace in the south."

South towards the White Palace, where her father and siblings resided. She had never been close with any of them, but to think the Dragon would slaughter them all filled her with fear. She had never felt so helpless in her life.

"You did not mean what you said before about killing my family, right?"

He did not respond and instead stomped over to the torii arch that separated the shrine grounds from the road leading up to the mountain. He stopped beneath the arch. A string of ofuda on the archway twisted in the wind. He stared at them for a moment. Suzume crept up behind him, crossed the threshold onto the road, and with a hand on her hip, she faced the Dragon.

"You've been here for centuries, are you afraid to leave?"

He narrowed his eyes at her. She did not know what she expected to get out of taunting him, but it made her feel better at least.

He took a step, his mouth pressed closed. She may have imagined it, but it almost looked like he was expecting something to happen. When nothing did, he took off at a fast pace down the road. Suzume stared after him. *I do not understand him at all.* He was moving so fast he was nearly around the bend. She watched him go for a moment, wondering what would happen if she refused to follow him. Then he stopped, turned around and beckoned to her.

"Come, Priestess, I haven't got all day."

She balled her hands into fists. "I am not your pet to command."

"But you are mine."

She rolled her eyes and crossed her arms over her chest. She'd be damned if she would come chasing after him like a dog. She did not know he was beside her until he was lifting her up into the air and threw her over his shoulder. "If you will not come, I will bring you," he said.

"Put me down!" she shouted, beating on his back with her fists.

He laughed but ignored her threats. Her skin prickled and heated where his hands wrapped around her calves, but no matter how she tried, she could not summon the same power to defend herself. *It would be helpful right about now.*

The journey down the mountainside was tedious and not worth mentioning, in Suzume's opinion. When she gave up fighting him, he let her down to walk on her own two feet. She insisted on numerous breaks, which he argued against, but she won in the end. It was nearly sunset by the time they reached the foot of the mountain.

By then her limbs ached in a way they had never done before. She dawdled behind the Dragon as they meandered over the hilly countryside. Trees blocked the dying sun and a breeze rippled through their branches, the wind cool as the sun descended below the horizon. The glare reflected off the water of a nearby river and blinded Suzume. She shielded her eyes with her forearm and scowled at green shoots of river grasses growing along the water's edge, struggling to break through the murky water and reaching towards the sky.

"By the way, what's your name?" the Dragon said from atop a small rise.

She stopped and squinted at him. *That's it,* she thought, *I cannot walk another step!* The coarse fabric itched and sweat plastered it to her skin. Her feet hurt from these inferior bamboo sandals the high priestess had given her and the straw hat and veil she wore kept slipping forward. Her arms were tired from adjusting it and carrying this infernal pack. A fly had also gotten under her veil and buzzed near her face.

They had been on the road for hours now and it *just* occurred to him to ask her name? She forced down a string of curses that were on the tip of her tongue. Not only were they not appropriate for a lady of her stature, but she didn't need another reason to incite the mercurial Dragon's wrath.

"Suzume," she ground out and took the opportunity to try to adjust the sandal on her foot. She missed her platforms and her palanquin. Small blisters had formed beneath her dusty socks.

"Soo-zoo-me." He rolled her name around on his tongue and

she regretted telling him immediately. He repeated her name several more times—only to further infuriate her, she suspected.

She knew she should stay on his good side. He had threatened to kill her and her entire family, after all. *I would fry him now and walk the rest of the way if it meant I could return **home**,* she thought. *If I knew how,* she amended.

The Dragon laughed suddenly. He startled her and she threw her arms out, throwing her shoe. She almost fell over and saved herself by rocking forward on the balls of her feet.

"What is so funny?" she asked with hands crossed over her chest once she had regained her balance.

He was bent over taking large belly laughs and did not respond right away. When he did, it was halting. "Your... name... means... sparrow!" As he said this, he laughed harder and clutched at his side.

Suzume frowned and considered throwing her other straw sandal at him, the head priestess' warnings be damned.

"Why would a sparrow be so funny?" she asked again. She took a deep breath and tried to keep her own temper in check.

"It's not the sparrow that's funny. It's you! A loudmouthed arrogant woman! You're nothing like a sparrow." He pointed at her as he said this and Suzume colored and turned away to hide her embarrassment.

She sat down on a nearby fallen tree, removed her other sandal and pelted it at the Dragon. He dodged it and continued to laugh uproariously. *I don't care what he thinks. He's just a lying fool.*

"*Then* what is your name, oh Great God of the Mountain?" she said.

He stopped laughing and stared straight at her, and storm clouds seemed to gather behind his eyes. Suzume shrank back. *What's gotten into him? The slightest thing upsets him.*

"A Yokai's true name is a secret no mortal shall know, but I was once called Kaito." His voice echoed through the valley, rippling along the river. She stared him in the eyes and refused to be cowed. He measured her, staring her up and down before turning to walk away without another word. *Probably something to do with that woman again,* she thought and fought the urge to roll her eyes.

She was perplexed by his reaction, but pleased; her short temper and violence towards the false god had not summoned his wrath, not yet at least. *Nothing worse than a man scorned!* Suzume thought. *They probably had a spat and she rightfully locked him up.* She sighed. *And now I am cleaning up the mess.*

She scanned the area for her sandals and found them floating along the river's edge, tangled in the reeds along the shore. She cursed aloud this time and went to find something with which to fish them out.

Down the road Kaito called out, "You shouldn't wear socks with those, you'll get blisters!"

"Thanks a lot," she muttered as she hoisted a sopping-wet straw sandal out of the water with a twig.

As she pulled the other sandal out, something else came out of the water with it. A green webbed hand held onto the sandal as well.

Suzume screamed and dropped the stick and fumbled backwards, falling onto her rear. The sandal landed in the water with a splash. The hand grasping the sandal was followed by an indented head, almost as if the creature had a dish in its skull. It emerged from the water's surface and blinked large black eyes at her. Suzume screamed again and the creature opened its beak and squawked at her.

Suzume, over her initial fear, grabbed the stick and struck the thing with it.

"Get out of here! You strange creature!" She shooed it.

The Yokai flailed and splashed about, trampling the reeds.

"What's all this commotion?" Kaito asked, coming over to Suzume, who was actively hitting the creature now.

"This toad thing attacked me!" she said, pointing an accusatory finger at the creature, who had sunk down in the water. Only his black eyes and indented head were above the water's surface.

"This?" Kaito pointed to the creature. He knelt along the shore. The creature sank beneath the surface, leaving a ripple in its place. Kaito reached in after it and pulled out the squirming creature, which continued to wail a high-pitched shriek. It was a pale green all over with a turtle shell and webbed hands and feet. "Stop your noise, insect. I am your lord returned after many centuries' sleep."

The creature flailed and beat at Kaito's arm with its webbed hands. He sighed. "Use your words. I know you speak the common tongue."

The creature looked at him, blinking its large black eyes. "You no eat me?" it asked with a trembling squeaky voice.

"No, I will not eat you," Kaito said with a smirk. "If you behave and answer my questions."

The creature nodded its head furiously and it was a wonder the water in the indent on its head did not spill out onto the ground.

"What is it?" Suzume asked as she wrinkled her nose.

"This?" Kaito said as he dangled the creature in front of Suzume. "This is a Kappa. A little insect that lives in bodies of water and has a bad habit of drowning unsuspecting idiots, don't you?" He shook the Kappa, who nodded its head in eager agreement as if blindly agreeing to Kaito's insults.

"Are you saying I'm an idiot?" Suzume asked with an arched brow.

"No, you just did." He smirked and then turned his attention back to the Kappa. "Now tell me, who has been ruling this region in my absence?"

"Many come. Many go. Humans multiply. Big ones disappear but for one." The Kappa looked back and forth, not meeting Kaito's gaze.

"Answer me straight, you little water beetle! Who is it, the

47

monkey clan? The ogres? No, wait, they're both too stupid to even put on pants, it wouldn't have been either of them. "

"This region is ruled by Governor Kitayama," Suzume interjected but was quickly cut off.

"Not your paltry human 'rulers', one of the one hundred thousand, the earth's first children, an immortal. We owned this land before Seikatsu accidentally unleashed you pests upon the earth. And now look how you've spread across this land like a disease." He shook the Kappa again. "Who is the remaining 'big one', then?" he growled.

The Kappa shrank into itself, making a compact little ball. "He has many names. Many faces. No one knows for sure."

Kaito sighed. "I'll let you live this time, but if you try to drown something of mine again, I'll use your shell as my soup bowl!"

He dropped the Kappa. It landed on its turtle shell and rolled over before scurrying into the water. The last they heard was a splash. All that marked his escape was a small ripple on the surface of the water. Suzume stared at the place where the Kappa had been. *Why have I never seen things like this until now?* She looked back to the Dragon. *Everything changed when he woke up.*

"What does he mean, 'big one'?" she asked.

He crossed his arms over his chest as he scanned the horizon. His eyes narrowed, looking in the distance. Suzume shaded her gaze beneath her hand to try to spot what he was looking at but saw nothing.

"What are you looking at?" she asked impatiently.

After a few minutes of silence he answered her. "There are different types of Yokai. They range anywhere from beings like me down to insects like that thing. My kind rule over the smaller ones and keep them from devouring each other. If there were another being like me in this area, I would feel his spiritual pressure or at least a trace if he were disguising himself."

"Well, do you sense anything?" she asked with a hand on her hip.

"No," he replied.

"Well, isn't that a good thing?"

"It is as if there is no Yokai here at all, expect for these dumb creatures. Which cannot be possible, there should be *someone* here. It's possible whoever this 'big one' is, he's powerful enough that he does not even leave a trace of his spiritual energy. That would make him as powerful as me." He frowned.

She did not like the sound of two of Kaito. Suzume snatched her sandal off the ground and shoved her foot into it. It squished unpleasantly as she walked, but there was no time to complain or she would be left behind.

"Where are you going?" she demanded.

"An old friend of mine is nearby. I think it's time we paid him a little visit and found out about this 'big one'." He smiled at her over his shoulder.

Suzume sighed. Somehow she did not think this encounter would bode well for her. Maybe if she was lucky, Kaito would meet this big one and they would somehow kill one another and take care of her problem for her. She could only hope.

# 7
---

Suzume's eyes refused to stay open. Her head bobbed as she followed Kaito. Her body ached, and her bottom and back were bruised from sleeping on a lumpy mat. She had tossed and turned throughout the night. Every call of a wild animal and even the sound of the wind through the trees had her bolting upright.

The Dragon had been awake most of the night as well. After the sixth time being awoken by an animal screeching, she had seen him sitting by the campfire, staring into the flames, lost in thought. The light had danced in his eyes and gave him a haunted, dangerous look. It was no wonder he did not sleep, she wouldn't want to sleep either if she had slept for five hundred years. He had not acknowledged her and she had not said anything about the sullen looks he gave her.

In the morning he was his same chipper self, urging her to hurry along like the happy sadist he was.

Kaito turned away off the road and down an embankment. She was in a daze and nearly walked past him until he grabbed her by the wrist and tugged her down with him. She lost her footing and slipped down the side, staining her clothes with mud and losing her hat in the process. It flipped end over end before plopping in a particularly large mud puddle with green algae clinging to the edges.

"What did you do that for!" she snapped. The sleepless night wore her temper thin.

"You were wandering off."

She looked forlornly at her ruined hat. The sun would fry her pale skin for sure. "Well, you could have said something instead of grabbing me."

"And miss an opportunity to see you fall in the mud?"

She clenched her hands into fists and tried to find a reasonable response, but that was impossible with Kaito. "Where are we going?"

He did not answer her and instead leapt along a few rocks across to the other side of the river. From her vantage point, she could see large trees, their roots exposed by the water rushing beneath them. *Is he really leading me into a swamp? He has to be joking.* She waited for him to turn back around and tell her it was a joke. When he didn't, she knew she had to follow.

Though Suzume had never had the displeasure of stepping foot in a swamp before, she imagined this was the worst of them all. There were no pathways, so they were forced to jump from slippery, slime-covered rocks across bubbling brown mud that somehow constituted water.

Suzume slipped at least ten different times and her pants were soaked up to the knee. Hundreds of thousands of tiny buzzing insects had made a feast of her, and her skin was already marred by angry red welts where they had dined upon her. *Now would be a good time to learn how to zap things with my powers,* she thought as she swatted at another insect that had landed on her neck.

As Suzume questioned her sanity in following the Dragon into this swamp, her foot slipped on another slick rock and she went into the boggy mud. She landed with a plunk up to her waist.

Mud flew into the air and landed on Suzume's face and neck. The thick brown water squirted and squished as she clawed at the fragile ground, which slid through her fingers, coating them in a slimy residue as she tried to climb back out. The mud that had landed on her face rolled down her cheek, leaving a filthy trail on her skin.

Kaito stood a few feet ahead of her at the edge of a rare patch of earth.

"We don't have time to stop and play in the mud," he called out to her.

She scowled at him, but it lost some of its power when she was covered head to toe in muck. "I am not *playing* in the mud. I slipped. Why does your friend have to live in such a disgusting place anyway?"

"Looks like you're playing in it to me." He smirked.

She had no rebuttal and decided to revert to more childish antics. She stuck her tongue out at him.

Kaito laughed and then said, "I don't mind this place so much. It's tranquil." He held up his hand and a dragonfly with shimmering blue wings landed on the tip of his finger.

Suzume huffed and dragged herself out of the mud, which made a sucking sound with each labored inch as she pulled herself out. Her pants clung to her thighs and her long sleeves were weighed down with saturation. She trudged over to him on the island in the center of the mud.

"Your idea of tranquil and my idea of tranquil vary *greatly*." She shook her hands and mud went flying in all directions. Kaito dodged a particularly large glob that she had aimed at his head. "How much farther is this place?"

"We're here," he replied with a wave of his hand to indicate the dirt patch on which they stood.

Suzume looked around. They were on an island perhaps the length of her arm span before it widened to maybe twice that at the far end, where a grass-covered mound sat.

"You brought me into the middle of the swamp for... this?" She swept her arm across the landscape. The trees were different here than anything she had seen before. Their roots were above the waterline and they looked like hundreds of coiling snakes curling and jutting out of the brown muddy water. Land was a rare sight and it was predominantly water and trees. The island they stood upon spearheaded into the river that ran through the swamp, and unlike the areas they had trudged through, the water was relatively clear here.

"That I did. Maybe we can make this our summer home."

She narrowed her eyes at him, but before she could snap back a retort, something else spoke instead. "I know this voice, though long has it been since I heard it."

Suzume glanced about, looking for the speaker, but there was no one there but Kaito and her.

"Did I hear someone talking just now?" Suzume asked.

"You did. It was I," the voice said.

Suzume spun around in circles, flinging mud every which way as she did so. "This isn't funny, Kaito."

Kaito laughed so hard that tears streamed down his cheeks. He clutched his knees and waved his hand towards the grassy mound at the far end of the island. It had moved closer. The front of the mound was diamond shaped and the back almost serpentine, but wider. Suddenly the front lifted up, revealing a crevice beneath. Suzume screeched and fell backwards onto her rump. Kaito was still laughing as she realized it was not a hill but a creature, which opened a wide mouth. It bellowed something akin to a laugh. The creature's breath stank like fish and the mucky water.

Suzume climbed onto her knees and frowned at the two of them. Kaito stopped laughing and went to kneel in front of the creature, which had raised itself off the ground by a few inches and sported short stubby legs that were draped in slimy moss. Two tiny black eyes stared at her from the flat head, and smooth skin covered its body. The creature's feet were webbed and greenish brown and sank into the soft earth. His body was covered in the same glistening skin, and a large bulbous tail was sunk into the water at the edge of the island. *It's a giant salamander. Yuck.*

"I have not had quite this much fun in a long time. The way she spun and mud went everywhere." It rumbled and croaked. "My old friend, I thought you were gone for good," the thing said in a deep booming voice.

"You should know better than to doubt me." Kaito grinned.

The creature nodded its massive head. "You're right. Perhaps it is a sign of the times. Once long ago I was sought after for my wisdom and knowledge; now I waste away here in my swamp, sometimes dreaming and sometimes listening."

"Please tell me we didn't come here to hear the swamp monster's life story," Suzume said.

Kaito ignored her and addressed the creature. "Well, I hope your ears are as sharp as they once were. Tell me what has happened in my absence? Everyone is gone, even the small ones are scarce."

The giant salamander shook his head back and forth, and clumps of grass and mud slid off his brow and revealed brown mottled skin beneath. Suzume wrinkled her nose as the creature sighed and a gust of foul-smelling wind hit her.

"They've fled south to warmer climates, east and west to the sea, and north to the island. They were trying to get as far as they could from here."

Kaito frowned. "What are they running from?"

"A new Yokai appeared when you went to slumber. The small ones claim it devoured the less powerful to absorb their energy, but that sounds like small ones' nonsense to me," the giant salamander scoffed.

"What is it, then?" Suzume asked. She had no patience for this chitchat in the swamp. The sun was rising high and so was the humidity. The insects buzzed about and she waved her hands in front of her face to bat away the swarm of gnats that were circling her.

"I can only speculate, as I have never seen it myself, but I would wager it is a shape-shifter. Those that came through my swamp described it in different ways: Tall as a mountain, small as a gnat, as powerful as a dragon, or as meek as a small one. I would have left my swamp to search myself, but I could not leave it unprotected. The small ones I have managed to catch say this land is cursed."

"What could you possibly protect in this swamp?" Suzume said with her arms crossed over her chest. "It sounds like you're just afraid of this powerful Yokai."

The giant salamander stared at her for a moment and she did not like the way its slimy eyes felt on her skin.

"Did you learn what you wanted?" Suzume asked Kaito to end the silent appraisal of the swamp monster.

"Not quite. When the shifter rose, where did it come from?"

The creature lowered its head and hummed a rumbling sound that rippled the muddy water around it. "Now that is a good question. It happened so long ago I think my memories are foggy."

"He doesn't remember—let's go. I am being eaten alive here!" Suzume snarled as she slapped another bug on her arm.

"That's right!" the salamander interrupted. "From the north, near Mount Kitayama... wait, weren't you..."

Kaito did not wait for him to finish. He leapt across stones and flew from stepping-stone to stepping-stone faster than Suzume could ever hope to keep up with. Suzume sighed. *Damn him, can he not remember for a second that I do not possess inhuman speed and balance?*

"Girl," the salamander called out to her.

Suzume turned hesitantly. "Me?" She pointed at her chest.

"There is no other human here that I see." He opened his mouth in what Suzume took to be a smile.

"Yes?" She arched a brow. She did not like to make a practice of talking to a swamp monster. *Good thing no one is here to see me talking to this thing...*

"What became of the child?"

She looked at the giant salamander askance. *Not only is he disgusting, he's confused as well, great.* "I don't know what you're talking about." She looked at the rocks, trying to decide how to best escape from this situation.

She saw a rock that was not covered in moss and moved towards it to make her escape.

"Oh, my mistake. I thought I recognized your spiritual energy. It is so like hers. But now that I think of it, she was a human and you do not live quite as long as we do."

She hesitated. He could only mean Kazue, but what did the Dragon's former lover have to do with her? She was tempted to ask him more, but Kaito had backtracked a few feet and peered at her from beyond the draping vines hanging from one of the large trees nearby. Judging by how he had reacted when she brought up Kazue before, she figured he wouldn't want Suzume asking questions.

"Coming? Or do you plan to marry my friend here? You would be his sixtieth wife!"

"One hundred!" the creature called. "I remarried a few more times since you've been gone."

"You have my congratulations. How did the last one go?"

"I cannot remember—probably drowned or maybe eaten by one of the other creatures in the swamp. It's hard to keep track."

Suzume did not hear any more. She scurried across the stones at a surprising speed. *I would rather be Kaito's bride over a swamp monster's any day.* She was nearly to him when her luck ran out and she slipped on a rock and almost went headfirst into the muck. Kaito caught her about the waist and kept her from falling. He pressed her to his chest and she could smell the masculine scent that was unique to him. *This is nice, compared to the swamp smells.* Her newfound defense mechanism did not even stir, so she assumed he did not mean any harm, at least for now.

"Were you sniffing me?" Kaito asked.

She blushed and then pushed him away and stomped over to the next series of stones. "Not on your life," she called out. *Never mind. I'd rather marry the swamp monster.*

# 8

"Don't fall for me, Priestess, it will only make it more difficult if I have to kill you," Kaito called after her as she stomped away.

She scoffed. *Maybe if he wasn't such an arrogant jerk.* "You keep saying that, but I don't think you will kill me."

He grabbed her hard by the wrist and spun her around. Her feet landed in a mud puddle and water splashed over her ankles. Where his hand encircled her wrist, her red aura rose up and tangled around his hand. His touch was a cold burn and the chill crept up her arm. She yanked her arm back, trying to break free of his grip, but he only pulled her closer.

"What do you hope to get from taunting me?" he said, his voice a low rumble.

She didn't even know the answer to that. The rational part of her knew it was a foolish thing to do. But the more she felt like she was spinning out of control, the less reason she seemed to have. Inciting anger in the Dragon was the only control she had left. His cold breath brushed against her cheek. Only a few inches separated them. Her breath came out in a cloud as she stared up at him. *You will not defeat me.*

"You were sealed by a human before," she replied. Her voice sounded much more confident than she felt. She had no control over her powers and no possible way to defeat him. But if she let her facade slip, he would use her weakness—she just knew it.

He grabbed her chin, rubbing his thumb across her skin. She shivered from his touch, and not from desire. Frost gathered along her skin, he was trying to freeze her out. But where he touched her, warmth followed, melting the ice. It was a constant battle between them, their powers seemingly at odds. She grabbed his wrist with her free hand and he stared down at the connection. He must have felt the flame that focused on her palm burning into his flesh—she could feel the residual heat radiating from her own skin.

"You've got some nerve, I'll give you that." He dropped her hand and she let him go as he brushed past her.

He leapt over a puddle of swamp water. And when he landed on the other side, he turned back to face her. "Coming?"

She stared at him, arms crossed over her chest. *I should run. Why follow him when he'll likely kill me?* But like a moth drawn to the flame, she obeyed him. Who was she kidding? She had nowhere else to go. Just thinking about what horrid creatures might be lurking in this swamp made her skin crawl. At least with Kaito she had some measure of protection.

They trudged through the swamp, and Suzume avoided puddles, but still more mud ended up splattered on her already filthy clothes. *I feel as if I will never be clean again.* Kaito, on the other hand, seemed to repel dirt. His clothes that the priestesses had given him were still pristine. The bright blue silk looked out of place against the brown and green of the swamp.

As they traveled, Suzume distracted herself from the biting insects and the squishy wet feeling between her toes by wondering about the swamp monster's parting words. Whatever Yokai had taken over this region sounded dangerous. Perhaps even more dangerous than the Dragon, as hard as that was to believe. *If I could find this shape-shifter, I would ask him to take out the Dragon for me.*

She tripped over a root that jumped out to tangle in her pant legs. She stumbled and fell hard into a puddle, her hands squishing in the mud. She pounded the ground. *What is wrong with me? A week ago I thought Yokai were just a myth and here I am plotting to find one to destroy another.*

The Dragon stopped ahead of her. He looked down at her from his dry perch and grinned at her current state of affairs.

"Maybe I should leave you here with the swamp creature, you look like you would fit in."

Suzume pushed back the curtain of filthy hair from her eyes. She was tired. Tired of being dirty, tired of feeling helpless. "I should fry you for that." She meant it as a joke, but the Dragon's moods were volatile at best, he'd probably take her seriously. She held her breath, waiting for his response.

"I'd like to see you try." He jumped in the air and rushed towards her. His feet did not even need to touch the ground; it was as if he could fly.

Suzume did not take her eyes off of him. Her power moved to defend her, cloaking her in red energy. She braced herself for the attack, but it did not come. He stood in front of her with his arms crossed across his chest.

"This will all go much smoother if we make a few things clear."

"What's that?" she said, climbing to her feet.

"Do not make threats you cannot follow through on."

"Who says I can't make good on that threat?"

He smiled thinly; it sent a chill down her spine. She had awoken his temper.

"Be my guest." He made a sweeping gesture with his hand.

"Fine."

*Why did I open my big mouth? I cannot control these powers; they only show up when I'm threatened.* Suzume closed her eyes and tried to picture the power, as she had done back at the temple. It felt like fire in her gut. She pictured a candle flame; nothing happened. She tried a brazier; when that didn't work, she pictured a fire she had witnessed when she was a girl, which had burned down an entire wing of the palace. She could still smell the smoke and see the amber glow of flames as they danced against the inky black sky. Nothing happened, she could feel the burning embers of her powers deep inside her, but they were just out of reach. *I will not be made a fool of, I can do this.* She tried to picture flames, lightning, anything that might awaken the powers. But without the Dragon directly attacking her, she could not go on the offensive. *I cannot let him show me up this way.* But no matter how hard she concentrated she could not find the source of the power. She scrunched her nose and balled her hands into fists.

The Dragon laughed. "Don't hurt yourself."

"Shut it," she snapped.

And then she felt it, an ember, a mere pinprick glowing in her gut. Even as soon as it sparked to life, it threatened to peter out and die. *Maybe when I get emotional, my powers react.*

Kaito stared at her with arms crossed. She concentrated on him, his smug smile, the arrogant tilt of his head so he always appeared to be looking down on her. *I should be the one looking down on him; I am the daughter of the emperor. He thinks I am weak.* It wasn't enough. Because right now, cast aside by her family and the shrine, and covered head to toe in mud, she felt worthless. The ember flared up for just a moment then faded.

"Give it up. This is a waste of time," he taunted.

Suzume, eternally stubborn, would not give in. "No."

She was determined to prove her worth, not only to the Dragon but to herself. She concentrated on searching for something that really angered her. She thought of her mother, specifically the last time she had seen her. It had been in the courtyard of the palace. She could picture it clearly: her mother sat in her golden palanquin. At the time Suzume did not know it would be the last time she saw her. As it was, it had been nearly a year since they had spoken other than through the occasional letter.

Her mother had pulled back the curtain and stared down at Suzume. Her long ebony hair fell over her shoulders like silk and she wore so many layers of bright-colored silk she rivaled a rainbow. She smiled down at Suzume, but the gesture felt more like playacting than genuine affection. They both danced the dance of pretending, her mother acting as if she cared for her daughter's welfare and Suzume pretending she didn't want her approval. She had been secretly anticipating her mother's visit for weeks. Her mother so rarely had time for her children, but now Suzume had won her attention by landing an important marriage for the family. She had expected her mother to praise her for her cunning, and reward her for her service to the family by giving Suzume some of her precious time. But her mother did not even step out of the palanquin. Her men came to a halt and she stared down at Suzume.

"I'm leaving the palace," her mother said.

Suzume bit back her hurt. Weeks of planning and anticipation dashed in just a few words. Her mother had done it so many times before, it was a surprise it still hurt, but it did. "Goodbye, Mother," Suzume said.

"You will leave the palace too. The emperor knows everything and none of us are safe."

That familiar rage started to bubble in Suzume's gut. Just a few words and her mother had brought her entire world crashing down. All of Suzume's plans and hard work ruined in an instant. She didn't even bother to explain. She learned later of her mother's infidelity. How the legitimacy of all of her children with the emperor was called into question. And so she and all of her brothers and sisters were shipped off to the far reaches of the kingdom. Her mother's clan's loyalty had been called into question; many of them were in high-ranking positions thanks to her mother's marriage to the emperor and now they were all being looked at as traitors. And it was all her mother's fault.

She had not even cared to see to Suzume's upbringing, had hardly batted an eye when she had landed a marriage contract, and with a flick of her finger she ruined Suzume's life. The ember in her stomach burst into a flame and then grew into an inferno. The feelings that she had locked up came pouring out, just as the fire flooded through her like a dam being broken, and it reached to all of her limbs, burning her from the inside. Tears fell onto her cheeks but evaporated beneath the heat of the flames. She had no control as energy burst from her fingertips and the ends of her hair, which rose up and swirled around her as if she were a gale force. She threw her arms out in an attempt to control the energy that rushed out of her, scorching her, threatening to burn her down to nothing but ash.

Kaito jumped out of the way just before a beam of red energy shot towards him. Everything inside Suzume came pouring out of her like a volcano erupting until there was nothing left. Her hurt, her anger, the fire that seem to be the core of her being and all the tears were burned from her. She felt the last of the energy escape and her knees gave out in the same instant. She collapsed and her limbs trembled.

*Well, that was not what I was expecting.* She hoped Kaito had been too distracted by the fire to notice her tears. *And that's what I am more worried about, not having someone see my weakness, even when I catch on fire.* She slumped over onto the ground, too weak to even sit up. She stared up at the canopy of the trees. She could feel water creeping into her clothes, soaking them through, and it was possible something was wriggling across her knee, but she had nothing left to fight it with.

Kaito leaned over her and peered down at her. "You're never going to defeat me if you cannot control your powers."

She bared her teeth at him in a snarl; that was all she could manage, she felt too weak to argue. He was right, of course. She could not stop her mother and she could not stop Kaito from taking her from the temple. She rolled her head to the side. She did not want him to see how badly this failure hurt. How once again her mother had caused her even more humiliation. The plants surrounding them were charred black and the water had dried up, leaving cracked and barren earth behind. Wavy black soot marks scored the earth. She squinted and realized they were in the shape of her body.

Kaito picked her up. Normally she would have fought him off, but she did not have the energy to do even that.

"Why is this happening to me?" She did not mean for her question to make her sound so vulnerable and weak, but it had just come out.

He did not answer straight away. Or perhaps he was just toying with her; it was difficult to tell where he was concerned. She did not even want to question why he was carrying her or where he was taking her.

"I don't know," he said at last.

It was probably the most honest thing he had ever said to her. Her eyes drooped as he carried her. *What if I fall asleep and he takes advantage of me?* Her lids would not stay open, no matter how much she didn't want to trust him. *He watched me sleep last night and nothing happened.* She felt hollow and empty, and the beating of his heart and the swaying of his stride lulled her. *I'll just rest my eyes for a moment.*

# 9

He stared down at the weakened priestess. *What a fool to fall for such a simple trick. I wanted to test her ability, but she really has no control.* I would be better off leaving her here with the salamander. Not that she would stay put for long. She was stubborn enough that she would come chasing after him.

The swamp had changed since he had been there last—the course of the river bent a different way and the inhabitants were all but nonexistent. He sensed a Kappa nearby and other low-level Yokai that would never reveal themselves to him. But there were far too few for an area so thick with wildlife. *Something has been hunting here.*

He glanced around, spreading his spiritual power outwards, probing the surrounding swamp and forest, but his power was limited. His imprisonment had left him weak, his power curtailed by hundreds of years surrounded by the spiritual energy of humans. *I should have recovered by now. What has Kazue done to me?* Then he felt it—a cluster of energy not far, just beyond his current reach. As soon as he sensed it, it retreated, disappearing into darkness. *We've been followed.* He had been so caught up in finding the salamander, he had not considered the possibility. *I wonder if it is whatever has been hunting this area.*

He looked down at the priestess once again. Her eyes were closed, the perpetual scowl softened in her sleep. *You cannot even tell what a nuisance she is when she's sleeping. Where do her powers come from? I've never seen that sort of untamed power before. Even Kazue when she was untrained was not nearly as dangerous.* Either way, he could not investigate with her dead weight and he dared not venture back into the swamp, for risk of losing the trail.

*There used to be a shrine somewhere near here.* He ran in the direction he thought it was, hoping his memory of the swamp still proved true. Carrying the priestess proved cumbersome, but he managed to leap over the river and up an embankment to the place he had remembered. A large tree dominated a small island in the river. It was much larger than he remembered—it was the width of ten men—and its canopy hung overhead, keeping the area for fifty meters in shade. Humans had tied ofuda around the trunk of the tree, but they were old and frayed. He laid the priestess down among the roots, her head cradled by them. He touched the trunk, searching for the Kodama.

At first, there was no response, and he feared it had left, perhaps scared away by whatever had been hunting in the area. Then it stirred, a small wriggle at first; then the energy rolled and stretched as if it was waking from a long sleep. A small translucent hand poked out from the bark, followed by another and then a head and feet. It appeared like a wisp of white smoke with almost humanoid features though they lacked definition.

"Sorry to disturb your slumber," Kaito said with a bow. "I have a favor to ask of you."

The Kodama bowed his head, indicating Kaito should continue.

"I need a safe place to keep this woman, will you watch over her until I return?"

The tree spirit floated downward and sat upon a twisted root beside the priestess' head. He tilted his round head from side to side, examining the priestess, and then looked up at Kaito with black eyes. He nodded his head again.

Kaito bowed once more. "I won't be long."

He jogged away, leaving the Kodama to watch over the priestess. As he ran over streams and through tangles of moss, and glided over the puddles of mud, he got a better sense of the watchers. *How long have they been following us?* He had been searching for signs of other Yokai since he woke. Either they had all cloaked their energy, or his senses were not what they used to be. He hoped it was the former. But as he closed the distance, he got a clearer read of their spiritual energy.

There were several of them, six in total, minor Yokai, from what he could sense. But he doubted they would prove a challenge for him, even when he was not at his full power. *How did they disguise themselves all this time? Have they been following just beyond my reach?* In the past they would not have ventured this close, but as he had learned since waking, things had changed. His kingdom had fallen into chaos since he had been sealed. *Once I get my revenge, I will set everything right.*

He reached an embankment, where he landed and spun around. They had stopped running away. They circled him, probably thinking they could overpower him by numbers. He smirked. It had been too long since he had a good fight.

He tilted his head back. "Come out, I know you're there."

Three figures dropped down from the trees. They were monkeys, or monkey Yokai rather, and they wore matching yellow haori and hakama. It was strange for a lower yokai to don clothes. They usually preferred to run wild like animals in the forest. And these three were a long way from home. They were mostly mountainous creatures. *They've followed us from the mountain, I suspect.* Though they were apelike in appearance, they moved like men and even grinned at him with identical smiles revealing their pointed canines.

"What are you all smiling about?"

"You shouldn't have left the priestess alone," said the one in the middle. He seemed to be their leader, but he would be giving them too much credit to say they were that organized.

Kaito narrowed his eyes at them. "Do you know who I am?"

They reached for short staffs that they carried strapped across their shoulders. They did not draw their weapons, but Kaito knew a threat when he saw one.

"We know who you are, Sleeping Dragon," the middle one replied.

"Is that what they've been calling me since I've been gone? I suppose Magnificent Dragon was taken? Was it my brother who styled himself that way? He was always vain."

They did not laugh. Kaito crossed his arms over his chest. "You're a long way from home, what brings you to this lovely swamp?" He gestured to the bubbling pools of mud and the moss hanging down like curtains from the branches of the trees.

"Business," the middle monkey replied. He shifted his weight from one foot to the others. And in unison the others did too.

Kaito pretended he did not see the small tell. "I bet, and that business has to do with me?"

"No. You are a minor annoyance. But draining you of what little spiritual energy you have left may help us ascend."

"Ascend? Pardon me, I know things have changed while I was away, but what does that mean exactly?" When the salamander had told him, he had thought it just rumor, but seeing a lower Yokai dressed like a human, it all clicked into place. *They really think they can gain more powers from other Yokai. Perhaps that's why they're so few left. They're devouring one another.*

The monkey grinned and clenched his hand tighter onto his staff. The monkeys flanking him did the same. *I knew it, they're just copies.*

"We are going to become as powerful as the Eight," the monkey replied.

Kaito laughed long and hard as the monkey glowered at him. This was just the sort of idiotic drivel he expected from a Yokai of his level.

"You will not be laughing when you're nothing but a husk." The monkeys screeched as they rushed towards Kaito.

He stopped laughing and twirled out of the way as they passed him. He shot icy blasts into the monkeys flanking the middle one. Two disappeared and pebbles clattered onto the ground in their place. *That's rather advanced, generating clones out of physical objects. Where did they learn such a trick? I wonder.*

The middle monkey remained and he pointed his staff at Kaito. "You saw through my deception."

They circled one another as Kaito uncapped his power, letting it flood his limbs. His hands transformed, tipped with claws. His breath came out in clouds of frozen vapor.

"Tell me," he rumbled. His voice deepened and sounded like the crash of thunder. "Who's been filling your head with lies about ascending?"

The monkey swung at Kaito's head with the staff. He sidestepped the attack and darted for the monkey, coming at him beneath his swing. He swiped a clawed hand at the creature, but when his claws should have ripped into flesh, the monkey disappeared with a pop and a stone clattered onto the ground. Kaito spun around; he had underestimated the monkey. A talking clone was very advanced indeed.

Five clones stared at him, with identical grins. He probed them with his spiritual energy, trying to find the real one, but they all blended together, sharing power without a source. He growled.

"You think yourself clever, but we have watched you prance around with the priestess, you are not as powerful as you think you were," the monkeys said in unison; their voices echoed and overlapped.

"I'll show you my true power." Kaito snarled and with a swing of his hand slashed through all five monkeys. Five stones fell to the ground, plinking one by one.

He clenched his hand into a fist. "Come out and fight me, coward."

Kaito spun in place. *They're playing games with me.* A monkey leapt at him from the trees, fangs bared and staff swinging. He batted it away as if it were a fly, but as he suspected, it was not the real monkey, and when one disappeared, another one replaced it. Two dozen monkeys loomed overhead in the treetops; half a dozen dropped down onto the ground surrounding him. He felt the power center nearby, but they moved about, darting back and forth, so it was hard to tell which one was the original and which were copies.

They screeched as they shook the tree limbs; others pounded their feet into the ground. The drumming and screeching and wailing made it difficult to concentrate, and while he tried to find the source of the chaos, the clones swung at him with short staffs, which he tried to fend off with his claws. If he had the room, he could transform into his dragon form, but they gave him not a moment to transform and they closed in all the time. For each clone he destroyed, another took its place. They kept coming like waves, one after the other, overwhelming him.

The real monkey was somewhere in the mix, and his spiritual energy burned brighter than the others. He would sneak in and land a blow to Kaito's stomach or his back before retreating into the mass, shielded by his many clones. Kaito's temper rose and he lost focus.

A staff hit him hard in the chin, knocking him backwards. He stumbled back, trying to regain his balance; the monkeys pushed their advantage, falling onto him in a pile. He staggered beneath them, his knees buckling as more and more climbed on top of him. He had overestimated his ability, just as the monkey had said. Had he had his full power, they would not have lasted a second against him.

He lost sight of anything but the bright yellow of the silk haori; their stink of musk and rotten fruit filled his nostrils. *I will not die this way. Not without my revenge.* He had one chance left, he had wanted to avoid using up what little energy he had. He concentrated on the river of energy flowing through his body, once a mighty river now more like a stream. He redirected the stream, pulling forth the energy deep in the pit of his stomach, and with an exhale he expelled it and they flew off him in a blast. Fifty monkey copies disintegrated into nothing. A cascade of pebbles fell onto his back as he lay panting on the ground.

Kaito stood, his legs weak and his head pounding. Among the rubble, one dead monkey, mouth open in shock, covered in ice. He stared down at the monkey. *Where did a monkey Yokai get this kind of power?* As he walked away, he staggered and leaned against a tree. The monkey laughed feebly. He turned back around to face him; the creature had only been stunned at first. He leaned over the creature and placed his foot against its throat.

"Not so cheeky now?" he panted.

The monkey grinned as Kaito glared down at him. "What are you smiling at?"

"The great Dragon fell right into our trap."

His senses had been numbed by the explosion of energy and he had not felt anyone sneak up behind him until it was too late. He felt the familiar spiritual pressure. *It can't be. I'm just imagining it. She's dead.*

Suzume screamed in the distance. *They were after the priestess from the beginning.* He whipped his head backwards, prepared to go and stop them. The source of the spiritual pressure stood in his way. A priestess in red and white stood nearby; in her hand was a charm, a white ofuda painted with black characters. He stared at her. *This cannot be real. This has to be a dream.*

She stared at him, stoic and removed. She lifted the ofuda and sang a few words. His feet would not move to stop her. Just as they had been that day Kazue had sealed him. Her song ended and the charm vibrated with energy twisting and tugging, trying to break free of her grasp. She looked down as she let the charm go. It came straight for him.

"Kazue?" he said—the words betrayed him. He should have been mad. He should have torn her apart for returning to him only to replay that final betrayal once more. But instead the charm slammed into his chest and he was thrown backwards as he uttered a single word. "Why?"

# 10

When she opened her eyes once more, she was alone in a strange place. Her head rested against the bark of a tree. She looked about for Kaito, but he was nowhere to be seen. *He left me! Was that his plan all along, to bring me to this forsaken place and abandon me?* Suzume grabbed the tree behind her, wrapped her arms around the trunk and pulled, but she did not have the strength to even lift herself off the ground. She slid back down to the ground and stared out into the forest. *I refuse to be left behind. I'll get out of here on my own. I'll show him that I'm not useless.*

She crossed her arms over her chest, trying to decide what to do next. She couldn't move, and who knew how long she could stay here without attracting some man-eating Yokai. *I'll just rest a while and then I'll go look for a way back to the road.* And from there, then what? She wasn't even sure she could find her way to the road let alone to any village or the governor's palace that she had never been to.

A twig nearby snapped and Suzume whipped her head in the direction of the sound. The branches rustled and then a pair of small brown birds burst from beneath the canopy. They twirled around one another, fighting over a piece of grass. Suzume exhaled a breath she had been holding. She hated to admit it, but the swamp monster's warning about creatures lurking about had spooked her. And now she felt as vulnerable as a newborn. A week ago she would never have worried. Then again, a week ago she did not know Yokai were real and had an appetite for human flesh.

*I cannot just sit here and wait to be made into a meal.* She wriggled her toes and flexed her legs. *That's it, I'm leaving.* She pushed hard on the ground with the palms of her hands. She managed to lift up by perhaps a meter before she tilted over to the side like an over-filled wagon. The ground here was harder and her only consolation was she did not get an ear full of mud. She rolled over and climbed onto all fours. *Come on, Suzume, if you can wake a dragon, you can walk out of this swamp.*

Her arms trembled as she crept on all fours. Her legs burned and her stomach muscles contracted. She made it to the other side of the clearing before collapsing face forward onto the ground.

Suzume lay head tilted to one side, too tired to care that she was filthy and lying on the ground. *How did I end up here? Where did I go wrong?* Suzume lay on the ground, listening to the burbling of the river nearby. A fish or some aquatic creature splashed in the water. Her eyelids had grown heavy, and the sun, which peeked through the canopy of the trees, warmed her back. She dozed off for a few moments.

She woke with a start when she felt a prickle race up her spine, as if an icy finger had been brushed against her skin. She gasped and rolled over, expecting to find Kaito leering down at her. But she was alone and the sun was high in the sky. She must not have slept for very long. She flexed her fingers, they were not as stiff as before, and her legs did not feel wobbly. She eased herself into a sitting position. It took more effort than it normally would have, but at least she wasn't face down in the dirt anymore. She looked around, the short hairs on the back of her neck pricked and a voice at the back of her mind screamed danger.

*I cannot stay here out in the open.* She maneuvered her feet under her and attempted to once more rise up onto all fours. She stayed like that for a moment, making sure she could hold her own weight. Then she heard a rustling sound behind her. She looked over her shoulder, her eyes darting back and forth. A frog hopped across her path. It stopped in front of her and stared at her with large bulbous eyes.

"Go tell your swamp lord to keep his subjects away from me," Suzume said.

The frog blinked at her before hopping off. She heaved a sigh. *It's now or never.* She lurched forward, and with more effort than she would like to admit, she climbed back onto her feet. She stood upright, wobbling with her hands out for balance. *I can do this.* She had started to chant it in her mind like a mantra.

She took a few steps, but she was so focused on walking she did not see the embankment that sloped down towards the river. She tripped and went tumbling down the hill. She splashed in a pool of water at the bottom of the hill, along the river's edge. She gasped and inhaled a mouthful of stagnant dirty water. She threw her head back, tossing water and mud around as she sputtered and spit out the brackish water. She shook her head as she clawed her way up onto the riverbank, where she proceeded to wring out her clothes. Though there wasn't much use. She was probably only going to land in another puddle or slip in more mud or, worse, get attacked by something that would cover her in goop.

She hated feeling this powerless. *Damn the Dragon for dragging me away from the temple. At least I was clean there.* She sat at the water's edge, watching the silt she had disturbed settle. Flecks of metallic-colored earth glimmered under the bright sun overhead. *I cannot stay here. He'll return and I can only imagine what sort of horrors he has planned for me from here. I have no intention of getting involved in whatever he plans; I have to get to the palace to warn them.*

She soaked up a few more rays before finding the resolve to stand once more. Her clothes were heavy with mud and water as she waded across the river. Before, she would have looked for a different way to cross, a drier way, but soaked and filthy, the direct route seemed best in this instance. Lucky for her it had been a dry summer and the river did not go much past thigh height, though the current tugged at her, trying to pull her downstream.

She lost her balance once and grabbed onto a river stone, scraping her hand. The scrapes weren't deep, but blood dripped from the wound just the same. She cursed and wiped it on her filthy clothes before reaching the far shore. She climbed up the embankment on the other side, grasping at roots and loose earth, which crumbled underneath her feet. She slid back after making it halfway.

She kicked a rock and hurt her toe. She hissed in pain as she hopped in circles. *You could go back and wait for the Dragon,* a small voice at the back of her mind said. She looked over her shoulder back across the river to where she had come from. It felt like she had been walking for hours, but it seemed she had only gone a few feet. *I'll be damned if all this effort was for nothing.*

She resumed her climb up the steep embankment, avoiding spots where the earth was mostly sand and loose earth, and used stones and roots as footholds. By the time she reached the top, she collapsed onto the ground in a patch of sun. Her breathing was ragged and her hands throbbed from grasping onto rocks, but she was one step closer to freedom. She lay sunning herself like a lizard on a rock for a few more minutes. She could already feel her clothes drying, her strength returning little by little. She rolled over and climbed back onto her feet. It was easier this time than it had been before.

She was at the edge of a forested area, dryer than the rest of the swamp, but long green moss hung from the branches. She marched forward, feeling better with each step. It felt good to take control. Perhaps this would be a new turning point in her life. She pushed aside the moss and ducked beneath it. This area did not seem familiar, but she supposed if she kept going in this general direction, she was bound to find her way.

But it did not take long before she was utterly and completely lost. She passed a tree with a hollow that looked like a face and then thirty minutes later passed it again. *I really hope that tree isn't alive and following me.* She stopped and stared at said tree for a moment; the eyes were jagged grooves as if a clawed hand had ripped them out, and the mouth a gaping maw.

"Are you alive and planning on eating me?" Suzume asked the tree.

It stared back at her without response. *That's it, I've lost my mind and I'm talking to trees.*

She sat down on a nearby rock. Her clothes had dried and stuck to her skin, and the air was so humid she felt like she was drinking it. She wiped her brow with the back of her hand. *Shouldn't I just have an innate sense of direction? I am a descendant of the Eight.* Perhaps this wasn't her best idea.

Then she felt it again, that prickling sensation on the back of her neck. Something deep down in her gut told her to move. She jumped up and rolled on the ground just as something went careening past her. It hit a tree at the same height as her head. She looked at the barbed sphere that had embedded into the trunk. *That could have been my face.*

She stood up, her arms raised in a would-be defensive pose. It was all for show. She was still weak from before. Laughter echoed around her.

"Who's there?" she called out.

The sounds of laughing came from all directions. She spun in circles, trying to find its source, only to make herself dizzy.

"A priestess has lost her way," said a high voice from above her.

"Tsk, tsk, tsk," taunted a second.

A tingling sensation raced along her skin, and the airs on her arm and neck stood on end. Which meant these were most likely Yokai that were watching her from the shadows.

"Don't you know better than to tangle with a priestess?" she asked.

The laughter continued; it had a crazed almost manic sound to it. It came from all directions, changing at random. She spun in circles, trying to focus on the source, but it was impossible.

"We do not fear you, Priestess."

"You should, I am a powerful priestess. I sealed a dragon just the other day." She planted her hands on her hips. If growing up in the palace had taught her one thing, it was never to show how afraid you were. Faceless Yokai could not be that much different than vapid courtiers.

The chittering laughter followed these words. *How many of them are there?*

"We know you are the one who freed the Dragon, you cannot fool us."

"Then if you know who I am, you know I am descended from the Eight. I am the daughter of the emperor."

They laughed again. Their laughter had gone from fearsome to somewhat annoying. Everything she said could not possibly be that amusing. She squinted into the gloom and spotted them at last. Three crouched figures watched her from the bough of a tree. All she could make out in the growing dark were their yellow eyes gleaming at her from the shadows.

"You seem to think you know everything."

"We do. We know your mother. And we know she betrayed the emperor."

She shrugged her shoulders. *Who would have thought Yokai keep up with human gossip?* "You and half the kingdom. A bride of the emperor does not get exiled without people noticing."

"Yes. But we know the *real* reason for her exile." Their voices echoed inside her skull. They meant to scare her, but she wasn't buying into this fearsome Yokai routine.

It was Suzume's turn to scoff. "You mean her wanton ways. I

know why my mother was exiled. She took a lover and got caught."

"Oh, how simple you are, to think that is the truth. You know the real reason in your heart, don't you, Suzume?"

Hearing her name on inhuman lips sent a shiver down her spine. This was more than a trick. Perhaps they did know what her mother did. She never believed the story being passed around the palace. Half the emperor's wives took the occasional lover. Her father had disowned all eight of her brothers and sisters. That was not the normal course of action.

Her spiritual energy was returning in spurts. She felt the sparks along her arm, but it would not be enough if these creatures decided to attack. She could not control it and if these things could read minds or whatever it was they were doing to gather this information, she wasn't sure if she had the power to defend herself.

"What do you want?" Suzume said.

"We want you."

Then they fell from the trees one by one, and the creatures stepped out of the shadows. They were ghastly with long hands and feet, and faces that were sunken in with yellow eyes rimmed with red that gleamed with their ill intent. Their bodies were covered in black slick skin that reminded her of the swamp creature but much more terrifying. Suzume stumbled backwards trying to flee the creatures, but she did not get a couple feet before she tripped and fell hard. She threw up her hands to shield her face just as they descended upon her.

# 11

They grabbed at her, and weakened by her earlier explosion, her natural defenses did nothing to deter them. She kicked, punched and scratched, but they only laughed at her attempts at self-defense. One of the monsters grabbed her ankles to pin them to the ground. She writhed back and forth as a second and third pinned her arms to the ground.

"What do you want from me?" She stared, her eyes darting between the three of them. *I never thought I would wish the Dragon was around, but he would be handy right about now.*

They grinned, revealing large white pointed teeth. Just the right sharpness to tear into flesh. *Are they planning on eating me?*

The one holding onto her ankles pulled and yanked her off the ground. He threw her over his shoulder like a sack. Suzume stared at the world upside down beyond the curtain of her tangled hair. The other two Yokai grinned at her in a lurid way. One reached out and placed something over her eyes. She may have imagined it, but it looked like a leaf. *What do they want from me?* She continued to kick and flail. But being upside down and blindfolded, she could not do much, and she felt like a fish on a line. Just the thought made her stomach squirm.

"I demand you put me down," she said. Even though she knew it was fruitless, her own stubbornness kept her from accepting her fate.

They ignored her protest and started to move. They were going fast from the way Suzume's hair flew about, and she swung back and forth, slamming into the creature's back over and over. She threw out her arms to try to steady herself and to stop the swaying that churned her stomach. It made no difference, and the contents of her stomach were threatening the back of her throat.

She tried to grasp onto any passing foliage, hoping to pull free of the creature, but all she could get a hold of crumbled in her grasp. The blood rushed to her head and the pressure built behind her eyes. The Yokai jumped into the air, judging from the rush of air past her face and the short feeling of weightlessness. Wind rushed through the trees as the Yokai leapt from branch to branch. Wood creaked as they landed on a branch and stopped.

"Careful, Hiro, don't break the branch with all the extra weight," one of her captors said.

Suzume tried to twist in their direction, but her limbs were losing feeling from being upside down for too long. Her entire body tingled.

Hiro, the thing holding her, laughed. "Oh, don't worry, if I go down, I'll just drop her."

"Are you saying I'm fat?" Suzume spat.

"You're not exactly light," grunted Hiro. And he hiked her up higher onto his shoulders.

"I'm a princess, how dare you speak to me that way."

"Go ahead and muzzle her, Jiro."

A hand descended over her mouth, intent on silencing her. When it got close, she lurched forward and bit it. She expected the hand to be slippery and maybe slime covered, but along with the coppery taste of blood, she got a mouthful of fur as well. She spat out the blood and fur as Jiro cursed. Suzume tried to get the hair out of her mouth, but it caught at the back of her throat. She continued to sputter as the other two creatures laughed.

"The little witch bit me!" Jiro said.

"Come over here again and I'll do more than bite," she replied. She imagined she sounded imposing. But in reality she looked like a fool—upside down, her hair in her face, and blood and mud smearing her cheeks.

"Just silence her and be done with it," Hiro said.

Suzume braced herself for them to try to cover her mouth again, but instead something collided with her skull and everything went dark.

Suzume awoke with a pounding in her head and a foul taste in her mouth. Her body tingled all over. She rolled over, groaning. *I feel like I've been wrung out like an old cloth.* That seemed to be her life since she met the Dragon.

She crawled into a sitting position and looked around. Night had fallen since she had been knocked unconscious. She was in a forested area, a ring of trees caged her in, and in the center of the ring a fire burned. She shivered, realizing she was cold. She scooted closer to the flames while looking around for her captors. *They kidnap me and then leave?* The flames cast long shadows on the trees, and beyond that lay darkness. She squinted, trying to catch sight of their yellow eyes peering at her through the gloom.

A stone circle charred black kept the fire in place. She put her hands near the flames and let the warmth seep into her. She closed her eyes, enjoying the warm current that rippled through her body. She hated being cold and dirty. She never realized how much she would miss simple creature comforts until she had to trudge through a swamp.

The all too familiar prickle against her skin alerted her and the whispered warning in her ear. *Be careful.* She opened her eyes again and saw her hands were rimmed in red light. A red current drifted from the fire into the palm of her hands. She skittered backwards, staring at the flames then at her hands, which looked the same as always. When she moved away from the ring of light, the red aura disappeared. The light around her hands faded. Suzume turned her hands over, looking for a clue as to what had caused the phenomenon.

A rustling in the dark forest beyond caught her attention. Suzume jumped to her feet. A man walked towards her from the darkness.

"Who's there?" she shouted. She looked around for something to defend herself with, but there was nothing within reach.

"You're awake, then?" he said as he approached her. He stepped into the light and she saw his face. He had the head of a monkey, covered in white and brown hair with bright pink skin circling his eyes and mouth. She had heard about monkeys and had been curious to see one since she was a girl, but this one wore clothes like a man, and from the way he grinned at her, she doubted he had her best interest in mind.

"Who are you and what am I doing here?" she asked. *I should have known it was another Yokai.*

"Why don't you sit down, Suzume."

She crossed her arms over her chest. She never took orders, especially not from a monkey in pants. "What do you want from me? Are you trying to ransom me to my father? Because it won't work."

The monkey huffed. "Why does everyone ask the villain their plans? As if I would tell you what I have planned just because you asked."

She eyed him suspiciously. She knew this type. She had met more than a few in her time in the palace. The man who thought himself exceedingly brilliant and everyone else was beneath his intelligence. *It's rather fitting that he's a monkey.* She laughed, thinking about a few lords back at the White Palace with a monkey face.

"What is so funny?"

She stopped laughing and replaced her expression with one of haughty contempt. A face she had perfected over the years. She lifted her chin and looked the monkey up and down. "Well, you're a monkey. Not the most intimidating creature."

He scowled, wrinkling his pink brow, which made him look even more foolish. Suzume laughed again. She imagined this monkey spent more time soaking in a hot spring than doing anything of real evil importance.

He marched over to her and she was too busy laughing to notice. He pulled his hand back and slapped her face hard. Suzume stumbled backwards and pressed her hand to her cheek. She looked at the monkey, too shocked to even find the right words to say. No one had ever dared raise a hand to her aside from the Dragon.

The fire in her gut sparked and the red aura glowed against her skin, encasing her in warmth. The fire nearby leapt and grew, casting the monkey's face into relief. He opened his mouth and showed off his canines. If she had the ability to control her powers, she would have fried the monkey to a crisp then and there, but for the moment she concentrated on keeping her temper contained. Who knew what would happen if she lost control like before.

"How dare you touch me, I am a descendant of the Eight!" she snarled.

The monkey stood back and eyed her, one brow raised. "You're also a brat who should mind her tongue."

"How dare you!"

"Silence or I will do more than slap you!" the monkey roared.

She snapped her mouth closed and glared at him instead.

"I could have tied you up. But I chose to treat you with respect because of who you are."

"Then why have your goons carry me upside down and knock me out?"

He ignored her question. "Sit down."

All her senses were on alert. She was not sure she could sit down without wanting to leap up again. She wanted to fight, to run, to burn. The fire in her felt like the campfire behind the monkey. It danced and twirled, trying to break free of the confines of the stone ring. She and the monkey stared at one another for a moment before Suzume did as he said and knelt down on the ground.

The monkey sat down as well, his hands folded in front of him. His actions were almost human. If it wasn't for the monkey face, she might have thought him a lord. He was arrogant enough to be one.

"Why did you kidnap me?" she asked.

Her first thought had been ransom, but she was starting to doubt this monkey would have any need of human currency or political favor. Which meant this had something to do with the Dragon. This was his world, after all. He had brought her nothing but trouble since she had awoken him.

He waved away her question. "Really, I thought we already covered this."

She rolled her eyes. "If you expect me to play along, you should at least tell me who you are."

"I am the elder of the Northern Monkey Clan."

That explained his superior air and manner. *I never knew Yokai were so organized. I always imagined them as wild animals without consideration for much other than tricks and destruction.*

He pressed his fingers together. "You'll find my kind can be very territorial." He smiled, revealing elongated canines. "You'd best listen to me if you do not want to be eaten by something along our journey."

Suzume eyed him, wondering if she should consider him a threat or not. The Yokai liked to threaten to eat her, but she had yet to witness them attacking humans. Everyone had heard the commoners' superstitions, but she had never heard of a human actually getting eaten by a Yokai. It was always a friend who knew someone who heard of someone whose uncle got snatched by an Oni, or some similar story. *I'm starting to wonder if it's all posturing just like humans do.* She had never seen any evidence of a Yokai until she had come to the temple. And even then not until she had awakened the Dragon. She had grown up at the White Palace and never stepped outside its walls until she was exiled, but she thought she would at least have seen some on the journey north from the palace. *Why did everything change all of a sudden?*

"Why have I never seen your kind before? Can you tell me that much?" she asked, not that she expected him to know.

"Our kind as a rule stay away from humans."

"I don't mean monkeys, I mean I've never met a Yokai until the past couple days. How is that possible?"

The monkey frowned. "That is very strange indeed." He examined her for a moment, dark eyes probing, searching for the answers to be written on her.

*Well, he's no help.* "Do you have a name, oh elder of the Northern Monkey Clan?"

"I'm glad you asked. My name is Kichiro." He puffed up his chest.

"So, Kichiro, are you just going to keep me here? What's step two of your nefarious plot?"

"That will come in time, once we can be certain the Dragon no longer poses a threat."

She leaned forward, curious. If this monkey could rid her of her dragon problem, she might be willing to help him.

"So that's what this is all about? You're using me to get to the Dragon?"

He stood and kept his back to her. "You don't even realize how valuable you are, do you?"

She scoffed. "I realize, but I don't think you realize how royally angry the Dragon is going to be when he finds out you poached me. Not that I care. I honestly would be glad to be rid of him."

"Then you have no need to fear, the Dragon will not trouble you again."

She should have been relieved, she had wanted to get rid of the Dragon, but somehow she felt like these monkeys would not be much better.

# 12

"Wake up."

Kaito dragged his eyelids open. He tried to move his arms but found his limbs unresponsive. Whatever spell she had put on him had him paralyzed. He rolled his eyes to one side and a priestess crouched beside him. She smiled down at him. *It can't be her. She should have died five hundred years ago. Is this her reincarnation?*

"Sorry for the spell. After the way we parted, I couldn't risk letting you up. Not yet." She smiled.

He opened his mouth with an effort and croaked, "Who are you?" His throat was dry and just forcing the words out felt like shards of ice were scraping against the back of his throat. He did not want to admit it aloud, but after five hundred years of dreaming of revenge, he thought his heart would be made of ice, but one glance from her and his heart had already begun to thaw. *I am a fool for loving her even after all she has done to me. And now she taunts me with a mystery and I want to forgive her.*

"Don't you recognize me, darling?" She brushed his face lightly with the tips of her fingers. He closed his eyes, relishing the feeling of her skin against his. *I've dreamed of you for five hundred years. No matter how I try I could not let you go.* Nothing had changed, just as he had been released, she came back for him. Drawn together by fate, they could not be parted. He tried to hold onto the anger, the bitterness, but it melted like snowfall in the spring.

"You were reincarnated, I assume?" he said. He turned his gaze inward, trying to access his spiritual energy, but her spell had locked it away, creating dams in the river of energy that flowed through him and gave him power. *She's learned new tricks.*

"Something like that," she said, and sat back, legs crossed, hands flat on her thighs. He wanted to trace her digits, relearn her body in this new form. She still braided her hair down her back. Kazue's reincarnation carried an uncanny similarity to the woman he had known. He had never known a reincarnation, but everything about this woman down to the shape of her lips was just as he remembered. It hurt to look at her, as if the barbs of their past love were lodged into his chest, making it difficult to breathe.

"Why did you not come to me, release me?" he asked.

She tilted her head and regarded him. "Why would I let you go?" A smile curved her lips as if she was holding back a secret joke.

A warning bell went off in the back of his head. That was not like the Kazue he had known. The sweet vision of Kazue had blinded him to everything else, to the subtle hints, powers she had not had before. Mannerisms that were unlike the woman who he had loved and had sealed him away. Intoxicated by the idea of seeing her again, he had let himself believe what he wanted. When he looked closer, he could sense something was not right. But weakened as he was, he could not place it. This was not his Kazue. His Kazue would never have done this. A part of him hoped even now that the woman that had sealed him away had not been Kazue. He wanted this woman—whoever she was—to be the one who had done the deed.

"Why did you do it?" He asked the question that had haunted his dreams, causing his restless sleep, and fueled his rage.

"You don't know yet?" She laughed. Her voice echoed in a manic, almost crazed way. This was definitely not his Kazue.

"For power, of course."

---

Three figures materialized out of the darkness. Suzume's eyes darted towards them as they approached and she half rose, preparing to protect herself. They were the same three monsters from the swamp, with black slick skin and yellow gleaming eyes. They saw Suzume and grinned at her. Kichirou saw her staring and glanced over to them. He stood to greet them.

"I've told you not to appear that way before me," he scolded.

The middle one grinned, displaying his pointed white teeth. He glanced in Suzume's direction before bowing to Kichirou. The three Yokai pulled at their foreheads, as if they were taking off masks, and when they did, they changed from gruesome swamp creatures to monkeys like Kichirou. In their hands they held leaves, the anchors of their disguise. Dressed in haori of lesser quality, with plainer designs, Suzume assumed these were Kichirou's underlings.

"Where is our brother?" Kichirou asked.

The middle one lowered his head. "Dead, brother. The Dragon killed him."

Suzume shook her head. *What did they expect when they tangled with a dragon?* As much as she wanted to be free of the Dragon, she doubted these baboons would be the ones to do it.

"The Dragon, has he escaped?" Kichirou asked.

"She has him," the one to the right replied.

"So is this woman your leader?" Suzume asked.

The monkey ignored her and she scowled at his back. He was

damnably persistent in keeping her in the dark. "Then we should move now."

"I want the Dragon dead as much as you four, but I seriously doubt any of you have the power to stop him," Suzume said.

Kichirou turned to face Suzume. "It is not one of my clan who has him now. She who has him is much more powerful than you can imagine."

"Who is she?"

"She has many names and many faces, you would be better served to worry about your own head. Forget the Dragon, he is as good as dead."

Initially, she thought the monkey was a bit of a joke, but his tone had her second-guessing. She did not think anyone was powerful enough to go against a dragon, but her knowledge of the Yokai world was woefully limited. And she hoped it would stay that way. Once she returned to her place at the White Palace, she would forget any of this ever happened; it would be all a bad dream. Either way, she had no intention of staying with these monkeys a moment longer than she had to. They were no better than the Dragon, and at least he was good looking.

The monkeys approached her, long-fingered hands grasping at her. Suzume felt her power rise like the tide within her. She had sat close to the fire, drawing the red aura into her, and she felt stronger by being near it. She pulsed with energy, and it rippled beneath her skin—she was full to bursting. When the two monkeys grabbed onto her arm, the power exploded out of Suzume and hit the monkeys, throwing them backwards.

The force of it had Suzume stumbling backwards as well. The warmth cocooned her but did not burn, though sparks jumped along her fingertips. The two monkeys who went flying collided with the third underling, who came too late to help. Suzume caught her balance and used the momentary distraction to run. She got a few feet before two more monkeys dropped from the treetops and grinned at her.

"You cannot run, Priestess." She shoved them with all her might. They screeched as if burned and fell down on the ground, writhing in pain. She ran around them and into the forest. The power coursed through her and the shimmering red aura surrounded her.

The monkeys, undeterred, followed after her but at a safe distance. She ran through the forest, blinded by the night, and she tripped over a fallen branch. She landed on the ground and scraped her knee. Cursing, she scrambled back to her feet, but the monkeys surrounded her on all sides. Hands up in the air, she spun around in a circle; the light on her hands had already begun to fade. Her reckless burst had used it all up, it seemed. *Great, so it's not limitless.*

"Grab her, Shiro," Kichiro said.

Suzume stood her ground as the monkey, Shiro, approached her. She held up her hands, preparing to zap him. "Like I am willing to go anywhere with you." She sneered.

"You would be wise to come with us," said Kichirou.

"Ha, and why's that?"

"Because the entire Yokai world is looking for you and not all of them will be as kind as us."

"You're lying. This has to be about the Dragon." *What could they possibly want with me?* She touted her divine lineage often, but Suzume doubted Yokai with their superstrength and powers cared one little bit about any of that.

Kichiro laughed, throwing his head back. The other monkeys joined in a whooping laughter. She placed her hands on her hips, having forgotten her intention to zap the monkey, which made no attempt to approach now.

"The Dragon has no power anymore. The priestess ensured that when she sealed him away long ago."

"What do you mean? He's back now."

The monkey shook his head. "You really know nothing."

"Care to enlighten me, then?" she asked.

They closed in once more and Suzume held up her hands to threaten them, but the power had faded to a couple sparks. If she was lucky, she would have enough to stop one of them but not all five. The one closest to her rushed her and the aura around her shot out and burned the monkey's hand. The fur on his hands burned away and left charred flesh, which split to reveal angry red muscles. Suzume stared at the injured monkey, wondering how this could have happened. Where had these powers come from and why could she not control them?

The leader looked to his injured companion.

"Why don't you ask the Dragon? He is with his beloved now. Perhaps she can provide the answers you seek."

"That's not possible, Kazue is dead. She would have died five hundred years ago."

"Who said it was the original Kazue? Can she not be reincarnated? Is that not why the Dragon set out on this mission?"

"You're tricking me," she replied.

"You wanted to know who our leader is, well, now you know. She is Kazue's reincarnation."

---

Invisible bindings crawled up his chest, constricting his breathing. Black creeped around the edge of his vision, and keeping his eyes open proved a challenge. He should have noticed from the start that this was not some human spell. *How could I be so blind as to not see it from the start? Kazue is dead, and even if she has been reincarnated, it does not change that betrayal.*

"Who are you?" he snarled from behind clenched teeth. Just opening his mouth to speak took all his effort and concentration.

She laughed, covering her mouth with her hands. "I've already told you, I'm your beloved Kazue, of course."

He glanced down and long strands of hair like tentacles wrapped around his body. *She's a shifter, a powerful one who uses*

93

*other Yokai's energy. This must be the Yokai the giant salamander heard about.* A Yokai like her usually stuck to luring human men in with their pretty face before they ate them alive. They were known to eat lesser Yokai when given the chance, but this one had grown powerful—more powerful than he had seen before—if she could read minds and take on Kazue's appearance based on his memories. *Kazue's spell did more than I realized if I fell for these petty tricks.*

He bared flat human teeth at her as she laughed at his struggles.

"Struggle all you like, you'll never escape."

"Since when does your kind go for bigger prey?" he said. He only needed a moment to refocus his energy and break free. Perhaps if he distracted her, she would loosen her grip enough for him to access his energy.

She threw her head back and laughed. "Much has changed since you went to sleep, Dragon."

"That is becoming quickly apparent."

"Don't worry, you won't have much time to lament the changes."

He grinned. Her admission, though indirect, weakened her spell; spells of this kind held power in the belief. The more the victim believed what they wanted, the stronger the hold. But this shifter was a vain creature and had not passed up an opportunity to gloat. If she had kept on pretending to be Kazue, he would not find the chink in her spell that he needed. He saw it like a hairline crack in a vase—running through the black hair that bound him was a single silver hair.

He refocused on putting all the energy he had into that one single hair, what little he had access to. Her tendrils of hair tightened around him, feeling the flow of his energy, trying to combat his escape. She had assumed her meal was coming to an end, she thought she had won. But beneath the bindings, he flexed his fingers and wiggled his toes. He could feel his energy locked behind invisible dams seeping out through the cracks and he unraveled her spell from the inside. She was so busy gorging herself on his spiritual energy she did not realize she was taking too much too fast. A dragon's spiritual energy was much richer than the average Yokai. And too much rich food could make you sick. Overstuffed, she loosened her bindings, getting lazy as she was satiated. He broke through her blocks, one after another.

"Tell me at least before I go, who is it that controls this area?"

She narrowed her eyes at him. "What does it matter?"

"Call it curiosity. I've been dying to know."

She leaned in close, whispering her mouth against his skin. She stank like rotting meat. "It was me."

"That was your mistake." He opened his mouth and icy blue energy poured out of his mouth and blasted into her face. She screamed and fell backwards, but her head, encased in ice, cracked down her forehead then a spiderweb of hundreds of cracks stretched across her face. The cracks grew until they split and broke apart in chunks. The pieces tumbled to the floor as she desperately tried to put her face together until one by one she fell apart until nothing was left but her headless torso and the slack bonds of her hair around his body. He tore it away with his claws and then stared down at the shriveled husk.

With her spell broken, she returned to her original form—blue skin, long hands and a humanoid body, shriveled and dried as an old husk. The spiritual energy she had absorbed seeped out of her and into the ground. The earth at his feet burst to life, plants poked through the ground, and flowers bloomed. The Yokai's black hair crumbled into pieces and then turned to dust. She had lived for thousands of years draining the energy of other creatures. These type of vultures usually preyed on the weak. But this poor idiot had finally bitten off more than she could chew.

"Damn Kazue," he said. If it wasn't for her, he would never have fallen for this creature's trap. *How can I cut her out of my heart?*

"How do I know you're not trying to trick me?" she asked with her hands crossed over her chest.

"What benefit would I get from lying to you?"

She shrugged her shoulders. *Everything, if you can win my trust, then you can please whoever is pulling all the strings.* She was not sure why, but something in her gut told her that Kazue wasn't the one behind all this. She suspected this was all a ruse to keep her here and it was working.

"All right. So say I believe it's Kazue, what does she want with me?"

"Your mother never told you?"

Suzume frowned at him. "What does my mother have to do with this?"

"You really don't know? I assumed because of your exile..."

Before he could finish his sentence, a bright blue light lit up the night sky. It encompassed the trees and the monkeys turned as one to face it. Suzume too stared as if mesmerized until something struck her in the back of the knee and she fell to the ground, encased in white light. She heard the energy rush by like a gale-force wind and the monkeys screaming in agony. After a few minutes the sounds died away. The white barrier that protected her shrank back down to size and a small figure no higher than her calf stared up at her with large black eyes set into a round head. He had no mouth but tilted his head back and forth as he regarded her.

"You saved me?" she said to the creature.

It nodded its head and made a sound like branches in the wind.

She was stunned, why would some spirit save her? "Thank you."

Suzume looked past the tiny Kodama. The monkeys were gone; only fragments of them remained. The trees were frosted—

even though it was summer—and the leaves had fallen off the trees, creating a blanket of frozen leaves. *What did this?* Her feeble energy sparked, mixing with blue energy that raised a chill along her spine. *The Dragon.* She looked up as he strolled into the clearing. He glanced around at his surroundings, bemused by the destruction.

"I told you to stay put," he said.

"What took you so long?" Suzume snarled.

"I had to take care of a Yokai, the one the swamp creature said was draining other Yokai."

"I hoped she would have drained you," Suzume replied.

He laughed and then knelt down to the small spirit, who jumped into his outstretched hand. "I've put you through a lot. Thank you, I owe you a debt."

The spirit bowed.

"You left that thing with me?" She did not think he cared about anything other than his revenge.

Kaito glanced at her. "I have to protect my pet."

# 13

"I've had enough!" Suzume announced.

Kaito, as usual, was further up the road. The moon was out but just a bare sliver. She had to squint to see him. He tilted his head to regard her.

"You've had enough of the sexual tension and you want to give yourself to me?" he asked.

She did not even have the energy to argue. *I am going to zap him for that later.* They had been walking nonstop since they left the forest. It had been a few hours since then, but it may as well have been days, for all she cared. Her hair was a matted mess, mud chafed her skin, and her blisters had blisters. She did a test sniff— she stank like monkey and swamp. She wrinkled her nose.

There was a grassy knoll topped by a tree. She stomped over towards it, sat down and leaned against the tree.

"This place is a bit public, but I like a bit of danger," the Dragon said as he loomed over her, his arms crossed over his chest.

Suzume closed her eyes and ignored him. *Maybe if I close my eyes, he and all of this insanity will go away. Even if I managed to get away from him and return to the palace, no one would believe that I'm the emperor's daughter.*

The grass rustled beneath his feet and she could feel the power radiating from his body as he leaned in close to her. His breath fanned across her cheek. Her powers reached out probing tendrils, testing his spiritual power with her own. He did not back down but let her power caress his. The sensation of their powers mingling raised the gooseflesh on her arms.

"I forget how weak you humans can be," he said in a husky whisper.

"That's because you're selfish and self-absorbed," Suzume replied. She kept her eyes closed. She couldn't see his smile, but she could feel his amusement in the commingling of their powers. Kaito's spiritual energy was sending off sparks like it had before; in fact, it seemed to be mixing with hers.

"You would know," he replied.

She peeked at him from one eye, wondering if she wanted to take that as the insult it clearly was.

"We'll make camp, but not here on the side of the road. We're too exposed."

"What are you afraid of? You defeated the Yokai that was hunting this area."

He frowned but did not respond. A chill crept down her spine, she wasn't sure if it was Kaito's mood or some other premonition. Whatever it was, she had the feeling they were not safe. Kichiro had said other Yokai would be looking for her. *What does my mother have to do with all of this?*

She looked up and he had disappeared. She sighed. *Where did he go now?* She glanced around in several directions.

"Where are you? This isn't funny!" She twirled in place, looking for Kaito. She inhaled sharply and wrung her hands. The night was dark and the night insects were the only sound. *If we get attacked by another Yokai...* A hand came down on her shoulder and Suzume screamed. A second hand grabbed her other shoulder and twisted her around.

"What are you screaming about?" Kaito asked.

Suzume looked up at Kaito and felt a hot blush stain her skin. *How could I let him trick me like this?*

"Nothing. A bug. A creature. Nothing," she said and ripped herself from his grasp.

He raised an eyebrow, but for once, he did not tease her. She ducked her head for a moment to regain her composure.

"Where did you go?"

"Why, did you miss me?"

"No. You said we couldn't camp here. Did you find somewhere for us to stay the night?"

He grinned. "I did, actually, and I have a bit of a surprise."

He held out his hand for her to take. She shrugged him off and followed him through the brush along the side of the road. They fought through low-hanging branches and tall grasses—or at least Suzume did; mundane things like struggling with undergrowth seemed beyond Kaito. It took a few minutes before they reached a clearing. The air was damp and smelt of sulfur.

"Is that?"

She ran towards the most glorious thing she could imagine. A group of craggy volcanic rocks created a pool of water. Steam rose from the water's surface in tendrils before dissipating in the night air. Suzume knelt down alongside the water's edge and the steam brushed against her skin like a kiss. She leaned over and dipped her hand into the warm water. The warm tingles raced up her arm and filled her in the same way the fire had. She did not see any of the red aura, but somehow she felt recharged just from the brief contact.

"A hot spring! I am saved." She sighed with delight.

"I thought you would like it." He leaned against a tree at the edge of the clearing, his arms folded over his chest.

Suzume got back to her feet, hands on her filthy hips. "What's your angle?"

"What? Can't I do something nice for my pet?" He grinned.

She decided to ignore the pet comment. "No. Not you. You're being too nice. Why?"

He uncrossed his arms and pointed. "You admit that you're my pet, then."

She scowled at him in response.

He laughed and then said, "You stink. I want to wash out that monkey stench."

She crinkled her nose at him. She hated to agree with him, but she did feel filthy and the water was calling to her. *There's always a catch. Dare I risk it to have skin free of muck?*

"You're not going to boil the water somehow and make me into a broth, are you?"

"I doubt it would be very filling." He smiled, but she knew a demon hid behind that smile.

Suzume looked to Kaito, then to the spring, and then back to Kaito. She just could not believe he was doing something nice for her. "Did you set this up so you could see me naked?"

He threw up his hands in defense. "There is nothing beneath those filthy clothes that I wish to see."

She folded her hands over her torso. "I'll have you know men have written poems about my body."

"Uh-huh." He strolled away. "Just hurry up and wash."

She watched him go with a suspicious glance. Once she was sure he was gone, she stripped down in a hurry. She peeled off her filthy clothes and dropped them onto the ground. Clumps of dirt came loose from the fabric and fell onto the ground with a plop. She shook her head, looking at the ruined clothes. She had no inkling how to clean them and she had no change of clothes. *I'll worry about that once I'm clean.*

She waded into the water. The water embraced her flesh and the gooseflesh rose on her arms and legs. She went to the center of the pond, it reached up to her middle, and she sank down to her shoulders. Dirty water swirled away from her in a murky cloud. She watched it go with a crinkled nose. *Did all that dirt really come off of me?*

She plugged her nose and submerged her entire body in the water. She burst through the surface and flicked her hair back, showering the rocks around the pool in water. She ran her fingers through her hair, trying to untangle the knots as she looked for a place to sit. All the while she kept one ear cocked for the sound of approaching footsteps. She found a smooth stone that made a natural seat at the water's edge. She sat down and the water came up to her shoulders. She leaned back against the volcanic rock and closed her eyes. *I am not coming out until I am a giant prune.*

The ground beneath her feet was smooth, like a polished stone. She rubbed her toes against it absently. A twig snapped and her eyes flew open. She peered past the rising steam but saw nothing waiting in the dark. *Maybe I'm being too jumpy.* With her luck, the monkey's relatives would have followed her here and were intent on revenge. She decided it was best to keep her eyes open. She stared at the steam as it rose off the surface of the water. *I would stay here forever if I could. No courtiers to worry about, no responsibilities and no dragons.*

Her vision blurred as she let her mind wander. Images danced through the steam and she smiled groggily. *It's almost like watching a dream while I am awake.* The longer she watched the images, the clearer they became. She watched as a priestess attended to a shrine. She leaned forward. *I know that place.* Suzume recognized the carved depiction of the mountain god above the shrine where Kaito had been sealed. The priestess had her back to Suzume, but she knelt before the shrine, hands pressed together as if in prayer. A second priestess approached her and put her hand on the priestess' shoulder.

"You shouldn't come here, what if you break the seal?" the second priestess said.

The first priestess looked up. She was beautiful in a classic way, round face, large eyes and ebony hair worn in a single braid. "I wanted to come here once more before I leave," she said.

"We will keep him safely locked away . Do not worry."

The priestess' hand drifted down to her belly. She rubbed her swelling stomach absently. "Thank you for this," she said. "You must never tell anyone the truth. Keep him here until I return for him. Promise?"

The second priestess bowed to her. "Even if it takes a thousand lifetimes, I will protect your secret."

The image dissipated in a swirl of colors. Suzume rubbed her eyes as another scene played out before her in the steam. This one was even clearer than the first.

The priestess from the shrine walked through the swamp they had just left. She had a long staff in a holster on her back, and instead of the traditional red and white of a priestess, she wore a long haori shirt in brown over brown hakama pants. She stopped at the edge of a clearing along a large expanse of water. The water bubbled and then parted. The giant salamander emerged and the woman raised her hand to him in greeting.

"You have some nerve coming here, Priestess." The giant salamander rose up on all fours in a menacing pose. He was five times the priestess' size and could crush her with one swing of his tail.

She did not even reach for her weapon. "Do not waste your empty threats upon me. I have erected a barrier to protect me. Now listen to me speak."

The creature shifted back and forth but appeared unable to move. "Very well, why have you come here?"

"For answers," she said.

He shook his head. "Many seek but not all find."

"I know. I wanted to know about—" She hesitated and touched her stomach. "Can a human ever become a Yokai?"

He sank down into the water and blew bubbles. After a few moments he rose up again. "No, it is not possible."

She reached for her staff but hesitated. "And a child born

between a human and a Yokai, will they be trapped also by this mortal coil?"

"Such a child would never be accepted by humans nor among the Yokai. It would forever be torn between two worlds. They are cursed with a long life of suffering."

"There has to be another way."

"You carry the Dragon's child, then?"

She had turned to walk away. "Yes."

"Is that why you sealed him away?"

She paused and looked the swamp creature up and down before answering, "Yes."

The vision ended and Suzume felt as if it took the breath from her lungs. She sank down into the water up to her nose and let her limbs float on the water's surface. *That was Kazue, then. She was pretty.* Suzume rose out of the water a bit. *She knew she was carrying Kaito's child. Why seal him away?*

"You have seen the vision?" a voice squeaked near her ear.

Suzume flailed in the water and splashed about, covering her naked body as best she could with her hands.

"Who's there? You pervert, you promised not to peek!"

"I do not care for your human body," the tiny voice said again. It sounded close, but when Suzume squinted towards the forest, she could not see anything.

"Where are you? Who are you?"

"I am here. I am me."

She stopped flailing around and really looked. The sound was coming from her left. She stood up and looked around.

"Down here."

Her gaze went downward to a small shrine made of four flat stones, three for the walls and one for the roof. A short string of ofuda had been tied over the opening. And sitting on a clay offering bowl was a tiny figure. Suzume sank back down into the water to conceal her naked body and then swam closer to get a better look. She leaned against the ledge and came within inches of the smallest person she had ever seen. It looked like an old woman with a long robe of bright pink and white with tiny water lotuses embroidered on it. She had her silvery hair tied up on top of her hair.

"Who are you?" Suzume asked.

"I am the keeper of the pool and the guider of visions. You were brought here to me."

Suzume narrowed her eyes. "By whom?"

"The master, the Dragon who has woken from his sleep, of course," she said with a smile. She only had two or three teeth in a gummy mouth.

*I knew there had to be a catch.* "Why did he bring me here?"

"He is testing you. You woke him and that could only mean you are linked to the one who sealed him."

"Meaning what? Are you saying she's my grandmother or..." She could not choke out the words she was thinking. It was too ludicrous to even consider.

The tiny old woman shrugged. "I cannot tell you; that is for you to discover."

Suzume sighed. This seemed to be a reoccurring theme. "Does this vision have something to do with my newfound powers? That was Kazue in the vision, right? The woman that sealed him? Why would she seal him because she was pregnant? Seems like a weird way of dealing with a bastard."

The old woman shook her head. "You are not prepared to understand. Nor is he; when he asks you about your visions, tell him you saw nothing. Do you understand?"

"Why? I mean, I don't exactly like doing what he wants, but I don't want to be eaten either."

"It's best that he does not know about your connection to Kazue. Much more will be revealed in time. For now wait and watch, Priestess."

The long grasses alongside the pool rustled and Suzume looked up. Kaito came strolling into view.

"Are you done yet? I'm bored."

*That's why he wanted me to come here. For the vision. Well, two can play at this game. He may be a dragon, but he is a **male** dragon.*

"Almost." She swam to the edge of the pond nearest to Kaito and pulled herself up, baring the top of her breasts glistening with water. She covered herself just enough to keep a sense of mystery. "Join me?"

She pouted her lips and ran her hands through her damp hair.

He narrowed his eyes at her. "Anything strange happen?"

She had to fight the urge to roll her eyes. He was not very subtle. "No, I was just thinking I owe you for saving me from those awful monkeys. Is there any way I can repay you?"

He crossed his arms over his chest. "No, there's nothing you have that I want." He stomped away.

# 14

K aito stormed away. *The hot spring should have exposed her. I was sure she was the one. Well, she's hiding something, that's for sure.*

Since the shifter, he had been thinking about it. Kazue's reincarnation was out there, and only her reincarnation should have been able to unleash him. He knew Kazue better than he had ever known another living soul. She would only allow the seal to be broken if she was the one doing it. No mere mortal could have unleashed him. She was tied to Kazue, that he knew for sure. Whether she be her descendant or otherwise, he was going to find out and get his revenge. These feelings the fake Kazue had awakened needed to be squashed. His love for Kazue made him weak, and the sooner he closed this chapter, the sooner he could regain his kingdom. *I should kill her and be done with it. I am wasting time.*

He went back to the campfire he had built and plopped down on the ground, crossing his arms over his chest. He did not even need the warmth of the fire, he had done it for the priestess. She's worthless to me, mostly an annoyance, yet I continue to see to her comforts. Who's the pet here?

She shouted from a distance, her voice carrying, and in her

agitation her spiritual energy flared up. It washed over him like a wave; to a hungry Yokai it would be irresistible. He did not even lift his head, no matter how much she squawked. He stared intently into the flickering flames. *The fool will bring every Yokai in the area down upon us.*

She stumbled through a bush nearby, night blind to the pathway a few feet away. She grumbled and complained as she pulled her robes free of the reaching branches. He thought about teasing her for being clumsy but decided against it. Getting close to her would only end poorly for both of them. If he wasn't willing to kill her, then he should leave now. She was no use to him.

"What's wrong with you? I'm a highly desirable woman. I was going to marry my father's top general before my mother ruined it for me."

He did not respond but continued to stare at the flames. *She looks nothing like Kazue, and her energy feels different too. She's loud and crude, Kazue was demure and quiet. There's no way she's Kazue's reincarnation.*

"The silent brooding routine doesn't suit you," Suzume said.

Again his answer was silence. *If she's not Kazue's reincarnation, how did she break her seal?* While he dreamed, he had plotted and planned his revenge. He wanted to find her reincarnation, win her trust, then slowly destroy her. He wanted her to feel the betrayal he had felt when she realized he had done it all for vengeance. But just a few moments with an impostor and he had forgotten his anger and fallen under the spell of love. *These feelings are a cancer that is spreading throughout my body. What do I have to do to forget her?*

"If you're going to ignore me all night, then I'm going to bed."

She lay down and faced away from him. She probably expected him to chase her, to beg her forgiveness. He scoffed. Humans could be so vain.

He could not help but ask again, though he felt like a fool for doing so. "That hot spring is blessed by one of the Eight. Did you see anything special while you bathed?" he asked, his voice coaxing. She had to have seen something, a priestess with her power should have been given a vision.

"Other than you peeping? No," she replied while keeping her back turned to him. Her voice rose just a bit, and he knew she was lying.

He stared at the back of her head. *Kill her now and be done. Let these memories go.* But he could not move from his seat.

Without warning, he felt a probing tentacle of energy brush against his own. He looked over at the priestess, but it was not coming from her direction. He stood up, surveying their surroundings. The probe withdrew when they realized he had noticed them. He had felt from the brief connection that they were powerful, close in power to his own. *What did she attract?* Instead of drawing closer, they stayed in one place as if they were waiting for him. *Could it be?* He spread out his senses, using his own probes to find them, but when he brushed against their energy, they cloaked themselves. He growled in frustration and pushed harder, spreading his energy out further, trying to break their barrier only to find them further away, but still within reach. They were calling to him. Curious, he went in pursuit.

The priestess heard him leaving and shouted after him, "You cannot leave me here alone!"

He ignored her, consumed by the hunt. Whoever they were, they had mastery over their spiritual energy, which meant they were very powerful. Few were of an equal level with him, and he knew them all. But this energy was unfamiliar; there was a strange note to it. It was an imperfection that he could not quite place.

Kaito ran to the edge of the forest, where the energy vanished and did not reappear. He stood at the edge of the forest, the road stretching out in either direction, darkness enclosing him. Kaito turned in place, his senses on high alert. There was nothing here, not even a void to indicate someone masking their spiritual energy. Despite that, he knew they were watching him.

He felt a spark, a tiny insignificant burst of energy. Had he not been focused on finding something, he would not have noticed it. Casually he turned and shot a blast of icy energy in its direction. A crystallized ofuda materialized, hanging in the air before it fell to the ground, shattering into thousands of pieces. He walked over and stared at the fragments of frozen paper.

Someone clapped slowly. A peasant stood on the roadside, rake slung over his shoulder.

"That was impressive, how'd you make that beam of ice?"

"You can see me?" Kaito asked, narrowing his eyes. He probed the man's energy, but he appeared to be a mundane human. There wasn't even a hint of spiritual energy; he shouldn't be able to see him.

"Of course I can, I've always been able to see your kind." He grinned, but there was something off-kilter about his expression as if he was disconnected from his body somehow.

"You're lying," Kaito rumbled.

The man smiled in a sinister way before he rushed Kaito, swinging his rake at Kaito's head. Kaito dodged it, and as the rake went zooming over his head, he transformed his hand into a claw and popped up to swipe at the farmer. The farmer jumped backwards, laughing all the while. Kaito lunged forward, and though the farmer bobbed and weaved, he landed one claw on the farmer's face. Then like a crack in a door, a sliver of spiritual energy escaped from underneath the mask. The farmer noticed and ran a hand along the seam, hiding the energy. All that remained was a veneer of an average human.

Kaito jumped backwards; he had grossly underestimated his opponent. He had never met someone with this sort of power, hiding his spiritual energy as if he were human. Then it dawned on him, the shifter had been a diversion. This was the real menace the salamander had warned him about. "Who are you?" Kaito asked.

"A friend, an enemy? Only you can tell," the man taunted. He stood a few feet away, the rake held in front of him like a staff. He knew the pose because Kazue had fought with a staff.

"What are you?"

He peered at the farmer, but no matter how hard he tried, he could not break past the barrier he had created to mask his energy. If he didn't know any better, he would think he was human.

He shook his head. "I just came to see the famous Dragon, ruler of Akatsuki. I can understand how Kazue could seal you away now. You seem to have a soft spot for humans."

Kaito snarled and bared his teeth, he would rend this creature apart piece by piece, and maybe once his guts were exposed, he would know how he could hide so well. He tapped into his spiritual energy to unravel it and transform into a dragon. But though he could feel the energy, he could not unleash it. He looked at his hands and arms, there were no seals on him, nothing that could stop his transformation, but try as he might, he could not transform.

"She took more of your energy than you realized, and you're weak from being locked away in a holy place." The farmer sighed.

"You did this?"

"Sent the monkeys and the Aryūru after you?" He shrugged his shoulders. "They do what they want. That's how things are run around here now. All the leaders are gone, except for a few clans. There are no Kami, there are no emperors." He smiled.

Kaito was done talking. He had met enough tricksters in his life to know he wouldn't get a straight answer out of this fool. Kaito shot a blast of ice at the farmer, weaker than he would normally be able to do, but it should at least knock the farmer off his feet. But before it hit him, he disappeared.

The farmer laughed behind Kaito. "You think you can hit me with such a weak attack?"

He turned around to see the farmer standing on the grassy knoll where he and the priestess had stopped earlier. The farmer rested his palm against the tree and then pulled his hand away, rubbing his fingers together as if residue remained.

"The priestess is delightful, though." He inhaled deeply as he waved his hand towards his face. "So much power and so little control. She leaves traces all over. You shouldn't have left her alone. Who knows what will find her."

The sun started to rise behind the farmer, framing him in the morning rays. He had not even realized the entire night had passed while they fought.

"What do I care?" Kaito snarled. "She's just one priestess."

The farmer leaned on his rake and with his free hand waggled his finger at Kaito. "Now, now, there's no need to lie to me. I know all about her because I sent her to free you. In fact, you should be thanking me for setting you free."

"You're right, I'll thank you by ripping off your head."

He ran up the hill, but ever since the farmer mentioned it, he noticed how much weaker he felt, as if he couldn't reach the speeds he could normally. The farmer stood smirking as Kaito reached out to grab him. But as he was about to place his hands around his neck, a rip in the air behind him opened up, glimmering with a white border and on the other side a starry sky. The farmer stepped backwards into the rent in the air and gave a backwards wave to Kaito as he went through the portal.

His voice echoed after him. "We'll meet again soon, Dragon."

# 15

She closed her eyes just for a moment, too tired to stay up waiting for the Dragon to return any longer, when a shout woke her. She jumped out of her bedroll and looked around the empty campsite. When Kaito had disappeared, she thought it was to tease her again. Now he was nowhere in sight and all that remained were the smoldering embers of last night's fire. *Where has he gone to now? I thought for sure he'd be back by now.* She glanced around. There was no sign of him or who had shouted and woke her.

"You men hurry it up. We haven't got all day." The voice was nearby.

*It couldn't be.* Following the gruff order, she heard the nicker of horses and the trudging of many feet. Suzume ran towards the voices, thankful for her good luck. Over a hill and down an embankment, a dozen tents were arrayed in formation along three lines. Men hurried back and forth, carrying weapons and tending to horses.

She looked to the banners above the biggest tent at the back of the camp. A crimson banner with a yellow sun rising imposed on it flapped in the wind. She could have wept for joy. *This has to be a dream. I am saved!*

Suzume entered the camp with her head held high. At last, she was among civilized human beings again. A man walking by with a bundle of gear stopped when he saw her.

"Ho, girl, what do you think you're doing?"

Suzume placed her hands on her hips. "I am the emperor's daughter."

He looked her up and down, taking in her stained clothes and her disheveled hair. She had not even taken the time to braid it. Wisps fell into her face. She ran a hand over them, trying to flatten them down.

"What do you take me for, a fool?" he asked.

Suzume opened her mouth to give an angry retort; then she realized no self-respecting noble lady would present herself to a soldier let alone dressed this way. *No wonder he does not believe me.*

"I demand you take me to your general."

The man shook his head. "We don't have any scraps to give you, now get."

He walked past her. Suzume scowled at him and stomped further into the camp, intent on finding the general on her own. She did not get three steps before a hand came down hard on her shoulder. And he spun Suzume around.

"I told you to leave," the soldier said.

"I demand you unhand me!"

She tussled with the young man, but he was much stronger than her, and he pushed her to the ground. She caught herself with the palms of her hands, scraping them on the ground, and she glared at him from behind the curtain of her hair.

"You will regret this when I am returned to my place," she spat.

He crossed his arms over his chest and just glowered at her, most likely expecting her to turn around and walk away. Perhaps she should have. But after spending a few nightmare days with the Dragon, she was not about to pass up an opportunity to return home. She was even willing to risk him chasing after her, her father's army could protect her, surely.

"I demand I speak to the general!" she shouted. "I am Suzume, daughter of the emperor and his wife Izuki!"

A few more men passing by stopped to stare.

Suzume shouted louder. "I am a daughter of the divine emperor. You will be tortured for seven days and nights if my father learns that you left me here like this."

A crowd gathered. Suzume looked to each of them. None of them moved to help her but instead whispered to one another behind their hands. *At least I've got their attention now.*

"What is all this commotion?" said an authoritative voice from behind the crowd.

The men parted and a pair of warriors strolled to the front. They wore painted masks in the shape of Yokai. The larger of the two men had a thick waist straining against his sash and his mask was red and decked with black hair made to look like an overlarge mustache. The second man had a blue mask with large horns on the brow and a pair of sharp teeth on each side. Suzume took a step back. The two of them were rather gruesome looking, and considering the things she had seen as of late, she was more than a little wary.

The first man stopped in front of her. He looked her up and down. Something about him seemed familiar.

"Speak, girl," he said.

*I know that voice. Could it be?* "General Tsubaki?"

"How dare you address the general directly, peasant!" the man to his left snarled. From the way the men moved out of his way, she had to assume this was his lieutenant.

Suzume glowered at the lieutenant. "I am not a peasant. I am Princess Suzume, eighth daughter to the emperor by his second wife, Izuki."

"The emperor set aside his second wife and their children were declared illegitimate," the lieutenant snapped back. "If you were Suzume daughter of Izuki, you would know that."

*I did, but I did not know every foot soldier in the palace did as well...*

"Seize this liar. Perhaps if she loses a finger, she will learn some manners," the lieutenant commanded with a sharp wave of his arm towards Suzume. She held her ground, but inside she was devising a plot to get away with her limbs intact. Running away seemed the most viable option and she took a few steps back as men approached her, hands outstretched.

*Now would be a good time for Kaito to jump in and save me.* She took another step and a spear poked her in the back. While she had been talking, the other soldiers had surrounded her. She yelped and rubbed the spot where the metal had pierced her clothes.

"Hey, watch that thing."

*Well, running away is out of the question.* She fell to her knees at General Tsubaki's feet. She bowed low to the ground, her face nearly in the dirt. It killed her to grovel, but she knew she could not hope to outrun them, and her powers had disappeared. Perhaps they didn't work on humans.

"Please, you must believe me. I am no liar. I was sent to the mountain temple when my father set aside my mother. A dragon awoke and killed all the priestesses. I barely managed to escape with my life!"

She looked up at General Tsubaki with pleading eyes, or at least she hoped it was him behind that disturbing mask. "Please, Daiki. We were to be wed. I was planning on going to you. I still want to be your bride, if you will have me." She peered up at him through her lashes and hoped the general could see beyond the dirt and grime and remember her.

He held up his hand and the soldiers who had been chattering amongst themselves fell silent. "Bring her back to my tent," he said.

"Sir," the lieutenant interjected.

"That is an order," General Tsubaki growled.

He bowed to the general. Then with a stiff bow he motioned for Suzume to follow him. When Suzume passed by the general, she nodded her head at him with a coy smile. It shocked her how easily she slipped back into her role from the palace, sly trickster and manipulator of men. The lieutenant led her through the aisles of the tents. Cook fires rose into the sky in serpentine shapes. *I wonder what the Dragon will do when he realizes I have gone missing. I hope Daiki's army is enough to defeat a dragon.*

They reached the largest tent in the encampment. Three times the size of the smaller soldier tents, this tent was decorated with all the opulence she expected of a palace dweller. Red and gold silk decorated the door, which the lieutenant pulled back to allow her to enter. The lieutenant held open the flap, and when Suzume passed him by, she felt his glare on the back of her head. Inside, bamboo mats covered the ground. One side held a sleeping area full of plush goose-feather-filled pillows and a proper futon. The cushioned sleeping mat made Suzume's own traveling mat look like a strip of fabric. In the center of the room sat a low table with cushions arranged around it. *This is the right way to travel.*

"Wait here. The general will come to you when he is ready," the lieutenant said before leaving her alone.

Suzume just scowled after him. Then she stood in the center of the room. Even after bathing in the hot spring, she felt too dirty to touch anything. After a few minutes of indecision, she sat down on the cushion nearest to her. She relished the touch of silk on the pillows. She ran her hands over the expert weave. She admired the soft futon where the general slept, wondering if she had time for a quick nap. At the back of the tent she found a small shrine with incense burning in it.

*This is nearly a luxury after all the camping and swamp adventures.*

Soldiers shouted and she thought she heard a voice calling her name. She got up to investigate, but as she did, a servant entered through the flap, carrying a tray with a kettle and a cup. She knelt down beside the table and poured the tea into the cup, and the tendrils of steam wafted towards her, bringing with it an earthy aroma. *The soldiers will handle it, I'm sure,* Suzume thought as she settled in.

Alongside the tea were pastries made of soft dough and filled with a red bean paste that Suzume had adored back at the palace. She grabbed one of the pastries and bit into it. The creamy, sweet taste filled her mouth. Suzume devoured it then licked her fingers clean after she was done.

Hours later, after Suzume poked around the tent, glanced over maps and skimmed a few letters with boring topics about strategy, General Tsubaki returned. The sun had started to set and the orange light pushed through the walls of the tent, casting the tent in a diffused warm light. Suzume sat at the table, reading an old novel that she found among the general's things. It was a scandalous tell-all about court life. She was rather surprised the general would read such a thing.

He stood in the entryway, not speaking for a long time. He had removed his mask and helmet and held them under his arm. She stood up to greet him, but when she did, he turned his head away.

"Thank you for saving me," Suzume said to end the silence.

"This is not right. I should not be able to look upon your regal face," General Tsubaki said.

Suzume wanted to laugh. She could be vain, but she did not think she was much to look at, at the moment. She had managed to braid her hair and the servant had washed her clothes, but a few of the stains would never come out. She wore none of her usual makeup that accentuated her best features, like her lips and eyes.

"I am no longer royalty," she said in a small voice—that was not entirely playacting.

"You are to me. What your father did to you—" He hesitated. "I advised him against it, but he swore I had been beguiled by your charms."

Suzume smiled to herself. *That's probably true.* "You must believe I never gave up hope that you would come for me and that we could be together."

He did turn around then. His face flushed and his squashed nose was bright red. She looked at his receding hairline and gut that nearly burst out of his clothes. *He is not handsome like Kaito, but he could give me a secure home, a place back at court. I should count myself fortunate I got away. The Dragon would kill me if he had half the chance.*

"Princess—" He stopped and twisted his hands in front of him, not looking at her but looking at the bamboo mat beneath their feet.

*Say something,* she wanted to scream. *Why will you not look at me, see me? Kaito saw me, all of me, and he never cared. The general cannot even look upon me clothed without breaking into a sweat. Is it because he is a mortal?*

Suzume turned her head away. She could not stand to look at the general any longer. She kept comparing him to Kaito's broad shoulders, trim physique, his long hair and dark eyes.

"Princess, if your father knew that I had you here, alone in my tent, he would have my head."

"What does my father care for me? I was sent to the temple and out of his sight forever," Suzume said.

"He is an honorable man. He is the son of the Eight; his judgment is divine."

Suzume resisted the urge to roll her eyes. Her father was no more god than she.

"Then I am to be left here to die?" She looked up at the general. Sweat rolled down to his jowls and pooled in his sideburns.

He fell to his knees beside Suzume. A sticky sweet perfume wafted off him and his foul breath made her stomach churn.

"No, I would not allow it. Never. I will take care of you. I plan to have some men escort you back to my estate."

She searched his face. *He's serious. He's willing to risk my father's wrath for me.* "What, as your concubine?"

His eyes darted around, looking anywhere but at her. "Well... I..."

Suzume held up her hand. "I may have been dishonored, but I have not sunk that low, even for you, Daiki."

"I meant no offense, that is to say..."

She strode away from him and crossed her arms over her chest. "I think I would like to retire for the night. Do you have a suitable place where I may rest?"

He jumped up and swayed on his feet as he did so. "Please, use my tent. I will use my lieutenant's."

He did not move to leave but instead came closer to Suzume and took her hand in his chubby and sweaty one. A shiver of revulsion swept over her and she had to look away to avoid showing it on her face.

"Princess... no. Suzume, I want you to be my bride. I will send you to my estate, and once I win this battle, I will go to your father and beg for him to allow us to marry."

She looked up into his eyes. He squinted and his gaze, shadowed by his heavy eyelids, made him look like he struggled to see. His proposal was everything she had hoped for, it was what she had been plotting from the start, yet now that it was here... she didn't want it. But this was her last chance to return to the palace.

"Yes, Daiki!" she said with all the fake sweetness she could manage without retching.

# 16

He arrived at the camp to find it empty, the priestess' vacant sleeping roll the only clue that she had been there at all. The fire had died down to embers and a thin trail of smoke curled up from the ashes. He stretched out his spiritual energy, looking for the priestess. He felt her in the distance like a flickering flame. Whoever had taken her, they did not have the power to cloak spiritual energy the way the fake farmer had. He could only assume the stranger's intention had been to distract him while his accomplices took his priestess. Well, whoever had taken his pet would soon meet a gruesome end.

He followed her spiritual energy like a dog following a scent; all around their campsite was evidence of humans. Hoofprints in the ground, and everywhere the stench of sweat and horseflesh. Broken branches and tamped down grass made an obvious enough path to follow. Still weak after the Aryūru, he was forced to walk on foot. As much as he hated to admit it, if he were to face this many humans in this form, he would not be in the best position to defend himself.

He put the thought aside and followed the path they left behind and found their encampment down the road. Going on foot, it took him nearly a half hour and the sun was beginning to rise in earnest. The camp had started to stir, and from his vantage point on a hill overlooking the encampment, he could see the soldiers going about their business, carrying buckets and armor on their way to one task or another. The energy of hundreds of humans muddled his ability to track. He probed them all, searching for Suzume, but found it difficult to untangle the energy from one human to another; they were all so similar. After a few moments of this, he gave up and decided a more direct approach was in order.

"Humans!" he bellowed, and the sound of his voice rolled over the encampment. Horses whinnied and humans shouted, dropping armor, and buckets of water splashed on their toes.

Tent flaps opened as late risers stumbled out half dressed. Kaito waited, hands on hips, surveying the humans. The rising sun fell on his face, illuminating him, giving him an unearthly glow that would be sure to impress the humans.

They gathered along the edge of the camp, speaking amongst themselves. None dared come closer. He kept his expression impassive, it had been too long since he had masses of humans at his command. He thought of his army of Yokai and wondered how hard it would be to recall his subjects to his side. That was a thought for another time.

When a sizable crowd had gathered, he spoke. "You have taken what is mine! Bring me the priestess and I will spare you."

The men looked to one another in confusion. And then at the back of the group, he saw a man pressing forward. Not young or handsome, with a round pink face and hair that was pulled too tight on top of his head. But when he strode through the crowd, the men parted, letting him through. It was their leader, he assumed.

The man stopped at the foot of the hill. He wore a sword at his hip, but made no move to draw it. "We have no priestess," the man shouted up to Kaito.

Kaito blew out an icy breath, which rolled down the hill and created icicles on the men's hair and mustaches. They shivered, pulling their arms around their bodies. He could turn them all into solid ice if the mood struck him. But he might freeze the priestess by accident and that would not be a satisfying way to fulfill his need for revenge.

"You lie to me, human, I know she is among you. Bring her to me and you shall be spared."

The round pink man puffed out his chest. "I will never give her to you."

Kaito shrugged. Humans were too easy to manipulate; he should never have admitted to having her. Not that he wouldn't have razed their camp anyway. "Wrong answer."

While he spoke with them, he had felt his energy start to return, enough that he could access his innermost well of energy. He jumped up into the sky, using his superior strength to propel him. Had they been closer to a body of water, he could have used its energy to rejuvenate himself, but seeing as he only had the clouds in the sky, that would have to be enough. He pulled from the precipitation in the sky, gathering the water he needed to destroy them all. When he had enough absorbed, he transformed into a dragon and floated in the sky, circling around clouds, gathering them to him. Sucking in their energy, like fresh clean breath.

He turned his sights down on the humans, like a number of ants on the ground, and he expelled dark clouds, which were the by-product of his use of their energy, leaving them crackling with lightning. He descended on the humans, but before he could get very far, an arrow flew towards him. He dodged at the last moment, but more followed. He did not care if they struck him, no human weapon could harm him. Or so he thought, until an arrow lodged itself in his shoulder. He lost altitude, mostly from shock, but recovered quickly. No human arrow should even pierce his skin. But this embedded in his flesh and burned, and the pain spread as if it were laced with poison.

He peered down at the ground, looking for the person who had shot the arrow. Does the priestess know how to use a bow and arrow? He did not imagine she would have had time to learn in between being pampered. But he could not see who had shot the arrow. All the humans looked the same, arrows notched and waiting to let them fly. He had barely enough energy to maintain the transformation to stay in the sky; he could not waste it on finding the one with spiritual energy.

No matter. I can defeat them even if there is someone who can wield spiritual energy among them.

He roared, anger clouding his judgment, and he unleashed raining shards of ice down upon their heads. The men did not flee and a new bevy of arrows were shot towards him. This time three different arrows lodged into his torso. The pain was immense; these were no mere arrows, they were imbued with spiritual power. The pain spread through him like fingers pressing into his wounds. He forced back the pain with a stubbornness only he could manage.

He shot more ice spears at them as he drew moisture from everything around him, trying to keep himself up. The wind picked up as the sky reflected his mood and turned a slate gray. He would find the archer and rip his head from his spine.

"Run, humans, or lose your lives," he snarled. Thunder roared behind him.

Then when he was not looking, another arrow came shooting towards him. He had no time to dodge or move as it came careening towards him and shot him in the chest. He lost altitude quickly and went flying for the ground in an out-of-control spiral. He made contact with the ground and his long serpentine body flopped about. Before the spiritual power could further corrupt him, he transformed into a man. The arrows jutted out of his chest and his thighs and his arm. He yanked at the one on his chest first, but his hands burned to touch it. It glowed faintly green as the energy in it pulsed.

He looked about, his vision swimming. Damn these humans for tricking him, and damn that creature who had lured him out. With another yank, he pulled the arrow from his chest, but the energy had done its job. Already weak from the Aryūru, he was further weakened by the arrows. He staggered as he pulled free another arrow from his thigh, then his arm. When the arrows all lay scattered on the ground, that was when the humans found him, bearing weapons and determined expressions. They would not leave him be until they had killed him. Which was fine with him. He was not done with them yet.

He stood up to his full height, drawing from his last well of energy. He may not be able to transform and was weak, but he was still more than a match for a few measly humans. Masked men stared at him through hollowed eyes, caricatures of the real Yokai they emulated.

"You wish to fight me?" Kaito asked. Blood ran in rivulets from his wounds, and he wiped sweat from his brow with the back of his hand.

They did not respond, but he didn't need one. He rushed them, prepared to fight, hoping a surprise attack would scatter them. They came at him with swords swinging and a shout in their throats. He dodged them, but just barely, their blades nicked him and tore his robe to shreds. He managed to get behind one soldier, whose neck he twisted, and killed him in one swift move. He plucked the sword from his hand as he fell to his knees and then turned on the others. They took a collective step back, surrounding him. He spun in a circle, waiting for an all-out attack. Even with a dull human blade in his hand, he would be able to defeat them.

"Do you fear me?" he asked, looking at them one by one. "You should, I am the Dragon, ruler of this land, and you should be praying to your gods, because you will be reborn soon."

They shouted as one and attacked as one, like numerous arms of one beast. His speed gave him the advantage, and he missed most of their thrusts, but the edge of a blade would nick him and then heal over. Then another would slash at his robe, tearing it. But he did not care about the clothes. He cut them down by the dozens, and they kept on coming.

Then he felt it, the burning energy. Someone in the crowd had spiritual energy. But in the press of bodies with the constant distraction, he could not say who among them it was. It had only just occurred to him that this had been their plan from the beginning and he had played into their trap. As he fought, a blade filled with spiritual energy made cuts that would not heal, not straightaway like the others. Each time the blade bit into his flesh, he would turn to find the culprit only to find another inferior blade swinging at his face. They were playing with him.

He growled, swinging haphazardly in his haste to get to this priest who could fill a blade with his energy. But while the men fell, so was his energy flagging. The tiny nicks, at seemingly random places on his body, were taking their toll, draining his energy. He stumbled, and a regular soldier caught him on the shoulder. He snarled, but he moved as if through mud. *What is happening?* His blade fell from his hand as he fell to his knees. Then the men stepped back, and from the crowd, a man stepped forward. He wore a mask over his face, so he did not know who he was, but his blade glowed green with spiritual energy. He brought it down towards Kaito's neck.

*Is this how it ends for me? I did not even get to see her face one more time.*

# 17

Things were moving too fast. The next morning, Suzume was taken to General Tsubaki's home. To her great dissatisfaction, she was personally escorted by the lieutenant. He had yet to take off his mask, and he rode ahead of her without speaking. His shoulders were stiff, and from time to time she saw him glance around him, waiting for an attacker, perhaps. The lack of conversation and the steady rocking of her mount made her sleepy. Mostly, she was bored. She watched the swishing of his horse's tail as they road down the dusty track.

"Where is General Tsubaki headed?" she asked to quell the stretched silences. She could not stand it any longer. The lieutenant was colder than the peaks of the highest mountain and just as dull.

"To war," was his blithe reply.

Suzume scowled at his back. "I'm not a complete idiot."

He scoffed under his breath, but Suzume heard him.

She ignored him. He was the general's second in command and she didn't want her intended to think less of her. She had spent a long time building her reputation and she didn't want it ruined by this prickly warrior. Her mother had done enough of that already. "Who are we at war with?" Suzume elaborated.

The island that her father's kingdom encompassed was massive and hundreds of leagues from the continent. At times there was internal strife within the kingdom, but that was infrequent and limited to small rebellions. Attacks from the continental countries were a concern, but those battles would be fought at sea or at least along the coast. The general's army was headed inland away from the ocean. *Are they going to challenge that shape-shifting monster the salamander mentioned? Do the people at the White Palace know Yokai even exist?*

"With our enemies," the lieutenant replied.

It was Suzume's turn to scoff. "That is obvious. Is a clan lord trying to rebel?"

The lieutenant glanced over his shoulder at her. It was the first time since they had left the camp that he had done so. His dark eyes stared out at her from behind his blue mask. The horns adorning the mask glinted in the sun. The effect was meant to be intimidating, but Suzume thought he looked foolish. Having met real Yokai, these caricatures were laughable. The grimacing expression carved into the mask were unrealistic and nothing compared to Kaito in a fury.

"What does it matter to you? You're no longer part of this world," he said without inflection.

He turned back around and kicked his heels into the ribs of his horse, cantering away before Suzume could snap back a response.

She shouted after him anyway. "I will be soon. I am going to marry the general and then I'll have him bring me your head on a platter." She scowled after him. *How dare he say that, doesn't he know who I am? Who I will be...*

The lieutenant did not respond and continued on ahead. She urged her mount to follow him. The mare tossed her head in protest as she followed Suzume's commands. After a few more silent moments, Suzume reassessed her previous declarations. *In truth, I don't know if I want to marry Daiki. He's a good man, to be certain, and powerful, which is very appealing, and yet...* She shook her thoughts away. She was being foolish. This was a golden opportunity to return to the palace and get her revenge—without the fear of being eaten by a mercurial dragon. She was still furious at him for abandoning her, but that was of no matter now. She was on her way back up in the world.

Suddenly, Suzume felt a ping, like a lightning bolt shooting through her skull. She looked around; she had felt that same feeling right before she had unleashed Kaito. She looked around and saw nothing to be worried about, but she could not shake the feeling that something was off. After a couple more steps, the horses stopped. She dug her heels in, trying to get it to move, but it would not budge.

The lieutenant turned back to her. His own mount obeyed, but its ears were pressed flat against its head. "We don't have much more time, hurry along," he said.

*What's the rush? Are they afraid my father will find out?* Out loud she said, "This stupid horse won't move." She pulled and tugged on the reins to no effect. The animal swiveled its ears back and forth. Suzume huffed and crossed her arms. The lieutenant rode over to her and pulled on the reins, but the animal would not budge, and then the lieutenant's horse started to shift beneath him, dancing in place, making it difficult for him to maintain his seat. She felt it again, that spark of energy, and it was more powerful this time. Her skin prickled and the hairs on the back of her neck stood on end.

She scanned the forest beside them, but nothing seemed out of order. *I know something is wrong.* Then without warning, her horse shot off like a rocket. The lieutenant called out to her, but Suzume put all her energy into holding onto the neck of her mount. Their flight was interrupted by a large black mass with glowing red eyes. She was so panicked she could not even see clearly what it was that filled the roadway or seemed to block out all the light. Her horse reared and she fell off the back of it and landed hard on the ground. She hit her head and her vision swam.

The lieutenant had caught up at last and he shouted as his sword was drawn from the scabbard. He ran towards the black thing. Suzume saw hairy legs, lots of them, and turned and ran in the opposite direction. She did not get too far before she found the horse tangled up in something, screaming and rolling its eyes. She felt bad for the animal, but she could not delay to save it. She tried to go around only to get tangled up in something sticky. The more she fought it, the more entwined she became. She heard the screams of some unearthly monster and screamed in reply, hoping the Dragon would come and save her. There was no such help coming and she struggled in vain.

Then she felt the spark again, but her energy burning along her skin could do nothing against what she was wrapped up in. It numbed her skin and she lost feeling in her fingers and toes. Then the energy under her skin started to throb as something, a shadow, leaned over her. She saw glowing red eyes before a sharp pain poked her in the neck and she lost consciousness.

---

The old priestess knelt in front of the shrine, hands pressed together as the incense rose in a spiral towards the sky. She felt his spiritual energy, knew it as well as her own, though she pretended not to. He came here often, but never spoke, just sat back and watched. Long ago, she would have tried to coax a few words out of him, just to hear his voice again, but he never responded, and if she did look at him, he would turn and flee—running from the past. Nevertheless, his visits had increased in recent years. Sooner or later he would give up this stubborn act;

they could not remain silent forever. Now that she was alone in the world, she needed his companionship more than ever.

She did not need to see him to know he had taken the form of a white wolf, larger than an average wolf, with golden eyes. They stayed like that for a time. An old woman in her priestess garb and a strange wolf who watched from a distance but never approached, too afraid to bridge the space between them. The masks they wore protected them from the truth, from the hurts they had endured; neither of them were as they appeared, not that they would admit that out loud. After a few moments, she got up on wobbling knees. Acting infirmed had become so natural to her, she forgot what it was to have a young body. She turned to face him, expecting him to flee, but he just stared at her with unblinking golden eyes.

It had been centuries since she had seen his other form, but his smile was still engraved into her memories. So while he denied her his presence, she indulged these moments where she could remember the old days. Tears brimmed along her lashes; centuries among the humans caused her emotions to hover closer to the surface. She turned her back to him, to hide her tears. *I wish you would speak with me, show me your real face at least once, that will be enough.*

She took a few steps when he spoke. "The Dragon has been awoken."

She stood very still. It had been so long since she heard his voice.

"Shin?" She started to turn around.

"Please don't turn around," he said.

She held her wrinkled and frail hand to her breast. Her heart was slamming in her chest. *I've been hoping for this moment for so long, and these are the first words you choose?* "Why now after so long do you let me hear your voice? You know I have missed you."

"You know why," he said.

She inhaled. They were just three words, but they sliced to her heart. "How do you know he is awake? We've heard rumors before…" She wanted so badly to turn around to look upon his face, but she knew if she did, he would run away before she got the chance and she might never get another opportunity to speak with him. He was just stubborn enough to punish her for her choices for eternity. *I should have saved you, I'm sorry.* But as always, the words got tangled up in her throat.

"This time it's true. I heard it from Akio. He was beside himself with rage."

She took a deep breath. After all this waiting, her master was awake at last, and Shin had come to her. If only Hikaru had lived to see it. The tears were flowing freely now.

"Why do you keep this form? The human has been gone for twenty years," Shin asked.

"You know why," she replied, throwing his words back at him. She could not help it. She had known her time with Hikaru would come to an end. She had known from the beginning that she was immortal and he was not, but when he died, she had died with him. She had hoped Shin would return to her, but he had not, and she felt as if she had been abandoned twice. Fate was cruel. She had not realized how Hikaru's death would cripple her, leave her without purpose. All she had was this shrine and the hope that she would find Hikaru in the next life.

"The world has changed while he slept. He will need you now more than ever," Shin said.

She laughed. "He does not need me. My place is here."

"Where you can pretend to be an old woman?" he scoffed. When had he become so bitter, so cruel? Time had changed them both.

"I will think about it."

"That's all I can ask, I suppose." He paused and the silence was charged with words unsaid, but neither of them dared to speak. "I should be getting back," he said at last.

She listened to his footsteps as they receded, then and only then did she look to see his tail as it disappeared down the temple steps and out of sight. If only she had seen his face. She sighed and turned to the shrine and the burning incense once more.

"The Dragon is back, Hikaru, should I return to him?"

# 18

Suzume woke with a start. Clutching unfamiliar blankets to her chest, she looked around the well-appointed room. In a fog, she remembered the day before, the black looming figure and being tangled up when something stabbed her in the neck. She rubbed at her neck. It was tender, but there were no wounds. She threw back her blankets, surveying her body. Though a little dirty, there was no indication that she had been injured, not a single wound could be found. *I know I was in danger just a few minutes ago. How did I get here?*

She rubbed her eyes. This had to be some sort of hallucination. The room she had woken up in had all the comforts of the one she had enjoyed in the palace, a soft futon, a painted screen, and trunks, which when opened revealed a multitude of different robes for her to wear. Someone had lit the braziers in the corners of the room, and they cast flickering shadows on the walls.

The futon had a screen around it, trimmed in red fabric, and beyond the sleeping area were a sitting room and a veranda that looked out into a garden with a koi pond and cherry blossom tree. *Am I back at the palace? This is almost identical to my room. Were the temple and the Dragon all a nightmare?* She pinched herself just to be certain.

"Ow." She smiled, realizing she wasn't dreaming. She had returned to civilization.

The door at the far end of the room slid open and a servant shuffled in. Suzume wiggled in place as the young woman walked in with eyes downcast.

"My lady, I hope you slept well."

Suzume smiled, something she would never have done back at the palace. It was too familiar and too unrefined. But now she did not care. She was where she belonged. She tamped down her emotions, just barely, and said, "Well enough." *What if this isn't real? I don't even remember arriving.* She thought how to next frame her question. "Remind me, where am I again?"

The servant was well trained because she did not react but kept her head down. "You are at the home of Lord Tsubaki, my lady."

She resisted the urge to rub her hands together with glee. However she got here was not relevant. She was where she was meant to be. Which meant this dragon ordeal was well and truly over. "Excellent!" She marched over to the servant and threw up her arms in a T shape. "I am ready to be dressed," she said.

"Perhaps a bath first, my lady?"

Suzume looked down at her filthy hands and had to agree. Two more servants carried in a bath, and after soaking until the water was cool, they scrubbed her until her skin was raw. And when they were done, they brushed her hair.

She felt worlds away from how she had when she woke. Suzume could not keep the foolish grin from her face as the servant dressed her. The woman moved with delicate but assured movements, smoothing the fabric and pinning layers in place. She was glad she had taken that bath; otherwise she would have ruined this fine silk with her filth.

When the servant slid on the soft white socks, she swore to

herself, *I will never walk again. I will demand a palanquin, even if it is to go a short distance.* The servant made no comment about the blisters on Suzume's feet, but she still feared she would get callouses from her brief stint walking. She wriggled her feet in the socks and marveled at how soft they were and how the silk of her robe glided against her skin. She sighed, content.

After dressing her, the servant left and returned with a sumptuous meal—all of Suzume's favorites. *Daiki must have remembered and sent word ahead,* she thought as she devoured her marinated fish. She ate without reservation, and then when her meal was finished, the servant opened up the doors onto a garden beyond. She went out onto the veranda and looked at the koi swimming in the pond. It was peaceful and perfect.

But like most things, the tranquil moment would not last forever. Unwelcome thoughts invaded. *If I want to stay here, I'll have to marry Daiki. But it's my only way of returning to my place in the world.* Before, that would have been the height of triumph, but that was before she had awoken a dragon and been claimed as his bride. After spending time with the Dragon, she felt like the koi in the pond, swimming in a small space, going in circles. As wonderful as these fine clothes were, and having servants attend to her every whim, everything was tainted.

The Yokai would not go away, and now that she knew they existed, she wasn't sure she could pretend any longer. Before, she would have been content to sit and gossip for hours; now she felt restless and worried. What had happened on her way to Daiki's home? What was the creature that attacked them and how had they escaped?

She was given an unexpected reprieve from her troubled thoughts when the servant appeared with an announcement. "The lieutenant wants to speak with you, my lady," the servant said.

As boorish as the man was, his visit was a welcome break in the monotony. She gave the servant leave to show him in. While she waited, she arranged her outer layer and placed a fan in front of her face. He may have seen her at her worst, but now that her star was on the rise, she would have him remember his place. The lieutenant came in briskly, still wearing his warrior mask. *Does he ever take that thing off?*

He bowed briefly before saying, "I have received word from General Tsubaki that I am to stay with you."

She pursed her lips. "You have?"

He nodded in reply.

If this was all he had to say, why not send a servant? It didn't matter. Now that he was here, she had a chance to get answers to some of the questions that had been troubling her. "What was that thing that attacked us, and how did we get away?"

He looked past her at the cherry tree when he answered, "I do not know." *He's lying.*

Fear grabbed a hold of her throat and she took a few gulping breaths to ease her racing heart. Even here she wasn't free of the Yokai. Was the lieutenant one of them? She peered at him, not having the slightest idea how to figure out if he was. She decided the direct approach was best. "I will be mistress here soon enough, it will not do well for you to lie to me."

He turned to face her straight on. "It was a Yokai, my lady. I did not want to frighten you. Forgive me, I did not know you could see them."

"How could I not, it was huge!"

He nodded. "We are safe within these walls, you have no need to fear."

She narrowed her eyes at him. There was something more he was not telling her. "And you defeated it?"

"I did."

She touched her neck, wondering how the wound had healed so quickly. She pinched her wrist again just to be sure. When she felt pain, she knew this could not be a hallucination. She could not see his expression beyond the mask, but she thought he must think she was insane. She turned her back to him; she did not want to drag out this discussion any further.

"You may go."

He left without a word, leaving Suzume with a bleak and boring garden to contemplate.

The day droned on much the same. At night, she was summoned to dine with the rest of Daiki's clan who were in residence. Daiki had a senile old mother, who stubbornly clung to life. When their original engagement had been announced, Suzume had come to visit as part of the arrangements for their soon-to-be wedding. That was when she had met the old witch, who looked down her nose at Suzume and loudly voiced her critiques of everything about Suzume, from the way she wore her hair to how she walked. Now she was being summoned once more.

It had been months since Suzume had left court, and this would in essence be her reemergence into court life. She dressed but with a hint of nervousness twisting her gut. The old woman had lived at court for a long time before retiring upon her husband's death. She was no stranger to scandal and not out of the loop despite living in the country. Would Suzume's mother's scandal follow her here? Everyone knew she had been exiled. If anyone was going to prevent her marriage to Daiki, it would be his mother.

The servant guided her into the large dining room. As the door slid open, the clan members, sitting in a horseshoe shape facing inward, turned to look at her. The butterflies turned into Yokai battling one another in her gut. She glided into the room, wearing false confidence as her shield. As she walked down the parallel rows of noblemen, she headed for the front, where one empty seat had been left next to Daiki's mother, Lady Tsubaki.

She looked even more old and feeble than the last time Suzume had seen her. Dark eyes were sunken into her skull, surrounded by layers of papery white skin in folds that hung down her jowls. Her neck was like loose rice dough and her white hair had started to thin on top. But her eyes were sharp and intent on Suzume.

She sat down next to the old woman with a polite bow of her head. "Mother," she said.

The old woman pursed her lips before taking a sip of her tea. *Probably wetting her mouth so she can criticize the way I walked into the room.*

"Daiki says he wants to marry you," she said in a reedy voice.

"Yes, Mother," Suzume replied. Her entire body felt on edge, waiting for the blade to fall.

"I don't approve, I am sure you're aware." The room was silent, everyone abandoning the pretense of eating.

She wanted to snap back an angry reply. But that was how she spoke with the Dragon; at court, she would never be so crass. It was more difficult to relearn the old habits than she thought it would be.

"Yes, Mother," she said again.

"I do not want a whore's blood in my line. It would be different if you were still the emperor's child, if you ever were at all."

"Yes, Mother."

"But your mother spread her legs to anyone who was willing. A shame. When she had the honor of being the emperor's wife. I was almost chosen as the previous emperor's bride. But fate worked out differently."

"Yes, Mother."

"Can you say anything other than 'yes, mother'?" the old woman snapped.

"If you stopped prattling, I might be able to contribute something more," Suzume shot back. And slapped her hand over her mouth. The silence that followed was deafening. She could hear her heart pounding in her chest. The guests took an inward breath, waiting to see how the old woman would react.

The old woman laughed. It was something akin to a cackle and it rang up to the rooftops. The others followed in nervous laughter. Then the old woman reached across and patted Suzume's hand.

"I think we will get along just fine, if you do not pretend to be anything other than who you are." She winked.

It shocked Suzume, the old woman she remembered would have struck her across the mouth for such insolence. But perhaps things had changed? She did not question it. Dinner went along smoothly after that. The clansmen made their greetings, giving her well wishes for her upcoming wedding. She should have delighted in their attention, she was back where she belonged. But there was an uneasy feeling in her gut, something telling her this was not right.

When dinner was over and she was being led back to her chamber, the lieutenant caught up with her.

"My lady, may I have a word?"

She stopped and turned to face him. She scowled, but he was undeterred.

"I wanted to congratulate you on winning over Lady Tsubaki. That is no easy feat. She thinks no one is good enough for her son."

The unexpected compliment shocked her. "Thank you—" she stuttered.

He lingered a moment longer. "Honestly, I was hoping she would reject you."

Suzume's hackles rose and she had to force her hand down or else she would have slapped him. "Are you ready to get rid of me?"

"No, I just hoped you would be free to marry whoever you liked. Not who your father chose."

She frowned at him. "Why would I marry anyone other than who my father chose for me?"

"You made a promise to someone once, do you remember it?"

She stared at him, uncomprehending. "What promise?"

He removed his mask and revealed a handsome face bisected by a diagonal scar from his right temple to the left end of his jaw.

"Do you remember me?"

She stared at him, squinting, trying to recall where she had met him, if ever.

"I don't." She shook her head.

"It has been a while, I suppose. And I am a different man than I was. You called me Akito."

The name unlocked a flood of memories, a handsome young man, stolen kisses when her chaperon was not looking, and a deep aching pain when he disappeared. The memories felt foreign but consumed her nonetheless. *Where did these come from? It's as if they belong to someone else.*

She closed the gap between them, overcome by emotion. Words fell from her lips unbidden. "Akito, you never said good-bye. I've been wondering where you've been all this time!"

"Well, I've returned now, but I suppose it's too late because you will marry another."

Her heart constricted. How could she choose between the love of her life and the man her father had chosen? *What am I saying? When have I ever been in love? Who is he really?*

*"Hush, hush, listen to my song, it will not take long. Hush, hush, if you are strong, you will find where you belong,"* a voice crooned.

She looked around but could not find the source. "Do you hear that?"

Akito only looked at her in confusion. She glanced over her shoulder as a wordless song flooded over her. It was soothing, and she found as she listened, her worries disappeared. The foreign memories filled her head, lodging in place until she forgot about everything else but the man in front of her and the fabricated history he evoked in her.

# 19

Daiki returned in triumph. Banners flapped in the wind as the army in orderly rows marched into the outer courtyard of the palace, an army at his back. Suzume awaited his arrival with a heavy heart. Now more than ever she doubted her decision to marry the general. After being reunited with Akito, her heart was in torment.

Just a few days ago, she would have happily married Daiki and lived the life she was meant to live. But now she was not sure. Marrying for love had never been a part of the plan, but Akito filled up every space in her chest, making it difficult to breathe. When he entered a room, he drew her eye without trying, and in the halls when they would pass one another, he would brush her hand behind the back of her vigilant chaperon. These short encounters were bittersweet because they could never be together.

When Daiki pulled in through the gates, she plastered on a fake smile. His mother watched her like a hawk, and though she had passed the first test, she knew there was more to come. She could not risk faltering. She put aside her concerns about Akito.

This was her future, and there would be no place for her in the world by Akito's side.

When Daiki walked up to her, she acted as a girl in love should. She lowered her eyes demurely and hid behind her fan. To her left, she felt Akito's eyes on her, full of withdrawn resentment. Should she have waited for him and hoped that they could beat the odds to be together? *This melodrama is not like me at all. I chased after Daiki, and it took forever to win him over. There never was anyone serious before.* But those thoughts surfaced only to be buried once more. *You chased after Daiki to forget about Akito, don't you remember?*

Competing memories warred inside her head, loud enough to split it in two. She resisted the urge to clamp her hands on her head to stop the chatter, and then suddenly it stopped.

*"Hush, hush, listen to my song, it will not take long. Hush, hush, if you are strong, you will find where you belong,"* a voice crooned.

She looked again for the source. *Did Yokai follow me here to Daiki's home? It would be just my luck for a bloodthirsty Yokai to want to put me under a spell and make me look like a lunatic in front of important people.* No one noticed the singing but Suzume. As she looked about for the source, Daiki's mother frowned in her direction, probably thinking Suzume was impatient to have the greeting over with. She smiled and looked back forward.

Suzume's vision blurred, and for a moment she did not see Daiki and his marching army. Darkness enveloped her and a chill ran up her spine. She peered into the gloom and she swore she saw something move in a shadow, but as quickly as the darkness had descended, it disappeared. The song grew louder, drowning out all other thoughts and concerns.

"Do not worry," someone whispered in her ear. "I will take care of you."

She returned to a sunny day, and a sweaty army led by their pink-faced leader marched towards her.

Daiki bowed to her, and his topknot almost touched the

ground. She had to bite down on a smirk. *Focus on Daiki and nothing else.* It felt good to have others bowing to her again, her father's general no less.

"I have returned triumphant!" he declared.

Suzume smiled patronizingly. "What was it you were going out to do?"

"We defeated a dragon!"

Her chest constricted, but she could not explain why. Dragons were not real.

"You joke, surely."

Daiki shook his head in confusion. "No, we went to defeat the Dragon. Your father heard that a dragon had been unleashed from the temple where you were staying. The one that killed all the priestesses."

Suzume scrunched her nose in concentration. That sounded familiar, but her brain felt muddled all the sudden. She looked to Akito, and he shrugged his shoulders. He had no idea either.

Daiki looked to Suzume and then looked to Akito. A frown fluttered across his face, but he hid it when Suzume looked back at him with a sweet smile.

"Let me greet you properly," she said. "Welcome home, husband," Suzume said with her best fake sweet voice.

His face flushed bright as a beet. She had managed to distract him from Akito, but who would distract her from dragons? It seemed like there was something important she should remember. She showed Daiki inside, where they parted with promises to see one another later. She followed after her chaperon, wondering what Daiki had meant about killing a dragon. Strangely enough, she felt bad for the Dragon. Normally she did not care about these sorts of things, but this time it shook her.

A hand grabbed her wrist and tugged at her. She looked up in surprise to see Akito, his expression grim. She gave a fevered look to her chaperon, who continued on, oblivious. Akito pressed a finger to his lips and dragged her along after him into a nearby empty room. Her heart raced as he held onto her wrist without letting go. They stared at one another, locked in a silent contest. She did not want to ever take her eyes off him; even pretending she could give him up made her miserable.

"You cannot marry him," Akito declared.

She looked away, full of shame—which was very unlike her. She had never been ashamed of her ladder climbing before. Marrying Daiki would be a great match for her. It would return her to her place at the palace and remove the stain of her mother's infidelity.

"I have to. What do I have left if I don't have a place in this world?" she said to the ground.

She wanted to lift her head to say it to his face, but she couldn't make her body obey. Her limbs felt leaden as if they were bound up by something.

"You have a place by my side," Akito said.

She looked up now, shock written on her features as was a blush that stained her cheeks.

"We can't—" But before he could say more, he pushed her backwards and pressed her back against the wall. He leaned one hand against the wall, trapping her in place.

He moved in close; she could see all the stubble on his face. "You have the right to decide your own destiny."

She looked away. But he surrounded her, his body angled to press against hers just enough where it was not inappropriate but made her realize he was a man. The only thing was his scent. It was not quite right, it smelled too sweet, like burnt sugar cane. Shouldn't he have a more manly musk? She tried to remember what he smelled like, but other than that initial flood of memories, of passionate embraces and promised words beneath the moonlight, she had no other memories of Akito. Trying to find details was like trying to see through smoke.

"Why do you look away from me, when before you only saw me?"

Words just spilled out of her mouth as if she was reading from a script. "Because if I look at you my heart will break, knowing I cannot have you."

"I'm here now, just look at me." He grabbed her chin between his thumb and forefinger. "Choose me."

She looked into his eyes, but something wasn't right, this wasn't her, it wasn't how she acted. And his eyes were empty somehow, they lacked an element she could not place. Suddenly, the door at the far end of the room slammed open. They broke apart, rushing to put distance between them, but the damage was done. A red-faced Daiki glared at them, heaving for breath as if he'd run there. He looked between them, accusation in his eyes. Though they tried to hide it, Daiki knew the truth. *Everything will be ruined.* She waited for him to shout, to call her a whore like her mother.

Daiki took a deep breath, and the color in his cheeks returned to normal. But when he spoke, he enunciated each word slowly as if it took great effort to control his temper. "My lady, I was looking for you. I thought we could walk through the garden together."

A blush bright enough to burn spread across her face and down to her arms. "That sounds lovely."

She dared not look at Akito, and each step she took, she felt his eyes on her back, watching and waiting. She joined Daiki and he put his arm around her. Forgetting the burning in her heart and chest, she focused on the man she was to marry. But she could not help but wonder, was this what love felt like, this nearly painful constriction in her chest? She felt as if she had been set on fire from the inside, as if her entire body fought against an unknown force. *What else can this revolution inside me be but love?*

The men closed around him in a circle. Their masks obscured

146

their faces, and as his vision blurred, he saw Yokai he had known, creatures he had ruled for centuries before Kazue had trapped him inside that tiny prison. There were too many regrets to name them all, but the one that floated at the top of his mind was seeking revenge. No matter how he tried to cover it up, Kazue had his heart and always would. Her betrayal cut him deep, but even now, as he prepared to die, he wished he could hold her once more, forgive her for what she had done. He had never imagined he would die at the hand of humans, but life had a strange way of taking turns he never expected. Kazue had taught him that.

As he looked up, waiting for the final blow, he thought he saw her face. Furrowed with concern, those perfect bow lips and the sweep of her brows. Dark hair framing her pale face.

"Kazue," he whispered.

He closed his eyes and braced for the killing blow. Seconds ticked by like hours. *What are they waiting for? Let me die so I might be reborn a more fortunate soul.* But the strike never came. Silence greeted his ears. He could not even hear the creak of armor or the clink of weapons. He opened his eyes and found he was alone, the gray sky overhead and trees rustling in the wind. *What's going on?*

He rolled over; every part of his body ached. The wounds inflicted by the priest did not sting as badly as before. He ran a hand over the chest wound. It had stopped bleeding and closed up. He sat up, his head pounding, and his limbs felt weak, but he was not dead. *Where are the soldiers? Am I dead?*

"Morning, sleepyhead," said a familiar voice.

Back rigid, he glanced over his shoulder. *I am dead.* Kazue wore the same kimono she had been wearing the day they met, pink with red cherry blossoms, and a red pin pulled back her tresses and exposed her ear.

"This is a dream?" he said.

She laughed and pushed her hair behind her opposite ear. "Oh, me? Yes, I'm not real. I just thought you would appreciate this form." She ran a hand along her front with a smirk, that same disjointed evil smile the farmer had.

"You're the farmer!"

"Well, I am many things," she said.

He clenched his hands into fists. He had fallen for the same trap again. Had he the energy, he would have done more than just grit his teeth. But as it was, he felt weak as a newborn. "Who are you really?"

She laughed. "Ah, such a complicated question without a real answer. I think I'll wait a bit longer before telling you."

"Did you save me from those humans?"

She looked away, pretending to be embarrassed. "Yes."

It was all a cruel farce. Wearing Kazue's kimono, the shifter mimicked her seamlessly. For a moment, he almost believed she was here in front of him. But stepping back from the brink of death, the anger and hatred refilled the cracks where her love tried to push through. *She betrayed you. She chose power over you. Kazue never loved you, don't forget that.*

"Why save me? I thought you were trying to kill me."

She shook her head. "I have no sway over the humans. They do as they please these days." She held up her hands in a helpless gesture. "I need you to protect the priestess. I warned you not to leave her alone."

He wanted to reach across and choke her. This was all the shifter's plot, to taunt and tease. She had drawn him out in the first place and let the humans take her.

"There's no reason to get yourself killed over her. She's not Kazue," the shifter said.

"Of course she's not Kazue, she's her reincarnation. I do know the difference."

He shook his head and waggled his finger at Kaito. "Tsk-tsk. So easily deceived. She's not her reincarnation."

"Then how did she unleash me?"

She chuckled and flicked her hair behind her shoulder. "What would be fun about telling you? I want you to find out on your own." She stood up and dusted off her kimono. "She's not with the humans anymore, but not safe, not yet. Better go quick."

Before Kaito could ask anything else, she opened another portal and stood on the threshold, unnatural light highlighting her features. She had an uncanny resemblance to Kazue. The slight tilt of her lips and the shape of her hands as she waved goodbye, every movement an exact copy of her. This shifter was nothing like the Aryūru who had tried to devour him. This one was much more powerful, or was it a he? You could never tell with their type. The shifter stepped through the portal, leaving him to contemplate their words. *If Suzume is not Kazue, could the shifter be her?*

## 20

Hands and feet bound in stringy white webbing, her mouth hanging open and a bit of spittle dribbling down her chin, the priestess looked harmless. *How can one human bring this much trouble?* Kaito wondered. The shifter claimed Suzume was not Kazue. Then why should he continue wasting his time here. He could travel faster on his own and draw fewer Yokai to him. He didn't have time to babysit an untrained priestess. Her untamed, raw spiritual energy drew Yokai to her like flies and she seemed to have a knack for trying to get killed.

Footsteps echoed from down the cave. He crept back into the shadows, taking care to mask his spiritual energy, making him invisible. A giant spider scuttled out from down a web-lined corridor. She loomed over Suzume and tutted over her body, fidgeting with the priestess. She undid her hand and foot bindings and then bound her arms and legs to her sides with long spindly legs and then encased her in webbing.

"She is powerful," she crooned to herself. Pulling a long thread of web from her abdomen, she patched charred holes in the webbing. The priestess' power sparked against the webs, burning them almost as fast as the spider put them on. "She's getting weaker, and now the cocoon should hold. But I must be more diligent, she continues to fight my spell. Oh, what a meal she will make when she succumbs."

The giant spider had her back to him, but he recognized her method. He had seen this type of Yokai before, a spider whose venom could induce hallucinations. Perhaps this was his chance to get some answers. It was also rumored they had the ability to put their victims under a truth spell as well. Kaito had no reason to trust the shifter's words; in fact, he had every reason not to. He needed confirmation.

He moved out of the shadows, startling the spider, who skittered backwards with a hiss. The spider dropped Suzume in her hurry to get away from Kaito. The priestess fell to the ground with a thunk. Her head lolled to the side and a slight frown creased her brow, but otherwise she did not stir.

"What are you doing in my domain?" she screeched as she clacked her mandibles at him.

"I go where I please. Do you know who I am?" He uncapped his spiritual energy and let it flow over the spider, and he saw recognition dawn in her numerous black eyes.

She dipped a hasty bow, bending her forward legs and lowering her head. She did not take her greedy black eyes off him for a moment. He could see her desire for his spiritual energy. "My lord, then the rumors are true, you have awoken."

"Yes, and you have in your web the priestess who freed me."

Her mandibles clicked together in excitement. He could practically see her salivate. She probably thought she had them both cornered and could make a meal of them. Though his power was diminished, he felt confident he could overcome her, if it came down to it.

"Pardon me, I found her traveling with a human. I did not know she had done our lord such a service." She made no move to free the priestess, not that he expected her to. She inched closer, venom dripping from her fangs. For a creature that lived off draining others, the priestess was a great prize, but a dragon would be an even greater one. His spiritual energy alone would feed her for centuries.

"Don't worry, I have no intention of taking back the priestess. I just have a question for you."

She stopped her slow crawl towards him and stood up a little straighter. "For me?"

"They say you cause hallucinations, but also you draw the truth out of someone, is that true?"

She rubbed her front legs together. "Yes, it is possible my venom could do such a thing."

She looked to the priestess and then to Kaito. With his back to the wall, he was at a disadvantage. He could not transform, he was still too weak, and the spider knew he had been sealed for a long time. He redirected his energy, creating an invisible barrier around himself, in case the spider got any ideas.

"Do not think about making a meal out of me, or it will be your last." He pressed upon her with his energy, encasing her, cutting off her air. She squirmed uncomfortably, overwhelmed by the weight of his power.

Panting, she said, "I can try to have her tell you what you want to know. But she has been under my spell for quite some time and it may not make sense."

He released her from his crushing grip and the spider inched over to the priestess, with another backwards glance in his direction. He stayed back, arms crossed over his chest. He playacted an impatient ruler, but it was to hide his shaking hands and the beating of his heart. Just that brief display had taken it out of him. *I need to find a large body of water soon before I am completely depleted.*

The spider suspended the priestess in her web, across the archway of the cave. Her neck and face were exposed and she bit the priestess in the neck. The priestess moaned in response. At first nothing happened until she started to shift restlessly. She rolled her head up and then her head popped up and she looked at Kaito with blank unseeing eyes.

"She will answer any question you have, without reservation. But you don't have long before the other spell takes hold again."

He nodded his understanding, and when the spider moved out of the way, he went to stand in front of the priestess. He stared at her face at his leisure as he had never done before. He searched it, trying to find a hint of Kazue, but there was not even an echo of the woman he loved. Perhaps it was as the shifter said and Suzume was not Kazue. But he had never met a reincarnation of a human he had known before; he had never been close to humans. Maybe they did not look the same, or was he hoping too much for another chance to see Kazue?

He kept track of the spider with his spiritual power, he still did not trust her. She hung back unobtrusively, but he felt her want radiating off of her.

He focused on the priestess. "Where are you right now?" he asked.

She groaned and mumbled under her breath.

"Answer me, where are you right now?"

"I'm with Daiki's mother, planning the wedding ceremony," she said.

*Daiki?* "Who is that?"

"My betrothed, but I do not love him, I love another man."

Kaito's gaze flickered towards the spider, who leaned in close, eating up every word. If this priestess confessed her feelings, it would ruin the few scraps of reputation he had left. He could not show weakness by caring for a human again. Never again.

"You know that isn't real, you're under a spider's spell," he said.

She furrowed her brow and her unfocused eyes looked all around. "It is real. I can feel the wind and hear the birds singing."

"My spell is powerful. The more she believes it is reality, the more tactile it becomes. She can even feel pain in the dream world I have created for her," the spider explained.

"Where is she in the dream?"

"Only she knows, but for most people it pulls from their memories."

As much as he did not want to expose the scars of his past, he was curious what the priestess was dreaming about. Something about this hallucination reminded him of Kazue.

"Why would you marry a man you do not love?" he asked.

"Because it is what my father wants," she said. But it was not her voice, but Kazue's voice speaking through her. *She said that to me long ago, when she was betrothed to that lord.* He shook himself. *It could not be Kazue; she is dead. I am imagining things.*

"These memories, are they always from a current life?" he asked the spider.

She clacked her mandibles in macabre laughter. "Sometimes if there is business left undone in a past life, they may have visions of the past."

The priestess mumbled, oblivious to the spider and him. "He came back for me, and he wants to run away together."

She may as well wave a flag declaring herself Kazue's reincarnation. This was their story, how he and Kazue met. How he stole her away from another man. Kaito leaned in close, hoping to keep the spider from hearing. "Who is it that is coming back for you?"

"Akito."

Akito... his stomach sank. A part of him hoped he would be in her delusions, if only to prove she was indeed Kazue. It must be a coincidence, then. He had been secretly hoping and he had twisted her answers to fit his own desire. *Do not be fooled. She would betray you just as Kazue did. Humans cannot be trusted. They fear what they cannot control.*

"Ask her the real question," the spider suggested.

He glowered at her for a moment before turning back to the priestess.

"Who are you?"

She scrunched up her face. "I'm Suzume, daughter of the emperor, and..." She fidgeted as if fighting her bonds.

"And?" the spider prompted.

"In the past I was Fujikawa Kazue, but the Dragon cannot know." Her eyes closed and he knew he would get no more answers from her.

"Well, Dragon, you got the answer you were looking for. What will you do now?" The spider had crept closer all the while he talked to the priestess.

He stared at the unconscious priestess, his thoughts spiraling out of control. It was one thing to suspect she was Kazue reborn and another to have her there in front of him. He balled his hands into fists, unsure of what to do next. He had dreamed of his revenge, but now that it was within his grasp, he was having second thoughts.

"How does your spell work? What happens?" he asked the spider.

"She is tangled up in my song. She will reach a conclusion in the story, whatever it may be, rekindling an old love, marriage, who knows. But once she makes that final decision, one which she cannot turn back from, she will be mine." The spider laughed.

Kaito looked down at her sleeping face. He felt nothing but distant hate for the woman. She had freed him, but she had also sealed him. When he first woke up, he had wanted to inflict the slowest torture possible. Seeing her like this, he wanted to walk away and never look back. The spider closed in for attack; he could feel her energy colliding with his. She had seen through his bluff, and she knew he was weak. But even weakened, she could drain him of what energy he had left and have plenty to last her a hundred years or more.

"You know you cannot escape," she breathed, mandibles clacking in his ear.

He smirked.

"Ah, but I may have one more trick up my sleeve." He spun in place and, catching her unaware, kicked her hard on her soft underbelly. She screeched and flipped over. He may not be in full capacity, but he still knew how to fight. Overturned, her numerous legs thrashed about as she tried to right herself. He ran past her and out of her reach.

"You tricked me," she shouted as she struggled to her feet.

He laughed as he ran out of the cave. "Take care of that priestess for me." He waved as he ran down the maze of web-lined corridors.

*Is this the revenge I wanted, really?* But it was a passing thought. If he couldn't get the revenge he wanted originally, at least he would be free of a pesky priestess.

---

"Are you listening to me?"

Suzume snapped back to attention. While the old woman had droned on, she had been miles away. Thinking about what, she could not recall. It was as if she had been in a different world entirely.

"I'm listening," Suzume replied.

The old woman scoffed. But she made no further comment on Suzume's lack of focus. "I was going to tell you we received news from the palace, but perhaps you have more important things on your mind than your marriage to my son. I begin to wonder if you want to marry him at all."

The truth was there for Suzume to pluck from the air. To come clean and leave this farce behind, but she was a coward who could not reach for her own happiness. "You have to tell me, please." She forced a desperation in her tone that fell flat on her own ears.

The old woman sniffed. "Well, I don't have to do anything I do not want."

Suzume rolled her eyes, and the old woman, seeing, smacked

the back of her head. "Do not roll your eyes at me like a petulant child."

She wanted to do more than that but decided to bow her head in fake penance. The old woman appeared appeased and turned to her servant. She whispered in their ear and the servant departed on some unknown errand.

"Before I tell you, I must ask you a question."

Suzume looked to the old woman, holding her tongue on impatient words.

"Now you must answer me truthfully, or I will know you are lying to me."

She raised an eyebrow but said, "I promise to hold nothing back."

The old woman smiled, the sides of her mouth creasing over. "Do you love my son?"

The words tangled in Suzume's throat. *Of course not, I love his power, his influence, and that he can get me back to the palace.* How could she say that to his mother, who loved him more than anyone ever could.

She must have seen the answer in Suzume's expression because she said, "Don't answer, I cannot bear to hear the truth. I know he is not the most handsome or the most charming, but he is a good man. He would never beat you or mistreat you. He would cherish you until you are older than me, that I can tell you. But I was a young girl like you once upon a time, and like many maidens, I was torn between love and duty." She sighed, a far-off look in her eye.

The idea that this ancient woman could have been Suzume's age once and caught in some sort of love triangle was almost laughable. But since she was already walking the line of her future mother-in-law's patience, Suzume trained her expression to polite interest. The old woman came back to the present and finished with, "In the end, duty always wins; that is the way of the world."

*Does she know about Akito? What if they send him away?*

"How do you know the choice you're making is the right one?" Suzume asked.

"You don't, until it's too late. But duty will never forget the service you've done unto it. Where love may fade and leave you behind."

The pain of abandonment was a familiar one to Suzume, but lost loves was not what initially sprang to mind. She thought of her distant father, who she had interacted with only a handful of times over her lifetime, and her mother, who was beautiful but cold. She had seen her more often than her father, but she had felt no affection there. *She's right, even if I do not have love, if I at least have power, I have something.*

Suzume looked up and across the courtyard. Akito watched her from a distance along the veranda. He did not look like himself, his scar was gone, and instead of a sullen expression, he grinned at her in a mischievous way. And she was transported for a time to a place she did not recognize, but it felt familiar all the same. He wore a uniform in blue, and his face was different, more handsome and charismatic. He looked familiar, as if they had known one another in a different lifetime. He walked over to her, arms swinging, and as he did, her heart swelled with unfamiliar emotion.

*My dragon,* she thought.

"If you continue to ignore me, I may call off the wedding altogether," Lady Tsubaki said.

Suzume looked away from Akito and back to Lady Tsubaki, her mind reeling. Who was that? Why do I keep seeing things?

"No, please tell me, Mother," Suzume said with genuine sincerity this time. Anything to distract her from these horrid visions.

The old woman sniffed. "We've received word from the palace. Your father has given his permission for you to marry my son. The wedding can commence."

# 21

Things moved too quickly. Suzume felt frozen as time sped past her. She felt disconnected from reality—even her own emotions. The tormented feelings of love and betrayal should have stung more, but they felt distant, as if she were observing a theatrical dance. Suzume stared at the falling maple leaves as they skated across the pond. A koi broke the surface of the water and opened its mouth, looking for bugs. The maid hurried about the room. A second maid tugged and pulled at Suzume's white robe, tying the sashes and flattening the folds.

Today was the day she would marry Daiki. All her scheming was coming to fruition and all she felt was empty. She could not even triumph in her soon return to the palace—Daiki had promised to take her there after the wedding. None of it felt real.

They were to be married at the local shrine. The same shrine Daiki's parents had been married at; Lady Tsubaki had insisted. Suzume smiled and pretended to be excited. The setting was picturesque. A traditional shrine, not unlike the one she had been exiled to. It was crowded by maple trees full of burnt red leaves that melded with the red archways, which led to the shrine proper.

Everything was perfect, except for Akito. He hung around like a ghost, watching her. Her feelings for him made as little sense as her melancholy over marrying Daiki.

*I've always gotten my way. I've never been passive. Why am I not standing up for what I want? I do not love Daiki. I love Akito. He is the man I should be marrying.*

"I am almost done, mistress," the maid said as she put on the outer layer of the robe. The ceremonial hood was held by a second servant, who was standing by with eyes averted.

"I want a moment alone," Suzume announced.

The servants looked at her with large liquid eyes, without emotion or concern. *They're just like empty dolls. They do as they are told, dancing to his whims. I hate them.*

"Mistress, it is almost time to leave for the shrine," the maid replied in a flat tone.

"Leave me," she snarled as she threw her arms out to exaggerate her point. She had hidden her less flattering tendencies since coming to Daiki's compound, but now she did not care what they thought.

The maid holding the hood set it down and the maid at her feet rose with simple grace. They bowed to her in unison and left. The paper-screen doors closed with a soft thud.

Suzume sighed. She hoisted up the thick layers of her robe and went out onto the walkway that faced the inner courtyard. She stared out at the garden. It was pristine. Not a stray stem or a leaf fallen in the wrong place. *I never see gardeners, yet it is always perfect.* The wind blew through the courtyard and chilled her to the bone despite the numerous layers. *The wind is too cold for summertime.*

Footsteps fell on the landing and Suzume turned in time to see Akito. He had put aside his military uniform and wore formal clothes that she remembered from when they had both been at the White Palace. He wore a long outer robe in a brilliant cerulean and white billowing hakama. His hair had been brushed and styled into a topknot. The scar across his handsome face gave it a menacing quality when he frowned, as he was now.

"Suzume." When he said her name, it made her knees buckle. It was intimate and caressing and wrong. He should not be here now to see her in her wedding clothes. If Daiki found them together again... she had to send him away but could not find the words to do so.

"Akito, what are you doing here?" She looked away, turning to go back inside. She could not face him. The guilt suffocated her.

He grabbed her by the shoulder and she glanced back at him. "You don't have to go through with this. It's not too late for us to run away together."

She slipped out of his grasp and kept her back to him. She shook her head. "It is too late. I am promised to Daiki, and this is the only way I can return to my place."

"Your place is with me," he snapped.

She hated hurting him. Akito was so calm and remote. To raise his passion like this, her rejection must have truly hurt him. She needed to apologize, to make him understand. Suzume turned back around to face him, but Akito was gone and the garden was gone. All that remained were blank stone walls, which were slanted at a strange angle. The walls were covered in a white substance tangled up in thick strands.

Something clicked behind her. Suzume tried to move, but her whole body was bound up tight. Her extremities were numb and only her eyes rolled around in her head. Something scuttled past her. She could not see it clearly, but she realized the walls were slanted because she was lying on the ground.

"You're stronger than I thought, Priestess, but they all succumb in the end," a high-pitched female voice crooned. The same voice she'd heard singing to her.

She heard the click-clatter again. Suzume felt her stomach roll. *Where am I? Where is Akito?*

She felt something, a tingling at the back of her neck. Whatever was behind her shifted in place. Suzume rolled her eyes around in her head but could not see anything other than the walls with the thick sticky strings in front of her. Then something pierced her neck. Pain flooded her body. Every inch was alight with pain. It radiated like liquid fire in her veins, and when she opened her eyes, she was standing outside a shrine.

The red arches loomed above her. Down a path, the temple shrine waited. She could smell the incense in the air. She spotted the red and white of the shrine maidens waiting for her at the end of the walkway. She looked down at her wedding robe. Her hood had been put on. She had to turn her head far left to see past the hood to Daiki, who stood beside her. He smiled at her shyly and his round cheeks were flushed with pleasure. His gut pressed against the black groom robes. His belt was cinched so tight it looked as if it might burst. *I am marrying Daiki. I must be tired from the sun. I am imagining things.*

They walked through the archways, and with each step, her body felt leaden, taking an enormous effort to move. Sweat rolled down her spine and she resisted the urge to wipe her brow, which was dewed with perspiration. She didn't want to smear her makeup. *This feels familiar.* The shrine loomed before them, with a sweeping arched roof and curled eaves like a fall leaf.

The doors to the shrine were open and flanked on each side by shrine maidens. She glanced at them and they seemed familiar as well. The woman on the right had white hair that was held in a loose ponytail down her back with one piece of white ribbon tying it. To her right on the other side of the door, a dour-looking woman scowled at Suzume. *I know these women, but how? I only just viewed this shrine the other day with Daiki—we did not even meet the shrine maidens.*

Inside was the shrine and, in the center, the altar, which held the host of the god: a sphere. Suzume stopped, she knew this. This all had happened before. She pressed her fingers to her temple. Her brain felt foggy again like she was forgetting something important. She glanced up and a man was sitting on the edge of the altar. His legs crossed over one another. He was the same one she had seen in the courtyard.

"So you're going through with this, huh?" he asked her.

Suzume looked to Daiki and the shrine maidens. They did not seem to see the man sitting on the holy altar.

She decided, in that case, it was best to ignore him. She joined Daiki as he bowed to the shrine. The man only grinned. The shrine maidens said an invocation, their melodious voices twining together. Suzume closed her eyes and tried to focus on the ceremony. She peeked at the man, who continued to grin at her.

"Is this what you've been wanting in your heart of hearts?" he asked her.

Suzume gave him a haughty sniff in reply.

The white-haired shrine maiden brought Suzume and Daiki the ceremonial rice wine. Daiki took three sips and then Suzume took her three sips. It burned the back of her throat, not unlike the pain of the bite from her nightmare.

The man on the shrine stepped down and paced around Suzume and Daiki. Daiki did not notice and smiled a goofy smile.

"I don't know why you're so intent on ignoring the truth," the man said as he paced.

Suzume glowered at him but did not reply.

"You can keep on pretending, but what I am dying to know is: Who's Akito? You've never mentioned him. There's never been an inkling of you being capable of real love."

She scowled at the apparition, because that is what she was sure it was. She was under a lot of stress lately, it had to be her imagination.

The apparition laughed softly. "Here he is to stop the wedding."

Akito stood to one side of the room along with the other servants. He watched her with hooded eyes. The apparition had a point. Until he had revealed himself, Suzume had forgotten about him. How could a love so passionate be forgotten like a lost trinket?

Daiki offered his hand to Suzume and the pair of them approached the altar. He read his invocation. The ceremony was nearly finished. Soon she would be his wife. She felt that everything would be back to normal once she was Daiki's bride. Akito would return to the battlefield and she would continue on with her life.

"Is that what you want?" the apparition asked. "To be tied to a man? Owned by him, subject to his whims? In another life, in another time, you were the greatest of the priestesses. A look from you could destroy men like this."

Suzume glanced at the apparition. Half of his face was Akito and half was the handsome stranger.

"Who are you, really?" she asked.

He smiled and it sent a chill down her spine. "I am everything you've ever desired. Everything you lust for. I am all your sins and mistakes, and I am your destruction."

Suzume took her hand out of Daiki's and stumbled backwards. She was trapped inside her nightmare again. This was a dream and she needed to wake up. The old shrine maiden approached with the ritual branch, moving automatically, not noticing the rising panic in Suzume.

She looked into the face of the woman. "I know you. You're Chiyoko, the head priestess at the temple in the mountain."

The woman did not respond. She handed Suzume the branch and stepped back. Her eyes were blank like that of a doll. The second shrine maiden glanced at her and she was the second in command at the temple shrine, Zakuro. She whirled around to look at Daiki and he was gone, replaced by a large looming spider with dripping fangs.

"You weren't supposed to wake up, Priestess. You're much too powerful. If the Dragon hadn't woken you to question you, this would not have happened. He should learn not to meddle, it would have made your passing so much quieter." The spider sighed or that's the closest thing she could compare it to coming from a monster.

"What did you do to me?" Suzume screamed.

"It doesn't matter now, Priestess, your end has come." The giant spider hissed as she dove at Suzume with her poison fangs.

## 22

Suzume screamed, her last defense. She wriggled in her bindings, but the strong sticky fibers had her bound up tight. She closed her eyes and waited for the attack that didn't come.

Her skin tingled all over and turned into a slow burn, which grew until she felt like she was ablaze, as if she was at the center of an inferno. The spider screeched and Suzume opened her eyes. A shield of red light surrounded her. Through an opaque red barrier she saw the spider pacing back and forth.

The temple and everything else had disappeared and she was inside the cave once more, but she was no longer bound. Her clothes were shredded and she was covered from head to toe in stringy, sticky remnants of the webbing that had cocooned her previously. She pulled a string of webbing from her face with a grimace. *Disgusting, how did I end up here?*

The spider scuttled back and forth outside the barrier, clicking her mandibles and hissing at Suzume.

"You shouldn't have a drop of spiritual energy left," the spider hissed. "My spell should have drained all of it out of you."

"Your spell didn't work very well," Suzume said, climbing onto shaking feet. She tried to gain her bearings. *Why am I in a cave?*

*Where are Daiki and Akito?* The spiritual shield around her was weak. In certain spots it was an opaque crimson, in others a faint pink. *Not good.* If the spider noticed, she did not know how to reinforce the weaker spots. She didn't know how she had made the shield in the first place, it had happened instinctively.

The spider lunged for the weak part of the shield. On reflex, Suzume threw up her arms to protect herself. But when the spider came in contact with the barrier, shafts of tentacle-like energy shot out, burning the spider's legs. The spider fell back, making a horrible screeching sound. *At least she can't get through the shield.*

Suzume's head spun. Whatever the spider had done to her, it was affecting her still, though the effects were fading. She was beginning to remember things. She remembered the attack on the road and the large shadow that descended upon her after getting caught up in a web. *It was the spider's spell all along. None of that was real. What a relief.* Suzume looked up at the spider, whose long legs and bulbous body blocked the only exit. *Now how do I get out of this mess?*

The spider taunted her, "You're weak from my spell and you cannot hold that shield for long. I will wait for it to fail and then you will be mine. You are just delaying the inevitable."

Suzume sneered at the spider. "You talk too much," she said, unable to stop a snide remark from slipping out.

The spider only laughed, convinced she had Suzume beat. Suzume concentrated harder on her barrier. Back at the mountain temple, when Kaito got too close, she was able to send probes of energy toward him. Seeing as her spiritual energy burned the spider, perhaps if she could control it now, she could get past this spider. She imagined the energy reaching out from her shield and attacking the spider—as she had once done with Kaito back at the temple.

A weak tendril, the size of a thread, slithered off of the shield. It floated over to the spider and brushed against one of the spider's legs. The spider retracted her smoking leg.

"That tickled," the spider said and clicked her mandibles menacingly.

Suzume hid her fear with a smirk. *Maybe she'll think I have a plan if I keep smiling like this.* The truth was, she didn't have a plan. The shield was starting to flicker again, her head was spinning, and her knees were bound to buckle beneath her at any moment.

The spider crept closer, and her fangs were dripping with more of the hallucinogenic poison—Suzume was sure. *I cannot believe I am going to die in a filthy cave, eaten by a giant talking spider who puts you into the middle of a melodramatic fantasy before you die.* Suzume's knees locked and she fell down, scraping them on the stone floor. The barrier had faded to a dusty pink, and when the spider loomed over her, it hardly flickered in her defense.

"You never should have left your shrine, little Priestess. You should know there are much bigger and badder things waiting to eat you."

"Thanks for the advice," Suzume replied—despite her current situation, she still couldn't guard her tongue.

The barrier flickered once more and died. Suzume scuttled backwards away from the snapping jaws of the spider. In her haste, she tripped over something on the ground. She landed hard on her butt. She looked down to see a human skull with a mask over the face. The same mask the lieutenant had been wearing. Nothing remained of the man but a husk of human flesh stretched over a skeleton. She screamed.

The momentary distraction was enough for the spider to close the distance. The spider dipped her pincers towards Suzume's neck. She didn't even have the energy to fight her off. She was too tired—she used the last of her energy in that lame attack. She closed her eyes and waited for the burning sting of the bite. Instead she felt something prickle across her skin; the gooseflesh on her arms rose up. She opened her eyes just as a blue light illuminated the multitude of eyes on the spider's face before flinging her backwards.

The spider was overturned with all eight legs flailing in the air. From over her shoulder, Suzume saw the Dragon in his true form. His long sinuous body filled the cave. His head and forelegs poked through tattered webbing that had blocked a different hidden passageway. In his open mouth, rows of sharpened teeth framed a glowing ball of blue energy. It illuminated his face, casting it in relief, and sent long shadows dancing on the walls. His long whiskers brushed against the web that covered the walls, and wherever they touched, the web froze and cracked.

The rush of relief that filled her would later be eclipsed knowing that the Dragon would hold this against her. For now she was happy he had come to rescue her.

"How dare you try to take a bite out of my prey." He spoke in a rolling voice full of thunder.

His energy crashed over Suzume like the tide on the shore. Normally her body's defense would have fought him off, but this time with her defenses down, she let it roll over her. His energy felt like raindrops or the first snowfall. Surprisingly, it felt nice.

The spider regained an upright position and crouched down low. Her legs were bent above her body, making her a harder target to hit. The two postured and sized one another up. Suzume was left pinned between the two mammoths. *Why am I always the one in the middle?*

"Dragon," the spider hissed, "I thought you agreed to not interfere."

"I changed my mind. The priestess is mine, and I do not like to share."

"How dare you!"

"I will dare what I will," he rumbled in reply. "I rule this land and you must obey me."

The spider laughed. It was a wet clicking sound. "You've awoken from your slumber and found the world changed. You are weak. You may have regained some of your strength, but the others will see you for what you are, as I have. The powers have shifted while you slept. You are no longer lord here."

"Silence, insect," the Dragon roared and the sound filled the tunnel and Suzume thought her ears would burst. She clamped her hands over her ears to silence them, but his words seemed to echo around in her skull.

The spider took a step back, backing into the dark web-lined tunnel behind her. "Master, I apologize. I meant no offense," she groveled.

*You say that now that you realize he could snap you in half.* Suzume shook herself. *Wait, she said he left me to her. He could have saved me sooner and he didn't!* She rounded on Kaito. "You knew I was in here and you almost let her eat me!" She pointed at the spider.

The Dragon stared at her with his large blue eyes. They looked like storm clouds over the churning sea.

He did not answer Suzume. He lifted his head to look over her at the spider. "You should be punished for your insubordination. But I will spare you so that you may spread this message: I have returned to regain my kingdom, and if anyone attempts to challenge me, they will die."

"Yes, master," the spider tittered.

"Also, the priestess is mine, no one shall touch her."

"I do not belong to you!" Suzume interjected.

The spider did not acknowledge Suzume's interruption. "Yes, master, of course." She bowed again.

"Now return the energy you stole from the priestess."

The spider hissed and hesitated, looking from Kaito to Suzume. Then with a resigned sigh, she opened her mandibles and a stream of red energy flowed out from her mouth and slammed into Suzume's chest. She doubled over as the power overwhelmed her for a moment. Then her head cleared and she felt her strength return.

*I almost get sucked dry and that's all she gets, a little slap on the wrist?*

Kaito turned his head and walked down the passageway. *I almost die and he doesn't even ask me how I'm doing?* Suzume got to her feet and stomped after him. She wasn't paying attention to where she was going, however. Her foot got caught on a stray web and got stuck. She tugged on her foot, but she couldn't pull herself loose. The more she fought, the more tangled up she got.

"Yuck." She yanked at the sticky webbing only to have more and more attach itself to her. "I could use some help here," she called out to Kaito, but he was out of sight.

The spider came over. "I'd be happy to oblige."

A long hairy leg brushed against Suzume's arm. She shivered with revulsion. She got the impression the spider wasn't looking to free her. Suzume turned to try to unleash the spiritual energy and fry the spider, but she couldn't. *These powers would be a lot more convenient if they worked on command.* She batted away the spider's leg, but she was already wrapping Suzume's legs in the sticky web. The web climbed up her legs and bound them together.

"He has gone soft in his time of imprisonment. The Dragon from before would have smote me where I stood." The spider clicked softly as she wound up Suzume, who beat on her leg with both fists.

"And you're upset about that?" Suzume asked as she tried to wriggle free, but it was no use, the webbing numbed her extremities.

"His compassion is my gain. Once I absorb your spiritual power again, I will be strong enough to fight against *him*."

"You mean Kaito, the Dragon?"

"No, not the Dragon, he is no longer a threat. There is one much greater, one who holds the power, and to defeat him would make me ruler of—" She did not finish her sentence because a flash of icy wind zinged past, forming ice crystals on Suzume's hair and turning the webbing brittle. She smashed through it with ease, though she shivered afterward. As for the spider, she shattered into hundreds of frozen pieces.

Suzume's eyes went wide as she glanced over to Kaito, once more in human form. His hand outstretched and his expression blank. He walked over to her and ripped off the brittle webbing and helped her to her feet.

"You killed her," Suzume said.

"She was playing with my food." He showed her his teeth, and though they looked like normal human teeth, she saw the threat behind the gesture.

She knew better than to tempt his temper, but she had to know. "You knew everything was fake, you knew that the compound, none of it was real. The spider had me under her spell that entire time, but you never stopped her until now, why?"

He kept walking without answering, and she thought he would not, as he so often did not. "I was too weak to fight her. I had to go and find a water source to replenish my energy."

For the first time in her life, Suzume was struck mute. She had viewed the Dragon as infallible, just the fact that he was subject to weakness surprised her, but he had told her as well...

"I guess I'm lucky you made it back in time."

He stopped, turned and faced her. "I didn't come back to save you. After she absorbed your energy, she would have been too powerful. I had to get rid of her or she would have been a nuisance."

"Are you saying you left me to die!"

He shrugged as he smirked. "It would have been nice to be lighter one troublesome priestess."

Suzume balled her hands into fists. "You... you..."

"Me?"

"You're just selfish. No wonder Kazue sealed you! She probably couldn't stand it anymore. How could anyone love someone so arrogant!"

His expression sharpened. She knew she had said too much,

but she didn't care. Suzume brushed past him and down the corridor. She did not know where she was going, so she let her angry thoughts chase themselves in circles. *I know Kazue loved him because I lived in her memories; that's what the spider's hallucination was, reliving my past life. What I cannot understand is **how** Kazue could have loved him.*

She reached a fork in the passageway and did not know where to go. Who knew what waited down these dark passageways.

Kaito caught up with her and said, "Running away from an argument doesn't make you the winner."

She scowled at him without answering.

"What are you waiting for? Do you expect me to apologize for leaving you? Because I won't."

She crossed her arms over her chest, it wasn't like she thought he would say sorry. She had just thought for the first time in her life, someone cared whether she lived or died. But it seems that had been her own wishful thinking.

"I wouldn't expect you to apologize," she scoffed. "I just don't know the way out of here."

He laughed and with it the tension eased. "Follow me, Priestess."

# 23

They emerged from the cave into blinding daylight. Suzume lifted her hand to shield her eyes as she looked at the sun's elevated position in the sky. Kaito, ahead of her as usual, strolled down a narrow pathway that weaved down the hillside in which the mouth of the cave was set. *How long have I been unconscious?* Kaito had made no special concessions despite the fact that she had just been sucked dry of her spiritual energy only to have it shoved back into her.

*I should zap him to teach him a lesson.* She reached for the inner well of power only to find she could not control it. She could sense the power, like a slumbering animal inside her, but she could not harness it at will unless she was threatened. *What kind of power is only around when you're in danger?* She huffed.

She stomped down the pathway after Kaito. Since she had stopped to try to access her power, she had fallen even further behind. She ran a bit to catch up and her feet slipped on loose gravel along the path. She threw her arms out to stop herself from falling.

Despite her attempts at reorienting herself, her leg slipped out from beneath her. She changed the angle of her body, preparing for a collision, when an arm slipped around her waist. Kaito had caught her and stopped her from falling. *He's always doing that.* She scowled at him.

She pushed him away. "I don't need your help," she snarled. He confused her. First he left her to the spider; then he came back for her and told the spider that no one could touch her. *Make up your mind, do you hate me or not?*

He gave her a half smile. "You say that, but is it really true?"

Rolling her eyes, she stomped past him and down the path. *I really wish I could control my powers right about now.* No amount of wishing was going to give her that ability, however, and to make matters worse, her dramatic exit was ruined by the switchback trail down the hillside. Each bend turned her so she and Kaito were facing one another, and he watched her from above, with a half-smile that rankled her.

"What are you smiling about?" she demanded.

His smiled broadened. "Wouldn't you like to know."

She huffed again and hurried down the path. But yet again as she rounded a bend she was facing him on the higher pathway looking down at her with a smirk. She lifted her chin and continued without making eye contact. She suffered through several more switchbacks before reaching the bottom of the hill.

Once she was back on flat ground, she hurried her pace to get away from Kaito—at least for a moment. She didn't want him going too far in case there were more giant spiders lurking about. He may have attempted to leave her behind, but in the end he had saved her. Until she could control her powers, she would need to keep him around. He did not seem to sense her need for space, however, and he jogged to catch up with her.

"Are you going to tell me about Akito?" he asked.

She rolled her eyes and didn't respond. The spider's dream world troubled her. Suzume had planned to use Daiki as a means to an end—a way back to the palace and her honored place as the daughter of the emperor. *I wonder what happened to Daiki. Did the spider get him and his men too? He might still be out there looking for me.* But if that was the case, she wasn't sure she wanted to see him again. She thought she wanted to marry him, but after the dream, she realized that might not be the case. *His mother is wretched.* On the other hand, she missed being the center of court gossip, flirting with courtiers and being admired in poetry and song.

In the dream, she wasn't content. The romantic notion of Akito had been an exciting twist to her onetime reality. The very idea of him was like something out of a story—a soldier who was sent away but never gave up on his love. *Sounds like an idealized woman's fantasy.* She snorted.

"Something funny?" Kaito asked. He jogged ahead of her and then walked backwards so he could face her. There was no way to avoid his knowing smirk. *If Akito was a representation of Kaito, does that mean he was different with Kazue?* It was hard to imagine Kaito saying the things Akito had said. *Maybe it really was just a fantasy and I am reading too much into it.*

"Nothing that I would care to share with you." She lifted her head imperiously, jutting out her chin.

"Fine, then if you won't tell me, I'll fill in the blanks." He hummed to himself as he tapped his chin. "Akito was a childhood friend, a boy you met by chance when you were young—" He smiled and Suzume looked away and towards the thick trees that surrounded them. "He was always quiet and mysterious, but you couldn't stay away from him. You watched him go from a stoic boy to a courageous young man and it wasn't until he was beyond your reach that you knew how you felt about him. Did I get it right?"

Suzume stopped walking and put her hands on her hips. "Akito never existed. I've never been in love. Are you happy now? I knew my father would choose for me from the time I was young and I never held onto the illusion of love. In the White Palace, as a woman, your value is in your ability to bear sons and marry well. Love doesn't come into the equation."

He appeared momentarily stunned as she stormed past him. Her eyes burned from unshed tears, but she told herself it was just leftover effects from the spider's poison. *I don't care about love. I don't need it. Power is what matters and I can control that. I just can't marry Daiki... because of his mother...* It was a lame excuse and she knew it.

She didn't hear his footsteps behind her and she was glad that for once he was giving her space. Suzume walked at a determined pace for quite some time until she came upon a roadside shrine. It was made of plain unvarnished wood with a slanted roof and an open front that looked out onto the road. There was a bench beside it where travelers could rest under the shade of a tree with low-hanging branches. Since they'd been walking for quite some time, Suzume decided it was time for a rest. She put on a brave front, but after everything that had happened, she was exhausted.

She plopped down on the bench and rubbed her sore feet. *I really need to get better shoes and soon. I wish I had some thicker sandals that were meant for travel.* She glanced down at the ground and a pair of sandals lay at her feet. She glanced around in either direction. *Were these here before?* She shrugged and picked them up. They were thick sandals made of a tight weave without any visible wear.

*Why would anyone leave such good sandals here?* She shrugged again. *Their loss.* She discarded her worn sandals by tossing them over her shoulder and put on the new sturdy travel sandals. She wriggled her toes and admired them. *Much better.*

She sighed and leaned back. From her vantage point she could see inside the shrine. An idol sat inside. It was the image of a short fat man with a necklace made of large coins, an empty offering bowl lay before him, and beside it incense burned down to ash. The shrine was relatively clean, aside from the empty bowl and incense. Unlike some roadside shrines, there were no discarded offerings or debris. Someone must come here often to keep it clean.

Suzume eyed the shrine. The empty bowl made her think of her own empty stomach, which rumbled in protest. She hadn't eaten in—well, she wasn't sure how long. The dream food had been nice, but it hadn't actually made its way into her stomach. She glanced down the path from where she had come, but Kaito was nowhere to be seen.

*I'm starving. I wish I had something to eat.* Suzume sighed. Suzume looked down the road in the direction they were headed, and a hunched form approached. She stood up, prepared to run, but as the figure scooted closer she realized it wasn't a monster but an old woman who hobbled down the pathway. She wore a plain brown robe and her back was bent, so she had to lean on her cane to walk. With her free arm she carried a basket. The blanket over the basket blew back and revealed several large dumplings. Suzume's stomach growled audibly. *She's probably going to leave that as an offering.* Suzume contemplated stealing them once she was gone. Then again her history with shrines hadn't been a good one. *I'd hate to unleash another dragon because I stole his offering.* She grimaced at the thought of two Kaitos.

The old woman reached Suzume and the shrine. She nodded in Suzume's direction and then went inside the shrine and knelt before the idol. She folded her hands and prayed. Suzume pretended to be enjoying the scenery while watching the old woman from the corner of her eye. As a test, Suzume made a cursory probe into her well of spiritual power but found no change from earlier. It remained dormant despite her proximity to a holy place. The old woman finished her prayers and then cleaned up the ashes from the old incense. She then reached into her basket and extracted a few dumplings, which she set down before the shrine in the bowl. She lit a new stick of incense and stepped back to admire her offering. *I bet she's the one who's maintaining this shrine. And she can barely walk.*

The old woman got to her knees and Suzume pretended to be admiring her nails. They were ragged and dirt caked the beds. She pulled a face looking at them. Never in her life had she had such filthy nails.

The old woman hobbled over to Suzume and stopped in front of her. Suzume glanced up at the old woman and forced a smile. She was never very good with the elderly or children.

"You look hungry," the old woman said, "Here, have a dumpling." She proffered the plump white dumpling. It was still warm with steam rising off of it.

Suzume raised a skeptical brow in the old woman's direction. She was offering her the food from her basket. "Isn't that for your offering?"

The old woman shook her head and the wisps of her gray hair fluttered back and forth. "Not all of it. I always bring extra in case I run across a hungry traveler. We get quite a few merchants who come through this area from time to time." She took Suzume's hand and placed the dumpling in her hand. "Enjoy."

The old woman hobbled away without another word. Suzume stared at the dumpling in her hand. Its warmth seemed to run up her arm, revitalizing her. She was beginning to wonder if she hadn't escaped the spider dream at all and now she was trapped in some kind of world where her every desire was instantly met.

"There you are," Kaito called out to her. "I'm shocked you didn't get into trouble while you were alone."

Suzume glanced up to see him a few feet away, grinning just as he had been when they were coming down the mountain.

Suzume prepared herself for the torment. *Sometimes I wish he was more like Akito from my dream. At least he would be nicer to me.*

As he approached her, his expression changed suddenly. "Suzume, you shouldn't wander off like that."

She frowned. "You left me in a cave with a spider who wanted to eat me and now you're worried about me getting ahead of you? You should get your priorities in line."

He cradled her hand in his. She yanked it backwards as if it had burned her. Suzume glanced up at him with a skeptical brow

—not unlike the one she'd given the dumpling lady. *What game is he playing?*

"*Oh behold beauty / With hair like the ebony night / How I adore her.*"

Suzume snorted. "What was that?"

"A poem inspired by you, my dearest one."

Suzume's eyes grew large as she looked at the dumpling in her hand and the shoes on her feet, then at Kaito, who looked at her with a simpering expression. *Oh no, what have I done?*

# 24

"You look pale, dear one, why don't you sit down?" Kaito asked as he approached with a hand outstretched towards her.

Suzume wasn't sure what feeling was stronger, repulsion or frustration. *This has to be a joke. He's mocking Akito from the spider dream.* He grabbed her shoulder and she batted it away before scuttling backwards.

"This isn't funny; I told you Akito wasn't real. You don't have to keep mocking me!"

He shook his head as he smiled. *How do I fix this? He's acting crazy.* She took a step back and the backs of her knees collided with the bench and they buckled beneath her. She wobbled on her feet, throwing her arms out for balance. Kaito snaked his hand around her waist and brought her to his chest, her heart resting against him. The scent of his musk filled her nostrils as his hand crept up to the small of her back. Surprisingly, she did not feel that telltale tingling or a rise in her spiritual defenses when he was touching her. She tilted her head back and stared up into his dark eyes.

*He's like a different person.* She sighed. *Why is this always happening to me?*

Kaito brushed a stray hair away from Suzume's face and she shivered. A new feeling was bubbling up, one that needed to be squashed immediately. She had seen what lengths he would go to, to deceive her, like back at the temple when he had tried to seduce her for the fun of it. *This isn't like back at the temple. He's not trying to seduce me. He is genuinely acting like Akito from my dream.*

He dipped his head close to her and his breath stirred the loose hair that had fallen across her face. "Are you all right?" he asked.

Having him this close with his arms around her was doing strange things to her head. He was an attractive, if not infuriating man, and she found when they were close together, her body made decisions that her head did not agree with. Suzume shoved him away before she gave way to her conflicted desire. He took a step back and his expression reminded her of a lapdog she had back at the palace. In particular the face it made when it was in trouble.

"What's the matter, Kazue?" he asked, with his palms facing up in a gesture of pleading.

*Did he just call me...?* She was too shocked to respond. *Kazue! Is that why he's acting this way, because he thinks I'm her?* Maybe he wasn't pretending to be Akito. Maybe he was lost in some kind of delusion as she had been. Could the spider have gotten him with her poison when she wasn't looking?

Suzume snapped back to reality as Kaito reached out to grab her shoulder and twisted away from him. "I am not Kazue. I'm Suzume, remember? I broke your seal." She crossed her arms over her chest.

His smile was not mischievous like usual. He sat next to her on the bench, his thigh brushing against hers. She scooted away. "I know that is not your name now," he said as he chased after her as she moved away from him—she thought it might not be a good idea to run, considering how mercurial he could be. "That was your name once."

She slid away from him, and he followed down the bench until she ran out of room and fell onto the ground. She muttered a curse as Kaito jumped up and offered her a hand up. She ignored him and brushed off her pants. He kept grinning at her in a dopey way. Her stomach was in knots and she couldn't say why. She had met more than her fair share of charming men, the ones that thought they could win over every woman with a glance. She loved to trick them, let them believe that she was under their spell, and then expose them for the fools they were. But when Kaito did the same thing, it made her heart race. *It must be an aftereffect of the spider dream. It has to be.*

He frowned. "I know it's difficult for you to accept, but you're Kazue's reincarnation. Where did you think your spiritual powers came from? Why do you think it was so easy for you to break the seal? Because your soul sealed it five hundred years ago."

Suzume shook her head. To save her own skin, she had to keep denying it. *How did he find out?*

"You can't deny it. The visions, the memories that don't belong to you but feel real nonetheless, those belong to Kazue, they are a part of your past." His tone was soothing, almost as if he were coaxing her into believing him, which only made her more wary.

*This is the Dragon that woke up eager for revenge. He wanted to kill all of Kazue's descendants! How can I possibly trust him?* "I don't know what you're talking about, none of those things have happened to me."

"From the moment I awoke, I knew it was you. I was blinded by my anger. I did not want to admit it, not even to myself, but I can see the truth now. Fate has brought us back together and I refuse to lose you again." He opened up his arms to envelope her in his embrace. Suzume ducked and scrambled backwards out of his reach.

"No," Suzume shouted and then covered her mouth with her

hand. *Why does this bother me so much? What do I care if my supposed past self sealed him away?*

And yet, she refused to believe it.

"You can't stop destiny. We are meant for one another." Kaito grinned and there was a hint of his old self in the expression.

Staring at a reality she did not want to face, Suzume did what she always did in these situations, she ran away.

"You're lying, I'm not her." She didn't wait for him to respond. She turned around and walked briskly down the pathway, away from the little roadside shrine.

"Wait, Suzume, we should talk about this," Kaito called out to her.

She spun around and fixed him with a hard stare. "Just give me some space. I need time to think about this."

She expected him to force her to stay or to argue more. Instead, he lowered his hand to his side and nodded. It was unexpected but welcome, and she all but ran down the road, with no direction in mind, just needing distance to breathe and to think. She could not accept Kazue was her past life; she refused to be believe destiny bound her to the Dragon. She was the master of her life, not some intangible force like fate. Kaito was confused by whatever spell had ensnared him, and once she figured out how to break it, everything would go back to normal. She hoped.

*What if it is true?* a voice at the back of her mind whispered. *How did you unleash him from his seal? You've never shown any signs of spiritual power until you entered that temple. What if your soul was waiting until you went back to where it all began?*

Suzume shook her head again, hoping to dislodge the unwanted thoughts. There was no way. Once she was a fair distance from Kaito, she slowed her pace. Her legs, unused to so much abuse, screamed in protest. In fact, her entire body ached, the dumpling had only curbed her appetite, and her stomach grumbled again. *I can't do anything to fix Kaito in this condition, and if I just run away, he'll come after me eventually. There's no escape.*

She collapsed onto a log on the side of the road. She glanced around her—there was nothing but a dirt road and paddy fields in either direction. Further down the path lay a village made up of tiny rows of wooden houses.

*I bet the old woman came from this village. Maybe I can convince someone here to feed me and give me a place to rest. I doubt it will be too hard, these country folk never see regal beauty like mine.* Suzume preened in her mind while conveniently forgetting that she had just spent the better part of a couple days wrapped up in a spider's web.

Suzume arrived at the village as the night was beginning to creep in. Orange light filtered through the collection of huts. Farmers with their tools slung over their shoulders trudged in after a hard day's work. Suzume also stumbled into the village. Children ran out to greet their fathers with shrieks of delight and were carried in swinging from their father's arms. People walked past her without so much as a second glance. *So much for entrancing them with my regal beauty.* Then she spotted the old woman outside a tiny hut at the edge of town. She walked over to her and the old woman looked up as Suzume approached.

"I saw you at the shrine today," said the old woman. She looked even smaller and more bent in the dying light of the day. "You look ready to fall off your feet. Do you have a place to stay for the night?"

All Suzume could manage was a shake of her head.

"Come with me, I can give you a place by my fire." The old woman motioned with her hand for Suzume to follow.

Suzume followed her wordlessly. The old woman's hut was not far away. It was a small one-room dwelling with a fire pit sunk into the center of the room and a hole in the roof where the smoke escaped. The old woman waved to a place across the fire pit for Suzume to sit. Suzume sat down, her legs burning from overuse and her joints complaining like that of a woman twice her age. The old woman hummed a tune under her breath as she ladled broth out of a pot that was boiling over the fire.

"Here, something warm will make you feel better," the old woman said as she handed Suzume the steaming broth in a lopsided bowl. "You look like you could use a wash and a change of clothes. I think I have some old clothes of mine around here," the old woman muttered to herself as she went to find means to accommodate her guest.

Suzume took the soup without a word. She held it in her hands, letting the warmth seep into her fingers.

The old woman shuffled about the hut as she hummed, leaving Suzume alone with her thoughts. She was still surprised Kaito had not come after her. It wasn't like him, but then again whatever this spell was, it made him into a stranger. *What can I do to turn him back when I can't even unleash my own power at will?* She frowned as she stared into her broth.

After Suzume finished eating, the old woman brought a small bucket of cold water for Suzume to wash in and a change of clothes. They were too small, and Suzume's ankles and wrists peeked out from beneath the fabric, but it felt good to be in clean clothes, even if they were a bit itchy. Clean and dry, Suzume sat by the fire, warming her hands. *I might as well see if this grandma can give me any information about the shrine, since I'm here.*

"That shrine by the road, do you visit it often?" Suzume asked.

The old woman nodded as she swallowed a mouthful of food. "Yes, I used to go daily, but now that my bones are getting older, I go much less, perhaps once a week. Why do you ask?"

Suzume shook off the question and lapsed into silence for a while. A thought had begun to form in her mind, but she feared speaking it aloud. It was too ludicrous, yet it wouldn't stop gnawing at her.

"Do you know who built that shrine?"

The old woman looked into the fire, thoughtful for a moment. "The first villagers would have constructed it, and I believe my grandfather once told me it was blessed by a wandering priestess. It's dedicated to our local Kami." The old woman gave her a gap-toothed smile.

Suzume swallowed hard. "Do you know the priestess' name?"

The old woman thought for a moment and then shook her head. "I'm afraid I don't. It's said the shrine brings good luck, though. There are stories of it granting wishes and things like that."

Suzume choked. *That's it! The shrine was granting my wishes. I wished for sandals and they appeared; I wished for food and she showed up with dumplings. I wished Kaito was more like Akito and...* Suzume groaned aloud.

"Something wrong, child?"

"Nothing," she blurted before clamping her mouth shut. *First thing in the morning, I am going back to that shrine and demanding that idol turn him back.*

---

Leaving her shrine after five hundred years had been difficult. She labored over the decision for days, sitting in front of the shrine she and Hikaru had built in contemplation. She had kept the guise of an old woman for too many years, and it scared her to think about resuming her place among the Yokai. *Who will watch over the clan when I am gone? Who will clean the shrine?* But knowing the Dragon was alive, she could not stay idle here.

She put her affairs in order, spoke with the Kaedemoris' current patriarch and told him she would be leaving on a journey. She promised to return, she wanted only to see to the Dragon and come back. Lord Kaedemori would not protest, she knew. He knew about Hikaru and her, though he had been a young man when Hikaru died. Only the elders of the Kaedemori and Shin knew. To the rest of the Yokai world, she was as good as dead. Dedicating your life to service to humans was unheard of, but

Hikaru had sworn to protect his former clan and she had done the same.

While she had watched the Kaedemoris spin out their brief lives, generation after generation, the world had changed around her. She had kept herself separated from the world of her birth. In part to keep Hikaru safe and in part because she had never felt like she belonged. But while he slept, the Dragon's kingdom had fallen, and though Rin had remained safe in her shrine, the Dragon would have many enemies. The Dragon would need a guide. So she had left, with nothing on her back but her clothes. She had traveled at first as an old priestess, helped by passing humans and travelers, given places to sleep around the fires of villagers, treated like a respected guest. It was a sham; had they known what she was, they would never have let her into their homes.

She went first to the place where the Dragon had slept, where Kazue's spell put him into an endless slumber. The shrine was at the top of the mountain, and the songs of the priestesses filled her with memories of better times. She never expected him to linger there, but what better place to begin her search than where it all began. She felt his power surrounding it, leaving traces of him in every stone. It may not have started out as a holy place, but it was now.

She did not stop to talk to the humans there and passed by with her spiritual energy cloaked. But upon seeing the empty shrine building, she knew it was true at last. And in that moment she gave up the guise she had lived under for nearly five hundred years. From then on she journeyed in something akin to her true form, following the Dragon's trail.

She heard the whispers from her kind on the road, others like her who had adapted by cloaking themselves as human to move about unseen. They saw her and recognition would spark in their eyes. For a brief moment they were kindred, lost and wandering without a home. When the Dragon was sealed, many lost the security they once enjoyed. More than once she joined a Tanuki or a Kitsune at a roadside teahouse. They would eat and drink and talk of better times, though they had never met before. They would swap rumors and give warnings about powerful creatures and how to avoid them.

"There's a dangerous Yokai north of here," said one Tanuki as he slurped his tea. He disguised himself as a merchant, a pack on his back and a straw hat strapped onto his chin.

"Is it the Dragon?" she asked.

He shook his head. "No, though I have heard he is awake and travels with a priestess. Those who have seen him say he is not as strong as he was before. He uses the form of a human, and his energy seems depleted. He is no longer a threat."

"Do you know where he was headed?"

The Tanuki scratched his chin in thought. "East, I think."

Rin nodded. She was headed in the right direction.

"I wouldn't worry about him. The one you should stay clear of is the shifter. He takes any form and can change his spiritual pressure. You will meet a human on the road and not realize what he is until it's too late, or so they say. Be careful, I heard he has been seen east of here as well."

She nodded and smiled. "Thank you."

They parted and she continued on her way. The world was not a safe place for Yokai anymore. They were not the masters they had once been. After days of travel she finally found a trace of the Dragon's energy, mixed with humans as well. The earth was browned in places where his ice had frosted it over prematurely. Hoofprints in the ground led in the opposite direction. *The humans know he's awake and they're looking for him.*

There were signs of him everywhere. She followed his trail through the hills, into a spider's den where she found a dead spider, and out down the hill and to a roadside shrine. That was where the trail had gone cold once more.

She stopped to rest, and a prickling sensation raced down her spine. The energy within the shrine churned like a pot about to boil over. She stood and went to the opening that faced out onto the road. The figure inside, a squat fat man with a chain of gold coins around his neck, rocked back and forth on the pedestal. She tilted her head as she looked at it. She crept closer, wondering what was causing the disturbance. She did not feel anything living coming from it, but the figure itself seemed to be cloaked in the spiritual energy of a priestess.

She reached out to touch the figure, but before she could, the figure cracked on the top of the head. The crack grew, shuddering through the entire idol down the middle. Then the two halves split apart and a man the same size as the idol stared at her. She was so surprised she screamed. The idol screamed as well.

Then she backed away as the idol leapt up and over her shoulder out into the night. She stared after it, wondering what had awoken it. She looked back at the shrine once more. *The villagers will be devastated when they find it empty like this. What should I do?*

# 25

The hut was small and the old woman did not have much in the way of bedding. She gave Suzume some blankets and a place by the fire. After sleeping on the ground for weeks, even the blankets and a warm fire felt like a luxury.

Suzume curled up in a ball beneath the blankets. She emptied her mind of thoughts of Kaito's strange behavior and let sleep claim her. She had just closed her eyes when something soft brushed against her face. Suzume's eyes flew open. She peered up through the darkness to see Kaito leaning over her. He grinned and his white smile flashed in the darkness of the room. She shot up and slammed her head into his chin. She hissed through her teeth, rubbing her tender head. Kaito massaged his chin, without his smile faltering. *He should have moved out of the way.* She stared at him, wide-eyed, more than a little disturbed to find him watching her sleep. *Was he stroking my face?* She touched her cheek. *What kind of lecher watches someone sleep?*

"You disappeared," Kaito said in a stage whisper.

Suzume's back was towards the old woman. The old woman snorted in her sleep but did not seem to be disturbed by their late night visitor.

"What are you doing here?" Suzume hissed. Her voice was louder than she intended and she froze, afraid she would wake her host. She glanced over at the old woman, who rolled over in her sleep but did not wake. *Good thing she's a heavy sleeper. I don't know how I would explain this...* Suzume eyed Kaito suspiciously.

"I came looking for you. I was worried. When you said you wanted your space, I figured you would come back eventually," he said. He caressed her cheek with his fingertips. The touch of his flesh against her bare skin sent a chill down her spine. *He's gentle when he wants to be.* She shook her head. *It's the spell, don't let it fool you. This is **not** the real Kaito.*

"Stop doing that." She slapped his hand away.

A sad-puppy expression crossed his face and Suzume had to chide herself for feeling guilty about yelling at him. *If the Kami could make Kaito this way, then he should be able to turn him back to his annoying self once again. I never would have imagined I would want him back. But I kind of miss the teasing.*

"Are you still upset about learning that you're Kazue's reincarnation?" Kaito scooted closer to her on his knees. His hand brushed against hers as he took a seat beside her.

She recoiled and sat back on her knees. *He's a crafty one. I'm going to have to keep an eye on him, or he may try to seduce me again.*

"I am *not* her," she snarled to avoid the uncomfortable feelings his close proximity elicited. "You're under some kind of spell that's making you sappy and emotional."

He shook his head. "No, this is how I really feel." He pressed his hand to his chest to emphasize his point. His fingers were long and elegant and she thought about the way they brushed her face or pushed her hair behind her ears. She had been trying to figure out why it felt different when he did it. Men always thought she wanted them to touch her, as if they were giving her a gift with their attention. But Kaito like this was different. It seemed genuine and that's what scared her the most.

*Wow. Get a hold of yourself. This has to be an effect of the spell. It's making me crazy.* She clapped her hands onto her cheeks. It hurt more than it helped her focus.

Kaito regarded her with a bemused expression. "You should rest. I'll keep watch until morning."

She opened her mouth to argue, but talking to him in this condition was like arguing with a wall. Despite that, her inherit stubborn nature kept her from seeing reason even if it was staring at her in the face.

"Then keep watch outside. I can't sleep with you leering at me all night."

He laughed and her stomach fluttered. *Come on, body, don't start betraying me now.*

"I'm not letting you out of my sight. Remember the spider? I can't risk losing you now that I've found you."

Suzume resisted the urge to groan aloud. *Talk about sappy... earlier today he was planning on letting the spider have me.*

"What am I supposed to tell her, then?" Suzume jammed her thumb in the direction of the old woman, who slept on unaware across the room. Despite the increasing volume of their voices, she had not stirred.

He shrugged and there was that familiar mischievous gleam in his eye. "Not my problem."

Suzume glared at him. "You're really not going to leave, are you?"

He grinned. "Nope."

She sighed and crossed her arms over her chest. They sat for several moments, just staring at one another, waiting for the other to crack. After about twenty minutes of this, Suzume's eyes grew heavy as if weighed down by sacks of grain, and her head drooped forward. She startled awake and resumed glaring at Kaito, only to have her eyes slide shut and her head bob again. *I can't fall asleep with him here. How do I know he's not playing some kind of trick on me and he's just waiting for my guard to be down...* Her head sank onto her chest, and she snapped back up, shaking her head and glaring at Kaito, who grinned back at her.

"Fine," she announced. "Be a creep and watch me as I sleep." She lay down and rolled over to face the fire.

After several checks over her shoulder and a lot of restless shifting, Suzume managed to fall back asleep. She awoke to the smell of frying fish and sunlight streaming through the door flaps that led into the hut. Suzume sat up, stretched, and yawned. The old woman was humming that same tune again. It was starting to grow on Suzume.

After Suzume rubbed the sleep out of her eyes, she looked for Kaito. She expected to see Kaito watching over her, waiting with a bowl of rice to force-feed her.

"Sleep well?" the old woman asked. She turned the fish over the flame.

Suzume sat up and pushed her thick hair over her shoulder. "Well enough." She paused, looking around for Kaito once more. "Anything interesting happen this morning?" *I would think she would scream or something if she found Kaito standing over me as I slept.*

The old woman poked at the fish with a long pair of metal chopsticks, checking if it was done. "Just an average morning." She smiled her gap-toothed smile at Suzume once more.

Suzume frowned. *Where did he go now? He's slipperier than an eel.*

"Any plans for your day?" The old woman came over to Suzume with the fish on a platter and a bowl of rice to accompany it.

Suzume looked down at the fish and the rice. *He was so adamant about not being parted from me, yet he runs away at the first opportunity.* She picked up the chopsticks the old woman had laid next to the bowl and poked at her fish with it. She broke off a piece and chased it around her plate.

"Nothing in particular, I was planning on visiting the shrine before I leave," Suzume replied evasively.

"Well, don't hurry away on my account. I was planning on heading to the shrine again today. I feel more energy since you are here, and I thought I might do a bit of tidying up. It's good to offer prayers to the gods before beginning a journey."

*Well, that's convenient. Maybe I can get more information about the shrine if we go together.*

"I guess it wouldn't hurt," Suzume said with feigned nonchalance. The old woman seemed to be rather devout, and maybe she knew how to communicate with the Kami. "Last night, you said that the shrine grants wishes."

The old woman was chewing when Suzume asked the question; not willing to wait for her to finish, Suzume continued on without waiting for a reply. "Have you ever known someone to have their wish granted... or wishes?"

The woman swallowed at last. "My grandfather said he got this house when he wished for it from the shrine, but I'm not sure if that wasn't a story he just liked to tell." She smiled and her eyes wrinkled as she did so. "Do you have a wish you want granted? Perhaps there's a young man you are fond of."

Suzume had to restrain herself from snorting. "No, nothing like that." She held up her hands. "I'm just interested in old customs is all," she lied. She couldn't bring herself to tell the old woman about the wishes, it was too ludicrous.

The old woman winked and said no more. They finished their meal and the old woman went to a small pen out back to feed her chickens before they headed back to the temple. Suzume paced the inside of the hut as she waited. She thought Kaito would come back, but he hadn't, and she was starting to get worried. The last time he had disappeared, she was trapped inside her own nightmare. *Please, just no spiders this time.*

The woman came in after finishing her chores and they finally left for the shrine. As they traveled, Suzume tried to access her spiritual power and see if she could sense anything. As usual it produced no results.

The old woman hummed the same tune, perhaps it was a case of getting a song stuck in your head. But the song seemed oddly familiar to Suzume.

"What's that song you're singing?" Suzume asked.

"Oh, just an old tune. I don't even remember the words anymore. I think it used to be something they sang at festivals when I was a girl. It's been so long that all I remember is the tune." She smiled and Suzume smiled back.

*This woman has practically nothing, but she's very content.* She thought back again to Akito. In her dream she had denied him because she had been so enchanted by the idea of wealth and power, but when it came down to it, she did not want to marry Daiki, even though he was probably the only person who would take her. *I bet if I went and found him and explained about the spider, he would take me straight to the palace.* Her opportunity was waiting, Daiki might even have the power to defeat the Dragon, but she couldn't do it. For whatever reason, she was sticking with the Dragon, even going out of her way to get him back to normal. *I hope I don't regret this decision later on.*

"Hmm," Suzume replied, not sure what else to say. They arrived at the shrine and the old woman went inside to offer her prayers. Suzume hung back and examined the bench where she had sat and the building itself. Nothing was unusual about it. It looked like a regular shrine. *It's hard to believe a roadside shrine could have that much power.*

"There you are, beautiful." She could hear Kaito's voice but could not see him.

She spun around in circles, looking for him. *He can turn himself invisible!*

He laughed somewhere behind her and she turned in that direction. "That's not fair! You can turn yourself invisible... did you use this power at the hot spring to peep on me?"

"I'm up here," he said.

Suzume tilted her head back and saw Kaito squatting on the

roof of the shrine with that same mischievous smirk in place. *Maybe he's back to normal?*

"What are you doing up there? I thought you said you did not want to leave my side," Suzume asked. It was silly to be upset over him disappearing, but her emotions had been all across the spectrum as of late, so she allowed herself the indulgence.

"I felt a powerful spiritual energy coming from the shrine, so I came to investigate." He smirked. "She's not going to like what she sees."

Suzume didn't like the look in his eye. The mischievous grin coupled with the compliments were too weird.

"What's inside the shrine?" she asked slowly.

"It's more like what isn't there."

Suzume frowned but took the bait. She had a bad feeling about his taunting but decided to take the risk. Suzume stepped inside the shrine. The old woman knelt on the floor.

She turned to look at Suzume as she entered; her face was pale. "I don't know..." She trailed off and turned back to look at the place where the idol had once been. It was gone and in its place a single acorn remained.

The Kami was missing and with it her hope of turning Kaito back to normal.

## 26

"What did you do?" Suzume spun around and pointed an accusing finger at Kaito.

He leaned against the doorway to the shrine. "I think you should be asking yourself that question, Kazue."

"Don't call me Kazue!" she snarled.

*I wish he would decide on a personality and stick with it.*

"Why would I stop when you make that adorable face whenever I call you by your old name?" He winked at her as he flicked his hand in her direction to indicate said face.

Suzume scowled at him. Even when he was acting out of character, he was infuriating.

"Miss, who are you talking to?" The old woman spoke up.

Suzume turned back around to look at her. *She's got to be joking. How can she not see him? He's a head taller than me, at least.* Suzume glanced between the old woman and back to Kaito. The old woman's brow furrowed and she glanced in Kaito's direction, but just past him out to the road beyond.

"Him." She pointed at Kaito. "He's standing right there." She jabbed with her finger for emphasis.

The old woman's frown deepened as she shook her head.

"There's no one there."

Suzume's eyes widened and she turned back towards Kaito. He examined his nails and raised a brow at her when she gave him a questioning look. *She can't see him? Why? Does it have something to do with this spell?*

"Maybe you've had too much sun," the old woman said, though her expression was cautious. She inched backwards towards the empty pedestal.

*Great, now this old lady thinks I'm crazy,* Suzume thought.

"I need to head back to the village and tell the villagers. They'll be upset that the shrine has been disturbed. You are a priestess, please pray here that the Kami is not angered. The Kami blesses our crops and brings the rain. If he leaves because of this desecration, then that would mean disaster for the village." The old woman wrung her hands and tears gathered along her lashes.

Kaito snickered from behind Suzume. Suzume balled her hands into fists at her sides and did her best to pretend to be interested in what the old woman was saying. She even nodded a few times as the old woman continued to babble about the importance of the Kami to the village. *How much more can she say about this Kami? What I don't understand is how a statue just up and walked away. There's some strange things going on around here and I'm not sure I want to stick around to figure out what.* Going back and finding Daiki was starting to sound like a good idea right about now.

Suzume glanced at Kaito. He strolled around the shrine room, pretending to inspect the pedestal before stopping behind the old woman and mocking her as she spoke. He used a fake old woman voice as he repeated her words, "I have been coming here for years, how could this happen! My grandfather said the gods could be mercurial, what will we do!"

Suzume snorted then covered her mouth. The old woman did not notice and continued on with her monologue. *This has to mean the Kami is behind the spell. It's the only logical explanation.*

"It would mean a lot if you could help," the old woman finished and Suzume realized she had not been paying attention for most of her long-winded speech.

"Sure," Suzume said without thinking, just so she wouldn't be caught not paying attention. It was Kaito's fault, really. If he hadn't been mocking the old woman, Suzume would have been able to focus.

The old woman smiled and took Suzume's hands in her own. It seemed the old woman had gotten over her concerns about Suzume's sanity. The old woman shook Suzume's hands violently. *She's surprisingly strong for someone that has to be pushing a hundred.*

"Thank you so much. I know you'll be able to find the Kami." The old woman beamed. Tears fell down her cheeks.

Suzume's mouth dropped open. When did she agree to look for this wayward Kami? *Oh, that's right, when grandma here took too long spitting out her request.* Suzume sighed.

The old woman had already grabbed her basket and shuffled down the pathway back towards the village. Suzume watched her go, at a loss for what to do next. *Well, I guess I needed to find this Kami anyway.*

"You're very generous to help those villagers; Kazue was like that too. She was always looking out for others." Kaito had snuck up behind Suzume and had his arms wrapped around her waist. His lips brushed against her neck and the feel of his mouth so close to her flesh sent a shiver down her spine.

*Stop it. Don't be lulled by his sweet words.* She broke free of his grasp and faced him, with her hands on her hips.

"Let's get a couple things straight here. I am not Kazue. I am not helping these people out of the goodness of my heart. I am doing this because I need to find that Kami to have him remove the spell that's on you. And I need you to explain why that old woman couldn't see you!"

He barked a laugh. "That's simple, because she doesn't have any spiritual power. If I do not choose to let a human see me, then they cannot."

It was Suzume's turn to raise a skeptical brow. "But everyone at the shrine could see you..."

"And they were all priestesses. Unlike you, many of them were chosen for their powers, not as a punishment from their father."

She glared daggers at him. "How do you know that? I never told you why I was at the temple."

He laughed again. "I heard things while we were there. I know that your mother was found in bed with another man and she was exiled for it. I know that your father also disowned you and all of your siblings that he had with your mother."

Suzume crossed her arms over her chest. She didn't like the idea of Kaito knowing more about her than she knew about him. "You shouldn't pry into my personal business," she snapped at him before spinning away to face the empty pedestal where the Kami's idol had once sat. A lone acorn lay there. It would have been funny if she wasn't frustrated.

Kaito came over and leaned against the pedestal in Suzume's line of sight. "I know more about you than you know about yourself, Suzume."

Her back grew rigid and she recoiled. *He called me by my given name. He hardly does that. Not without mocking me, anyway.* Ever since the spell had fallen on him, he had been alternating between calling her Suzume and Kazue. "Or so you say." She brushed off his apparent affection. It was all a trick anyway. "How do we find this missing Kami, then?"

"Who said I was going to help you?" He sat down on the pedestal with his legs crossed.

"Why wouldn't you? You've already declared your devotion to me—even though you keep disappearing and playing tricks on me as usual." She made a sweeping arm motion as she spoke.

He chuckled. "This is who I am. I'm a dragon, it's in my nature to be a trickster." He jumped down from the pedestal and took a step closer to her. "It doesn't change the way I feel about you, though." He brushed her cheek with his thumb and for a split second she leaned into his touch, letting herself get lost in his warm hands. *Why do you have to be so confusing?*

She pulled away. No good could come of falling for his charms. "We're never going to get anything done if you keep falling into this romantic melancholy all the time," she snapped to hide her own desire.

"Melancholy's a pretty big word for you. I'm impressed."

"Shut up," she growled. "Tell me, where would a Kami go if he was not in his shrine?"

Kaito pressed his finger to his chin and tapped it. "Well, what do we know about him?"

"Well, he's a Kami."

"Or the villagers perceive him as one. As you remember, not all gods are really what they claim." He smiled at her, showing all his white teeth. She looked away, ignoring the way his smile made her feel. *This needs to stop before I turn into an emotional mess like in the spider dream. Now **that** would be a nightmare.*

"Okay. So he's a god or godlike creature," Suzume amended.

Kaito preened as if she were talking about him. He ran his hand over his hair, which was styled in a sleek topknot.

*Damn former 'god'.* Suzume rolled her eyes. "The old woman said he controlled the crops and the rain, so he must have some sort of control over the elements. I also think he can grant wishes."

Kaito snorted. "Do you know how many immortals claim that very thing?"

"Since I haven't met many, I'll have to go with an 'I don't know'," Suzume deadpanned. He may act like he loved her, but he was still condescending as always.

He ignored her quip and continued. "Let's just say a lot. Granting wishes is not something just any immortal can do, not really. A lot of them like to pretend they can—like giving a farmer gold that turns into dirt a week later and things like that. A true wish can only be granted by a very powerful god. I'll tell you right now, this village is way too small for something that powerful to be watching over it. Most of these villagers just get something they call a god and pray to. Sometimes immortals will take up residence and eat the offerings, listen to the prayers, then leave. There are hardly any real gods living in shrines. My guess"—he picked up the acorn from the pedestal and rolled it around in his hand—"we have a thief who stole an empty idol."

"Why would they do something like that?" Suzume asked. "What would be the point?"

Kaito shrugged. "There's lots of different reasons, but most likely because they thought it would be funny. My gold coin is on it being a Kitsune." He flung the acorn into the air and caught it.

"You mean those little furry things with the big ears?" Suzume held her hands together to indicate the size of said creature.

Kaito patted her on the head. "No, this wouldn't be an ordinary wild fox. This creature would have a human form—most likely with ears and a tail. When a human without spiritual powers saw it, they would only see a regular fox, but for someone like you or me, we would see the creature's true form."

"How did you figure all of that out just from an acorn?" Suzume asked with a puzzled expression.

"Because the culprit is behind you." He motioned with his hand and Suzume glanced over her shoulder.

A woman with auburn hair down to her waist and matching ears poking out of the top of her skull stood outside the shrine. She had red lips and long lashes. She wore a robe hitched up to her hip, revealing a long shapely leg.

"Well, long time no see, Dragon," the Kitsune said. "I'm disappointed that you would jump to the conclusion that I am the one who stole the idol."

She sauntered over and brushed past Suzume, bumping her and almost causing Suzume to lurch forward.

"Hey," Suzume snapped. "Who do you think you are, coming in here and interrupting?"

The Kitsune pressed herself against Kaito, and he looked down at her with a bemused expression. The Kitsune rested one hand on his chest as she turned back and looked at Suzume as if she was just noticing her for the first time.

"I felt something coming from this shrine last night and came to investigate." She gave Suzume an innocent smile. "It was a bonus to discover my dragon here as well." She purred.

Suzume scowled at her.

"Rin, what are you doing in this region?" Kaito's voice wasn't harsh necessarily but not affectionate either.

Rin nuzzled into his chest. "I heard about your resurrection and I came looking for you." She looked up at him, batting her long lashes. "Why didn't you come get me the moment you awoke?" She pouted.

Suzume thought she was going to be sick. Who was this tramp, and why was she practically throwing herself at Kaito? *Why do I care?*

"I hate to interrupt your *reunion*, but I need to find whoever stole this idol so I can reverse this spell that has Kaito acting..."

"Like he's in love with you?" Rin asked.

Suzume glared at her. "How do you know?"

"Because I've been listening while you two bickered." She grinned. "I can help you break the spell and find the idol."

Suzume sized her up. Rin stood with a hand on her hip and her body turned to give Kaito the best view of her generous curves. Suzume looked at her own ill-fitting borrowed clothes and flat chest and nonexistent hips. Suzume hated Rin, she decided.

"We don't need your help. Come on, Kaito," Suzume said as she motioned with her hand.

Rin pulled a face and then a slow smile spread across her features. *What is she smiling about?*

Suzume turned to walk out, but as she did, Kaito stopped her with a word. "Wait."

Suzume was opening her mouth to argue when he gave her a quelling look. The thunderclouds were in his eyes again. The tell-tale prickle of her powers raced over her skin and she clamped her mouth shut. She wasn't going to argue with him when he was in a mood. She had seen what he did to that spider. Rin watched the exchange, smiling to herself.

"What did you see?" Kaito asked Rin.

Rin shot Suzume a smug, triumphant grin. "Last night, I was on my way to find you when I stopped at the shrine. I felt a strange energy and went to investigate. The idol broke apart and there was a little bald man sitting there." She pointed at the pedestal where the idol had previously sat.

"Are you saying the idol came to life?"

She shook her head. "I'm saying something unleashed the immortal that was inside that idol."

They both turned and looked at Suzume, who threw her hands up. "Well, don't look at me."

## 27

Suzume shook her head furiously; her hair whipped back and forth as she did so. "You can't blame this one me!" She stopped shaking her head and jabbed a finger towards Kaito. "I was at the old woman's hovel all night. You saw me, you were there! There's no way I could have awakened the god... if it even was a god. I'm still thinking this *Kitsune* has something to do with the missing idol. Why was the acorn here? Maybe we should be investigating other explanations!"

The pair of them stared at her with identical dumbfounded expressions. "Are you finished?" Kaito asked. He grinned and it only intensified her embarrassment.

*There's no way I unleashed that Kami. Sure, a couple of strange things happened when I was here yesterday, but when I broke Kaito's seal, I felt something. I felt my powers reaching out to the seal. I didn't feel anything here.*

She glared at him, but it had lost some of its intensity. "Yeah. I'm finished." Her shoulders sagged.

Kaito looked at Rin. "Tell us, other than that, what did you see last night?"

Rin sat down on the pedestal where the idol had been. She

crossed her leg over her knee and her robe hitched up nearly to her hip. Kaito's eyes flickered in that direction and Suzume's temper, already frayed, reached a boiling point.

"Cover yourself. You look like something from the red district," Suzume snarled at Rin.

Rin gave her a placid expression and pulled her robe down an inch. She cleared her throat. "I told you all of it, basically. The god —or whatever he was—was sitting here where the idol used to sit, I'm assuming." She shrugged. "He had a chain around his neck made of large coins, and when he saw me, he screamed; then I screamed. He bolted past me before I could get anything out of him."

"That's all?" Kaito asked. He looked at Rin like he was chastising a child.

She smiled up at him and batted her long lashes. "That's all, master."

The way she said master made Suzume's skin crawl. *Get it together. You don't care who he flirts with or how trashy she is.* "I have to know, how do you two know each other?"

"That's not important right now," Kaito said, waving away her question. "If you did unleash this immortal, it means your powers are not under your control in the least, which explains why you were so irresistible to that spider..."

Rin's ears perked up and swiveled towards Kaito. She looked at him with wide fearful eyes. "Spider?"

"A huge one whose poison caused vivid hallucinations before it drained its victim of all of its life energy." Kaito wiggled his fingers and moved towards Rin.

She shrieked and ran away from him. He chased her around the pedestal. *What is wrong with these immortals? Is everything just a game to them?*

Suzume stepped in Kaito's way. He nearly collided with her but caught himself at the last minute. She jutted her chin towards him. "We don't have time for your flirting. We need to find this idol."

"Jealous?" he purred.

She dodged his hand before he could touch her. She scoffed. "Hardly."

Suzume stomped out of the shrine and out onto the road beyond. She looked both ways. *If I were a god, where would I go?*

"He went into the woods behind the shrine," Rin said. She pointed at a wooded area that led up the hill behind them.

Suzume bit her tongue to keep from saying a sharp retort. Rin's input may have been unwanted, but it was at least helpful. *I'll make a onetime exception to listen to her.*

"What do we do once we find him?" Suzume asked.

"Well, I for one want to know what unleashed him," Kaito said. His expression was pensive.

Suzume stared at his profile. His brow crinkled slightly and his lips were parted. She had not seen him look so thoughtful before. It softened his face and she could see the handsome man beneath the taunting, infuriating creature she had come to know. *Why does he want to know who unleashed the idol? Does it have anything to do with me breaking his seal?*

A sharp pinch on her arm brought Suzume back from her musings. "Ouch!" she shouted and spun around to see Rin grinning at her. "Why did you do that?" Suzume demanded.

"Do what?" Rin swished her tail behind her and flattened her ears. She gave Suzume a look that belied innocence. *She's anything but innocent.*

"You pinched me or something..." Suzume rubbed her arm where the pain had started.

Rin scoffed and tossed her auburn hair over her shoulder. "I did not. You're delusional."

Suzume considered scratching her eyes out when Kaito intervened. "Ladies, you don't need to fight over me."

"This has nothing to do with you," Suzume snapped.

Rin coughed and it sounded like she was saying "liar". Suzume scowled at her. Suzume thought of saying something rude in return, but for once common sense overruled. In a battle between her and two Yokai, it was better that she bite her tongue. Rin swung her tail back and forth, and whistled. *I'm onto you, Kitsune.*

"Enough bickering," Kaito said, with a half-smile. "Let's go find this Kami, or whatever he is."

Kaito headed towards the woods. After another snotty glance between the two women, they followed after him.

The forest behind the shrine was thick with undergrowth. Plants tangled in the roots of the massive trees that towered overhead. Sunlight pushing through the trees' canopy, creating fractured shadows on the forest floor as the daylight struggled to break through. Suzume had the impression that the villagers did not come this way very often. While she fought through the undergrowth, Rin and Kaito seemed to have no trouble. The hairs on the back of her neck rose up and the skin on the back of her arms prickled.

She rubbed the back of her neck and looked over her shoulder. She heard nothing but birds calling to one another and the wind rustling through the trees. *There's nothing here. It's just my imagination.* After a few feet, the undergrowth gave way to a steep incline. Kaito and Rin chatted together, oblivious to her struggle. *Damn Yokai. I bet she's loving watching me flounder, too.* Suzume glared daggers at Rin's back.

Too focused on Rin, she did not see the loose earth and her foot slid and she stumbled, landing on her elbow. Pain shot up and down her limb. She cried out in pain and Kaito stopped. When he saw her, he doubled back, leaving Rin farther up the hill. Rin pulled down her lower lip, mocking Suzume behind Kaito's back. Then Rin feigned falling to the ground, and rubbed her fists over her eyes like she was crying. Suzume pushed up onto her knees with her good arm and brushed off her hands as Kaito reached her. She held her arm close to her body and pretended it didn't hurt though it was throbbing and bleeding.

"If you want, I can carry you. It's only going to get more treacherous the higher up we go." He held his hand out for her, but Suzume ignored it and climbed to her feet.

"I don't need your help. I can climb on my own." She held her head up high, like the princess she was.

He smiled but made no comment. He hurried back up the hill to a waiting Rin. Rin took Kaito's hand as he approached and he didn't shake her off. *I'd like to see her smile when I rip her hair out,* Suzume thought. *What does she want with him anyway? I cannot believe he just lets her hang onto him. Didn't he say he loved Kazue? He must have been unfaithful and that's why she sealed him away.*

Suzume liked this idea and it helped her climb the remainder of the hill. By the time she reached the top, the forest had begun to thin and she could see the mountains in the distance and specifically the mountain where their journey had started. She couldn't see the temple from this distance, but she could imagine it sitting against the backdrop of the blue-gray mountains, clouds swirling around it. *I thought we had gotten farther away than this.* She sighed. *Are we ever going to reach the palace at this rate?* With everything else that had happened as of late, she had almost forgotten her original motives. *I don't even know what I'll do once I get there anymore.*

She could not chase this thought further because the forest had grown silent. She could not hear the birds nor the wind in the trees. She glanced around for her companions, but they were nowhere to be seen. *Not this again.*

"You know, I'm really starting to get tired of these hide-and-seek games," Suzume shouted.

"Tired of the games?" a voice echoed back at her.

Suzume spun around, looking for the source. Nothing was there. "This isn't funny!"

"Not funny!" The voice cackled. It sounded like it was right by her shoulder. She arched her head in that direction.

There was nothing there but a slow-rolling fog.

"Kaito, Rin? Where are you?"

"All gone, they left the priestess alone."

A chill ran up Suzume's spine. She didn't like this, not even a little bit. She stepped forward. The fog swirled around her ankles like a veil and it obscured the forest floor.

Something brushed against her leg inside the fog and Suzume shrieked and backed away. She ran into something solid. She felt up and down and realized she had been backed into a tree.

"Tasty, pretty, tasty," something hissed inside the mist.

*Why is this always happening to me?*

Whatever it was drew closer. She could smell the decay hanging from it like a cloud. Her heart hammered in her chest and she felt the tingle on her skin, the fire under her skin coming to her rescue. Her power burned her fingertips. Suzume concentrated and listened for the sound of the creature. A twig cracked nearby and she focused on the spot where the sound came from. She pointed her hand in that direction. Flickering flames burst from her fingertips in the direction of the sound. It burned through the mist, and for a moment she saw a hint of mottled skin before it disappeared.

Heart pounding in her chest, she strained her ears, listening for the creature. Then she felt something like a beacon in her head, telling her to shoot to the left. She aimed both hands in that direction. The creature hissed and squealed in pain before everything went silent. Frozen in place, she could only hear her blood thundering in her ears. Then slowly, very slowly, the fog began to dissipate.

Suzume stayed with her back against the tree for a few moments, letting her heart slow down. She could hardly believe she had reacted that quickly. Once she regained her composure, she went over to look at the creature. It looked like a hunched-over old man, with a sparse covering of hair on its head and long pointed teeth in its mouth. In the middle of its chest was a burn mark where her power had hit it dead on.

*Well, at least my powers came to my rescue when I needed them.*

Footsteps fell on the soft ground covering and Suzume jerked her head up, hands at the ready to shoot fire at whoever approached her. A very short bald man with a round belly stood at the edge of the clearing.

"You! You're the idol from the shrine." She pointed at the bald man. Her voice seemed to echo back at her in the empty silence of the forest.

The short man gave her a serene smile. "That I am, and I've been looking for you."

"For me?" Suzume asked and pressed her hand to her chest. *Why me?*

"I owe you one more wish."

---

"What are you doing here, Rin?" Kaito said, breaking the silence.

She smiled to herself. She had been having so much fun teasing the human, she had forgotten the Dragon would be expecting answers. Slipping into the role of the trickster and flirt had been a good disguise to find out the priestess' intentions. She was surprised to find the Dragon traveling with a human, and one he seemed fond of. The look he gave the priestess was the same he had given Kazue all those years ago. *I've been quite nostalgic lately.* Of course, for the Dragon, it would not seem nearly as long. When Rin and the Dragon had parted ways, she did not think they would see one another again. But here she was by his side once more, and again he was in love with a human. It seemed history really did repeat itself.

"I thought you would need my help," she replied with a wink.

"You're not acting like yourself."

She laughed. "I'm just having some fun with the priestess. She's easy to tease. I could see she has a temper right away." She looked at him from the corner of her eye with a smirk. "And she's rather jealous."

He frowned. "She's different from Kazue in that way. But then Kazue knew I had eyes for no one but her."

Rin hesitated to ask. Everyone knew Kazue had been the only human to win the Dragon's heart, but she had betrayed him in the end. *I'm surprised he's willing to open his heart to another human.* But perhaps that wasn't quite right, they didn't seem like lovers. Maybe he had not accepted his own feelings yet. He had been hurt before. *It's a good thing I am here, maybe I can help him heal by finding happiness with another.* It would be a distraction while she waited for her own happily ever after. *Is this our fate? To keep falling in love with mortals only to have our hearts broken over and over again.*

"Who is she?" Rin asked.

He looked at her sidelong. "She's the one who broke the seal."

"Really? An untrained priestess?" Her raw power was evident. It radiated off of her like a beacon. She was not surprised they had run into trouble thus far.

He nodded his head. "She's Kazue's reincarnation."

Rin stopped in her tracks. *He forgave Kazue after she betrayed him?* "How can you be sure it's her? How can you tell someone has been reborn?" Her chest constricted, thinking of her own lost love, maybe out there somewhere.

"The Hanyou, he's gone?" he asked.

Rin looked at the ground. "Hikaru died twenty years ago. I've been living at the shrine we built together. I thought I would know when his soul returned, that I would feel it..." Rin pressed her hand to her heart. "But I've felt nothing. Perhaps he'll never come back."

They walked in silence for a moment. "We both knew the price of loving a mortal."

She nodded. "Knowing doesn't make the pain less."

Kaito did not answer and she left him with his thoughts. Her own had turned introspective. She had found him to forget the past, she did not want to waste any more time waiting on Hikaru's rebirth. She would find him, one way or another. But in the meantime she could support the Dragon, as she had done long ago. She could help him in the new world.

"The priestess must have broken the seal on the Kami in the idol. It's the only explanation. Is that why you want to find him so badly?"

"No, I want to know who sealed him."

"What good will that do?"

"Because if he is powerful, as I suspect, that means there is only one who could have sealed him."

"Kazue."

He did not answer.

"So you are not positive Suzume is Kazue's reincarnation, then?" Rin asked.

Birds called to one another overhead. The Dragon's gaze focused ahead, scanning the horizon, searching for the missing Kami. Or was he in search of answers? She did not expect him to speak; he did not owe her any explanations. But when he spoke, his tone was low as if pitched for her not to hear. "I want to hate her, but each time I try, she makes me laugh or yells at me. She's nothing like Kazue, which makes it harder to think of her as the same woman." He smiled to himself.

Rin could not help but feel as if she had invaded his private thoughts. The Dragon she had known would never show this vulnerable side before. *His imprisonment did change him.* She had to ask, however, "Have you forgiven Kazue, then?"

He responded with a frozen silence. They continued their climb, jumping over boulders and around thick groupings of trees and bushes. The only sound was the crunch of debris and the priestess' heaving breathing behind them.

"Why did Kazue do it? I never knew why. I thought she loved you, I thought you loved her."

"So did I."

They ducked beneath low-hanging branches, and down below, the priestess in question huffed and complained. It was true this woman had none of the power and grace Kazue exuded. *Will I recognize Hikaru in his new form? If Kazue's reincarnation is so different from her, perhaps Hikaru will be a stranger to me.* She had assumed that when he was reborn, it would be the same man she had known. Now she was not so certain.

"I thought you were out for vengeance. What changed?"

He paused and looked over his shoulder at Suzume struggling up the hill after them. Her hakama had gotten tangled in a low-hanging branch and she was tearing at the fabric as she tried to break free, distracted and beyond hearing distance.

The Dragon said to Rin, "The priestess, Kazue's reincarnation, was trapped by a spider. I had a chance to walk away and let her die. All the evidence indicated she was Kazue's reincarnation. Originally, I had planned to draw out my vengeance, mete it out in small doses. I wanted to destroy her life before killing her. I thought that was the only way to fill this hole inside me that Kazue's betrayal left behind. But perhaps I've grown soft during my imprisonment. I decided on the coward's path, and I left her behind."

He looked away from Rin, across the forest and at the fractured light falling onto the forest floor. The sun was high in the sky, their shadows looked like dwarfed miniatures of them. The Dragon sighed and then said, "I kept thinking about her after I left. I couldn't get her out of my head. I had to know for certain she was Kazue, or else I would keep hunting down her reincarnations for all of eternity. So I rescued her, but I'm still not sure. I don't know what to do with her now. She thinks I'm under a spell, so I'm playing at being in love just to lower her defenses." He ran his hand along the top of his head and then held it there. "I want to believe she is Kazue, but she can't be."

Rin sighed. She wished she knew how to advise him. Once upon a time they had been close, if only for a short while.

The Dragon would not meet her gaze. He looked back again to the priestess. She had been unusually quiet for some time. But when they looked, she had disappeared.

Kaito swore. "I shouldn't let my eyes off her for a moment." He balled his hand into a fist. His eyes clouded over, and she felt the moisture gathering in the air around him. *He wants her to be Kazue because he loved her, but he's afraid of getting hurt again.*

"She seems like an awful lot of trouble. What will you do if she is Kazue?" she asked.

He looked at her, a complicated series of emotions on his face. "I want to start over. She is not her predecessor. Maybe we can heal the wounds of the past together."

# 28

Suzume's mind spun for a moment before the words could come out properly. *This has to be a trick or a dream or a hallucination.*

"Then turn Kaito back to the way he was!" she shouted.

He shook his head. "I cannot."

She placed her hands on her hips and looked down at the small bald man. He didn't come up much higher than her hip. She gave him a scowl that turned most men into a puddle—except Kaito, but he wasn't most men. "You made him into a simpering idiot, so turn him back into the arrogant boar he was before."

The bald man, Kami—or whatever he was—chuckled and smiled at Suzume. "It was not my power that changed the Dragon." He frowned slightly as he looked into the distance. It gave Suzume a sinking feeling. "You've been hurt before, I can see that."

She scoffed.

"You've been hurt many times."

*Is he insane? What is he talking about?* "What do you mean? I've never been hurt, not really..." Her father's impassive face as he delivered her sentence floated to the surface of her mind, and her mother's indifference. She shoved it down where it belonged. *I don't care what my father thinks or about my mother.*

"No? You've lived your entire life alone, isolated from those around you by your birth. Used by everyone trying to get closer to your father. And then because of the sins of your mother, your father disowned you and sent you into exile. Did that not hurt? What about your mother choosing her lover over her children. Did that not sting?" the Kami said with a raised eyebrow.

Suzume shivered. *It's like he can read my mind. I don't think I'll ever get the hang of these immortals.* "Hey, I thought you were going to grant my wish, not analyze my personal life," she said, hoping to redirect the conversation away from painful memories.

The god shook his head, smiling.

*What's so amusing?* Suzume narrowed her eyes at him.

Ignoring Suzume's suspicious glance, he elaborated, "Your real wish is not simple, I fear. Your life has many folds like a lily." He opened his hand and a white lily bloomed there. It unfolded its multitude of petals, revealing a pink center.

A few weeks ago, that might have impressed Suzume. But after everything she'd gone through thus far, she was not going to be distracted by something so simple and nonthreatening.

"How do you know what my wish is when I haven't even asked for anything yet?" she said, with her arms now crossed over her chest. He spoke in too many riddles for her liking.

He closed his hand and the lily disappeared. He folded his hands and rested them on his belly. "It is my gift, as a creator and giver of life."

She eyed the supposed Kami up and down. The top of his head would reach her chest and he was thick around the middle with chubby fingers and short stubby legs. *This guy is a creator? I find that hard to believe.*

"Is it so hard to believe one as small as me could bring life?" His voice, though mellow, had a sharp edge to it hidden beneath his calm words. For a brief moment she felt an overwhelming pressure, enough to knock her to her knees. But it was brief and she only wobbled slightly on her feet.

"You can read my mind? That's not fair!" She pointed an accusing finger in his direction as she took a step back. This Kami was powerful, maybe even as powerful as Kaito, which was difficult to believe. *How many more scary things are out there that I don't know about?*

He laughed long and loud this time and his round body shook with the force of it. The silence absorbed the sound, leaving not even an echo. *This place is bizarre—why is it so quiet here?*

He took a moment to collect his breath before looking at her. "I know what your wish is because I do not need words to grant a wish. How else did you think I granted your earlier wishes, when they were never spoken aloud?"

"But I didn't mean to wish for anything," Suzume replied in her defense. "I was just tired and hungry and..."

"Lonely," the god supplied.

"No." She shook her head forcefully and her hair whipped around her face.

He clicked his tongue. "Come with me, child." He swung around and waddled down a pathway that appeared with a wave of his hand. *I'm still not sure if this is a trap or not.* The body of the Yokai that had attacked her lay on the ground a few feet away. Its blank eyes stared up at the blue sky.

"I can assure you, I am no more danger to you than that was." The Kami stopped up the path from her and motioned towards the dead creature. "If your predecessor was able to capture me at my full strength, you would have no trouble overcoming me in a weakened state."

"You mean Kazue? I am not her!"

He shook his head. "In time you will have to accept the truth of your destiny, but that is a tale for another day." He shrugged before continuing up the path.

Suzume hung behind, uncertain if she could trust him.

"Are you coming?" he called.

*I might as well follow him, it's better than hanging around this thing.* She nudged the dead Yokai with the edge of her sandal. It shifted and rolled over, making a sickening crunching noise. Suzume screeched before blushing and hurrying to follow the Kami. *I hope I never have to kill another Yokai again.*

"You'll face many such creatures on your journey," the Kami said, replying to her thoughts.

"Quit doing that," Suzume chastised. She looked down at his gleaming bald head, it looked shiny enough to reflect the light. "Why are these things after me?" she asked finally.

"Because they desire your power. Your untapped spiritual energy is a tempting prize for those who seek it. And in these times, there are many," the god explained without looking up at her.

"Then how do I learn to control my powers?"

"That is not something I can answer. I can only grant your wish."

"And telling me about the creature is part of this wish?" she asked. *That's awfully convenient.*

"I am sorry, Priestess, but these are the laws for my kind." He sighed and he seemed very weary.

"There are other wish-granting... Kamis?" Suzume asked. *If I had known I had wishes, I would have asked for a handsome but stupid husband, a palace of my own and my position returned at the palace.*

"That is not your true wish; if it was, I would grant it."

"Really, you need to stop reading my mind." Suzume stopped in place.

The god turned around to face her. "I am sorry, Suzume, it is not often I meet a priestess of your caliber and one whose mind I can read as easily as an open book. You must forgive me for peeking at the pages."

She wasn't sure if she should be flattered or offended, so she decided to move on. "At least tell me this, when I freed Kaito, I felt the power hit the holy object. But when I freed you, I wasn't even there. How is that possible?"

He did not reply at first and they continued walking down the forest path. Suzume did her best to remain patient, but her patience was wearing thin. As they walked, the path changed and became more refined and gave way to a courtyard garden.

"There is a piece of you that acts of its own accord. It moves in ways you cannot understand yet. When you unleashed the Dragon, it awoke, and from now on your powers will grow. Once you learn how to control it, you will see the signs. But I cannot say any more."

The path led them into an empty palace. The style of the houses was different, more rustic than what she was used to. The garden was less refined but rivaled the emperor's in its opulence. It was full of exotic plants, and a large maple tree overlooked a koi pond. *This is just like the garden from my spider dream when I saw Kaito dressed as a soldier.* Suzume shuddered.

"Are you sure you're not trying to steal my soul or anything?" Suzume walked over to the maple tree to inspect it. This was much more lifelike than the one from the dream. She reached out and grabbed a waxy leaf from the tree. She rubbed it between her fingers, marveling at the tactile sensation.

The god shook his head. "I promise, I am not. Please have a seat." He motioned to a bench beneath the maple tree that over-looked the koi pond. Suzume sat down hesitantly and the god jumped up beside her. "You know this place?"

"I dreamed of it, but I don't know where it is."

"Think harder."

Suzume gave him a puzzled look. "It's a palace, I don't know what else it could be."

He patted her hand. "This place"—he motioned across the courtyard and towards a manor house—"is the original clan house of the Fujikawas, more specifically, Fujikawa Kazue, your past life."

Suzume shot to her feet. "No. I don't believe you."

"It's true," he said. "Priestess Fujikawa Kazue is a part of you."

Suzume groaned. "Then all those sappy things Kaito has been saying, they're true? He really..." She couldn't finish the sentence. The feelings wrapped up in it were much too confusing for her to face, yet.

The Kami smiled. "Yes and no. There is a battle raging within him."

"Is that why he hasn't killed me yet?" Suzume's stomach sank.

He nodded gravely. "The Dragon never loved a human until Kazue. She changed him and the way he thought about humans. Despite his anger, he still loves her. But when Kazue sealed the Dragon, it set in motion a great upheaval, one even she did not understand the gravity of."

"Great. So he's looking for revenge and I am the reincarnation of the woman he hates." She sat back down and cradled her head in her hands.

"Therein lies the problem. Before Kazue sealed him, Kaito ruled over this land. The Yokai and the humans were in balance, but the Dragon and I are not the only ones Kazue sealed away. There are more of us hidden away. You must break them free and return balance to the world."

"What does that have to do with Kaito?" Suzume asked.

"If he cannot forgive Kazue for her past sins and help you, you will never defeat the darkness."

"What darkness?"

"In each man's heart there are five elements: fire, water, earth, air and the void." He ticked each one off on his fingers. "When Kazue sealed us, she threw the world into discord and gave rise to the darkness—the void. The two of you, when in harmony, can defeat the void."

Suzume threw her hands up. "What am I supposed to do? You don't know Kaito like I do. Anything that has to do with Kazue makes him mad. If he knew, he'd never forgive me. He'd kill me first. Sure, he's acting sweet now, but that's because he's under a spell."

"And here we come to your wish."

Suzume peered at the Kami. "What about my wish?

"Your soul's desire is to protect Kaito—" Suzume snorted, but he held up his hand to stop any interruption. "You must choose how you will protect him."

"Great, more riddles." How could she choose when she didn't know the options? "Why do these things happen to me!" Suzume huffed and ran her hands through her hair. It was tangled and dirty. *I should have stayed at the temple, at least I wouldn't be in this mess.*

"Whether you will it or not, it is your duty as Kazue's reincarnation to correct the imbalance. You must return the world to its proper order or it will destroy you both."

"I don't want to. I don't want any of this, I never asked for this destiny. I just want to have my normal life back."

"You cannot say that. This is your fate." The god looked frazzled for the first time during their encounter.

"I refuse it! You said I have a choice, well, here it is: I wish Kaito never realized that I was Kazue's reincarnation."

The god's face grew pale. "Do you understand what this means? He may never heal. And there is no guarantee that he won't learn the truth eventually. This could mean dire consequences for both of you."

"I don't care." Suzume glared. *The god said it himself. I'm a powerful priestess, and if Kazue could seal him away, so can I. I'll just find a way to lock him up again and be done with it.*

The god lowered his head. "Then I have no choice. Your wish shall be granted."

## 29

A blinding white light surrounded Suzume and she threw her arms up to shield her eyes. It faded just as quickly as it had appeared. She lowered her arm and glanced about. The garden had disappeared, and so had the Kami. She blinked, letting her eyes readjust, and her gaze fell on a simple wooden structure. *Is this the shrine?* She went inside. The idol sat on his pedestal, face serene and hands folded in his lap. *How did I get back here?*

"Don't take all day," Kaito called from outside the shrine.

Suzume peeked outside the shrine door. Kaito leaned against a nearby tree, waiting for her.

He glanced up at her as she peeked around the door. "You've been taking forever; I never figured you for a pious woman." He grinned and her stomach constricted. *Does he know, does he suspect the truth about me, or did the god's wish come true?* "Why are you staring at me like that?"

He strolled over to her and she took a step back. Her powers did not flare up to protect her. They had stopped trying to defend her when he acted sappy. She studied his face, looking for a hint of change.

Kaito frowned in return and then snapped his fingers in her

face. "Don't tell me you've fallen for me. Oh, little Priestess, I'm sorry if I've led you to believe—"

"Shut up," she snarled and pushed past him. *He's back to normal, I think. At least he's not caressing my face any more.*

"A bit testy today, aren't we?"

She could just imagine the expression he wore while he spoke. There was probably an ironic twist to his mouth and an eyebrow cocked. His dark eyes most likely were dancing with laughter.

*I didn't think it was possible, but I miss the gentle way he looked at me.* Suzume blushed; then, mortified by her maidenly actions, she shook her head and smacked her cheeks with her palms. Now her face was red and her cheeks stung. *Get it together. Everything is back to normal, just like you wanted. Now I just need to learn how to control my powers and seal him away once more, and then all my problems will be over.* She inhaled deeply and closed her eyes to gather her thoughts.

While she tried to regain her composure, Kaito sneaked up behind her. He rested his hand on her shoulder. His touch sent electricity shooting down her arm, but not like before. This wasn't a defensive action, more like reactive. She stiffened and twirled around to face him. He loomed over her and she had to tilt her head up to meet his dark gaze.

"You're acting strange, are you feeling all right?" He searched her face and the softening of his features reminded her of the Kaito under the spell. *He really loved Kazue. That's why he acted that way. He can never love me because I am not her. Even if we share a soul.* She shook her head again. *No. Now is not the time to go soft. If he knew, he would kill me for sure. It's me or him, and I am not going down.* She shoved him away and with it her own guilt over wiping his memories.

"I'm fine. What's wrong with you? You're acting awfully senti-mental. Are you falling for me maybe? Because I'm sorry if I gave you the wrong impression, Dragon, because I have no interest." She gave him a cocky grin.

He smiled back at her and she bit her lip to distract herself from the butterflies in her stomach.

"Do you two need a moment alone? I think I'm going to puke," Rin drawled.

Suzume sighed in irritation. *Great, maybe I should have modified my wish to get rid of Rin too.* Suzume rolled her eyes towards the sound of Rin's voice. The Kitsune sat on the roof of the shrine, her robe hitched up to her hip, displaying her pale thigh.

"Rin, what are you doing here?" Kaito called out.

Rin stood up on the roof with hands on hips and regarded them. "I came looking for you, master. I heard that you had been released from the seal and I came to avow myself to your service once more."

*I feel like we've had this conversation before.* Suzume frowned.

"You were always faithful, Rin." Kaito chuckled. He threw his arms open to receive Rin in an embrace. She jumped down and landed neatly on her feet. Then she picked up the edge of her robe and ran over to Kaito, flinging herself into his arms. The speed at which they collided was a blur to Suzume's human eyes. The two Yokai laughed as Kaito spun Rin around, and Rin's tail flung about in the wind. After an overlong embrace, in Suzume's opinion, Kaito set Rin on her feet.

Rin giggled as he did so. She turned her back to Suzume and tossed her auburn hair behind her shoulder. Her long red tail twitched behind her, mocking Suzume as she brushed Kaito's hair back onto his head.

Suzume scowled at the pair of them. *My wish turned the clock backwards. Meeting Rin, everything that happened in the village, it all went back to normal.* She sighed. *I'm beginning to feel like this journey will never end.*

Rin brushed against Kaito, fussing over his topknot, which had come loose while they were playing around. He only laughed and playfully asked her to leave it be.

"Master, I cannot believe you've gone without someone to

style your hair and your clothes." Rin tutted as she brushed her long-fingered hand along Kaito's sleeve.

Suzume bit her lip and kept herself from a scathing retort. *What does it matter to me if that harlot is all over him?* Suzume couldn't stand to watch any further and turned her back to the pair of them, only to continue to watch them over her shoulder. After a few moments, Kaito remembered Suzume standing there.

"Oh, Rin, where are my manners? This is my pet priestess," he said while motioning with a loose wrist in Suzume's direction.

She scowled at the pair of them.

Rin looked over at her. She gave Suzume a once-over before turning back to Kaito. "You're keeping a pet human again? Are you sure that's wise, after last time?"

Kaito pushed Rin back and held her by the shoulders. Her fox ears flattened to her skull and her posture shrank. Suzume could see why; Kaito's eyes had clouded over like thunderclouds. "You forget your place, Rin."

Rin fell to her knees and placed her forehead against the ground. "I'm so sorry, master. It's been so long since you've been gone and there's been no one here to correct my impertinence. Can you forgive me?" She glanced up at him and smiled, revealing her white teeth and a pair of canines. Her ears were pointed towards the back of her skull. If Suzume had really been meeting her for the first time, she might have thought Rin chastised, but Suzume knew enough about the Kitsune to know this was an act.

Kaito patted her head and she sat back on her haunches to regard him with a sly grin.

"I never could stay mad at you, Rin. I'm glad you came back to me. But as I'm sure you've realized, my kingdom has fallen and the world has changed while I slept. I have no need of your particular services..."

"What do you mean by services?" Suzume interrupted. This had been the last straw. What other service could this promiscuous-looking woman provide a male like Kaito?

Kaito glanced at Suzume. "I was wondering when you would butt in. Rin here is one of my former vassals. As for her services, that I'll leave up to your imagination."

Suzume glanced up and down Rin. From what she'd witnessed of the fox-woman thus far, she did not think she was his maid.

"Well, what is she doing here?" Suzume had been hoping Rin would go away now that the Kami matter was settled—not that anyone remembered other than Suzume.

"Like I said, I've been looking for my master—"

"Kaito," Suzume corrected. *If she calls him master once more, I am going to puke.*

Rin looked at her and gave her a toothy grin. Suzume gave her a questioning look in return.

Rin's smile only grew. "Right. Kaito. I planned on returning to his service, but now I'm not sure what I'll do since he's rejected my vows." Her bottom lip quivered and she looked to Kaito, who stood with hands on his hips.

"That's too bad. We really should be going," Suzume said.

She strolled past the pair of them and down the path a few steps before Kaito's next words stopped her. "I think Rin should join us."

Suzume whipped around. "Absolutely not!"

"Do you let the human tell you what to do?" Rin asked Kaito innocently while giving Suzume a narrow-eyed look.

"Rin has skills that we could use on our journey. I can't watch you all the time, and since you seem apt to get into trouble..." He motioned vaguely in the direction from which they had come.

She couldn't argue with that logic, but she tried anyway. "Well, if I had a better mastery of my powers, then I wouldn't need you to babysit me."

"You should be honored to be under Master Kaito's protection," Rin interjected. Her ears were back flat again and the hairs on her tail bristled.

Suzume ignored her and continued. "What can this concubine

do for us? What can she do that I can't? I was handling the spider just fine before you showed up. Plus I killed that monster thing in the forest all by myself."

"I will not be insulted by a mere mortal woman." Rin raised her voice.

"Enough." Kaito's voice cracked across the squabbling women.

They both twirled to face him and his expression was foreboding. He seemed taller than Suzume remembered and his shoulders broader. The clouds behind him were gathering and looked gray and ominous. Suzume glowered back at him, even if she knew better than to challenge Kaito when he was in a foul mood. *I just fixed everything too.*

"You would be dead if I hadn't saved you from the spider, and if you're so sure you'd be better on your own, then I'd be happy to find another spider for you to battle. As for this imaginary monster in the forest, you haven't been out of my sight long enough to find a Yokai to kill, and besides, if you had killed anything within a mile of here, I would have sensed it. Your lies might work on humans, but they will not work on me, Priestess. Rin is coming with us and there will be no further arguments." Kaito gave Suzume a pointed look and for once she clamped her mouth shut. Then to Rin he said, "You will treat my pet with respect and not eat her."

Rin looked at Suzume with a toothy grin. "She looks like she would be stringy and flavorless anyhow."

"Fine." Suzume huffed.

"Good, now let's head out." He turned and stormed down the pathway.

*He seems more on edge than usual.* When Kaito was out of earshot, Rin fell in beside Suzume. Suzume turned her head away and hurried her pace, but Rin kept up with little effort. *Damn Yokai.* Rin cleared her throat and Suzume pretended the rice paddy fields were of intense interest. Rin ran in front of Suzume and waved her hands back and forth. Suzume stopped to adjust the strap on her sandal and Rin squatted in front of her.

Suzume sighed in defeat. "Can I help you?"

"It's more what I can do for you," Rin replied.

"I doubt you can do anything for me." Suzume stood back up and continued walking, thinking the conversation was over before it began. She was wrong.

Rin laughed. "I know what you wished for, and if you hope to make it out of this alive, you'll need to trust me."

Suzume stopped in her tracks, truly shocked for the first time. Rin looked at her, with her foxtail twitching back and forth. *I was right. The spell only worked on Kaito. She knows.*

"Why would I trust you?"

"Because if you don't, I'll tell the Dragon what you did."

## 30

W hat is she getting at? Why not tell on me? What does she stand to gain from blackmail? Suzume wondered.

Rin walked ahead of Suzume, her long red tail swishing back and forth. Kaito had disappeared shortly after they left the roadside shrine, without an explanation other than to tell Rin to watch over Suzume. *As if I am a child that needs babysitting. I may not have complete control over my powers, but I'm getting better... sort of.* Rin glanced at Suzume over her shoulder and grinned at her.

Suzume scowled back at her. "What is wrong with you Yokai? Do you live to make my life miserable?" Suzume growled in frustration and threw her hands up. "Speaking of annoying Yokai, where is Kaito? We've been walking for days and we haven't seen any sign of him. He said he wouldn't be gone long." Suzume's voice had reached a high-pitched tone.

Rin flattened her ears against her head as she shrugged. "I don't question the master's motives. He told me to lead you east and that's what I am doing."

"Where are we going? There's nothing out here but farms and villages. I thought he wanted to go to the White Palace and seek his revenge."

Rin's tail twitched from side to side. "Why would he want to go to a place full of humans? Personally I cannot stand their stink."

"I resent that."

Rin ignored her and continued. "If the Eight hadn't been sealed by Kazue, then your people would never have been allowed to flourish like this." She motioned towards the fields that surrounded them. "It's disgusting. You're inferior in every way possible, yet you continue to breed like vermin."

"I am not vermin. I am the daughter of the emperor, I'll have you know, and a descendant of the Eight," Suzume snapped. True, she had been disowned, but that didn't change her lineage. Besides, Rin didn't need to know all the details.

Rin laughed. "Human rulers mean little to me. Back when the Dragon ruled the biggest island of Akatsuki, your people had just barely crawled out of holes in the ground a couple centuries before."

Suzume rolled her eyes. "Nice story, Grandma, how old are you, one thousand?"

"Three thousand, thank you," Rin corrected with a smirk.

Suzume's mouth hung open. How could she look this good after thousands of years? *I'm jealous of Yokai if they get to live forever and look like this.*

"I bet you wish you had these good looks at my age." Rin preened.

Suzume scoffed. "I have no desire to be anything like you."

"It looked like you were rather jealous to me, especially when it comes to the Dragon." Rin leaned in close, peering up at Suzume's face.

Suzume flipped her hair and looked anywhere but at the Kitsune. "You're delusional. There's nothing between me and the Dragon."

"Humans are so sensitive. Maybe that's what makes you so delightful to tease." Rin smiled again, showing Suzume her fangs.

If Suzume had been a bit more sensible, she would have shut

her mouth, but she never did think before speaking. As she was about to reply, a roar from above stopped her. A strong wind picked up and whipped her hair around her face. She pushed back the flyaway strands and glanced up to the sky. Rin ran past Suzume and towards the serpentine body of the Dragon as he landed on the road nearby.

Suzume shuddered to see Kaito in his dragon form. He always appeared more menacing as a dragon. Maybe it was his massive jaws or the powerful coils of his body. It might also be the fact that he could squish her like a bug if he wished.

"Master!" Rin cried. She ran to greet Kaito as he transformed back into his human form.

Kaito held Rin at arm's length as she wiggled her tail back and forth. It reminded Suzume of a lapdog.

Suzume giggled and covered it with a sleeve. She cleared her throat to further cover up her laughter and said to the Dragon, "Nice of you to join us. I was starting to hope that you'd never come back."

Kaito pushed Rin aside to get a better view of Suzume. His expression was serious, and for a moment, he scrutinized her, his brows furrowed. Suzume paused. *This isn't like him. Does he suspect what I did?* Rin pulled a face at Suzume over Kaito's shoulder as if to say, 'I know you really missed him.' Suzume ignored her, instead focusing on the Dragon. *Let her think I care for Kaito. It will be that much easier to learn about my powers in secret and subdue both of them once I know how.*

"I'm glad to see you missed me, pet." He grinned, breaking his solemn expression. Kaito reached out to presumably ruffle Suzume's hair, but Suzume dodged the action and the air crackled with Suzume's power. Red sparks flickered and died between them.

His smile faded once more and he watched her gravely for a moment. She leveled an arrogant look at him. *I guess everything is back to normal if the sparks are back.*

"I have good news," Kaito said at last, breaking the awkward tension. "I found a place for you to train."

"What?" Suzume asked and then quickly schooled her features to neutral. "What do I care about these powers? All I want is to go back to the palace. A general's wife doesn't need a mastery of spiritual power," she scoffed.

"You'll need them if Akito comes to take you away and the general challenges him to fight for you. I doubt any man you would choose could fight for himself," Kaito replied, and Rin sniggered behind him.

Suzume opened her mouth to retort and then bit her tongue. Kaito did not realize just how close he had been to Akito. *And he'll never find out if I can help it.* Distracted by this fact, she couldn't come up with a snappy retort fast enough and Kaito jumped his advantage.

"Did I leave you speechless?" He laughed and Rin joined in.

Suzume threw both of them a dirty look, which they promptly ignored because they were too busy mocking her. Suzume huffed and pouted until their laughter died away.

"So where is this place? Who is going to train me, oh Great Dragon?" Suzume asked with her arms crossed over her chest. She turned away and watched them from the corner of her eye.

Kaito wiped laughter-induced tears from his eyes. "It's a temple not far from here. The priests there are well known for their mastery of spiritual powers. The best part is their order used to be dedicated to my worship." He puffed out his chest.

Suzume rolled her eyes. "So we're going to a temple run by your minions. Great."

"What a brilliant plan, master," Rin piped up.

*On second thought, I hope they can teach me how to fry one annoying Kitsune.*

"Thank you, Rin." He patted her on the head. Rin closed her eyes and leaned into his hand.

"Well, are we going, or do you two need a moment?" Suzume interjected.

She turned so she couldn't see Rin. She was undoubtedly giving Suzume another look. *I really don't like that woman.*

"We're leaving right now. Follow me." Kaito strolled down the road before turning to cut between two fields. The path he was taking faced a distant mountain range.

*Great, more mountain climbing.* "Can't you just fly us there or something?" Suzume asked.

Rin gasped. "How could someone as low as you ask something like that of the master?" She pressed her hand to her chest as she spoke.

"We're going to walk all the way over there? Why can't he transform and fly?" Suzume asked with a puzzled expression. It made perfect sense to her.

"Sure, you can ride," Kaito said with a devious gleam in his eye.

Suzume raised a brow. "What's the catch? You're being too nice."

"No catch, get on." He transformed in a puff of smoke.

His forelegs straddled the two fields and bent grain sideways under his feet. The coils of his body wrapped back and forth across the fields rising and falling under the tall grasses. His whiskers brushed against the ground and rustled with every breath. His breath brushed over Suzume's skin like a cool breeze. Rin wriggled back and forth, her tail swinging to and fro. She held her hands to her chest as her body swayed while staring at Kaito in adoration, while Suzume eyed him with suspicion.

"I don't trust you," Suzume declared. Nothing was ever this easy with Kaito. Nothing.

He laughed and the sound echoed off the hills and rumbled like thunder. "Well, I do have less control of my human mind in this form and I have been known to drop riders from great heights. Oh! And I sometimes eat them."

"Never mind, I'd rather walk." *There's always a trick with him.*

He laughed again and the sound reminded Suzume of a babbling brook. He transformed back into his human form and said, "Well, if there are no other arguments, let's head out."

Kaito led the way and Suzume hung back, concocting a plan in which she could learn more about her own powers and somehow seal Kaito away—and maybe Rin for good measure. *Yeah, it should be simple enough.* She almost believed herself. Almost.

The trip took the remainder of the daylight before they arrived at the temple. The temple itself was at the top of a flight of stairs. When Suzume saw them, she groaned. The stairway disappeared into the treetops.

"Why is there so much climbing! Can't they just make temples easy to reach?"

"They're high up so the unworthy cannot reach them," Kaito replied.

Suzume shot Kaito a dirty look before they proceeded to climb the endless staircase. As it was with the mountain by the roadside shrine, Kaito and Rin climbed with ease while Suzume huffed and puffed, taking the occasional break.

When they neared the top of the stairs, it had gotten fully dark and Suzume had to squint to find her way. *I can't see a thing, not even Kaito and Rin.* Then out of the darkness, hanging lights appeared. She followed them the rest of the way. When she arrived panting at the top of the stairs, priests in brown robes greeted her, holding onto lanterns attached to strings at the end of poles. They nodded to her as she joined the others. Rin and Kaito were standing nearby. Rin looked around with interest, and Kaito, in the dim yellow light of the lanterns, looked bored.

The priests led them to the temple courtyard. More priests lined up in rows in front of one of the shrine buildings. The man in the forefront was ancient with deep creased wrinkles on his face and a completely bald head. Despite his great age, he stood upright and had a certain glow to him.

"Lord Dragon, thank you for honoring us with your presence." The priest bowed low from his waist.

The other priests followed suit and bowed in unison to Kaito. He smiled down at them before lifting his hand. *He's loving this.*

"And this must be the priestess you mentioned." The old priest approached Suzume and brushed his hand against her face. His hands were deceptively soft and gentle. She normally didn't like people touching her, but she found the priest's touch soothing. He felt familiar, as if they had met before. "You have a very old soul. It has seen much over the centuries."

He smiled down at her and Suzume felt a warm glowing feeling grow in the pit of her stomach. A yellow light haloed the old man's head and she gasped in wonder.

"It would appear we have met in a previous life." He smiled at her.

"How do you know that?" Suzume asked.

"Souls recognize one another, even if the vessels do not," the priest said. His eyes flickered towards Kaito for a brief second and Suzume's heart raced. The priest looked back to Suzume and then took a step back. "I think there is much we can learn from one another."

Suzume avoided looking at Kaito, but a smile was creeping over her face. *I hope so as well.*

---

Rin could not sleep. The energy of the temple felt wrong. It filled her head with thoughts of Hikaru, and each time she closed her eyes she thought of that last day. After an hour of trying, she gave up and paced her tiny chamber for several minutes. She never spent too long indoors and the walls were closing in on her.

She exited her chamber in the dark of night, padding silently down the hall in search of the Dragon. When they had talked before, he had thought Suzume was Kazue's reincarnation, but ever since the flash of light, he had been acting strangely. At first she thought it had all been part of his plan to trick the priestess, but she slowly realize he had forgotten everything. How this untrained priestess had this sort of power, Rin had no idea. *Is it a good idea to train her? I do not trust her. Kazue betrayed the Dragon, what's to stop her reincarnation from doing the same?*

Outside the Dragon's chamber, she hesitated. Memories from a lifetime ago swam through her thoughts as her words caught in her throat. *He does not remember our conversation in the woods, what if he gets the wrong impression as to why I am here?*

"Come in, Rin, I know you're there," he called from beyond the doorway.

She swallowed her anxiety and went inside. As to be expected, the Dragon's room was slightly larger than her own, with a single futon against a far wall and a window that looked out to the garden beyond. He sat on the futon, his back against the wall, his knee bent and one arm dangling over it. He looked out the room's only window to the night sky.

"Why did you come here?" he said. His voice was distant and remote.

It broke her heart to see the great Dragon brought down this low. His kingdom torn apart, and the lower-ranking Yokai ruling their own tiny micro-kingdoms. He would not admit it, but he had yet to return to his full strength and still struggled to be the man he had once been. Betrayal, anger, and the priestess' spell had changed him.

She knelt down beside him as she said, "I could not sleep and I figured you would still be awake as well." *I should tell him what the priestess did. I cannot believe she has his best intentions at heart.*

He did not look at her when he spoke. "I did not mean this evening, I meant why did you come to me when the seal broke? I released you from my service long ago."

Rin pushed her hair behind her ear and thought of how to answer. When she had been in the Dragon's service, she never would have come to him in this way, approached him as a friend, but time changed her. Hikaru changed her, and she no longer felt like the unworthy servant she had been.

"We were lovers once." She paused. "I thought perhaps you needed an ally, someone you can trust."

"How did Hikaru die?"

The question was unexpected, and one she did not want to answer. She shook her head. "It doesn't matter, he's gone now."

He rested his hand on hers. She looked into his face, and she saw the man who for a brief time she had thought she loved. What an innocent she had been in those days. She had experienced true enduring love, and what she shared with the Dragon so long ago had been an infatuation. A brief and glorious fever.

"You're lonely, I can see it." He leaned in and she did not back away.

She had been lonely. With Hikaru dead and Shin haunting her like a yaori, she had lived twenty years as an old woman at the shrine, waiting for the rebirth, never knowing if she would ever feel the touch of another. Dying for contact but afraid she would be betraying the man she loved.

When Kaito leaned forward and kissed her, there was no passion, no spark. Just a hot meeting of lips. With one hand on the back of her neck, he held her close, and with the other he pulled loose the ties on her kimono. Her heart raced as she thought to that brief tryst, those passionate nights when the most powerful Yokai in Akatsuki had worshiped her body, had been hers, if only for a short time. But now everything about it felt wrong. She did not love him, and as desperate as she was for that intimacy, she couldn't, not with him. They were two damaged people, and she was not the one who could heal his wounds. If they got tangled together now, they might both unravel.

She pulled away. "Don't," she said with her hand on his chest. Her kimono had slid down and hardly covered her breasts.

He looked at her with a hunger in his gaze. But it wasn't her he was looking at. He was looking for something to fill the void Kazue had left in him. She had seen a hint of it in the forest; now she saw it displayed on his face. That raw vulnerability that so few glimpsed, the hurt that shook him to his core and even now stopped him from recovering from his imprisonment.

They were interrupted from further awkwardness by a knock on the door. Kaito rose to answer it, and he locked away his emotions, shut tight behind his mask of power. Rin exhaled. *How can I tell him about the priestess now when he's like this?*

The door slid open, and Kaito said, "Oh ho, come to sneak into my bed late at night, Priestess?"

Rin looked around, sitting on the Dragon's bed late at night, her clothes falling off of her, she knew how it must look. And she saw the accusation in the priestess' eyes. She did not trust the priestess, she feared her intentions, but when she saw her expression, she knew she had misjudged her. The look on her face was that of betrayal.

# 31

K aito rested his hands on his hips as he stared down at Suzume. Despite her deep mortification from finding Kaito and Rin alone in his room, her eyes traveled over Kaito's well-defined chest. Her sight skimmed over the top of his pants before shooting back up to his face. Too bad he's too annoying to even consider taking as a lover. She had to shake herself. *Get it together. Why did I come here in the first place?* She couldn't remember and looked to Rin, whose kimono hung off her shoulder. *There can only be one explanation, of course. Just because he had a human lover does not mean he turns away his own kind. Rin is beautiful, and I knew from the start what she wanted.* But still her chest hurt. She shouldn't care what the Dragon did or who he slept with, but it hurt just the same.

"Well, I guess I've discovered what Rin's service to you was," Suzume said. Her hand trembled and she realized she was holding a clean robe for the Dragon.

Rin came to peer over Kaito's shoulder, her robe hanging off her shoulder and the top of her breast revealed beneath the silky fabric. Her auburn hair was tousled and she looked at Suzume with a half-lidded smile. Neither of them attempted to deny their actions, which stung more than Suzume thought it should.

"It looks like you're both busy. I won't bother you, the priest asked me to give you this." She shoved the clothes against Kaito's chest and turned to walk away. Bad enough she was being used like a servant girl and then to be humiliated on top of it.

"Wait!" Kaito called out to her.

Suzume's heart clenched and she chastised herself. *Stop it.* She took a breath before glancing back at him with what she hoped was an indifferent expression. "Yes?"

"There's room for one more if you'd like to join us." Kaito grinned and pulled Rin under his arm and held his free hand out to Suzume.

"No, thank you," Suzume said with an icy tone.

The smile left Kaito's face. The spiritual energy crackled around her, electrifying the air between them. They held one another's gaze for a moment. If she hadn't been embarrassed and upset, she would have said something to turn the shame back on them, but she couldn't think of anything to say. She twirled away, her wet hair flipping behind her just in time to hide the flush of her cheeks.

She stomped away, making sure to make every footstep echo off the walls as she withdrew. *They're perfect for one another. They're both annoying beyond reason and they're both immortal.* Suzume arrived at her room. She threw open the door. Once inside, she slammed it behind her and the paper screen shuddered beneath the force. Suzume flopped down onto the futon that had been laid out for her.

She lay on her back, her arms and leg spread-eagled, while staring at the ceiling. *It's not like I care who he has a relationship with. He loved Kazue not me.* She rolled over onto her side and brought her knees to her chest. *Sure, he can be charming when he wants to. And he's not ugly...*

"That's some dangerous thinking," she said to herself.

The silent shrine did not answer. Even the wind through the trees was hushed as if it too had witnessed her humiliation.

*Kaito may be handsome, but he has also sworn to kill me if he ever finds out who I was in a past life. Not the ideal start to a relationship. I am better off sealing him before this gets out of hand.*

Eventually, Suzume fell asleep. She woke early the next morning on top of the futon, wearing the robe from the night before. She had a crick in her neck and her hair was a tangled mess since she hadn't brushed it out after the bath. Suzume groaned and climbed to her feet. The temple air vibrated with energy. She heard distant chanting. The words were too low to decipher, but they caught Suzume's attention despite her sleep-addled mind. *What is that? Please tell me it's not something trying to kill us all. I'd like to eat something before having my life threatened today.*

She closed her eyes and tried to fall back asleep, but the chanting kept weaving in and out of her thoughts. With a heavy sigh, she climbed off the futon, ran her fingers through her hair, and tied it back hastily. She rubbed her eyes with the back of her hand as she opened the chamber door.

When she opened her door, she could hear the chanting better. The words, though incomprehensible, still took on a defined shape and they seemed to be coaxing her, drawing her to them. Suzume slipped out of the chamber and followed the sound down the hall. The chanting seemed to be coming from a building that adjoined the sleeping quarters. A covered walkway separated the two buildings. Suzume crossed it and glanced about the grounds that surrounded the buildings. Gingko leaves covered the large square courtyard ringed by gingko trees beyond.

The buildings were large and square as well. The entire temple seemed to be made of squares within squares, even the hallways and rooms followed the same geometric pattern. The red roofs of the buildings met at a sharp incline. On the other side, the torii arches framed a narrow walkway. At the end of the path was a small shrine building. *I am not going anywhere near that shrine. Shrines and I do not have a good history.*

Suzume faced a large building with open doors on all sides. Inside, the priests sat on the floor in rows, their legs crossed and eyes closed. Suzume stepped up to the threshold and listened to the haunting sounds of the chanting.

The head priest sat at the front of the group, wearing ceremonial white and black. *What are they doing?*

"You came just in time for their morning prayers."

Suzume spun around to see Rin leaning against a beam that supported the covered walkway. Suzume glowered at her and turned back to the priests, pretending the chanting was of deep interest to her. But even the soothing sound of the priests' chanting could not calm the anger that festered in her chest. She hoped Rin would get the hint and leave her alone. Suzume feared speaking, in case she said something incriminating and added fuel to the fire. She hung about for another moment, waiting for Rin to leave. She didn't. Instead, Rin came closer. She stood close enough to Suzume to brush against her sleeve. Suzume withdrew her hand and scowled at Rin from the corner of her eye.

"This order is known for their ability to transcend into the spirit world. They also have the best mastery of spiritual power manipulation," Rin explained.

Despite Suzume's interest in learning more about spiritual powers, she feigned disinterest.

"They draw on water; that's their element of choice, you could say," Rin continued, heedless of Suzume's lack of engagement. "It's Kaito's element as well."

Suzume had to stop herself from questioning Rin further. She didn't want to give the Kitsune the benefit.

Rin stepped in front of Suzume and tried to force her to meet her gaze. Suzume turned to walk away.

Suzume heard Rin sigh behind her. "Suzume, we need to talk."

"I have nothing to say to you," Suzume said without stopping to look at the other woman. Suzume headed at an angle away from Rin and toward the courtyard where the priests had met them the day prior. Suzume tried to put distance between herself and Rin before she figured out how to use her powers and turn Rin into dust. Suzume took a deep breath. *I don't care who he wants to be with. It does not matter to me.*

Suzume had almost reached the courtyard penned in by large ginko trees when Rin grabbed her by the shoulder.

Suzume spun around and wrenched herself out of Rin's grasp. "I would appreciate it if you would keep your filthy hands off of me." She tried to walk again but found she could not move. Suzume glared at Rin. "What did you do to me?"

"Just a simple charm. It's time you stop being so pigheaded and listen up." Rin tossed her auburn hair over her shoulder and gave Suzume a firm look.

Suzume prepared an angry retort, but before she could, Rin placed her hand over Suzume's mouth. She tried to dodge, but the Kitsune was too quick. When Rin removed her hand, there was a leaf covering Suzume's mouth. Suzume tried to shout at her, but her entire body was frozen.

Suzume groaned at Rin, who smiled. "If you don't like it, then just use your powers and break the charm."

Suzume groaned again and struggled, trying to break free of the charm to no avail. Her powers did not even rise up to defend her. After a few minutes of fruitless struggle, she sighed —or as close as she could get to a sigh without use of her mouth.

"Are you ready to listen?" Rin asked.

Suzume rolled her eyes and looked away from Rin. At least she had control over that.

"Too bad, you're going to have to," Rin replied. "First of all, what you saw last night wasn't what you thought it was."

*I know exactly what I saw!* At least that's what she wanted to say, but couldn't. The response that came out was more like a grunt.

Rin held up her hand. "We were talking, nothing more."

Suzume rolled her eyes in response. *Like I'm going to believe that, when you were half dressed and alone with him.*

"I know you think we're lovers, but we're not." Rin crossed her arms and it pushed up her breasts.

Suzume tried to scoff, but it came out more like a groan.

"We were at one time." Rin smiled to herself and looked out into the distance as if she looked into the past. "But that was before Kazue. We had our time and we parted ways, the way most immortals do. We don't often stay with one person for long."

*Is that why Kazue sealed him away? Because she was afraid of being left alone, and her pregnant with his child, once he was done with her?*

"I told you before that I would keep your secret if you trusted me, well, here's your chance," Rin continued, once more back on topic.

Suzume regarded the fox woman intently for the first time. Rin twitched her tail back and forth for a while, not meeting Suzume's gaze.

"Kaito doesn't know this, but I witnessed Kaito and Kazue's courting—briefly." She smiled faintly. "Not long after we parted ways, Kaito left his palace. He often took on the guise of a human and seduced human women. That's how he met Kazue. She was the daughter of a clan elder and betrothed to marry the heir of another clan lord. She resisted his seduction because of her betrothal. Well, Kaito never backs down from a challenge and he pursued her even more, to the point where it stopped being a game and it turned into real affection."

Rin gave Suzume a pointed look. She had been so enthralled by her story, she had forgotten to pretend she was not interested. She looked away, but waited for Rin to continue.

"What Kaito wasn't expecting was that this woman had spiritual powers. She was not even aware of them herself. But being an immortal, he felt it and he knew it would put her in danger. He brought her to this very temple to train. Here is the place that she learned how to control her abilities and here they fell in love."

Suzume glanced about the clearing. She tried to imagine Kaito training with Kazue, walking beneath the gingko trees together. Did they embrace beneath the falling leaves, or did he caress her face with careless affection? She imagined all the things the bespelled Kaito had done and tried to picture him doing something like that for her in earnest. *I can see how she could fall in love with that Kaito.* Jealousy twisted knots in her stomach.

"Much of what I know is from what I have heard from others. But what I want to know from you is how you made him forget you're Kazue's reincarnation. You must realize he is going to find out again. Can you not see it? He's brought you back to the same temple. Everything is repeating over again. I can't let the Dragon go through that again, I will not see him sealed for another five hundred years or more because of some human. I know deep down you care for him, don't make Kazue's mistake."

Suzume grunted, trying to reply.

"I guess I can't get answers out of you if you don't behave. Do you promise to be a good girl?" Rin asked.

Suzume nodded.

Rin yanked the leaf off Suzume, almost taking her lips along with it. Suzume's lips tingled and she rolled her jaw as she massaged it. "That hurt," Suzume said.

The Kitsune waved her hand in a dismissive gesture. "You'll live."

*It's easy for her to say I should forgive him, trust that he won't kill me. But she wasn't there when he woke. She hasn't seen the way he reacts each time Kazue's name comes up. If I am her reincarnation, when Kaito finds out, I am dead. The only way I can make it out alive is if he is sealed. Period.* Out loud, Suzume said, "Well, I don't care what you want. Once I learn how to use my powers, I am going to seal Kaito."

"Is that so?" Kaito asked.

Suzume's stomach dropped and the air crackled with energy around her. She spun around. Kaito stood at the edge of the courtyard and storm clouds gathered in the sky overhead.

# 32

As a rule, she would not be cowed by Kaito, but her body wasn't willing to listen to her stubborn brain. It felt like the spell Rin had placed on her but much more terrifying. Suzume's skin tingled with the untamed spiritual energy rippling off her. Flames danced over her skin and burning coals were stoked in her gut. Her power did not go on the offensive as it had before, but she could feel it clinging to her like a protective second skin. *This would be a really good time to be able to control these damn powers.*

"You think you can seal me away?" Kaito asked. His voice rumbled over her.

When he finally spoke, the spell broke and Suzume found her tongue once more. "Yes. Once I master my powers, I am going to seal you like Kazue did." Suzume met his stormy gaze and the darkness in his eyes should have been enough to make her guard her tongue, but her reckless side had a hold of the reins and there was no turning back now.

"Quiet, you idiot," Rin hissed and attempted to grab Suzume. The crackling energy running over Suzume's skin burned Rin. She cursed and pulled her hand back while examining the charred flesh.

Suzume ignored her and continued to gaze at Kaito. "Try to stop me. I'm sure you can already sense my powers flaring to protect me from you. You cannot—" Before she had an opportunity to finish uttering her sentence, Kaito darted forward.

Suzume took a step back to dodge him. She was too slow and he grabbed her by the shoulders. Kaito slammed her against a nearby tree. Suzume gasped as pain shot up her spine. Kaito's hands bit into her shoulders hard, pinning her against the rough bark of the tree. A few gingko leaves broke free and floated down. Suzume glanced at the parasol-shaped leaves as they fluttered and then back at Kaito. *He actually attacked me. I cannot believe it.* She was too shocked to even move. She was paralyzed both by his anger and her inability to stop him.

"Master, stop this! She didn't mean it!" Rin shouted at Kaito and pulled at his arm, trying to separate Kaito and Suzume.

*Why is she coming to my defense? Shouldn't she be on his side?* He knocked Rin aside as if she were an insect buzzing about, without moving his blazing blue eyes from Suzume. She tried to meet his gaze. She didn't want to show any fear, but she couldn't—she was terrified of him. She had seen the storm clouds gather in his eyes before; this was nothing like those other times. His eyes reminded her of a thunderstorm that was gathering overhead. Fat gray clouds blocked out the sun and cast everything in darkness. She was afraid where the lightning was going to strike. Her powers had gone dormant, numbed by shock, leaving her helpless.

"You," he growled, "are not Kazue. Do not presume to have her level of power." He dug his nails into her shoulder and Suzume gasped. "Do you understand? You are not her, nor will you ever be anything like her."

"I understand," Suzume snapped back at him. She bit back a retort with much more venom. From the way Rin frowned behind Kaito, Suzume figured it was best not to anger him further. She was lucky he hadn't killed her outright.

He pushed off the tree and stomped away. Suzume slumped to

the ground as her knees gave out beneath her and she watched him stalk away. Rin watched Kaito go, hand pressed against her chest.

"Go after him," Suzume said. "You know you want to."

"You fool! What are you trying to do? Get yourself killed?" Rin shouted.

Suzume lifted a shaking hand. She was too shocked to respond. *The power was there in my hands; I felt it protecting me. Why didn't it stop him when he attacked me?*

Rin knelt down in front of Suzume and peered into her face. Suzume looked past her to where Kaito had disappeared back into the building. Rin touched Suzume's shoulder. Suzume winced with pain. Where Kaito had touched her it burned. Not like fire, it was not warm but more of a cold burn. Suzume brushed Rin's hand away and the cloth of Suzume's sleeve and shoulder were ice cold. Crystals of ice had formed on the fabric. She had been so distracted by the pain she had not noticed before.

"Don't touch that, it hurts," Suzume snarled at Rin. *I cannot believe she saw him humiliate me like this.*

Rin sat back on her haunches. "Well, at least you're not in shock."

Suzume ignored Rin's seeming concern. *If it wasn't for her, I might be dead right now.* She glanced at the Kitsune from the corner of her eye. Not that she would be admitting that to Rin. She would much rather focus on Kaito's reaction and, more importantly, the fact that he had not killed her as she expected. "Why did you defend me?" Suzume asked.

Rin stood up and brushed off her robe. "I honestly can't say. I can't decide if I sympathize with you or hate you. The real question is why didn't he kill you?"

"Maybe because he knows I am stronger than him." Her voice trembled as she said this. He had her beat and she knew it. No one believed her false bravado.

Rin laughed. "I bet whatever spell you put on him took away

the memories but not the feelings. Deep down he knows you're Kazue's reincarnation, and his feelings for your past life are holding him back from killing you. The Dragon would never have let you live otherwise."

"That wasn't my fault!" Suzume jumped to her own defense. "The Kami, or whatever he was, didn't give me a choice; I had to take away his memories. You weren't there when he first woke up. He wants revenge, and if he knows..." Suzume trailed off. Her excuses sounded lame even to her own ears.

Rin rolled her eyes. "If it was a Kami that put him under a spell, then it must be a powerful one and old." Rin frowned in thought.

Suzume scoffed. "He couldn't have been too powerful if Kazue sealed him away. She was only a human." She huffed; they were getting off topic. "Besides, it doesn't matter now. What's important is figuring out how we're going to fix this. He knows who I am!"

"Not my problem," Rin said with a twitch of her tail and a smirk.

"You said you were going to help me!" Suzume jabbed a finger at Rin's chest.

Rin easily dodged and alighted on a nearby tree branch. Suzume spun around.

"I said I would not tell him, and I didn't. If you are a threat to the Dragon, then I will not help you. Now you have to figure out how to get out of this mess," Rin said.

Suzume stamped her foot. "You cannot do this to me!"

Rin, crouched on the bough of the tree, said, "Sure I can. I'm free to do as I please, and you're now in a very serious position."

Suzume narrowed her eyes at the Kitsune. *I really hate her.* "What will it take to get you to help me?"

"Hmm." Rin hummed and rubbed her chin as she thought. She sat down on the tree branch and swung her legs.

Suzume's neck hurt from watching Rin.

"I want your firstborn son."

"What!" Suzume squawked.

Rin laughed. "I'm joking. Human children are too fattening. I need to keep my figure." She winked.

Suzume growled in frustration. Rin laughed harder. *I don't need her. I'll figure out a way to fix this on my own.* Suzume turned to walk away when Rin shouted out to her.

"Wait, I'm kidding. Come back."

Suzume turned around and glared at Rin. "What do you want, then?"

"I don't want you to seal Kaito," Rin said. Her face was somber and the usual mischievous twinkle in her eye was somewhat diminished.

"What does it matter to you?" she asked with an arched brow. *I am not going to fall for this Kitsune's tricks. She may seem concerned for my well-being, but I'm not convinced she's not trying to use me somehow.*

Rin folded her hands in her lap and twisted them together. "Because I know he can forgive Kazue, given the chance. We need him, the island has been in chaos since he left." She frowned. "And because I care about Kaito. He's more than a master to me, he is my friend. I'm afraid if he is betrayed again, he will not be able to recover."

Suzume snorted, but it was only halfhearted. *Is she serious? How can she consider him a friend when he treats everyone around him like they're nothing?* "What does it matter if I seal him? It wouldn't be a betrayal if there's no trust. He treats me like an animal. He should be expecting this."

Rin shook her head. "You don't know him like I do. He wouldn't keep a human around for amusement. He cares about you. He may not realize it yet, but he trusts you. I'm sure his soul is calling to yours. You're destined to be together."

Suzume forced a laugh while her heart skipped a beat. *That's ridiculous. There's no way he feels anything for me other than sick amusement from torturing me.* "I'm sorry, you must be confused. I am not destined to be with him. I am betrothed to General Tsubaki."

"Not anymore," Rin said. Suzume was not sure if she was referring to Suzume's banishment or the deluded idea that Kaito and Suzume were meant to be together.

"Right," Suzume replied, slowly drawing out the I.

Rin's eyes were shadowed. She kept staring at Suzume, perhaps waiting for Suzume to agree to the bargain. *She's giving me the creeps. There's no way I am going to promise not to seal him. It's him or me, and I like myself much more than him. What does that Kitsune know about my destiny? If you ask me, she is just a know-it-all trying to insert herself in my business.*

---

He stomped away, a storm gathering overhead, the sky reflecting his mood. *I should have killed her. I never would have let a human speak that way to me before. How much longer will I let gratitude and amusement distract me from the truth? I've grown soft.* She was no real threat to him, even once she was trained. He would never let his guard down to be sealed. He convinced himself that he would not let a human back into his heart. He did not fear betrayal; if you did not let anyone in, they could not get close to you.

He clutched his clawed hand into a fist. The harder he tried to keep Suzume at arm's reach, the more she crept into his head, filling his skull as he looked for new ways to taunt and tease her, to see that flush of embarrassment or the rise of her temper. Without realizing it, she had broken past all his best defenses. He could only lie to himself so much.

What he feared right now was Suzume's betrayal. His chest constricted replaying her words through his head. An echo of another time, of the woman she had been. The idea of Suzume betraying him cut him like a knife, deeper than the actual act, because for a brief moment he had thought he could open himself up again, even if it wasn't a romantic love, to let a human be his companion, to amuse him and ease his boredom and dull the edge of his rage. *I do not care for her. She is a means to an end. Once I find Kazue's reincarnation, I will have no further need of her.*

He leaned against the beam that supported the covered walkway, his hand half formed with claws bit into the wood, which splintered beneath his iron grip. Ice ran from his hands up the beam to the ceiling, frosting it over, spreading down the hall, turning everything into a winter wonderland. He took deep breaths to calm his nerves.

Up until a few days ago, he felt as if he had started to let his anger go. But now it slammed into him, demanding release, like a tsunami that threatened to destroy everything he touched. When would this hate be sated, would revenge even be enough? Even if he killed every living link to Kazue, it would never be enough. She was dead and he would never see her again, never know what changed or how their love had gone astray.

He blew out a breath, a cloud of ice that hung around him and frosted his hair and brows. Nearby, the priests chanted; their sonorous voices rose and fell like the undulating waves in the ocean. He missed the sea, his palace and his carefree life when he reigned over a peaceful domain. Loving humans had brought this. Since Tamashi had accidentally given birth to humans, they had been nothing but a pestilence upon the land. *We would be better to wipe them all off the earth.*

He tightened his grip and cracked the support beam. The walkway overhead groaned but did not fall, the weight held by the remaining beams. He spun around and started walking, but the song of the priests drew him closer. He thought of the high priestess' prayers at the Shrine of the Mountain god, their fervent prayers for rain, for peace, for prosperity. He never had the power to grant any of it. He could only dream, swirling in his hate and loneliness, but the songs had made the time pass easier, and being near it again, he was lulled, calmed by the melody. He floated closer, listening, letting his mind drift while his body changed, spreading and growing, changing from man to beast. And a voice whispered in his ear.

"You should get rid of the priestess before she does what Kazue did to you."

Kaito rolled his head, looking for the speaker, but his eyes were half lidded and it was difficult to see anything. His serpentine body stretched down the hall, filling the space. *Why did I transform?* His eyes slid closed.

"You need to stop her," the voice cooed.

He opened his eyes and tilted his head back to look up at the gray sky overhead. *I need to fly.* He rose into the sky, twirling and weaving about. But the voice did not leave his thoughts.

"You both cannot live; kill her now before it is too late," it said.

*They're right, this pain will not end until Kazue's reincarnation is dead.*

## 33

The priests filed out of the temple as Suzume approached. She stood off to one side, watching as the line of priests trickled past her. The priests seemed to have been too absorbed in their prayers to notice what had transpired outside. They wore serene expressions, with their hands folded in front of them as they passed her by. The scent of their incense clung to their robes and wafted over Suzume as they walked past, musky, with slight floral undertones.

While Suzume waited, she let her mind wander. *What if Rin is right? What if Kaito and I are destined to be together?* She shook her head. That was impossible. There was no way she was meant for someone as boorish and arrogant as Kaito. She was willing to accept the fact that she was Kazue's reincarnation; it explained her dormant powers, anyway. The fact that she was Kazue in a past life did not mean they had to share men. *No way.*

The last of the priests exited, closely followed by the head priest and his second. The head priest turned to see Suzume standing to one side, her arms wrapped around her protectively as she contemplated her unfortunate fate. The head priest smiled at her and nodded his head in greeting. He walked past Suzume and down the covered walkway before Suzume had the sense to speak.

"Excuse me!" Suzume called out. Her voice cracked across the hushed silence of the temple and reverberated back at her. The echo did not disguise the desperate whine of her tone.

The head priest stopped and turned to face Suzume. The second hung back behind the head priest's shoulder. The head priest addressed Suzume, "Young Priestess, how can I be of assistance?"

*Finally! Someone with some manners.* She bowed. "I was hoping I could speak with you, if it is not too much trouble." Suzume felt compelled to respect the priest, she could not exactly say why. Even back at court when addressing her father, the emperor, she had at times been haughty and disrespectful. But there was a magnetic draw she felt to him as if he had all the answers in the world.

"What a coincidence. I was hoping to speak with you as well. Shall we walk in the garden together?" He motioned towards the garden on the other side of the walkway.

Suzume smiled in response. "That would be lovely, thank you."

The head priest excused himself from his second and then offered a bended arm to Suzume. She took his arm and they walked together in the opposite direction from the other priests. They headed towards the shrine and Suzume's stomach clenched with fear. Before they got too close, however, they turned and walked down a few steps and onto a garden path. Suzume exhaled with relief. *I don't think I'll ever be able to go near a shrine again.*

There was a stone pathway that weaved among miniature, decorative bushes. They were silent for quite a long time. Suzume took the time to enjoy the serene surroundings. It was a refreshing change. No monsters threatening to devour her for her powers. No creatures lurking in the shadows, hunting her. And best of all, Kaito was off somewhere pouting, which meant Suzume had a moment of real peace for the first time in weeks.

She hoped he would be the one that could help her master her powers. They passed by a decorative pond with koi swimming about in it. There were more gingko trees here that shaded the walk. The umbrella-shaped leaves littered the ground in a yellow carpet. *It's almost too perfect here. I really hope this priest is really a priest and not the spirit of a priest who wants to use my eyeballs in an evil potion that will help make him invincible or something awful like that.*

"You have questions?" the priest prompted, ending the comfortable silence and dashing Suzume's twisted thoughts.

Suzume, by now used to mystical individuals seemingly reading her thoughts, replied, "Yes. You mentioned our souls met in a past life. What did you mean?" She wanted to keep asking questions, but something about the slow cadence of the priest's voice and the tranquility around them kept her from asking all her questions in a rush. She would get the answers she wanted in good time, her little-used patience reminded her. As much as she felt it would, waiting wouldn't kill her.

He patted her hand, which was linked through his arm. "I have been head priest here for many lives. Oftentimes souls that reincarnate will travel similar paths. For many of my lives, I have been the head priest here. Including five centuries ago when your soul was last here."

Suzume gasped, impressed by his intuition. "How do you know that?"

He pulled away from her so he could face her. "It was a guess." He smiled.

Suzume frowned at the old man. "That's not funny, you tricked me." *Maybe I misjudged him after all.*

He chuckled. "I apologize. I could not resist. Your soul and mine did indeed meet long ago. When you are trained as I am, you can sense these things. The reason I was able to deduce the time frame is because of the great Dragon."

"What does he have to do with this?" Suzume crossed her arms over her chest.

"Because your souls' paths are bound together."

"No, they're not!" Suzume shouted without thinking. She balled her hands into fists at her sides. *Why does everything come back to him and me? Can we all just move on from this destined souls thing?*

The priest's brow furrowed. Suzume hurried to cover her faux pas. She had been spending too much time with the Dragon. "I'm sorry. I don't think my soul has anything to do with the Dragon."

The priest folded his hands in front of him. He inserted his hands into the billowing sleeves of his robe. He regarded Suzume for a moment without speaking. Suzume squirmed beneath his gaze. It felt like when he looked at her, he could see right through to her soul, and for the first time she was afraid of what someone saw within her.

"There is a bond when two souls must share a journey. You and the Dragon share this bond. It does not have to be a romantic bond, oftentimes it can be merely friendship or even enemies. I said many souls travel the same paths, but despite that, no journey is the same. You may be the reincarnation of Fujikawa Kazue, but it does not mean you will love and live as she did. You are your own person. And as with High Priestess Fujikawa, when a soul has been damaged by a past life, it will often times drastically alter the future path to heal the old wounds."

Suzume was somewhat mollified by this. *Then I don't have to be with Kaito...* She was oddly disappointed, but she pushed the feelings aside. It was better not to analyze that thought. "What can you tell me about Kazue?"

"High Priestess Fujikawa?" he corrected, using her more formal form of address. "She is often called the first priestess. Though there were shrines and attendants before, she was thought to bring them together by traveling between them and sharing knowledge about the mystical world, and she is credited with founding many of the shrines around the kingdom, including the Eight High Deity Shrines, which includes the shrine at the White Palace."

"Is it true she was the mother to the first emperor?" Suzume asked. *What a strange twist of fate if I was my own great-great-great-great-grandmother.*

The priest shrugged. "It is difficult to say. During Priestess Fujikawa's time, the empire was made of many factious clans ruled by different lords. The early records were destroyed when the shrine that held them burned back in the two hundred years after the beginning of our empire. Most of those early days have been lost to the mist of time. There is no way to say whether she was the one who bore the first emperor or if it is truly myth. This I can tell you: she trained in this very temple and she died at a young age."

"How did she die?" Suzume asked, but as the question escaped her mouth, a roar ripped through the tranquility of the garden. "What was that?" Suzume twisted around to find the source of the sound.

The ground rumbled beneath Suzume's feet. It lurched and bucked and she had to focus just to keep her balance. Suzume threw her arms out to keep from falling. She looked to the priest. He had his head tilted up to the sky. He muttered under his breath and it sounded a lot like the prayers she had heard earlier that day. Suzume followed his gaze. Gray storm clouds fat with rain had blotted out the sun when just moments ago it had been a sunny day. Rain burst from the clouds and pelted Suzume and the priest like icy needles.

Suzume squinted as something writhed among the clouds. Lightning flashed and lit up the dark sky. Then she saw a flash of pearlescent skin and a serpentine body. *No!* The Dragon hovered far above them and he opened his mouth in another thunderous roar. His eyes were an electric blue like the lightning that cracked and sizzled behind him. He opened his mouth and ice

261

shot from it. The ice flung to the ground and impaled the earth at their feet.

A barrier materialized around her as Suzume threw her hands up just in time to protect herself from the falling ice. The dagger-sharp shards sizzled and clanked off her force field, melting the ice as it hit. Some of the ice daggers were so large they did not melt immediately but threatened to pierce it. The Dragon circled back around and disappeared behind the clouds. While he was gone, Suzume chanced a glance at the priest. He had fashioned himself a barrier as well and continued chanting under his breath.

"What's going on? Is that Kaito?" Suzume shouted to the priest.

He did not respond. The rain had solidified and now pelted their barriers as enormous balls of ice. The ice balls hit her barrier before sizzling and rolling off in rivulets of water as they melted.

The Dragon roared and coiled about the sky. It looked like Kaito in his dragon form, but between the clouds, it was hard to tell. All she could see was the writhing body of the Dragon seething among the clouds. *How many other dragons could there be?*

Then her questions were answered when the Dragon bellowed, "Kazue, I am coming for you!"

*Great, what have I gotten myself into now?*

# 34

The Dragon swooped down from the sky, and the wind, unhindered by the barrier, froze Suzume down to the bone. The bushes were fringed with frost, and the sky was thick with clouds so dark they blotted out the sun. The Dragon skimmed the edge of Suzume's barrier. Her barrier crackled as his clawed hand tried to grab hold of her. She panicked as he came near her and she stumbled backwards against her own barrier. It did not burn, but felt like a warm tickle. But she could smell the burning flesh on the Dragon; it smelled like burning rotten meat. He roared in pain and reeled back from her barrier. He opened his mouth and aimed a spray of ice at Suzume, which collided with her barrier and shook it. Steam rose off her barrier where ice had pelted it. Her barrier flickered for a brief second.

Slack jawed, she watched the Dragon's underbelly pass over her. She could feel the cold wind rolling off of him. *He came really close to taking my head off.* Her hands went to her throat. Her pulse jumped beneath her skin and her heartbeat was loud enough to drown out the sound of the pounding rain that followed the falling ice. The Dragon roared and twisted in the sky. His body coiled around without end like an endless mass of twisting flesh.

"Face me, Kazue! You cannot hide behind the barrier forever," the Dragon thundered.

"He's lost his mind!" Suzume shouted at no one in particular. She thought he would be upset after discovering her past life, but this seemed a little overdramatic.

"You need the staff!" Rin shouted from Suzume's left.

Suzume twirled around inside the barrier. Rin stood beneath a gingko tree, her mouth set in a line. Suzume had never seen her look so serious and it scared her. *She looks terrified.* Suzume's hands shook and she clamped them down at her sides to hide their shaking.

"What staff?" Suzume cried over the wind.

"It's in the shrine. It belonged to Kazue. It will help you focus your power."

Suzume glanced over her shoulder towards the shrine. It was a hundred feet away, at least. And on top of that she would have to get around the bushes and then cross open ground before reaching the shrine. She might as well paint a giant target on her back that said "come eat me". The barrier flickered again. *I don't know how much longer I can keep this up. I'm getting weaker every minute, and Kaito has gone insane.*

"Go, I'll cover you," Rin said. Before Suzume could even voice a complaint, the Kitsune ran out from beneath the tree and into the way of the descending Dragon.

As the Dragon descended, Rin transformed from woman to animal. Her fur was bright orange, her underbelly was white and her numerous tails whipped behind her.

*That's Rin?* Suzume gasped. She should have known Rin had a different form, but it still came as a shock. Rin bared her teeth at Kaito as he lunged for her. He was distracted by the introduction of the Kitsune. Rin lunged for Kaito's throat and caught him. Though Rin was perhaps a third the Dragon's length, she was able to get enough leverage to bring him crashing to the ground. The force of his impact shook the ground and he snarled at Rin as he gained his feet and broke free.

Suzume did not take another second to watch the battle and ran full speed for the shrine. Crossing the open ground took only a few seconds, but it felt like an eternity. She did not look back, but she heard the Dragon growl and felt each breath she took. Run. Don't look. Keep going. By the time she reached the shrine, she was panting for breath. She stumbled inside, tripping over her hakama as she ascended the steps. She saved herself from face-planting by grabbing the door frame.

As she took a moment to catch her breath, she looked around the shrine. It was a plain square building. In the center of the room was a rectangular pedestal. It was long and narrow, with sticks of incense burning at the four corners.

Inside the shrine, the outside noise seemed to dim and Suzume could focus on the staff. It lay on a stand that kept it propped up on the platform. She walked over to it hastily. Thankfully, unlike the other occasions when she'd been near a shrine, she did not feel anything stirring or her power reaching out for the object. She stood over the staff for a moment, examining it. It was surprisingly unimpressive. The staff was made of worn wood that was smooth around the edges and the middle where Kazue had gripped it. It appeared to have been painted red at some point, but the paint had long since faded to a burnt orange color.

*This is it?* She picked up the staff. It was light and fit in her hand. She stood it upright and it was the same height as her. *It's like it was made for me.* She twirled the staff and brought it down in front of her with a swipe. It felt right. Holding this felt natural as if she'd been trained with it her entire life, but she'd never touched a weapon before.

The fight outside invaded the tranquility within the shrine. A yelp followed a growl. There was no time to think about why the staff felt so right, she had to help Rin. She ran out the shrine doors. The sounds of fighting had faded away. She looked up into the dark sky and fat drops of rain fell onto her face.

The Dragon was nowhere to be seen. Suzume stopped and looked around, the staff held loosely at her side. *Why am I doing this? I should take this opportunity to run.* She didn't know how to explain it, but she felt compelled to help, to fight the Dragon. Then a disturbing thought occurred to her. Everything was too quiet—something wasn't right. Then she felt pain, bright and sharp, at the base of her spine where something had struck her. She collapsed to her knees from the pain. Low rumbling laughter filled her ears.

She spun around to face her assailant. A man with dark hair hanging loose around his face walked towards her. He had an angular face with high cheekbones and a cruel smile. He walked towards Suzume, with a smirk tilting his lips.

"We finally meet face to face, Suzume." He paced towards her.

"Who are you?!" she demanded as she jumped back onto her feet. She pointed the staff at him.

He did not answer and instead circled her with an almost bored expression. His eyes glanced up and down her, not in a lascivious way but almost as if he were sizing her up.

"I asked you a question." Suzume jabbed the staff in his direction.

He laughed again. The sound rolled over her and made her skin crawl.

"We'll just say I'm an old friend." He stopped pacing and faced Suzume. His eyes were narrowed as he regarded her.

"I doubt that," Suzume spat. "What did you shoot me with anyway?" Her back still throbbed and she could not massage it as she wanted to. Both her hands were being used to hold up the staff and her arms shook with the effort.

"Perhaps I should correct myself, I was a friend of Kazue's."

She scoffed, trying to ignore her fear. "Kazue's friends are not necessarily my friends."

"Then you no longer deny you are her?"

"I'm Suzume—if you don't mind. Maybe you could give me your name since we're such good friends now."

He clicked his tongue as if he were scolding her. "Let's make this more fun and keep that a secret for now."

*This guy is a creep. If I didn't have other things to deal with, I'd fry him, but as it is, I have a dragon to deal with.* He blocked her way back to Rin and Kaito. She swung the staff, hoping to get him to move. He dodged her swing easily. Instead of Suzume hitting him with her staff, he grabbed it in the center, swung it under her armpit and flipped her over. The staff slipped from her grasp, and he used it to pin her to the ground as he loomed over her.

Suzume glared up at him. "What do you want?" she snarled.

"Nothing... yet." He leaned forward and brushed his lips against Suzume's, despite Suzume wrenching her face away from him.

"What is wrong with you!" she shouted.

She tried to kick him or punch, but her body was not listening to her. All attempts at defense were nothing more than lame twistings of her limbs. Her barrier was curiously dormant and she couldn't call forward her power in her own defense. He eased off of her and then, with one more wicked smile, he disappeared through a glimmering mirror, stars reflected on the other side. *Wait, that's no mirror, is that a portal?*

*Who was that?* the Dragon roared and the sound of the battle came crashing down on her once again. Suzume did not have much time to consider her strange encounter before she ran back towards Rin and Kaito. Rin, still in her fox form, came bounding over the decorative hedges, with Kaito hot on her tails. Rin spun around to face Kaito. The Kitsune opened her mouth and blue flames shot out and met Kaito's icy breath.

Steam erupted around them, haloing their heads in clouds. Suzume rushed forward, using the clouds to disguise herself. It was not enough, however, and Kaito spotted her and roared. He flew up into the air before coming hurtling down towards her. Suzume realized too late she had no idea what she was doing. The mysterious stranger had proved that much. Kaito's icy breath brushed against her cheeks and the perspiration on her brow froze.

"What am I supposed to do now?" She looked at Rin.

The Kitsune was badly wounded, her shoulder torn open, bleeding profusely. Along with myriad other wounds that were in some state of healing.

"Just use the staff, focus your energy on it and hit him with it!" Rin panted.

Suzume stared down at the staff, the faded patterns and the worn middle. *How did you use this stupid thing, Kazue?*

Kaito lunged for Suzume, she couldn't create a barrier—she didn't know how unless it created itself. She only had the staff. She flung the staff up, holding onto it with both hands. She brought it down on Kaito's nose. The force rattled the staff and jarred her arm. It did little to deter him, but he was momentarily deflected. He spun away for a moment before he came twisting back around.

Suzume focused on the staff. She imagined the power slipping from her fingers and wrapping around the staff, as if it was an extension of her body and full of her power. She exhaled. *Here goes nothing.* She reached for the well of power she knew was hidden deep within her. Kaito roared and hail fell onto her head like hundreds of knives, tearing into her skin and obscuring her vision. Blood trickled down her cheek where one particular piece had sliced the skin near her eye. She could feel the power just below the surface, just beyond her reach. *Focus,* she told herself. *Focus.*

Then she heard something, a low hum, a melody. It was the same one the old woman had been singing back in the village. Suzume hummed a few bars and it was as if a dam within her had been broken—power flowed through her fingertips and into the staff. She was cocooned in power. It radiated from within her and it burned, scorching her skin, and her insides felt as if they were being boiled in a pot. She had to let it loose or it was going to destroy her.

Kaito was close now and Suzume pointed her staff. Her arms quivered, and like loosing an arrow from a bow, she unleashed the power. She felt it break free from within her and shoot towards Kaito. The staff worked like a conductor and it made a straight path, hitting Kaito square in the chest with a ball of red energy. He fell from the sky, plummeting like a rock before he crashed into the ground. Once the power left her, Suzume no longer had even the energy to stand. She slumped to her knees. Rin had returned to her human form and ran towards Kaito.

Suzume felt hands on her shoulder, comforting and warm.

"You did well," the priest told her.

"'Did I kill him?" Suzume asked the priest. She had almost forgotten he was there.

She felt conflicted. On one hand, she wanted Kaito out of her life. On the other, she did not want him dead. It was a surprising revelation, and one she would need to process, but not now, maybe not ever.

The priest did not answer right away. He glanced over to Rin, who sat by Kaito's side, stroking his muzzle and speaking to him. "No, he is stunned."

Suzume exhaled with relief. She ignored the look the priest gave her and focused on the real question. Now that this battle was over, there was only one thing left: what would happen when Kaito woke again?

# 35

The priests stood over Kaito in a circle as they chanted. The low reverberating sound resonated through Suzume and the short hairs on the back of her neck stood on end. Their chanting changed tempo, increasing in pace. Suzume's pulse raced with the fast-moving chant. Kaito's form blurred and shifted. His serpentine body shortened, twisting and writhing. Suzume watched with rapt attention. The song faded into one residual note that echoed around them and filled Suzume's skull. Kaito lay on the ground, back in his human form. The head priest had been leading the chanting.

He directed the other priests to pick Kaito up. *Must be easier than trying to pick up a one-ton dragon.* Two priests stood on opposite ends of Kaito and picked him up by his hands and feet. Slung between them, Kaito's head lolled backwards at an unnatural angle. He looked dead and the idea sent a twisting sensation through Suzume's stomach.

She turned away. The garden was in disarray. Bushes had been uprooted. The paving stones were slicked over with frost and pools of water had gathered in massive indents made by clawed feet. *What a mess.*

Across the garden, an elderly priest tutted over Rin's injury. He dabbed at the gash on her shoulder. Rin swatted at his hand, but he grabbed her hand and pursed his lips at her. Rin scowled back at the old man. They remained locked in a battle of wills for a moment before Rin rolled her eyes and let him continue. Rin caught sight of Suzume watching them, and smiled at her. Suzume reluctantly smiled back. Now that Rin had helped her, were they obligated to be friends? Suzume wasn't sure how she felt about that.

Suzume fidgeted with the staff in her hand. Now that the battle was over, it felt leaden in her grip. She looked away from Rin and towards the ground. Blood was spattered there and her stomach heaved. *He knows Kazue was my past life. If Rin hadn't intervened, this would have been my blood on the ground.* She looked away from the blood and back towards the retreating forms of the priests who carried Kaito away. *It happened just like I thought it would. But now it may be too late to get away with my life.*

Rin broke free of the priest and sauntered over to Suzume. "How are you?" Rin asked as she reached Suzume.

Suzume shrugged in response. She wasn't sure what to say—for once in her life. She felt deflated and humbled by her fight. By some miracle she had escaped with her life, but if it came down to it, could she repeat the performance?

Rin didn't seem to need an explanation and she continued, "I'll watch over Kaito until he wakes up."

*What happens when he wakes up? He'll most likely want to try to kill me again. I need to run away from here.*

"Yeah, that sounds like a good idea," Suzume said. She shifted the staff from one hand to another. "When will he wake?"

Rin shrugged. "Hard to tell, but I can keep him at bay if he's... aggressive when he does."

*I'll be long gone by then, hopefully. Maybe I can convince the head priest to give me food and a way to get away from here.* She was disgusted by her own thoughts. *When did I become such a coward? Even if I run, he'll find me.*

Despite her own fear, however, she had to keep up appearances. "Make sure you do," Suzume said. With a toss of her hair, she strolled away. Her hands shook. She tightened her grasp on the staff as she walked away.

She made a beeline for the head priest. She needed to keep moving; if she kept still, then her fear would catch up with her, and if that happened... well, she was not willing to consider that. The head priest was conferring with his second when Suzume approached. The priest looked up at her and smiled, but the smile did not reach his eyes.

"Suzume, I thought you would want to rest." He motioned for the second to leave with a wave of his hand.

"I don't think I could rest even if I wanted to," she replied with a self-deprecating laugh.

He chuckled softly and his eyes flitted towards the staff. "You were able to get her staff with little trouble."

She held up the staff for his inspection. "So this is Kazue's staff?"

"It is, I'm glad you were able to retrieve it. None of our order has been able to get near it for many years."

A feeling of foreboding settled over her, just another way in which being Kazue's reincarnation made her special. The words caught in her throat, choking her.

"I have a favor to ask of you," Suzume said, changing the subject.

"Oh?" the head priest said. His eyes bored into her, as if he saw through her to her soul.

Suzume shifted the staff so one end rested on the ground while keeping it within her control. She was feeling oddly possessive of the thing. "I need to leave here before the Dragon wakes. Can you help me?"

A slight smirk curled his lips. "The Dragon will sleep for now.

He shall not wake until we find a way to calm him, I can assure you."

*Am I imagining things, or does he not want me to leave?* "How can you be so sure? Have you put him under a spell?" He didn't seem that powerful, but maybe there was more to the priest than met the eye.

"Not indefinitely, but long enough to sort some things out." He smiled. Before his smile had been reassuring, but now that she felt trapped, she wondered if she had been drawn in too easily by the priest.

*This is a good opportunity to learn. If he **does** stay asleep, then maybe I can learn how to seal him before he wakes.*

"Can you teach me how to seal him away?" she asked without disguising the desperation in her voice.

"I am not sure that is wise…"

"He's going to kill me! Can you not see that?" She pointed towards the dormitories where Kaito had been taken. "He's realized I am Kazue and he will not stop until he has his revenge."

The priest nodded thoughtfully. "Perhaps."

"Can you at least tell me what's so special about this staff?"

"It was Kazue's," he replied.

"That I know, but there's more you're not telling me."

He rubbed his hands together and his gaze slowly slid from the staff to Suzume's face. "The legends say that Kazue embedded certain artifacts with her spiritual power. We believe this staff was one of those artifacts."

"You don't know for sure?"

"The staff was warded by Kazue before her death. And no one could touch it, except you…"

Suzume frowned. "Because I am her reincarnation?"

"Perhaps"

She fought the urge to shake the old man. Could no one give a straight answer?

"Well, I have the staff, now what?"

"Stay here, let us train you in its use. Together we will be able to unlock your true potential." Again she saw a hint of something more sinister in his expression. *I'm being paranoid, not everyone has an ulterior motive.* The fight with Kaito had shaken her. He was still the kind priest she had met. Nothing changed.

Suzume pursed her lips. "Alright, fine, but if the Dragon shows the slightest inclination of waking, I am out of here, got it?"

"Thank you, Suzume." The priest bowed deep and the hems of his sleeves scraped against the gravel at their feet.

Suzume fought an eye roll. *Feels like I am back at the palace.* A momentary pang of longing swept over her. *I'll get back there eventually, I guess.*

"When can I start learning?" Suzume asked while gesturing with the staff.

The priest glanced around them. Suzume followed his gaze; the place was in chaos. The ordered hedges were trampled and the ancient gingko trees had deep gashes in them. "I will need time to set things in order, but soon, hopefully." He looked doubtful.

She hated to wait, but it looked like she did not have much choice in the matter. The alternative, of course, was running away and hoping Kaito would not find her. The problem was he would wake eventually and he would come for her, of that she had no doubt. *I can't live on the run forever.*

"In the meantime, could you take that back to the shrine?" The priest nodded towards the staff. He still had a hungry look in his eye.

She held it close. She didn't want to let it go. "I was wondering if I could keep it?" Suzume asked.

The priest's frown deepened. "I will have to discuss it with the others. I know you are Kazue's reincarnation, but that is a sacred item, one that is imbued with power, and we cannot let it leave this compound lightly."

Suzume rubbed the smooth edges of the grip across the palm of her hand, contemplating it. This held immense power? It felt like a little bit of wood, but it felt right in her hands. She felt powerful while she had it. *Except for when that strange guy attacked me. Who was he?*

"I'll take it back to the shrine, then," Suzume said.

*I don't want to leave this lying around. Something is telling me I am meant to have it. If Kazue warded this five hundred years ago, it must have been with good reason.* She headed off towards the temple. *I wonder if that man will be there when I get back.*

She touched her lips where he had kissed her. Who was that creep, and what did he want with her? She reached the shrine without interruption. She was half-hoping she would run into the mysterious man. He did not make an appearance, much to her frustration. She had some questions for him now that the battle was over. Suzume set the staff back in its place and looked around the temple.

*What was so special about Kazue? Why did everyone revere her?*

The wind blew outside and ruffled the trees and leaves. Suzume felt a prickling along her neck. Her hand reached instinctively for the staff on its pedestal. It felt safer to have a weapon, rather than not. Right now her senses shouted at her that something was amiss. A floorboard creaked. She snatched the staff back off the pedestal and spun around. There was no one there. She rolled her eyes. *I'm getting paranoid. Rightfully so, my life was normal until recently...*

She moved to set the staff back down when sparks raced over her arms and neck. She rubbed her neck and looked over her shoulder. *There's definitely someone here.*

"Who's here?" She spun back around, staff held in a defensive pose crossed in front of her at a diagonal. "I know you're there and I am ready for you this time. I owe you payback for that kiss earlier."

Soft laughter, husky and feminine, replied. The gooseflesh rose on her arms. That was not the response she was expecting.

"Who's there?" Suzume repeated.

The laughter died, and from around a pillar on the outer veranda, a woman appeared. She wore a blood-red kimono, with long sleeves edged in gold thread, that dragged along the ground. Her ebony hair was coiffed on top of her head. Decorative pins stuck from it and small bells on the end of the sticks tinkled as she moved.

"My, you are a strange-looking priestess." The woman looked Suzume up and down.

Suzume pointed the staff at her. "Who are you?"

A strange energy radiated from the woman and Suzume had a sinking suspicion she was no woman at all.

"My, my, your manners are terrible." The woman strolled closer to Suzume. She had her lips painted a bright red, which flashed against her white teeth and dark black eyes.

Suzume took an unconscious step back and bumped into the pedestal. She steadied herself on the pedestal to keep from falling over. The woman came within an inch of Suzume and tilted her head from side to side as she examined Suzume's face. A faintly sweet smell clung to the woman. She brushed a long-fingered hand against Suzume's face. The touch crackled with energy but did not burn, more like tickled.

"You are her, I thought Tsuki was lying."

"Who's Tsuki?" Suzume asked. She was not sure if she was afraid or intrigued.

The woman's smile was a predatory flash of teeth. "My brother."

Suzume slid away from the woman's grasp and ran around to the other side of the pedestal. She tried desperately to remember the melody that had unleashed the power before, but it escaped her at the moment. *This is a great time to choke. What does this woman want with me? And her brother, for that matter.*

"What do you want? To drain me of all my spiritual power? Well, I'm not going down without a fight!" Suzume snarled. She tried to swing the staff to make a point, but it collided with an incense-filled lantern. Her staff tangled in the chain, suspending the staff from the ceiling. She jerked forward and stumbled, hitting the floor at the woman's feet. She yanked the staff free and it slammed into the ground with a thunk.

"I see you have the staff—you're making good progress, then. We've been waiting a long time for you to realize yourself." The woman's expression gave nothing away.

Suzume scowled up at her. Was the woman making fun of her? Suzume couldn't tell. "What are you talking about?"

The woman's perfect painted lips hung open for a second before she smiled again. "You've realized that you are Kazue. That's why you woke the Dragon. You should know..." The woman shrugged her shoulders.

"Well, I don't. Do you care to enlighten me?"

The woman laughed her throaty laugh.

"What is so funny?" demanded Suzume.

"It's just you look nothing like Kazue and sound nothing like her. Kazue always led. We never had to give her instructions."

Suzume's face flushed. She wasn't sure why it upset her so, but it did. "Well, I am not Kazue, and it would do you well to explain what you're doing here."

She stopped laughing, but the mirth continued to light up her eyes. "Well, seeing as I am your servant, I am here to help you finish Kazue's task."

"Her task?" Suzume prompted.

"You don't know?"

"No. That's what I am hoping you'll elaborate on."

The woman frowned. "What? I don't know either! Kazue said when she returned, she would break the curse and finish the task." The woman's eyes had turned red, a scorching red that looked like they would burn through Suzume. "Damn you, Kazue, you tricked me!" She snarled as she tugged at her coiffed hair. The pins came loose and clattered on the ground. Her black hair tumbled to her shoulders and she turned away from Suzume.

"Now, sister, calm down," a man's voice said.

He sounded like he was nearby, but as far as Suzume could tell, she and the woman were alone.

"Tsuki," the woman whined, all traces of her sultry voice gone, "I am tired of these tricks. Maybe we should kill the incarnation and be done with it."

"No." The man's tone was firm. "We have waited much too long for this. The priestess can be taught. Perhaps she has not regained her past memories yet."

"Ah, Tsuki, I think you are right." The woman turned back towards Suzume.

Suzume gasped and covered her mouth with her hands. The staff fell to the ground with a clatter. The woman strolled over to Suzume and picked up the staff off the ground. Suzume stared at the woman, she could not take her eyes off of her.

The woman's face had changed. One half, the right, remained the same—all sultry eyes and soft lips, but the other side was angular with a slight bristling of a beard.

Suzume screeched. "What is wrong with your face?"

The man's voice responded. "Sorry to frighten you, let us introduce ourselves. My name is Tsuki, and this is my sister, Akira."

Suzume's chin had hit the floor. *I must be exhausted from the fight, I could not have heard him—er—her correctly.* Words escaped her, she did not know how to process the sight before her. Even the left half of her body was different. The left shoulder was broad and instead of the elaborate robe, the left half wore a blue haori, the sleeves trimmed in silver thread over black hakama.

"Let me explain, brother, you're scaring the girl," Akira, or was it Tsuki, said in a feminine voice.

"Very well," the male voice said before it disappeared, leaving behind the seductive-looking woman, once more whole, in a single red and gold kimono.

Akira explained, "Kazue trapped us inside one body and bid us guard her staff until she came for it. She promised to return us to our separate bodies once the task was complete. When she died, we assumed her reincarnation would return to complete what she had started, so we have waited and guarded this place for many years."

Suzume shook her head. She had seen a lot of strange things, but this had to be the topper. A brother and sister sharing a body? Two people in one.

"Well, I don't know what you expect me to do," she said, staring at the woman in front of her, wondering at what point her other half would pop out.

"We can help you learn about your powers and teach you about your past life. We were... close... with Kazue."

Akira smiled, but something about it made Suzume's stomach turn. Despite her uncertainty, it was a tempting offer.

"What can you teach me?" she asked. *This very well could be a trap.*

The body transformed without warning from soft to hard. The robe receded and became pants and a long shirt. Suzume saw Tsuki's form in full. He was a young man with angular features and a wide sensual mouth that mimicked his sister's. His looks were almost androgynous, with long dark hair framing his face.

"Do you always do that without warning?" Suzume snapped.

"Forgive me, Priestess, my sister and I have not had company in a long time."

"What have you been doing all this time, then?"

"Waiting." His expression dropped. "Guarding the staff. We have not let anyone touch it until you retrieved it this afternoon. I saw you fight, you need a lot of work."

"What would you know about fighting?" Suzume snapped back at him. *Did he see me get knocked onto my back by that strange man?*

He grinned and his face lit up like a child's. "I know everything about fighting. I can teach you how to fight, and my sister, how to master your powers, and together we can help you finish the task, once we figure out what it is…"

He held his hand out to her, imploring. Could she trust him—them? She wasn't sure, but the alternative was being killed, and she liked her life, thank you very much.

"What's in it for you?" she asked.

"We want you to set us free from this prison, separate us," he said, his tone serious, his gaze wary.

*No big deal...* She had to fight the urge to roll her eyes. *I'll agree and then if anything goes wrong, I'll... well, I'll figure that part out later. What harm could they do? They can't be worse than Kaito. Can they?*

"All right, you've got a deal."

# 36

"Where do we begin?" Suzume placed her free hand on her hip and stared at the androgynous man.

"Well, your first move should be to seal the Dragon, am I right?" Tsuki said. He smiled and Suzume narrowed her eyes at him.

*He makes it sound like it's easy.* She shivered to think about the unleashed power of the Dragon.

"Unless you don't want to?" Tsuki drawled. He strolled past her and looked down at the shrine where the staff had been kept before. He bent over and picked up a stick of incense. He rolled it between thumb and forefinger as he regarded Suzume. He leaned against the shrine with his head tilted to the side.

"Why wouldn't I want to seal him? If I don't, he'll kill me," she snapped.

"Will he now?" Tsuki smiled and it was the same predatory smile his sister had given Suzume. *It's like they're the same person in more than one way. Like they've shared a body so long even their mannerisms are the same. As creepy as they are...*

Suzume frowned at him. "Do you really know how to help me, or are you just playing with me?"

"Perhaps a bit of both."

*I have a bad feeling about these two. I have yet to meet an immortal who did not like to play games, and it seems they are no exception.*

"On second thought, I think I'd rather go alone." Suzume hefted the staff onto her shoulder. There was no way she was leaving it with him. She hoped to sneak it into her room; perhaps the priests wouldn't come looking for it. She managed a few steps towards the door of the shrine before they shifted back to Akira. It was she who joined Suzume. She did not try to stop Suzume but walked beside her. Suzume glared at her from the corner of her eye. Akira's movements were fluid and her ruby lips were pulled back, revealing her white teeth.

"Ignore my brother, he likes to play games. I *can* show you how to seal the Dragon," she purred.

Suzume stopped. Akira turned to face Suzume. Akira folded her arms in front of her and tilted her head to one side as her brother had.

"I get the feeling you're both tricking me. Why would you know anything about spiritual power?" She pointed at Akira with the end of her staff. It brushed against the sleeve of Akira's crimson robe.

Akira pushed the staff away with her finger and sneered at Suzume. "Because before I was forced to share a body with my brother, I was something like you."

Suzume frowned. "You mean a human?"

"Not exactly." She looked away from Suzume.

"Then you're not human?" Suzume raised her eyebrows. *This has to be a trick.*

"We are something in between—not quite Yokai or Kami, but not mortal like a human. We have spiritual power, or something similar to it." She shrugged. "It's difficult to explain. Just trust me, I can help you."

"That's just it, I don't trust you," she shouted. Her voice echoed off the courtyard before fading away.

Akira regarded Suzume, her expression guarded, not giving anything away. She did not say anything for a few moments and Suzume thought she had offended her. *I can't believe I would care that I offended these tricksters.*

Akira whistled. It was a low mournful sound. The sound tickled the short hairs at the back of Suzume's neck. The sound grew louder and Suzume felt a tingling sensation spread over her arms to her fingertips; she felt as if every inch of her was alive with sensation. Akira raised her arms and then began to sing, her voice husky and low. The notes reverberated, combining and threading their song around the pair of them. Akira glowed, orange and bright as the sun. She turned into a burning ball of light so bright Suzume had to shield her eyes.

Then the song ended and the light faded. Suzume was left blinking and staring in Akira's direction.

"Now do you believe?" Akira asked.

Suzume shook off her shock and said, "How do you do that?"

"It's the song, it harnesses the spiritual energy. It gives it voice and purpose," Akira replied smugly. Suzume was impressed, though unwilling to admit it.

"Teach me how to do that!" Suzume commanded. She waved her hand as if Akira could plant the knowledge into her mind.

Akira laughed low and throaty. "Perhaps you're more like Kazue than I thought."

Suzume frowned. She did not like being compared to Kazue, she may have been her past life, but she was her own person— wasn't she? Akira strode across the garden path and towards the dormitories. Suzume had to jog to keep up. *What is she doing? I thought she was going to teach me the song to seal the Dragon.* When they reached the edge of the courtyard, Akira twirled unexpectedly in place to face Suzume. Suzume almost tripped over her own hakama trying to keep from colliding with her.

"I will need to disguise myself. The priests here have enough spiritual power that they will be able to see us and that will ruin the fun. You'll be able to hear us, but no one else will. Just keep that in mind."

Before Suzume could ask her to explain, Akira disappeared. Suzume blinked and looked around. The wind rustled through the trees nearby, but other than that, she was alone.

"Where did you go?" she hissed.

"We're here." Akira's sultry voice filled Suzume's ear.

Suzume jumped in place, startled by her close proximity. She scowled at thin air and tried to figure out where she was, but no matter how she tried, she could not locate them.

"Don't worry, little Priestess, we will not leave you," Tsuki crooned.

She felt a hand brush against her shoulder and it raised the gooseflesh along her arm. *What a strange feeling.*

"Don't do that." She swatted at the air.

Tsuki only laughed in reply. His laughter seemed to surround her, coming from all directions.

"I thought you were going to teach me how to seal the Dragon." She stared at the trunk of a nearby oak tree to have something to focus on while she talked. The entire thing made her feel insane. *I hope no one sees me talking to myself and swatting at imaginary foes.* She glanced around just in case, but the courtyard was deserted.

"The best way to learn is by doing," Akira said. "I want you to go to the Dragon's room and there I will instruct you on how to seal him."

She rolled her eyes. "You could have said so earlier before your little disappearing act."

They laughed—their combined laughter was both musical and husky. It was a strange combination and Suzume wondered how they could laugh together.

"Do you do this often?" Suzume asked as they strolled along the path back to Kaito's room.

"We have to find some way to pass the time. Five centuries is a long time to wait idle, Priestess," Akira said, her tone wistful.

Suzume nodded. *I can imagine. I wonder why Kazue did this to them. Am I right to team up with them, what if they're Kazue's enemies?* Out loud she asked, "Why didn't you leave the temple?"

"We couldn't," Tsuki said, his tone melancholy.

A heavy silence followed this statement. In the absence of conversation, Suzume heard the distant humming of activity around the shrine. The priests were repairing the destruction Kaito had wrought. The silence went on long enough that Suzume feared they had abandoned her. So she decided to fill in the silence with another question.

"If you're supposed to help me, then why didn't you help me when I was fighting Kaito earlier?"

"We did," Tsuki replied. "We gave you the staff."

Suzume stopped and scowled at the brush nearby. *They gave me the staff? That explains why the priests were never able to handle it before. Maybe they're not so bad after all.* "Thanks for that."

"You're very welcome, Priestess, it is what we are here for," Akira intoned in her husky voice.

Another thought occurred to her. "There was a man outside the shrine who attacked me. Is he a friend of yours?"

They hesitated before replying. "I did not see anyone other than you," Tsuki said. "But I was so excited you had returned, it's possible I overlooked another human in the courtyard."

*They know something they're not telling me. I know that man was no human. What is he, and why won't they tell me?*

"Suzume, I thought you were going to put that back."

Suzume twirled around to see the head priest regarding her with a confused expression. She paused. *How do I explain I am trying to use it to seal Kaito?*

"I was, but I sensed an evil presence in the shrine. I was looking for you. I think someone needs to exorcise the space before the staff is put back."

Tsuki snickered. Suzume flinched, afraid the head priest would hear, but he did not seem to notice.

His eyebrows rose to his hairline as he studied Suzume. "You felt an evil presence?"

"Yes." She held his gaze. *Don't back down.* She felt like a fool. *There's no way he's going to believe this story.*

"I see." His gaze slid over her and she felt that same possessive longing in his eyes.

"He's not what he seems," Akira hissed in Suzume's ear and she jerked backwards.

The head priest's gaze flickered over Suzume's shoulder in the direction of Akira's voice. Had he heard them after all?

"I'll take it back now. I am sure it was nothing. I was probably just paranoid after my fight." She forced a laugh. Invisible hands pulled and turned her around. She was forced to walk away from the priest. *He knows; somehow he can see them.*

"Come this way," Tsuki murmured near her ear.

Tsuki had released Suzume's shoulders. He took her hand instead and pulled her between buildings. Once they were out of sight, he dropped her hand. Suzume glanced around to regain her bearings. They were two buildings away from the dormitory where Kaito was being kept, just behind the bath house.

"What was that about?" She looked around, hoping they would reveal themselves so she could stop talking to thin air.

"That priest is not a priest," Tsuki explained.

"What?" Suzume gasped.

"Follow me." Tsuki tugged on Suzume's hand once more, ignoring her indignant questions and grumblings. They tiptoed behind a covered walkway and through a decorative garden alongside it. Suzume heard footsteps echoing down the hall. She hunched down to avoid being seen. "Wait here," Tsuki whispered and Suzume listened as light footsteps pattered on the walkway above her. She felt a light touch on her shoulder a few moments later. "The coast is clear. His room is this way."

Suzume climbed over the railing of the walkway and headed for Kaito's room. She gripped the staff hard, but her hands shook nonetheless. *What if something goes wrong and he wakes up?* She stopped outside the door to Kaito's room. The last time she had been here, she had discovered him and Rin in a compromising situation. *That feels like it was decades ago.*

She slid open the door. Kaito lay alone on a sleeping roll at the far end of the room. Rin glanced up as Suzume entered. Her brows furrowed.

"You still have the staff?" she asked.

Suzume put it behind her back. "The priest asked me to guard it. They felt a negative energy near the shrine. They asked me to come get you, they think you can help purge it."

Rin scrutinized Suzume while Suzume tried to keep her face free of expression, lest she give herself away. Rin sighed. "I should not have left you to deal with Kaito on your own. That wish did something to him. It's like he's not himself." Rin looked down at Kaito's sleeping form. "Promise me you won't hurt him, I know deep down he is trying to reconcile with his past. He cares for you, I know it."

A momentary pang of guilt struck Suzume in the chest. "What can I do to him? I think I proved today that I'm not strong enough to defeat him."

"You did a lot. If you hadn't gotten the staff, I think the damage would have been a lot worse." Rin stood up and came over, standing directly in front of Suzume. They were of a height and Suzume met Rin's gaze. "Thank you for sparing him, that blast could have been the end of him." She bowed to Suzume before exiting.

When she left, Suzume exhaled. *That was close.* Her chest felt tight, and it wasn't just nerves. *What does Rin know? If he wakes up, I am a goner.*

Once Rin departed, Akira reappeared. "That was close. We don't have long, she'll realize and come back soon."

Suzume looked down at Kaito's peaceful face as he slept. *He's handsome when he's sleeping. It's a shame I have to do this.*

"Are you ready?" Akira asked.

Suzume took a deep breath. She looked away from Kaito. It was hard to commit when she was looking at him. For all his annoying tendencies, and there were a lot, she had almost grown fond of him—almost. But after his attack, she could not risk her life. If he woke, he would kill her—there was no other choice. "Yes," she said.

"Take the staff and point it at him."

Suzume took the staff in two hands and pointed it at Kaito's chest. "Now what?"

"Concentrate. Think of the spiritual energy inside you as a river that is flowing through you."

"Alright." Suzume closed her eyes and imagined as Akira instructed. *I don't know how this helps, but I guess I can try.* She did not feel any different than before.

"Now imagine there are dams in the river with which you can redirect the flow of the river to different channels or different parts of your body."

"Okay." Suzume thought of small stone dams, like the ones she had seen in the fields while she and Kaito were travelling. *Don't think of him now.* She peeked at his sleeping face before closing her eyes shut again.

"Now close all the channels until they are focusing the force of the river into your hands and through the staff."

Suzume focused and used the visuals, the river of red energy burning through her, and then she channeled it. She focused it on the staff and her fingers. She felt a burning sensation, a rush of power flowing through her.

"Now to unlock it, follow my lead," Akira instructed. She hummed a tune; it was fast and powerful like the rivers she had made Suzume imagine.

Suzume breathed in and opened her mouth, preparing to mimic the song Akira sang. She opened her eyes one last time and found Kaito staring back up at her. He had awoken.

# 37

Suzume took a couple steps backwards in an attempt to get away from him. She stepped on the hem of her too-long hakama and lost her balance. In an attempt to regain her balance, she swung her arms out and lost her grip upon the staff in the process. It flew from her hand and across the room. At the same time she stumbled, Kaito's hand shot forward and grabbed her by the wrist. She was tugged in the opposite direction and down onto the sleeping mat with him. He rolled over and pinned her beneath him. Disoriented, he moved to defend himself without thinking. She swung her free hand to try to strike him. Kaito grabbed her by both hands and held her to the mat by her wrists, his thighs pinning her waist. Her hair fanned out around her. *Mmm. This is one way to wake up.*

"Let me go!" she snarled and wiggled beneath him. He tightened his grip in response.

He laughed. "Why would I do that when you're so adorable all trussed up?"

Suzume flushed. She was too easy to tease. Something about the flush of her skin and the way her brows pulled together in a scowl excited him. He laughed, and it rumbled in his chest. Where his hands touched her, sparks tingled along his flesh. Her latent protection system had always felt like a minor annoyance. *How did we end up here? The last I remember I was in the courtyard.* Then it hit him. Suzume threatened to seal him. *She is Kazue's reincarnation.* His fingers steamed, and the ice in his grip collided with her fire. He did not let go despite the burning flesh of his palms. He tightened his grip. *She is Kazue.*

"You were not supposed to wake up," she said, staring at him wide eyed.

His memories were foggy. He felt as if he had been drifting about in a dream, but he thought he had dreamed of Kazue singing again. "Then you should not have sung the song of awakening," he replied. A wicked grin turned up the corners of his mouth. *Now I have Kazue's reincarnation in my grasp, what should I do?* The endless possibilities stretched out before him.

Suzume's eyes grew large as saucers and she whipped her head to the side. He followed her gaze.

"You tricked me!" Suzume shouted.

Akira—he had not seen her in a long time. Then without warning, she shifted forms and became her brother, Tsuki. "I wouldn't call it a trick." He leaned against the wall with his arms crossed. "It was meant to help, honestly."

Kaito's grip tightened on Suzume's wrists, and she gasped in pain. He did not notice, but her wrists were freezing beneath his touch, burning from the cold. Her skin heated in response. The air sizzled as ice met fire where their skin touched and steam poured forth from their connection, haloing them in clouds.

"I should have known you two were behind this," Kaito growled. His eyes flashed blue for only a moment.

He let go of Suzume's wrists and eased off of her. *If they are here, does that mean Satsuki is nearby?*

Suzume jumped up and skittered across the room, towards her staff, gripping her wrist.

"Don't try pegging this on us, Dragon. We did as we were told.

We helped the priestess get the staff and we woke you before the false priest put you in an endless slumber. Don't you think you should be thanking us? How could you not sense him the moment you got here?"

Kaito's gaze was dark and dangerous. Suzume glanced between Tsuki and Kaito. He felt the rise of the priestess' energy as she tried to harness her powers. He had let his guard down for only a moment; he spun around and knocked the staff from her hand once more. It clattered on the ground, sliding across the reed mats and colliding with the wall.

"Hey!" Suzume shouted.

"Don't even think about it." Kaito glared at her. He stood between her and the staff and left her with little choice. *How can she be Kazue? She would never have been so careless.* He found it difficult to believe, even with all the evidence to the contrary.

The priestess glared at him with hands on hips. Then she opened her mouth and started to sing. The notes had been forever etched into his memory, the song of binding. Kaito's eyes grew wide, and he took a menacing step towards her. *She cannot, she does not have the power.* She kept singing. The haunting melody wrapped around him, reminding him of painful memories. Kaito lunged for her and attempted to grab her by the waist. She dodged him by ducking beneath his outstretched arms. Her song faltered. His fingers snatched at the hem of her sleeves as she ran past him in Tsuki's direction.

Tsuki shifted into Akira, his masculine form melting into the feminine of his sister. Her lips were bright crimson against her pale skin. Akira stepped in front of Suzume, blocking Kaito.

Kaito roared. *I do not need a long drawn-out revenge. Just killing her will be enough.* The notes of the song died, and with it his temper cooled. If only slightly.

"Out of my way, Akira, this insolent priestess needs to learn a lesson." Kaito slashed the air with his hand.

His anger had unblocked his power and he had half transformed, his skin turning blue and scaly. His hair was long and spiny and pointed in a ridge. A pair of horns sprouted from his brow and his face had elongated and was near muzzle-like. The priestess was panting for breath, and not from running. He knew his untamed energy overwhelmed her. She leaned heavily against the wall, perspiration on her brow. *I will squash her like a bug.* The air temperature dropped as the priestess' labored breaths came out in vapor form. Suzume shivered as the gooseflesh rose on her arm.

"Enough," Akira's voice whipped across the pair of them. "You know who Suzume is, but you don't know the whole story."

She had no power to command him, but she had piqued his interest. He put a stopper on his powers, and the priestess gasped for air.

"Yes, I know," Kaito snarled, revealing pointed teeth in his near canine mouth. "You do not need to explain. I can see Kazue's spirit has returned to finish what she started—as I should have known." *I never should have trusted humans. Even letting my guard down for a second was a mistake.*

"Don't stand in my way, Akira," Suzume said. She jutted her chin, but he could see how her hands shook. "He's right, I need to kill him before he kills me." Suzume tried to push past Akira, but she threw her arms out to stop Suzume.

"No!" Akira's voice echoed off the walls and the two fell still.

"They're just as ignorant as they were five hundred years ago," Tsuki said, using Akira's mouth—or their mouth, more like.

Akira sighed. "Truer words have never been said, brother."

"Don't insult me, I am not in a good mood," Kaito warned. He pointed a clawed hand at her. His fingers had melded into three and they looked strange on his humanoid body.

"We say everything out of love, Dragon." Tsuki said—once again using his sister's form to speak.

Kaito snorted in disbelief, but a smile tugged at the corner of his canine mouth. The blue scales faded and his hair fell limp at his shoulders once more. His muzzle retreated and his teeth were white and straight again. When he had returned to normal, Akira motioned for them all to sit.

"We need to talk." She looked to Suzume with an expression that broached no argument.

Suzume grudgingly sat down, legs crossed. Kaito did the same, wondering what Akira hoped to gain by playing mediator.

"Good, I hope we can all act like adults," Akira said with a smile at each of them.

Suzume only glowered further at Kaito like a petulant child. Kaito kept his arms crossed, his anger rolling off him in waves. He had returned to human form, but he was nowhere near ready to make peace. Sparks of red energy pulsed around Suzume and his own energy danced along his skin in reply.

"So the priestess has realized herself and you ran back to your mistress?" Kaito said, eyes narrowed at Akira.

"Yes and no," Akira said without flinching beneath the open hostility he displayed. "Suzume knows who she is, but she has not realized her full potential. Kazue bid us guard her staff and so we did. We were not the ones who brought her back to this sacred place." She raised an eyebrow in Kaito's direction.

"Why did you bring me here?" Suzume demanded. "Did you know all along?"

He would not look at her and instead addressed Akira. "I brought her here because her power was raw and she needed to learn to control her powers before she unleashed some other horror." He smiled at Suzume then, revealing his pointed teeth. "If I had known she was Kazue, I would have killed her on the temple mount."

Suzume frowned and, like a fool, tried to hide her fear behind arrogance as she said, "Then why don't you now?"

"Don't tempt me," he snapped and pointed his finger at her. His temper had faded, leaving behind only confusion. She was Kazue's reincarnation, but he hesitated to kill her.

"Enough." Akira pinched her brow with thumb and forefinger. "I do not want to hear you argue any further. Suzume and Kazue do share a soul, but she is not the one who sealed you. Besides, I suspect Kazue did it with good reason."

"Are you saying I deserved to be locked in a damn prison for five centuries?" Kaito half stood, rising up on one knee. He bared his pointed teeth at Akira and the temperature of the room dropped by several degrees.

Akira held up her hand. "No, Dragon. I am saying Kazue did nothing without intent and purpose. There was a task that she meant to complete, though I do not know what."

Kaito scoffed. "Kazue was a fool. She feared my power would eclipse hers, so she sealed me."

"No," Suzume whispered.

Kaito swung his gaze towards Suzume, his eyes narrowed. "Do you remember something from your past life?'

"No. I don't know anything about Kazue. Not really." She paused and looked to Akira, who smiled encouragingly. She looked back to Kaito, who frowned at her. "I think she did it to protect her child," Suzume finished, looking Kaito in the eye. The fear was gone, but even though his head was telling him this was the woman he loved reborn, he could not believe it. *They are not the same.*

"That's ridiculous." Kaito stood up and paced to the other end of the room. He wanted space; he needed time to think. He did not want to think about their child or the woman who bore no resemblance to Kazue, but their fates were entwined nonetheless.

"What child?" Akira asked, her brows pulled together in thought.

"Kazue was pregnant with Kaito's child," Suzume explained.

Akira's eyes grew wide. *Akira did not know?* Akira looked to Kaito. "Is this true?"

He was facing away from them. "Yes," he whispered, his voice edged with danger. They danced along a topic that he would not explore. With any luck the child did not know their parentage, and he would rather keep it that way.

"Then where is the child?" Akira asked.

"How do you think I would know?" he snapped. "I was sealed before the child was ever born."

"Wouldn't it have died long ago?" Suzume interrupted.

Akira shook her head. "Not necessarily. It would have been a half dragon, it may not live forever, but it would have had a long life span. At five hundred years old, it would perhaps be middle-aged?"

"That means Kaito and Kazue's child is alive somewhere?" Suzume shook her head in wonder.

"Yes." Akira nodded. "Could this be Kazue's task, to reunite father and child?"

"Five hundred years later? Why seal him in the first place?" Suzume replied.

"It sounds like something she would do. If she feared for the child's well-being, she may have sealed the Dragon to keep him from harming the child until it was strong enough to fend for itself," Akira replied to Suzume's question. She cradled her chin in hand in thought.

"What say you, Dragon?" Tsuki asked. He had shifted to dominance while Kaito paced the room.

"I don't care about the child. They are no concern of mine." He looked at Suzume. *I cannot kill her. I should stay away from humans, return to the palace, and fix what has been broken.* Suzume squirmed uncomfortably, and he suddenly realized he had been staring at her.

"And what about me?" Suzume bristled. "Will you kill me now that you know the truth?"

He looked at her for a long moment, studying her. He did not want to admit to his own weakness, that the love he bore for Kazue kept him from following through on his threats. *I may not kill her, but I cannot start over with her reincarnation either. That door closed when Kazue betrayed me.*

"Should I?" he said, his tone was low. "Will you try to seal me as your predecessor did?"

She blushed but did not look away as she said, "I only said I would because I thought you were going to attack me."

"Hmm," he replied.

"Which you did! So I was in the right."

"What are you talking about?"

Tsuki interrupted, "You don't remember? You attacked the shrine?"

Kaito looked between Suzume and Tsuki, a wrinkle forming between his brows. "The last thing I remember was hearing you say you planned on sealing me and then..."

"Then what?" Suzume asked.

"Something came over me, a blind rage, I blacked out. So I attacked you?" His tone was light, as if he were asking about the weather. *Who is powerful enough to put me under a spell?* He stretched out his senses, searching for a trace. He had an idea, but he feared the truth. If the shifter was here, then they might all be in danger.

"How could you forget that—you almost died, I almost killed you!"

He laughed to keep the others at ease, but his probes came up empty. "I doubt it."

Tsuki rocked back and forth on his heels. "Well, aren't you a merry pair. Perhaps you can pick up where Kazue and Kaito left off."

"No!" they said in a rounding unison.

She met his gaze and they both laughed. It was the only thing to ease the tension. *Do not let her work her way into your heart.*

Tsuki clapped his hands together. "Well, now that the boring parts are concluded—"

Tsuki was cut off as the sliding door slammed open and hit the end of the track with a thunk. Rin stood in the doorway, looking disheveled and heaving with each breath.

"The temple is under attack again!" Her eyes slid over to Kaito. Her brows pulled together in confusion. "What are you doing here?"

Kaito tilted his head, looking at her, puzzled. "What are you talking about?"

"I just saw you outside attacking the shrine."

# 38

Suzume looked from Rin to Kaito and back again. "Can someone tell me what's going on here?"

It was Akira who stepped up to explain. "It would appear someone is impersonating Kaito."

"I wonder why," Akira murmured. She tapped her chin in thought.

"I don't know why, but I have a good idea of who it might be, and I'm going to teach that bastard a lesson," Kaito snarled. He brushed past Rin and out the door to the hallway beyond.

Following his exit, the shouts of the priests and the roar of the dragon could be heard from within the small room. Rin shrugged her shoulders and followed after Kaito.

Suzume shook her head. "Would it be too much to ask for a few moments' peace?"

Akira had shifted into Tsuki and he smirked at Suzume playfully. "What would be the fun in that?"

Suzume scowled at him.

"Get your staff, Priestess, I think we'll be in need of it."

*He's a little too excited. Can I trust them? What if they created this fake dragon?* Suzume ran to grab the staff anyway. She would feel safer with a weapon. She retrieved the staff from where it had been tossed on the ground by Kaito. Tsuki waited for her by the door, smirking all the while. *I really don't like that secret smile of his, it's like he knows something about me that he shouldn't.* Tsuki motioned for Suzume to exit first. She eyed him suspiciously before the pair of them ran down the covered walkways towards the sounds of shouts and the crash of falling ice. *I can't believe I'm running to danger.*

They passed a few screaming priests who were fleeing in the opposite direction. Suzume watched them go. *If I had any sense, I would be following them, not this trickster.* Tsuki kept stride with her, but when Suzume fell behind, he slowed to let her keep up, smiling over his shoulder at her.

"Don't dawdle; dragons will not wait."

Suzume snorted. "Don't I know it." *Kaito has left me in the dust more than a few times.*

A roar shuddered across the temple, shaking the buildings around them. *It's louder than last time. It's as if it's getting stronger.* Suzume tilted her head back, scanning the sky. She couldn't see anything other than gray clouds fat with rain. *If that dragon isn't Kaito, then who is it?*

The answers would have to wait. The dragon roared again and icy rain pelted the shrine. Through the stinging rain, Suzume saw her first glimpse of the dragon. It was coiled about a cloud like some massive serpent. The length of his body weaved in and out of the clouds. Suzume tilted her head back, watching as the dragon emerged from the clouds to open his maw and spew hail and daggers of ice from his open mouth. *He looks just like Kaito. I would be hard-pressed to tell them apart. No wonder even Rin was fooled.* The brunt of the dragon's attack was focused on the courtyard, which was further off. Suzume was safe for the time being.

Kaito had stopped at the edge of the courtyard. He was hidden from the impostor dragon by the boughs of a gingko tree. He watched the impostor dragon, his gaze hooded. Suzume could only guess at his thoughts. He had not transformed, which Suzume found passing strange. She approached him, her staff held in a tight grip.

"Shouldn't you do something about this?" She pointed towards the sky where the dragon was streaming through gray clouds.

"It's an illusion," Kaito replied.

Suzume scrunched her nose. "That is not an illusion. Can an illusion do this?" She pointed at the spikes of ice impaling the ground, the overturned ornamental bushes and crushed buildings.

"A powerful one can." Kaito walked away towards the courtyard.

*Either he's brave or an idiot. I'm still not sure.* Suzume jogged to keep up with him. "This new mysterious thing isn't working. Care to explain what's going on?"

"Someone wants to frame me, or give the priests a reason to never let me wake again."

"You have quite a few enemies, don't you?"

Kaito wheeled around to face Suzume. His eyes were ice blue and full of deadly intent. "You could say that."

Kaito was being as mercurial as ever. "Either way, that thing looks pretty real to me. What if it's another dragon?"

"That's impossible—I would know them."

"Are you saying that you know every dragon? There's been quite a bit of time since you were sealed. Maybe he's new in town, maybe it's your offspring."

"Don't you dare," he snarled at her.

She took a step back.

"It can't be a half dragon," Rin said.

Kaito elaborated, "Dragons are tied to locations: bodies of water, rivers and lakes, things like that. I should be able to sense where he's from, who he is. I cannot sense any of that; he's not a dragon."

Suzume hated to admit it, but she was kind of impressed. *What other abilities does he have that he's holding back?* "Well, if he's not a dragon and he's definitely *not* an illusion, what is it?"

He scowled at her. "That's what we need to find out, isn't it?" He smiled and Suzume's stomach did an uncomfortable flop.

*I'm only feeling like this because I know somehow my life is going to be endangered, not because he's charming when he smiles.*

Suzume rolled her eyes. His smile faltered and she saw a flash of hurt and anger there. *I need to be careful. Now that he knows I'm Kazue's reincarnation, everything is different. When he smiles at me, I wonder if he's smiling at Kazue or if it's me he's smiling at.* Suzume shook her head. *Now is not the time.*

The group of priests ran past Suzume and Kaito, and Suzume spotted the head priest's second but not the head priest himself. When he saw her, he was flushed and gasping for air.

"Suzume, I am glad to see you... the dragon... he's..." His eyes landed on Kaito and they grew wide with fear.

"You!"

"Me!" Kaito returned.

The priest looked to Suzume. "What is the meaning of this?"

"I was hoping you could explain that." Kaito smiled, baring his teeth.

The priest took a step back. "The head priest said you would not wake. How can you be here and up there?" The priest pointed to the sky overhead. The dragon dived towards the nearest building. Its massive body undulated as the roof of the building erupted into a thousand splinters of wood.

"Maybe we should focus on destroying the rampaging dragon, then talk," Tsuki said.

The priest stared at Suzume and she remembered the priest did not seem to be able to see Tsuki or Akira.

"You're probably right." Suzume sighed.

The priest gave Suzume a baffled look, raising one brow.

"I think we should focus on the problem at hand rather than

worry about Kaito for now," Suzume said, paraphrasing Tsuki's thought.

The priest bobbed his head in acknowledgment. "Of course, I will leave it to you, then." He scurried hastily past Suzume to join his companions.

Tsuki came close to Suzume and whispered in her ear, "He's right—you'll need to take care of this one too."

Suzume noticed Kaito watching Tsuki and her with a faint frown. She turned her back to Kaito. *Why does it always have to be me? When did it come down to me to defeat all the dragons?* She withheld her thoughts and said instead, "Do you have a plan to bring this one down? I used my only trick and I don't think he'll fall for it."

"Well, if he won't come to you, there's always the option of going to him." Tsuki nodded his head skyward. His eyes danced with mischief at his suggestion.

"What?" Suzume squawked.

Kaito glowered at Tsuki. "Are you suggesting what I think you are?"

"Suzume has the power to dissolve the illusion and the sooner it's taken care of, the sooner we can get to the bottom of this," Tsuki said.

"Do you know how difficult it would be to get her up there?" Kaito asked Tsuki.

"Are you implying I'm fat?" Suzume interjected.

"No, I'm just saying I may not be able to lift off with the additional weight, that is all," Kaito replied to Suzume with a smirk.

She tossed her head and looked away. "I don't need you, I defeated you on my own and I can do it again." *Of course, last time Rin had fought him for me and kept him distracted while I looked for the staff, but I am not going to admit that to him.*

Rin shook her head behind Kaito but otherwise did not refute Suzume's version of events.

"Can you now?" Kaito crossed his hands over his chest.

"Yes!" she replied hotly with her hands planted on her hips.

"Be my guest, then." He stepped aside and swept his arm towards the courtyard.

She scowled and gripped her staff tighter. She stomped away towards the center of the courtyard, where the dragon had been focusing its attack. Suzume took a few steps towards the crater carved out by daggers made of ice. She stood at the edge of the hole scored into the ground, regarding the fresh-turned earth frosted over with ice. She tilted her head back once more. *Why can I not keep my big mouth shut?* She swung the staff back and forth. *What am I doing? I could have at least asked Akira for a song or asked Tsuki for fighting tips first.* She slashed the staff down in an arc. *What am I supposed to do now? Last time the dragon came to me. Well, it was intent on killing me; now it seems more intent on destroying as much of the shrine as possible.*

Suzume looked back over her shoulder at the others. Rin watched her with concern, her auburn eyebrows pulled together. Tsuki smirked while leaning against the gingko tree. This was all just a game for him. Kaito had his arms crossed over his chest. When Suzume met his gaze, he waved his hand, signaling her to get a move on.

Suzume squared her shoulders and shouted, "Hey, dragon, if you're looking for a fight, come and get one."

The dragon emerged from behind a cloud, reared its head and roared. The very sound echoed through Suzume and sent icy shivers down her spine. She wanted to run, but the idea of being ridiculed kept her planted in place. *Damn my pride.*

The dragon dipped down. She could see the rows of fangs and the long whiskers drooping on either side of his face. *What if this is Kaito's child? Maybe it doesn't have a river or lake because it's only half dragon.* That thought left her feeling conflicted. The dragon dived and Suzume spun around just in time to avoid having an arm torn off.

"Hey, no fair. You can fly!" she shouted at the dragon's retreating form.

It rose in the sky and flew behind a cloud and out of sight. Suzume spun around, eyes trained on the sky, waiting for another attack. *Don't let your thoughts detract from your focus.* She felt a prickling sensation at the base of her neck. She spun and struck the dragon as it swooshed past her on the right. The hit felt strange, like she was hitting something soft, not like before.

The dragon flew out of range again and Kaito decided to shout encouragement. "Keep it busy, I think I know what's going on here."

"That's easier said than done, you know!" she called back.

Tsuki tipped his head and chased after Kaito, who was headed towards the destroyed shrine buildings. Rin remained watching but did not move to assist Suzume.

"Now would be a good time for some help," Suzume shouted at her.

Rin shrugged.

"Damn Kitsune," Suzume muttered under her breath.

The dragon had not waited while Suzume bantered, and she nearly lost her head. The dragon swooped over her, his icy claws grazing the top of her skull. She ducked down at the last moment. Her power shielded her. She felt the burning sensation along with the crackle and hiss of a barrier being erected around her. *Now you decide to show up,* she thought. The power flew out from within her, released from the dams within, and lashed out at the dragon like a whip. It slashed the dragon across its serpentine body. The dragon hissed and reeled back, using the clouds as cover once again.

*Maybe if I could get a clear shot, I might be able to knock the dragon from the sky. If he was on the ground, we would be more easily matched.* This, of course, was easier said than done. Suzume watched the writhing form of the dragon as it wriggled between clouds. It appeared at random, feinting a few times before dive-bombing her. It collided with her barrier, which shuddered but held. *I need to focus my energy like Akira taught me.* She visualized the dams channeling the energy through her body and into the staff.

*If I sing the song, I should be able to channel the energy through the staff... I think.*

Her shot came at last. The clouds parted and the dragon was headed straight for her. Suzume dropped the barrier, pointed the staff at the dragon, took aim, and sang the first few lines of the song. The power surged through her and burned through and out her fingertips. It entered the staff and shot out like a beam. It ripped through the air, melting the ice that rained down.

Steam filled the air and reduced her visibility, but she could see her energy hit its mark. Like a crimson blade, it hit the dragon between the eyes. The energy sliced through the dragon as it approached her and it disappeared into a burst of mist and steam. Suzume's energy spent, she fell hard onto her knees, feeling the sticky hot moisture as it drew sweat on her brow and rolled down onto her cheek. Steam hung around her like a thick cloud.

"The dragon was made of water," she mused.

"Just like I said, it was an illusion." Kaito strolled over to her. He was carrying a singed piece of paper with archaic writing on it. Akira sauntered behind him. It seemed with the battle over, Akira had replaced Tsuki.

*I don't even get a thanks for destroying the fake dragon. What a bunch of ingrates.*

"A charm, it was anchoring the spell that created the fake dragon," Akira explained, unaware of Suzume's thoughts.

Akira plucked the burnt paper from Kaito's hands. She held it in her palm and it burst into flames before floating away as ashes.

"Is that why it turned into water when I hit it?" Suzume asked. Curiosity had won out over hurt at being disregarded.

"It would appear so," Akira replied.

"Who did this?"

"Who do you think?" Akira asked.

Suzume's first thought was the stranger she had fought when she found the staff, but no one seemed to know about him but Suzume. Then it occurred to her.

"The head priest! He was chanting the entire time I was fighting Kaito the first time. I was with him when it attacked." *Plus, Tsuki and Akira keep warning me about him—who else could it be?*

"That's no priest, then." His eyes iced over.

Suzume was glad his wrath wasn't directed at her for once.

"Why did he do this? I thought he was one of your devoted worshipers?" Suzume said. "He even said he knew me from my past life."

"I told you before, he's not as he seems," Akira said cryptically.

"Then who is he?" Suzume asked. *Is it so hard to give a straight answer?*

"I don't know, but I am about to find out," Kaito said. His eyes were ice blue and he had half transformed—his skin was scaled and his hands were clawed.

Suzume tightened her grip on her staff. *I hope I'm not going to have to fight a dragon for a third time today, I'm not sure I have the energy left.*

## 39

K aito walked back towards the shrine buildings, his stride long and full of purpose. Suzume had never seen this level of intensity from him before, at least not without it being directed at her. *He really does not like being impersonated—duly noted.*

The shrine was in tatters. The dormitory roofs that housed the priests had caved in and shards of wood were left behind, looking like gaping mouths opening up to devour the sky. The gray clouds had not dissipated, leaving the air damp and clammy. A breeze rustled across the temple grounds and chilled Suzume. There was an ominous feeling to the temple; something wasn't right.

"You need to be careful," Akira murmured in Suzume's ear.

"You don't have to tell me twice," Suzume replied as they followed after Kaito. He led them back to the main temple where Suzume had met up with the priest earlier that day.

*How does he know where to go?* she wondered.

Rin kept pace with Kaito. She had not said much since the attack. Akira was glued to Suzume's side, which could either be a good or bad thing.

"Do you care to explain about the head priest now?" Suzume asked Akira.

Akira lifted a thin shoulder in a shrug. "We do not know much —only that the priest who was here before changed subtly. The others didn't seem to notice it, but he's not the man he was before."

"How can you tell if no one else can?" Suzume asked.

"It comes with the territory, I suppose you could say. When Kazue bound us together, our powers merged. We see things regular humans cannot."

"Like what?"

Akira regarded Suzume from the corner of her eye. Her ruby red lips pulled up at the corners and revealed her white teeth. "Like a person's energy. Everyone has a different signature. For example, yours is red like fire. Kazue's was similar, yours is more vibrant."

"Hmm." Suzume sniffed. She still wasn't comfortable with being compared to Kazue.

"What about Kaito?" Suzume nodded in the Dragon's direction.

Akira's dark eyes flickered forward to Kaito. He had stopped at the edge of the steps of a walkway and glanced up and down the hallway. The priests were scarce and it made sense. In the wake of the attack, they must have all fled. Kaito remained half transformed and he lifted his muzzle-like head towards the sky, sniffing. *He looks like a dog when he does that.* The thought made her smile, but seeing the destruction Kaito could wreak in his true form was enough to wipe the smile right off her face, even if it wasn't Kaito who had done most of it.

"Kaito is more blue-green, like the ocean," Akira whispered in Suzume's ear. Her breath hot against Suzume's skin.

Suzume had never been to the ocean, but she had heard stories as a child. There was a nursemaid that used to tell her all kinds of fantastic tales. It wasn't until she was much older that she found out that half the stories she told her were made up. *Not the ones about the Yokai, those were true. They're truer than I like to admit sometimes.*

"What about Rin?" Suzume asked. She had gotten an impression of her own spiritual energy and Kaito's before, but she had never really seen Rin's.

Akira glanced over at Rin and regarded her for a moment before saying, "Orange, like the leaves when they turn in the fall."

If Suzume wasn't inclined towards being prideful, she might have told Akira she was impressed. Instead Suzume hurried to keep up with Kaito, who seemed to have caught the scent of something or had found a trail. She still wasn't sure how he was tracking or if he was tracking. They could be following him in circles for all she knew.

The group ran down a hallway. The pillars that held the ceiling of the covered walkway had been broken and splintered. There were puddles of water everywhere. Someone had walked through and tracked the water leading into the main temple where Suzume had seen the priests praying earlier in the day. *Was that really this morning? I feel like it was ages ago.*

Kaito stood at the doorway, his clawed hands curled into fists. His hair was blue and spiny again, his skin scaled and shiny. He slammed a fist against the wood outside the door.

"What are you doing? Go in," Suzume said.

He snarled and turned a dragon-like face attached to a human body to look at her. "I can't, there's a barrier."

Rin watched Kaito with a furrowed brow, her red lips turned down at the corners.

"So whoever made the charm is inside there?" Suzume asked.

"Yeah, but he's hiding, the coward."

Suzume stared at the door. There didn't seem to be anything special about it. The open sliding doors revealed the temple within, an altar at the front of the room had incense burning. Smoke curled in ribbons and rose up to the ceiling in offering to the gods who presided here. *Maybe I awoke the god here, like at the roadside shrine.*

Akira came over and tried to put her hand through the doorway. Her hand pressed flat against an invisible wall. She looked over at Kaito and Rin. "You both tried to cross over?"

Rin nodded in response.

"Of course, I'm not a fool," Kaito snapped.

Akira took the brunt of his anger with good grace. She turned back to Suzume. "You should try."

"Me? Why?"

"Because I think whoever built this barrier is waiting for you within."

Suzume scowled at Akira. Suzume hadn't trusted Akira from the first moment they met. Akira seemed to know too much and reveal too little. Now Akira was trying to convince Suzume to go into the unknown to meet whoever had attempted to frame Kaito. *What game is she playing at?*

"I don't know if that's a good idea," Rin chimed in for the first time.

Akira fixed her with a cool stare. "Believe me, it is very necessary."

A shiver rushed down Suzume's spine. Rin, her auburn brows pulled together, made no further protest. Kaito scowled, his features were even more menacing half-transformed.

"What say you, Dragon?" Tsuki asked, using Akira's face.

"Let her try. It's better than sitting here doing nothing." He waved his hand to the doorway.

Suzume swallowed past a lump in her throat. "Why am I always getting chosen for these dangerous tasks?"

"Because you're meant to do them," Akira said.

Rin nodded her agreement. "She's right; you should go in there."

Suzume shook her head. *They've all lost their minds. Some*

*psychopath is in there waiting to probably kill me and they all want me to waltz right in.*

"I'm not going—" Before she could complete her sentence, Kaito hoisted her up by the armpits and dragged her to the doorway.

"In you go, Priestess." He heaved her through the doorway. She felt a slight resistance, like walking through a spiderweb. The barrier clung to her skin like a sticky residue. She tried to rub it off and it dissolved beneath her fingertips, evaporating into the air. When she looked up, she was standing in the doorway of the temple.

Everything was silent. It was darker within than she had thought originally. As she walked across the tatami mat, her footsteps echoed back at her. She looked over her shoulder once to where her friends stood, but they had disappeared along with the door. *Oh no, what did he do to me?*

Suzume tightened her grip on the staff and walked towards the altar, where the incense burned. Smoke drifted on the air, but she could not smell it. It was as if she was looking at it from outside a window.

"You found your way in quicker than I thought you would."

Suzume spun around. A man leaned against a pillar at the back of the room, his face shadowed and long black hair falling down to his shoulder.

"You!" The man who had attacked her outside the shrine.

"I'm glad you passed my tests." He pushed off from the pillar and sauntered over to Suzume. She held her staff up in a defensive pose, with the length of it crossing her body at an angle. It wouldn't do much against this opponent, but it made her feel better.

"Put your toy away; I didn't come here to fight, I just want to talk."

Suzume scowled at him. "Talk like we did earlier, when you

shot me with something?" she snapped. "That really hurt, by the way," she added as an afterthought.

He chuckled. It was a dark and husky sound. "No, I promise to play fair this time."

He stepped into a shaft of light that came from a window in the ceiling. Suzume could see his features clearly for the first time, sharp features, a narrow nose and wide mouth.

"Where's the head priest? Were you working together to make the fake dragon?" Suzume pointed her staff at the stranger.

He chuckled and shook his head, his dark eyes intent on Suzume. "He's here." He wiped a hand over his face and it transformed from a young man to the elderly head priest.

Suzume hid her surprise. "Then this was all a trick from the beginning?"

He shrugged and transformed his face back to that of a young man. "More or less. You have to admit it was amusing."

"Why did you do this?"

He strolled around Suzume in a circle, like a cat batting around a mouse for its own amusement.

"Do I need a reason?"

"I suppose you don't need one, *per se.*"

He laughed again. "Oh, I like you, Suzume." The way he said Suzume's name was like a caress and it made her skin crawl.

"What do you want with me? There has to be a reason you would only let me through." She spun in circles to keep her eyes on him as he walked around her.

He stopped and regarded her, his thumbs hooked into the waistband of his hakama. "I just wanted to have a chat, that's all. We got off on the wrong foot before."

She snorted. "Do you make a habit of understatements? I'm pretty sure the dragon you created was trying to decapitate me back there."

"No, only seriously maim you." He shrugged as if losing body parts were a day-to-day affair.

*This guy is nuts.* "How reassuring." Suzume rolled her eyes.

He moved closer to her. Before she could back away, his hand darted out and grabbed a few strands of Suzume's hair. She twisted away and slipped out of his grip. She turned around and tried to hit him with the staff, but he moved too quickly for her.

"Don't touch me!" she shouted.

He only laughed. He had melted into the shadows of the chamber. For a moment all she could see was his white face against the dark before he was gone completely. Suzume spun around, trying to figure out where the stranger was.

"Oh, Suzume, you have so much to learn. They will let you believe you are Kazue, but you are so much more than that. Only I see your true potential, see you for *who* you are."

She knew better than to be lulled by this psycho's words, but she could not keep from replying, "You told me that you knew me when we first arrived at the shrine, that you and Kazue knew one another in another life."

"We did." His voice sounded distant as if he were talking to her across miles and miles.

"What was she to you?"

He did not answer right away. When he did, he sounded closer, as if his lips were pressed against her ear. "An enemy, of sorts," he whispered. "A friend, as well."

"What does that make you to me, a friend or an enemy?" Suzume asked.

He reemerged from the dark and rushed her. Suzume threw up the staff in a lame defensive move. He wrenched it from her grip and with one hand pinned her back to his chest and slung the staff over her arms, trapping her against him. She could not move and she felt his lips brush against her ear. She brought her shoulders up to try to defend herself from his offending mouth.

"Oh, no, Suzume, you are not my enemy. You don't have to live Kazue's life. Your choices are your own—that's why I showed you the Dragon. You could do what Kazue could not do and kill the Dragon. You have the power."

"Who says I want to kill him?"

She couldn't see his smile, but she felt it. With his face pressed against hers, she felt the muscles tighten along his jaw. "I can see it in your soul, Suzume. You have the bloodlust. Do it and I will teach you about power you've never imagined."

He moved around to her front, so they were face to face, but she remained bound in his arms, her arms locked against her body. He leaned in to kiss her like he had done in the courtyard. His lips mesmerized her; his hands weren't holding her captive any longer but holding her close, their hearts beating together. *Could I kill Kaito? I'm not even sure anymore. I thought he would kill me, but now that he knows I am Kazue, everything is different.* The stranger's lips were about to brush hers when there was a roar and shudder. The stranger pulled back and Suzume regained her senses.

"It looks like our playtime is at an end." He bowed to her. "Until next time."

"Who are you?" Suzume called.

He smiled at her and said, "My friends call me Hisato."

He disappeared into the shadows once more, leaving Suzume alone.

The building shuddered and groaned as bits of wood fell down from the ceiling. Then with a rip and the crash of broken beams, the ceiling came loose, and Suzume saw Kaito had transformed and ripped the roof off the temple. *He did all that just to help me?*

"What have you been doing all this time, you useless priestess?" he roared.

Suzume's hackles rose. "You're the one who threw me in here!"

He roared something that sounded like a laugh. She shook her head. For once she couldn't bring herself to get mad at him. She laughed as well, not because it was particularly funny but because her life had taken so many strange turns as of late and it only seemed to be getting stranger.

## 40

"Who is Hisato?" That was the question no one seemed to have an answer for. They knew he was a shifter, but where he came from and how he got his powers was a mystery. The group sat in a circle, discussing the possibilities. Tsuki was in control of his and Akira's body.

The priests had started to trickle back into the temple after Kaito had torn the roof off the temple. The second in command had taken over control. No one knew where the head priest had gone, and Suzume wasn't going to tell them that some shifter had been masquerading as their head priest, for who knew how long. The priest organized the cleanup and rebuilding, and it was going to be a massive undertaking. The temple grounds were torn to bits from three dragon attacks—Suzume counted the one where Kaito tore off the roof of the temple as an attack. Many of the dormitories were in ruins and the walkways were near impassable in some places.

The priests seemed trained to hospitality because despite the state of the temple, they still served Rin, Kaito, and Suzume a meal. For whatever reason, the priests still could not see Tsuki. Tsuki ate Suzume's noodles noisily while Rin sat with her knees pulled up to her chest, scowling. *We can't stay here much longer,* Suzume thought. *We've destroyed enough of the shrine as it is. Where do we go from here?*

Kaito paced back and forth, anger written in the lines of his body. Suzume watched him. She hadn't said anything, but she thought she knew who Hisato was. The Kami had told her darkness had risen when Kazue sealed Kaito. *That has to be him.* She kept this knowledge to herself. She was already dancing along a thread with Kaito and she feared bringing it up now would only shatter their fragile peace. For whatever reason, he was not going to kill her and that would have to be enough for now.

Tsuki slurped up the last of his noodles then said, "Could Hisato be a fake name?"

"Why give me a fake name? I think he wanted me to know him," Suzume said. Along with her knowledge of his potential identity, she had withheld the majority of her conversation with Hisato. She hadn't decided what to do about his offer yet.

"So the question is: how do we find out who this Hisato is?" Tsuki said. He leaned back on his forearms and watched the group with a half-lidded gaze.

"There are plenty of people we could ask," Kaito said. He stopped pacing and considered Tsuki. "What about Yasuharu?"

"Dead," Tsuki replied with a shake of his head.

Kaito's brows shot up to his hairline. "Really?" He shook his head as if he couldn't believe it. "What about Bunmei?"

"Also dead."

"You're kidding? That guy was the size of a mountain, literally! He was some sort of massive stone creature." Kaito's shoulders had relaxed, but it was more of a slump of defeat. "What about Naoki, Gengo, and Chiyuu?"

"Presumed dead, dead, and headless." Tsuki ticked off on his fingers.

"Shouldn't he be dead if he's headless?" Suzume asked. She scrunched up her nose just thinking about it.

318

Tsuki grinned. "Not for a Yokai. Sometimes they just wander round without heads, crashing into things. Seeing as he's missing a head, though, he cannot give us much in the way of information."

*I cannot get my mind around this world, creatures living without a head?* She considered telling them what she had deduced about Hisato, but seeing the pain in Kaito's eyes held her tongue. *Everyone he knew is dead. Did Hisato kill them? Why does he want me to kill Kaito? If he could kill someone as large as a mountain, then why not Kaito?*

Kaito and Tsuki went down a growing list of names and Tsuki ticked off more deaths, to Kaito's continued horror. Kaito crouched down on the ground, his head resting in his hands. He did not stop listing names while Tsuki recounted numerous gruesome deaths, his descriptions getting more graphic with each new name. Suzume felt a sudden urge to be away. She needed fresh air, she decided. She stood up and slipped out of the room. Kaito and Tsuki were so engrossed in their conversation, neither of them noticed her leaving.

Outside, the night closed in. Suzume walked towards the decimated temple where she had talked with Hisato. In the dark, the beams and broken shards of wood look like a barren forest. *Would I be willing to join Hisato if it meant I would be free of all of this?* The thought kept popping up in her head. Kaito, Akira and Tsuki, even Rin all saw her as Kazue. *I'm not her. I'm Suzume.* Hisato said he *knew* her, the real Suzume; no one had said that to her before. No one knew the real her, she hid it deep down where no one could touch it, yet Hisato had spoken her thoughts. He was right; she did have a bloodlust, a boiling anger that sometimes threatened to swallow her whole. *How can he know me? Or am I Kazue? And he is just telling me what Kazue was like before me?* She growled and raked her hands through her hair.

Footsteps fell on the landing behind her. Suzume spun around, expecting another attack. She had left the staff behind and she felt naked without it. There was no light in this part of the temple but the stars above. The shadows were long and reaching Suzume. She squinted in the dark, looking for an attacker. Rin approached, materializing from the darkness and shadows Suzume had been cloaked in. Rin wrapped her arms around her torso, as if fighting off a chill. Now that the clouds had dissipated, however, it was humid. The heat and moisture stuck to the skin and sweat rolled down to the small of Suzume's back.

"What do you want?" Suzume said. She would rather be alone.

"You're not going to do it, are you?"

Suzume froze up. Did Rin suspect Suzume of allying with Hisato? Suzume wanted to learn more about him, like how he knew things about her that no one else knew.

"What are you talking about?" Suzume's voice was high and squeaky.

Rin sighed. She walked over and surveyed the dark temple grounds. She was close to Suzume but not close enough to be considered a threat. Rin spoke to the darkness. "You're not really going to try to seal Kaito away again, are you?" Rin looked at Suzume from the corner of her eyes.

Suzume turned away. Even though she wasn't looking at her directly, Suzume got the impression Rin could see right through her, as if she were transparent. "Not if he doesn't give me a reason to," Suzume said.

The wind rustled through the gingko trees and there was nothing said for a few moments.

Rin exhaled. "I'm glad, I was worried..."

The relief in her voice irked Suzume for some reason. Rin had insisted there was nothing between Kaito and her, but Suzume couldn't help but wonder. *What does it matter if there's something between them? Maybe if there was, he wouldn't look at me like I'm Kazue, his reincarnated lover.* No matter what she told herself, however, she felt a twinge of jealousy.

"What do you think about this Hisato guy?" Suzume asked Rin just for want of a change of subject.

Rin did not answer right away. She leaned on an intact pole that held up what was left of the covered walkway.

"I don't know, but he gives me a bad feeling. He's very powerful if he can create an illusion that realistic, plus he fooled us all. None of us sensed his presence. I wouldn't say this to Kaito, but I don't think even *he* could do that."

Suzume laughed and Rin smiled. They shared a brief moment of camaraderie before Suzume cleared her throat and said, "What does he want with me?" She knew, of course, but she wanted to see what Rin thought.

Rin turned to face Suzume and she had narrowed her green eyes at Suzume. "I'm not sure. Are you sure he didn't say anything more to you while you were inside the shrine?"

Suzume met Rin's gaze, not flinching lest she realize she was hiding information. "No, he just taunted me without giving me much information."

Rin stared for a moment more, her eyes searching Suzume's face, looking for the answers there. She flashed a smile again. "I guess Hisato is a bit like Kaito in that—maybe he's one of the first children."

Suzume laughed. "I don't know about that; why would a Yokai that powerful want to taunt me?"

"Maybe he's in love with you," Rin replied with a smirk.

Suzume's eyes grew wide and she shoved Rin hard, as if pushing her away would avoid the truth. "That's not funny, Kaito loved Kazue, not me."

Rin's smirk only grew wider. "I know. I meant maybe *Hisato* is in love with you."

Suzume's neck burned with embarrassment and she was glad it was dark out and Rin couldn't see. "I know, that's what I meant. They're both so similar I got mixed up for a moment."

Suzume had to get away from this topic and fast before this conversation went down a road she did not want to take.

"Uh-huh." Rin chuckled.

Suzume was in desperate need of a change of subject. "Where do we go from here? How do we find out more about Hisato?" *How can I find out more about him?*

"Well, as you may have noticed, there are not a lot of people left to ask." There was a hint of sadness in her voice. Rin had lost friends, just as Kaito had. "A lot of powerful Yokai have gone missing or have died since Kaito was sealed, and lower-level Yokai tend to keep to themselves. They wouldn't know much."

"Why is that? Where are they all going?"

"My guess is someone is killing them and trying to gather power."

"But why?"

"Why else do people look for power? To be in control."

Suzume frowned. It made sense, she supposed. Where did Kazue fit in with all of this, and Kaito? Hisato had to be the one killing the other Yokai. *I wonder what he's collecting power for.* Kaito had told Suzume once that he ruled over a region, and the priests seemed to pray to him in some capacity.

"Do you have leaders, among the Yokai, I mean?" Suzume asked.

"Not in the human sense. Six of the first children each ruled over the islands. At one time Kaito ruled here, on the largest island. But they don't do much now. Most of the remaining stay locked up in their palaces, never venturing out. The Eight original Kami used to rule in ancient times, but they've disappeared."

"Where did they go?"

"No one knows; maybe to sleep. They've lived for centuries, since the beginning of time, and they tend to view time differently than us."

*This is all incredibly boring and unhelpful. None of it tells me what Hisato wants. Do I dare trust him?*

"Hey, girls, come back in here. We found some rice wine!" Tsuki appeared down the hall, illuminated by the light spilling from the open door. He carried a jug of rice wine in his hand and his smile stretched from ear to ear.

"Please come and make him show some restraint," Akira said, using Tsuki's form. "It's been a long time since he's drank and I fear he will get out of hand."

Rin laughed. "We're coming."

By the time Rin and Suzume were back, Kaito and Tsuki were already pouring rice wine into small porcelain cups. Kaito and Tsuki clinked glasses and cheered. Kaito tossed back his rice wine in one gulp, and Suzume watched his throat work as he swallowed. His early anger had melted away, but there was a sadness there that she hadn't seen before. *I'd want to drown myself in drink if everyone I knew was dead, too.*

Kaito saw her staring, and instead of scowling or pretending to flirt, he gave her a smile, a rare genuine smile. His eyes crinkled at the corners and he gestured to her with the cup. Suzume took a seat beside him and accepted his silent peace offering; they were in a rare truce.

"Bottoms up, Priestess," Kaito said, before drinking another cup.

Suzume drank it down, the liquid fire burning its way down her throat. She was no stranger to drinking. She had more than a few late night rendezvous with sake involved. Somehow, this time she felt like she needed to hold back. The others were not as reserved with their drinking and soon they were singing rowdy songs with lyrics that made even Suzume want to blush.

At some point, Rin passed out. A cup fell from her hand and the liquid poured out, soaking the bamboo floor. Tsuki had gotten up, saying something about wanting to relieve himself. Suzume and Kaito were alone for the first time since they had found out she was Kazue's reincarnation.

Kaito took a swig of the sake and set the jug down with a

plunk. "How long did you know?" he said, his words sloshing together like the rice wine in the jug. Despite his drunken state, his eyes were focused and intent on Suzume. It was disarming.

"Know what?" Suzume asked. She twirled her cup in her hands, avoiding his gaze.

"That you were Kazue."

She shot her head up, preparing to defend herself. Instead she saw him looking at her with a strange expression. He leaned forward. Crouched on all fours, he crawled over to her, wobbling slightly as he did so. Suzume scooted back against a wall to try to avoid him, but he came over and hovered over her, his arms placed on either side of her legs. They weren't touching, but she could feel that crackle of their powers colliding. She could smell the drink on his breath and she turned her face away from him.

"Your breath stinks. And I'm not Kazue, we just share a soul."

Kaito reached out and tried to touch Suzume's face. "You look like her, especially when I've been drinking."

She slapped his hand away, and sparks erupted where their hands contacted in blue and red. "As flattering as that is, I'd rather you didn't touch me."

He laughed; it was intimidating and thrilling at the same time.

"What's so funny?"

He leaned in close and Suzume felt the sizzle of commingling power, the heat that their combined energy seemed to create.

"You're funny, Suzume." He so rarely said her given name that it was always a shock to hear him say it. She spun her head sideways to look at him and found his lips very close to hers. Even though he was drunk, even though she knew it was a stupid idea, she thought about kissing him. Just to see what his lips would taste like, and to see if the sparks would erupt between them when their flesh met for real.

She closed her eyes and leaned in, intent on trying. *He won't remember; he's too drunk.* Kaito moved closer as well. She could feel his energy wrapping around her. The combat had ended and

324

instead their powers were melding together, swirling and becoming something different entirely.

The sliding door crashed open and Tsuki called out a drunken slur. Suzume wrenched her head back just in time to crack it against the wall. She rubbed her sore spot, staring at Kaito, who looked at her with a strange expression.

She looked away. "Your breath really stinks."

"You were going to kiss me and we both know it," he said in a husky whisper in her ear. He chuckled and sat back on his haunches.

Suzume's face burned with embarrassment. *I'm an idiot. I am not going to be like Kazue, no matter what they tell me.*

# 41

Suzume, hands on her hips, glowered at the young priest bowing in front of her. His bald head gleamed in the afternoon sun. His hands trembled. The man dared not speak. He had delivered the remaining temple elder's decree and silence had fallen afterward. Five minutes had passed since. Kaito stood at Suzume's shoulder. She could feel his smirk and she knew Akira was smiling with her red lips pulled back to reveal straight white teeth. Only Rin seemed to understand the implications of their eviction, because that was what it was; the priests wanted them off the temple grounds, the sooner the better.

"Where are we supposed to go?" Suzume said at last. "Do you think the creature that destroyed over half of your temple won't come back for more?" Of course, Suzume could not be certain they would stay away if she and her companions remained either. It appeared they had drawn Hisato here and he was not done with Suzume, not by a long shot.

She straightened her shoulders to look more imposing. If she looked confident, maybe inspiration would strike because she had not the slightest idea where to go next. The truth was, none of them knew where or what to do next. The trail, so to speak, had run cold. They needed answers, but as they had all concluded the night before, there was no one to turn to. Kazue had taken her secrets to her grave, it seemed.

"We are unable to host you any longer," the young acolyte said and his voice cracked. He did not invoke a lot of respect, and Suzume suspected he must have been at the bottom of the pecking order to be stuck with telling the dangerous visitors to skedaddle. He reminded her of one of her younger brothers. He had a round dumpling face with rosy cheeks and thick lips. There was not even a hint of stubble on his face. Suzume's fiery gaze slid over to him. The boy checked himself for a moment and visibly swallowed a lump in his throat. He had made a mistake in incurring her wrath.

Suzume had been in a foul mood since the night before. Kaito's fumbled attempt at a kiss had left her with a burning sensation. She felt on edge, and the slightest movement had her jumping out of her skin. *Kaito is playing games with me because he wants to disarm me,* she thought. She frowned and the boy mistook her lack of response for an invitation to continue speaking.

"You and your—" the boy fumbled with the right words "—friends, have brought evil to this place. Whatever possessed the head priest killed him. It left nothing behind, how will he reach the next life now if his soul has been destroyed by a Yokai?"

Kaito snorted.

The boy's eyes flickered in his direction and he licked his presumably dry lips. "You have to go," he said more firmly.

She had to give him credit—it took a lot of guts to stand up to a dragon, but maybe this boy was more ignorant than anything, it was hard to tell.

"We will leave, then, but do not seek us if disaster returns to this place." She turned on her heel, huffing with discontent.

Akira glided alongside Suzume, smiling to herself, as Suzume knew she would be.

"What is amusing about this situation?" Suzume snapped.

"You, Priestess; I think those priests are more afraid of you than they are of the Dragon." Akira laughed her throaty laugh.

"Well, they should be; I am the emperor's daughter." It felt strange to say that aloud. It seemed a lifetime ago she had been wandering the palace with nothing better to do than flirt and gossip.

"That's not why they fear you."

Suzume glared at the other woman from the corner of her eye. "Then why else would they be afraid?"

"Maybe they have heard the rumors about your past life."

Suzume stopped in her tracks. Rin and Kaito had been trailing a few steps behind Suzume and Akira, and Kaito nearly ran into the back of Suzume when she stopped unexpectedly. He caught Suzume around the waist, and for a moment, he held her close. She felt the beating of his heart against her back before the spark of her power fought him off. It was subdued for once, and instead of the electric feeling, it was more like glowing warmth wrapping itself around the two of them. She hated to admit it, but his arms holding her felt nice. She could not remember the last time she had been in a man's arms. A real man, not a hallucination or a dragon. *A normal life would be wonderful. I would give up my eternal soul for one regular lifetime, since it seems I've never had that luxury before.*

The others were looking at her. Rin quirked an eyebrow and Akira was smiling smugly. Suzume pushed away from Kaito and twirled to face him.

"Don't touch me!" she snarled.

He smirked in his infuriating way. "I wouldn't if you really didn't want me to."

Suzume stumbled over her retort. Could he read her thoughts? Then it hit her. It wasn't her thoughts he was reading but the change in her powers. When she didn't find him a threat but welcomed him, their powers melded together. His smile was borderline crude. He was obviously drawing the wrong conclusions about her welcoming his touch. Her cheeks were awash with heat. She turned away and shouted, "As if I would want my past life's leavings."

Kaito watched Suzume slip off by herself. He had been intent on following her when Rin touched him lightly on the shoulder.

"What are you doing?" she asked.

"I don't know what you're talking about."

Akira had drifted away and was pretending the wreckage was of interest.

"Playing with Suzume's emotions. I know you haven't forgiven Kazue for what she did."

He scoffed but could not meet her gaze. How had he not realized how intuitive Rin was before? For him, it had been a short time since they'd parted ways, his onetime messenger had left him for the love of a Hanyou, a half Yokai. Though they had been lovers, he had never considered her as anything more than a temporary amusement. But time had matured her, and she understood more now than perhaps even he did. He was at war within himself, simultaneously looking for Kazue in Suzume and trying to disprove the connection. He didn't want to hate the priestess, she amused him with her antics, but if she was her reincarnation, then he had to have his revenge. From the start, he had planned on winning Kazue's incarnation's trust and destroying her. This constant battle would not end until he got his revenge.

"Don't worry yourself with what I have planned," he said and hurried to catch up with the priestess.

He followed her to her chamber. Still naïve, she did not feel her eyes on him. He watched her pass through a clumsily made barrier that Akira had helped her construct. It would hardly even keep out flies and it still glimmered in the light. *Amateur. Kazue could have done better, even untrained.* He slipped through the barrier, it felt like a warm bath, but her spiritual energy was prevalent in the design, that spark of defiance that seemed to make up her being.

Suzume knelt on the ground near her futon. She held the staff crossways over her lap, her finger tracing the markings on the staff. Just seeing Suzume holding it recalled painful memories. He stamped those down; he did not need the priestess to see that weakness in him lest she exploit it.

"I wish you could tell me what I am supposed to do." Suzume sighed.

"You could ask her yourself," he said.

Suzume jumped up into a defensive position. She bent her knees and crossed the staff in front of her. She looked comfortable, as if she was born to fight. *That is Kazue.* Kaito leaned against the back wall of her chamber. She had not even heard him come in, had not even sensed him. *All this power and yet no sense. That's not like Kazue at all.* She did not lower her defenses for a moment. *Just like Kazue.* She had not trusted him at first either.

"What are you doing here?" She pointed the staff at him.

"I thought you would need some help packing." He laughed. He knew as well as she did that she had little more than the clothes on her back and the staff in her hand. "You don't look like you slept very well last night." He pushed off the wall and walked over to her tangled futon. He kicked aside the blankets then smirked at her with a cocked eyebrow. "Were you up all night thinking about me?" Pretending to be drunk had worked to his advantage. If only she had kissed him, things might have progressed farther by now.

Suzume made a retching sound. "You're much too full of yourself. What are you doing here, really?"

He shrugged. "Would you believe me if I said I'm concerned for your welfare?" He stepped very close to her. He could feel her energy, the spiritual power that was so uniquely Suzume. Wild and impulsive. It churned about her like an angry storm, and his own power rose to meet it, seeking a challenge. *Kazue was different; she melded with me, our powers in harmony. Like they were last night with Suzume.*

The constant back and forth in his mind was giving him a headache. He had never been this indecisive before. *Ever since we left that roadside shrine, I feel like there's something missing.* He reached out to touch her face, hesitating for a moment. *She cannot be Kazue, not really.* He brushed back a stray hair that had fallen over her eyes. Red sparks followed his fingers up her cheek.

Their powers warred, hot and cold, fighting for dominance, each reaching out and repelled by the other. *Different from Kazue, but not unpleasant. Hisato said you are not her, yet everything tells me you are.* He searched her face, looking for a hint, a sign. Suzume's eyes darted across his face, like a cornered animal.

He shook his head. "I know you think you're her, but I find it difficult to believe. You look nothing like her, for one thing, your eyes especially. They're too different." He wasn't sure who he was trying to convince more, her or himself.

"Well, according to Akira, I'm the genuine article."

"What should I do with you, then?" He pitched his voice low.

She leaned in towards him, enchanted by him. She shook her head suddenly and backed away, keeping the staff between them. "Nothing, I don't belong to you because I share a soul with Kazue."

He grinned at her, an interesting concept. "I wish it was that simple."

She stared at him for another moment, trying to decipher his cryptic words most likely. He smirked, easing the tension. He wasn't ready to make a decision where Suzume was concerned; he needed more time. His initial rage had ebbed, and his confusion only complicated matters.

"Where do we go now? You've been the one with an agenda this whole time," she asked.

Glad for a change of subject, he shrugged. "I'm not sure. I don't know much about Hisato, other than he's the shifter everyone has been talking about, and there isn't much we can find out about him beyond that."

"Is there any way we can find Kazue's descendants? Maybe she left instructions somewhere?"

"You mean my child?" he asked. She had an uncanny ability to anger him. *Just when I was considering sparing you.* The room froze over, the breath escaping Suzume's mouth came out in clouds, and frost crept across the walls.

"I take it you don't want a reunion with your long-lost offspring?"

"No," he growled.

The tension was palpable. She knew she had made a mistake in bringing up his child, but made no move to apologize. It was her stubbornness that normally drew him to her. But in this case, he would rather not be reminded of the embodiment of Kazue's betrayal.

"What about the staff? Do you think this might hold some kind of key to unlocking Kazue's task? She did leave it to be guarded by Akira and Tsuki."

"True, perhaps we should ask Akira about it."

"Ask me about what?" Akira said as she glided into the room, Rin following close behind.

"Please come in, I don't mind," Suzume said, her tone dripping with sarcasm.

"Thanks," Rin chirped as she took a seat on Suzume's rumpled futon.

"This staff," Kaito said, answering Akira's question. "Why did Kazue ask you to guard it?"

Akira shrugged her shoulders. "I could not say. Kazue did not deign to explain why when she chained me and my brother to it."

"Then you're bound to the staff, not the temple?" Suzume asked.

"We are the guardians. Until her task is complete, we must remain with the staff or who wields it." Akira smiled at Suzume.

Kaito did not trust them, but he trusted few people. There was more to their story that they were not sharing.

"There's markings here; I don't recognize them, do they mean anything to you?" Suzume asked.

Akira slid closer and examined the markings. "It's written in an archaic language which hasn't been used in centuries," Akira said after a few moments of examination.

"Great, what does it mean?" Suzume asked.

Akira shrugged. "I don't know. I can't read it."

"What?" Suzume shouted.

Akira held up her hand to halt Suzume's tirade. "But I can find someone who can. There's a man who lives up in the hills beyond the temple. He used to be a priest here, but he left the priesthood some years back."

"Are you sure he's still alive?" Tsuki asked his sister.

"How long ago was it?" Kaito asked.

"Maybe one hundred years? I lost track of time, this place can be deadly boring," Akira replied. She fanned out her hand, examining her nails.

"Wonderful. So we may or may not have instructions from Kazue herself written on the staff, but there's no way of knowing without finding this man who is most likely dead," Suzume summarized.

"Exactly," Tsuki said. Akira had shifted into Tsuki as Suzume was summarizing their predicament. Tsuki grinned from ear to ear.

Suzume threw up her hands.

*Ah, then that is their motive. There's something in the mountains they want. Fair enough, I'll play along for now,* Kaito thought.

"I think we should try. What could it hurt?" Kaito said to the group at large.

Suzume glared at him.

If anything, this quest for the missing priest might give him a chance to lure Hisato out of hiding. He wanted Suzume, and if he played his cards right, he might just figure out why.

# 42

According to Akira, the old man lived in the mountains behind the temple—that is, if he was still among the living. Either way, they had to get out. And chasing after this alleged expert was a good enough reason for now.

The priests followed the party off the temple grounds. Much to Suzume's dismay, they did not exit out the main gates with the red arches but out a small back gate like a group of lurking thieves. *This is humiliating. We saved their temple from complete destruction; it was only partially destroyed. No one has any gratitude these days.*

The rear gate, despite Suzume's fear, was not a crack in a wall. There was a small red arch with charms dangling from it and twirling in a slight breeze. Suzume tilted her head back, trying to read the black markings on the white paper, but she could not get a clear look at them. *What are they trying to keep out?*

Akira was the first to step through the arches, and when nothing cataclysmic happened, the others followed. A short stone walkway ended at the edge of the forest and beyond that was a twisting narrow forest path. It divided at random and ended without warning. It appeared to have been created by some forest animal. A wider path switched back and forth up the hill and disappeared into the forest.

Suzume looked up at the hillside. It loomed green and massive before her.

"How far exactly do we need to go to confirm this former priest is dead?" Suzume asked the group at large.

Kaito, a few feet behind Akira, grinned. *I bet he would not mind if we never found this priest; it's all about the journey for him.* He always seemed to enjoy the prospect of an adventure. Rin walked between Suzume and Kaito. She too looked to Akira for an answer, with a hint of skepticism. Akira was the leader for this hapless venture, it seemed.

Akira lifted a shoulder. "Until we find him," she said and proceeded to pick her way through the trail. She walked with confidence through the maze of animal trails, even though she had been trapped inside the temple for a very long time.

Suzume huffed. *Maybe if I lingered behind, I could find a reason to make the priests keep me. I am Kazue's reincarnation and this is her temple.* She looked longingly back at the temple to the line of priests who were blocking any attempt at return. Though she could not see it, she could sense a barrier being erected around the temple. There was a tingling in the air, and the wind didn't blow through the trees on the grounds of the temples the way it was through the trees outside of it. The four or so priests standing by the gate were chanting together. *No going back there, I suppose.* She heaved a sigh and continued after her companions.

The climb was long, hard, and endless. Her companions all were possessed of superior strength and stamina, and Suzume found herself falling behind more and more. Rin hung back, waiting for Suzume to catch up more than once, and at last Suzume snapped at her.

"Hurry up, or the others are going to get away without us," she said, picking up her pace though her limbs screamed in protest.

"You're not strong enough to keep up with them," Rin said matter-of-factly.

It was true. But it pricked at Suzume's pride, and when her pride was pricked, she struck back. "I don't need help from you. I know you're only doing this because you feel guilty about Kaito knowing I am Kazue. Or you're jealous and you feel guilty for that because you love him."

A complicated mix of emotions crossed Rin's expression. Suzume hadn't really meant to hurt the Kitsune. She had just lashed out without thinking, like she usually did. She did not really think Rin loved Kaito, not romantically, but Rin had taken the words to heart, it seemed.

"You know what? You're probably better off on your own." Rin turned, flicked her tail, and bounded up the trail, leaving Suzume in her dust.

Suzume swore and kicked a nearby rock. It slid down the hill and rattled the undergrowth as it rolled away. Suzume plopped down on the side of the road. *Forget them. Forget the probably dead guy, and forget Kazue and her task. I'm not going another step.*

She folded her hands over her chest and exhaled. Then she waited. It was shady under the tree and light filtered through the leaves, creating a mosaic of shadows on the ground. The wind whistled by, rustling the branches. Suzume looked around. From her vantage point on the hill she could see the temple. It was not as far away as she would have hoped for how much effort she put into climbing this hill.

The temple buildings spread out across the compound in neat rows. Well, they had been. She could see the full picture of the destruction Hisato had wrought. The splinters of wood scattered about contrasted against the remains of the formerly orderly gardens. Beams and support frames stood out against the blue sky like sentinels over the destruction. Priests moved about, carrying away rubble and sifting through debris. There were scars in the earth from where Rin and Kaito had battled. The main shrine was nothing but broken wood from when Kaito had removed the roof. *We really did a number on that shrine. No wonder they chased us out.*

Suzume turned away and surveyed the forest instead. She did not like the feeling of guilt that she associated with looking at the shrine. The forest was dense and massive. It stretched out in each direction further than she could see. It was like being in the center of a sea of trees. Off in the distance, she saw a flock of birds take flight just as the trees themselves began to convulse and bend over.

The trees parted, divided in half by what she could only assume was a huge creature. Whatever was breaking the trees was headed up the hill in her direction. She stood up and reached for her staff, which she had strapped across her back. According to Tsuki, having it strapped to her back would make it easier to draw when necessary. It also kept the staff from encumbering her walking.

She held onto the handle without drawing it. *Maybe it's nothing. Maybe it's the wind in the trees?* The crack and snap of trees breaking echoed over the treetops towards her, followed by a deep guttural roar. The ground beneath her feet trembled beneath the force of its footsteps. *Now is a good time to run.* Which way should she go? It would be faster and easier to go downhill, in the opposite direction, but that put them on even ground. With her luck, it was after her, and if she was going downhill, it would make her easier to catch. Her other option was uphill, which would be slower but might put some distance between her and whatever was breaking the trees.

She pondered for another moment until a group of deer burst through the underbrush, leaping and attempting to flee whatever was drawing closer. Suzume left her staff strapped to her back and ran uphill away from the creature that was tearing through the forest in her direction. Her limbs were tight and angry, her breathing labored. She forced herself to stick with the stream of deer and followed the paths they did, swinging around trees and stumbling through the undergrowth. They were much more agile and less prone to catching their clothes on low-hanging branches and they quickly outraced her. Suzume's energy flagged and she slowed down.

The creature was almost upon her. The vibrations of its stomping footsteps reverberated through her entire body. She would have to stop and fight or hope it did not blow her over. She considered climbing a tree, but hearing the sickening crunch of trees being destroyed behind her, Suzume decided against that idea.

She ran ahead as fast as she could. Up the slope was a fallen gingko tree. The tree had fallen lengthwise on the slope and gotten wedged on a boulder. Dirt had slid down the hill and gathered behind the log, making a natural platform. It was her best chance at gaining an upper hand—literally—against whatever was coming her way. There, at least, she could see her attacker and make an assessment as to her danger—with her luck it was almost absolute. She whipped her staff out from the strap on her back and put herself into a defensive position, feet spread apart and staff crossed in front of her.

The Oni burst through the trees just as Suzume prepared herself to stand and fight. It was massive, over twelve feet tall, with bright blue skin. Gray horns jutted out from his protruding brow and large fangs stuck out from beneath his bulbous lips. He smiled when he saw Suzume standing there and revealed several more sharp teeth.

"Priestess," he bellowed, "you should not have come to my forest. I smelled you the moment you left the temple. Now I will devour you!" He laughed as he slapped his enormous blue gut, which hung over the edge of his ragged loincloth.

His squat muscled legs were as big around as tree trunks. He held a battered and filthy giant club covered in what appeared to be dried blood.

*Now would be a good time for Kaito or someone to come and intervene.*

"I have no intention of being your meal. I would never let someone so ugly and stupid eat me," Suzume taunted. It wasn't her best idea, but she didn't have a lot of options at this point.

His beady eyes glowed red as he rushed towards Suzume. She twirled her staff and sang the incantation Akira had taught her to make a barrier. A shimmering barrier flew up to deflect the blow of the Oni's club just as he swung it in an arc towards Suzume's head. The club struck the barrier and red sparks flew where they collided. The Oni took a lurching step back. He had not been expecting a barrier, it seemed.

Suzume used his momentary confusion to her advantage and lunged forward with the staff. She jabbed at his gut with the end of it and focused her energy, channeling it through it as Akira had taught her. A red streak of light erupted from the tip and the Oni fell backwards onto his back before rolling down the hill a few feet.

Suzume panted. Unused to utilizing her powers, even the small burst of energy drained her. She wanted to run away, but the Oni was back on its feet, roaring with anger. It charged again towards Suzume when she felt the barrier flicker and die. She turned and ran up the hill. She weaved in and out of trees, but it did nothing to dissuade the Oni. It plowed through everything without stopping.

*I have to do something.*

Up ahead, there was a low-hanging branch. She grabbed onto it and with some difficulty climbed up into the tree. The Oni lumbered towards her. She held onto her staff with sweaty hands, debating her plan. The Oni grabbed a hold of the tree she was in and shook it. Leaves fell onto his head and Suzume wrapped her arms around the branch to keep from falling. *There's nowhere else to go.* With a blind leap of faith, she jumped down and onto the Oni's shoulders. She clung to his thick neck by swinging the staff across it and holding on to each end of her staff. She pressed her face against his rough back. It was like cuddling with a giant rock. Her powers were so depleted she felt nothing but a faint tickle as her natural defenses tried to protect her from close contact with the Oni.

The Oni swung his club wildly and shook back and forth, trying to get her off his back. *Now what?* All she could do now was pray she came up with a better plan before he tried to squish her against a tree. Her legs scrambled up his back, looking for purchase. But she couldn't find a toehold. Her fingers were going numb from holding on. *This is not how I imagined I would die.*

Then the Oni swung hard right with his club, seemingly having forgotten about Suzume, who was riding piggyback.

"Suzume, let go!" Tsuki shouted up to her. He ran back in forth in front of the Oni, trying to draw his attention.

"Are you crazy? He'll smash me to bits," she called back to him.

"Throw the staff to me; I can defeat him with it."

She hesitated. Not only was the staff the only thing keeping her on the Oni's back, she hated the idea of giving up the staff to anybody, even Tsuki. *He is the staff's guardian, though.* Then again, if it was down to her and the staff, she supposed she chose herself. Suzume used her flagging energy to climb up higher on the Oni's back and grabbed a fat fold in the Oni's neck. She let go of one side of the staff and tossed it as hard as she could. It fell to the ground a few feet from the Oni, between it and Tsuki. Tsuki scuttled forward to retrieve the staff. The Oni swung its club, and Tsuki rolled out of the way, the edge of the club just grazing the top of his head.

Suzume let go and slid down the back of the Oni like some grotesque slide. Her skin was raw and chafed from where the Oni's rough skin had brushed against her and her powers had feebly tried to protect her. She ran away from the thundering Oni, who twisted back and forth, trying to choose a target for his rage.

Tsuki jumped and hit the Oni in the head, drawing its attention at last to him. Tsuki held the staff horizontally in front of him. The Oni swung his club and brought it down hard on the staff. Tsuki deflected the Oni's attack with a forward thrust and pushed it back. They traded blows, Tsuki landing quite a few on the belly of the Oni, which had little effect.

The Oni caught Tsuki unaware as he tried to lunge for the Oni's shoulder, and knocked Tsuki onto his back. Tsuki jumped back up and narrowly avoided having his skull crushed by the Oni's club. After a while the Oni slowed down. His labored breathing was loud enough to shake the trees around him. Tsuki took his opportunity to attack the Oni's head as he leaned down in an ineffectual attempt to swipe at Tsuki. Tsuki struck the Oni in the eye with the end of the staff. The staff sank in deep and gore spilled out, soaking Tsuki in gray blood.

Suzume swallowed back the bile that rose into her mouth as the Oni stumbled backwards and collapsed on the ground, unmoving. Tsuki stood over the dead Oni with a grin plastered across his face, covered in gore, and a bit of something that looked suspiciously like brain matter clung to his long black hair.

"Why are you always such a slob?" Akira asked, using Tsuki's form. Hearing her voice coming from Tsuki's mouth was disturbing in itself, but seeing him covered as he was, Suzume had to turn away to hide her disgust. *They make killing look so easy.*

Just then Rin and Kaito arrived on the scene. They both surveyed the dead body and Tsuki's bloody person with relative calm.

"What happened here?" Kaito asked. His tone was difficult to read, and Suzume was not sure if he was upset, excited, or indifferent.

"This thing was trying to eat me, you know, the usual." She pointed to the dead body with a shrug of her shoulders. She hoped no one noticed her shaking hands. This was probably her closest brush with death yet.

"That's what happens when you fall behind," Kaito said in dismissal and he turned to head back up the hill.

"Thanks for the concern!" Suzume shouted after his retreating back.

"Anytime!" he replied.

*He always has to have the last word, doesn't he?*

# 43

They wandered around the forest until dusk fell. At which point, Suzume gave up the pretense and demanded they rest. Who knew what lurked about in the forest, waiting to come and try to devour her. Then again, she had been almost eaten so many times it was hard to get excited about it anymore. They set up camp, which wasn't much more than a fire pit and a few sleeping mats rolled out. Not for the first time, Suzume wondered why the immortals even pretended to rest. Surely they did not need sleep.

Suzume plopped down on her sleeping mat. She was considering rolling up in a blanket and forgetting the world when Tsuki came and sat down beside her.

"You did good today," he said with his characteristic grin.

Suzume scowled at him. "At what point did I do good? When I was clinging for dear life from the monster's back or the part when you had to sweep in and save me?"

Though she knew she did not have the skills to fend for herself, she was tired of playing the weak and helpless damsel in distress. *Whoa, that's a new concept. Before this nightmare started, I would have loved to play damsel in distress. Men like feeling as if they saved the day. Of course, I never knew what real danger was waiting beyond the palace walls. It's eat or be eaten out here, literally.*

"You have the raw talent. You just need to tap into your potential as a fighter," Tsuki said, and the surprising thing was he sounded sincere.

She snorted. "I have raw talent because I am Kazue's reincarnation, right? Everything flows from her." She could not hide the bitterness in her tone.

Tsuki shook his head and his long black hair swung from side to side. "No, that's not what I meant. You have fire in you. I can see Kazue in you, but I also see something different. It's a spark that sets you apart from her."

She narrowed her eyes and regarded him. It was no secret she despised the fact that everything about her life seemed to be predestined by her past life. Which begged the question: was Tsuki just trying to get on her good side? And why?

"What do you want?" she asked bluntly.

He had the good sense to pretend to be offended. He pressed a hand to his chest and opened his mouth in feigned shock. "Can't I pay you a compliment?"

"No."

He laughed. It was an almost sensual sound, dark and husky. That was one thing he had in common with his sister, oozing sex appeal. Though Tsuki seemed to lean more toward playful, Suzume could not shake the feeling that the entangled siblings had an alternate agenda.

"You caught me." He turned to look at her. His eyes were hooded and his lips parted slightly.

Suzume cocked her head back and gave him a look. "What's with the bedroom eyes?"

He leaned forward. "Maybe I'm paying you a compliment so I can get closer to you. It's been five hundred years since I've been near a woman I don't share a body with."

Suzume leaned back on her hands to put distance between

345

them. "Can someone explain why all of you immortals seem to have no personal boundaries?"

Before he had a chance to answer, Kaito stomped over and plucked Tsuki off of her sleeping mat and tossed him aside like a rag doll. Tsuki hit the ground, rolled, and then jumped back to his feet, smiling. He threw his arms out with a flourish.

"Did I hit a tender spot, Dragon?" Tsuki asked. He had his hands on his hips, but his body looked tense and ready for action. Kaito stood in front of Suzume so that she had to crane her neck around Kaito to see Tsuki.

"The priestess is mine, and I don't like to share," Kaito snarled.

Suzume jumped to her feet and shoved Kaito hard in the back. Her final nerve had been struck.

"How dare you!" she shouted. She balled her hands into fists at her sides, trying to curb the impulse to swing and hit Kaito. She could feel the rivers of energy coursing through her body. Flames leapt along her skin and sparks flew from the ends of her hair.

The two men swiveled to face her. Kaito raised an eyebrow in question, as if he did not understand her indignation. *This is all a game to the lot of them. I hate them all, the inconsiderate jerks.*

"I am not yours; I do not belong to anyone," she said through clenched teeth.

Kaito's expression was bland, but she could see the fire—or in his case, ice—burning in his eyes. She knew from experience what the result of pushing his buttons was, but she just could not stop herself. It was like a bad habit, one that she was powerless to correct.

"Have you forgotten you were given to me on that mountaintop? You were meant to be my bride." His tone rumbled with thunder. Had Suzume not known Kaito, she might have been afraid, but she knew this was all just posturing on his part. Something about Tsuki getting chummy with her had struck a chord with Kaito and this was the resulting pissing contest. *It's like he's jealous.*

She did not want to think about that possibility, so instead she shoved him again. And this time she pushed with a thrust of her power. She had recouped more energy since her fight with the Oni. The red streak of energy rolled over her skin, smashed through all the dams inside her, and grew into a tidal wave. The energy manifested in a ball in the palm of her hands and in her rage-filled push, she hit Kaito in the chest, sending him flying through the air and into the forest beyond the light of their campfire.

Kaito landed in a bush but leapt to his feet quickly enough. When he got back on his feet, the air temperature dropped several degrees. Kaito was mad. It had been a clear night before, but storm clouds started gathering in the sky—big, gray and ominous. This was quickly escalating beyond posturing and turning into a full-blown battle royal and she was the challenger. She knew she should step down, but she was too angry to do so. She stood with hands on hips, glaring at Kaito and Tsuki.

"All of you think it's fine to play games. That people's feelings don't matter. Well, here's the truth. I am not your possession and I am not a tool." She glared at Tsuki. "I do not want to be Kazue. I do not want *anything* to do with her task. I'm tired of having my life threatened by Yokai and I'm tired of the secrets. Now either everyone lays everything out on the table or I quit!" She finished her tirade and panted from the effort of forcing the words out.

Her power swirled around her, over her skin and through her veins. Every part of her vibrated with energy. It felt like she was made entirely out of flame. Red light fanned around her, flickering and moving like fire. Kaito stomped over to her, but as he drew closer, he stopped, his face washed in a red glow. Rin had been staying out of the fight, sitting on her own sleeping mat, but she rose to her feet now and stared at Suzume. Tsuki's eyes were wide and terrified.

"Why are you all staring at me like I am some kind of freak?" she asked them.

"You're on fire," Rin said.

Suzume lifted up her hand; it was tipped with flames. She did not feel the heat, but it rippled and contorted as she waved her hand back and forth.

"What is this? What did you do to me?" She looked over at the most likely candidate, Tsuki, but he looked just as shocked as the others.

None of them would move any closer to her; in fact, they all took a step back. *Thanks a lot, guys, for your help. What if I really had been on fire?* In truth, she would have fled the scene just as quickly had the roles been reversed. As it was, she was afraid to move for fear she'd ignite a forest fire.

Tsuki switched to Akira and she alone among the group was willing to cautiously approach Suzume. Akira stood a few feet away from the burning priestess. She reached out to touch Suzume. When she got close, the flames erupted, burning like an inferno around Suzume. Her hair whipped around her as if she was in the middle of a tropical storm. The flames that encased her lit up the entire clearing, casting everything in crimson light. The flames wrapped around Akira's arm like a vine on a tree, and unlike Suzume, it burned Akira.

Akira screeched as the flames scorched her skin. Her lips pulled back in a grimace. She batted at the flames that were crawling along her sleeve and catching fire on her clothes. She dropped to the ground and rolled around, but nothing seemed to deter the fire's ferocity.

"Do something!" Rin shouted at Suzume.

Suzume threw up her hands. She was locked in place, not sure what to do or how to stop the unnatural fire from killing Akira and Tsuki. It was Kaito who came to the rescue and blew on the burns with breath made of ice. The two combating elements met in an explosion of fire and sparks, steam and ice, as it extinguished the flames. Akira lay on the ground panting for a few moments. She trembled all over and her skin had pink and black burns vining up her arms from where the fire had touched her.

Suzume's anger had cooled into fear, but she remained engulfed in flames that did not burn her. Kaito turned back to Suzume and he tilted his head as he regarded her, less afraid and more curious. "This is not a skill Kazue had. What are you?"

"Believe me, I wish I knew," Suzume said in a shaky voice.

*I wish none of this ever happened. Damn my mother for doing this to me. If I hadn't been exiled, none of this would have happened. I wish everything would go back to normal.* She tried to fight it, but she was so mad and afraid that a tear escaped and rolled down her cheek. Once the tears started, she could not stop them. Suzume fell to her knees and hid her crying behind her hands.

The wind died down and she felt the storm inside her calm. The flames must have gone out as well because someone put an arm around her shoulder. She was mortified to have had so many people witness her moment of weakness. She did not want to open her eyes and face them, but if she kept letting one of them comfort her, she would look even weaker. She opened her eyes. She was surprised to find Kaito had put his arm around her. This led to a complicated series of emotions. Chief among them was the thought that he was only doing it because he still saw her as Kazue. *He did say he does not think I'm Kazue. Not that I care. He's an arrogant jerk.*

No matter what she told herself, she did feel comforted when he held her, as evident by her body not sparking to protect her. There was also the possibility that she had burned out all of her spiritual energy in her fire display. It was difficult to tell. She did feel empty at the moment, but she wasn't sure if it was because of her lack of energy or the feeling that she had lost everything the moment she had released Kaito.

She discreetly removed herself from Kaito's grip. But she did not give him any spitting insults and he did not leer or make any suggestive remarks.

"Well, that was interesting," Tsuki said using Akira's form.

Suzume laughed and it sounded insane to her own ears. The others were definitely looking at her in a new light.

"Any theories on what just happened here?" Suzume asked.

Kaito had not moved away. He was near enough to touch. Their fingertips were just inches apart. She looked down at their close proximity, considered saying something, then decided not to. She liked having him close, just in case anything decided to pop out of the woods and try to eat her. As weak as she felt, she wouldn't have the motivation to even try to defend herself. It was not because she wanted to be near him. At least that's what she told herself.

Everyone took a seat and they looked at each other. No one spoke for a long time.

Surprisingly, Rin was the first to speak. "I think you're some sort of fire creature, at least in part."

"That's not possible. Both of my parents are human!" Suzume protested.

"Your mother did get exiled for having an affair; maybe it's been going on longer than we initially thought," Kaito said.

She glowered at him. Leave it to the Dragon to drag up her past. *Thanks for kicking me when I am down.* "Yes, she was banished for her infidelity. But even if the emperor is not my father, how does that equal me lighting up like a torch?"

"Maybe the infidelity charge was a cover-up? Perhaps the emperor discovered that your mother was something less than human," Akira said reasonably.

It was a sound theory, but Suzume was not willing to believe her mother had been a Yokai. She tried to think of the few and far between times she had seen her mother. Her mother had, for most of Suzume's life, been the emperor's favorite wife. Though not his first, she was adored and often exploited her position to get whatever she wanted. Suzume was more inclined to believe her mother had an affair than that she had secret powers.

"Maybe we should find her after we find the forgotten priest," Kaito said. She could see his wheels turning, planning another adventure.

"No. Not going to happen."

"Why not? Don't you want to have a reunion with your dearest mommy?" Kaito teased.

She turned to face him and said, "Do you want to find your son?"

The smile was wiped right off his face.

"I did not think so." She crossed her arms and scooted a little further from him. She was not feeling as chummy with Kaito as she had been before. "Speaking of which, how do we even know this priest is alive?" Suzume asked.

"I just know," Akira said with an air of superiority.

"Well, I meant what I said earlier; I'm tired of the secrets. What are you two plotting?"

Akira stared at Suzume for a moment, giving her a steady look. "You want the truth?"

"No, I want more lies."

Akira sighed. "The priest we are looking for is like us. He will live trapped as he was the day Kazue cursed him until Kazue's spell can be broken."

"Okay, why would you keep that information from us?" Suzume had a feeling they still were not telling her the whole story.

Akira looked away. She and Tsuki appeared to be having a silent conversation. *I didn't know that they could do that. I wonder why they have all the other back and forth. Maybe it's for our benefit.* Either way it was creepy.

They concluded their silent conversation and Akira turned to face Suzume.

"The priest is not just cursed, he's our father."

**44**

---

"Wait," Suzume said as she put up her hand. "So you're saying this mythical priest is your father? Why didn't you tell us this before?"

Akira shrugged. "We thought you would doubt our motives if we told you."

"It's too late for that. I have doubted your motives from the moment I met you. I think an explanation is in order. What are the two of you after, really?"

Akira sighed heavily. "I was afraid it was going to come down to this. As you may realize, Tsuki and I want to be freed from the curse that bound us together, but we're not the only ones who were effected by Kazue's curse. She cursed our entire family. She bound us to the staff and forced us to share a body, and our father is being forced to guard Kazue's heart."

Suzume's head hurt, and she massaged her temples. "What do you mean 'Kazue's heart'?"

"What game are you playing, Akira?" Kaito snarled.

Suzume's head whipped to the side to watch Kaito. His hands were clasped at his sides as if he was using all his effort not to strike at Akira. Akira returned his snarling gaze with a tilted smile. *She loves taunting him.* Rin moved close to Kaito and put a hand on his shoulder. He did not turn to look at her, but Suzume could see his shoulders relax. Suzume looked away from them. Her angry words she threw at Rin earlier that day came back to mind. *I do not want her thinking I am jealous.*

"There's no game, Dragon. You should know that at times those humans who have exceptional spiritual powers are embalmed so their holy powers can be harnessed. What is hidden in this mountain is Kazue's remains. They are imbued with Kazue's spiritual power. You and I both know what danger that could mean if the power fell into the wrong hands."

Kaito's eyes had turned a burning blue that he only displayed when he was really angry. She had not seen him this angry since the temple, when he thought she planned to seal him. *What is he so worked up about? It's just her body.*

"Who did this to her?" he growled. The air dropped by a few degrees and Suzume shivered. She rubbed her palms against her arms.

"It was Kazue's choice," Tsuki replied, once more using his sister's face to speak. "There was something she could not finish in her first life, so she sealed her powers until her reincarnation was born and could take her place."

Three pairs of eyes swiveled in Suzume's direction. She threw up her hands in a defensive pose. "Why are you all looking at me?"

Kaito coughed and it sounded suspiciously like laughter. She scowled at him, but he would not look at her.

"We've already established Kazue had some great quest I am destined to complete, but why hide her powers up in the mountains? She seemed perfectly content to leave the staff at the shrine."

"I would assume this would be the best way to protect it," Akira said. She shrugged again. "Honestly, I don't know the whys of it. All I know is that Kazue's heart has the power to break this curse on my family, but only if the right person can access the power within."

"Meaning me?" Suzume guessed.

"Yes, she intended for her reincarnation to gather the relics of her previous life."

"What if I don't want to help? Ever since I unleashed Kaito from the seal, I've had nothing but trouble. How much worse will things get once I free Kazue's power?"

"You don't have a choice; this is your destiny," Akira said.

Suzume's hands clenched at her sides. Her building frustration had reached its peak. She was tired, hungry and, the worst offender, filthy. Bits of ichor and dirt clung to her torn and ruined clothes. She had gone along at first because she did not have any choice, but everyone had a breaking point and Suzume had reached hers.

"That's what's great about being human, I don't have to do anything I don't want to." She turned on her heel and stomped away from the group.

"You can't run away," Kaito called out to her, but she pretended not to hear.

Her fingertips crackled with power. Red sparks sputtered and flickered along her skin and her hair. She was afraid she was going to erupt into flame once more, and that was probably the only thing keeping the others from following after her. She expected Kaito to come after her despite that, but she made it out without anyone physically detaining her.

As the light of their campfire faded behind her, Suzume stumbled over rocks and tore her clothes further. She tripped over a bush and scratched her arm. She swore under her breath as she fell to her knees and pain shot up her leg. She looked over her shoulder, out of habit. There was no one behind her to see her fall.

The forest was pitch black. Overhead, the stars twinkled against the inky sky. The moon was a thumbnail and gave little light. As her eyes adjusted, however, she could see the silhouettes of trees. She got to her feet and continued on with her hands outstretched in front of her. *I'd rather deal with whatever is lurking in these woods than face another moment of my so-called destiny. I'm not stupid, I know they're just helping me because I can free them from their curse. I don't know what Rin wants, but I'm sure she has her own motives. As for Kaito, he just wants me to be Kazue...* That was the most bitter thought of them all.

Cicadas buzzed nearby as she bumped into tree trunks. An animal skittered through the underbrush and she saw a glimpse of luminescent eyes before they disappeared into the forest. A twig snapped nearby and she spun in circles. Her power swam to the surface, coating her skin in a pale red glow. It felt like a prickle along her arm, wrapping her in warmth. It was getting easier to summon the power. She held up her hand, hoping the glow of her skin would illuminate her path. *Which way back to the shrine? I'm going to force them to let me stay, even if I have to invoke my father's name.* She hadn't been able to do that in quite some time. The emperor would be upset with her if he found out, but it seemed worth the risk. It would at least give her enough time to figure out where to go from here.

The cicadas' song cut short and the following silence was deafening. Suzume spun around in circles, her eyes squinting in the dark, looking for a shadow, a hint of what had scared away the insects.

"Kaito, if that's you, I am not coming back. Go fetch Kazue's heart yourself. I'm done being your dog!"

A light flickered to life a few feet from her, a glowing orb hanging overhead. Suzume turned towards it as she removed her staff from her back sheath and pointed it in the direction of the unnatural light.

"Suzume, I thought we had agreed we would not fight one another," Hisato said.

A shiver ran down Suzume's spine. She knew she had not seen the last of Hisato. He stepped into the light. The golden orb hung above his head like a miniature sun and cast his face in shadows. She could see the sharp edges of his cheekbones contrasting with the sweep of his eyebrows and his lips, which were pulled back in a toothy grin.

"What are you doing here, back to taunt me some more?" She pointed the staff at him, but she suddenly felt very vulnerable. If her previous run-ins with Hisato were any indication, she was no match for him, and this time there was no one here to save her.

He strolled over to her with his hands folded behind his back. "No. I came for my answer, Suzume." He spoke her name, savoring every syllable.

"Oh yeah, you want me to do your dirty work, right?"

He stopped a few feet away from her, just out of striking distance. He chuckled. "Something like that. What's your decision?"

She was outmatched by him physically, but she knew she could talk to him. "Let me ask you, why don't you kill him yourself?"

"A good question with a complicated answer. Let's just say the universe has a certain... balance. I cannot raise a hand against Kaito because if I did, it would upset that balance."

Suzume frowned and let her staff drop a little. *That doesn't make any sense. He seems more like the type that loves chaos.* Hisato's gaze flickered to her lowered defenses. She took a step forward and jabbed at him with the end of her staff. "But you can kill all the other Yokai? Why is that?"

He spun away from her attack and disappeared into the dark. He reappeared behind Suzume and said, "As I said, it's complicated. Does this mean you agree?"

She had thought about it, seriously even. All Kaito had done since she met him was cause her heartache, put her life in danger, and drag her around like a lapdog. But she could not bring herself to kill him—she didn't have it in her. The only thing she had ever killed was the Yokai back when she was trying to find the wish-granting Kami, but that had been coincidental. The problem was she wanted out of this quest; she wanted nothing to do with Kazue, her task or the lot of them. *I am running out of options. They let me stomp off for now, but I know Kaito will come drag me back any minute.*

"I don't think I am powerful enough to kill him," Suzume said, as an excuse. She hoped if Hisato thought she was too weak, he would leave her alone. It wasn't likely, but she liked to stay optimistic.

"That can be remedied easily enough. All you lack is Kazue's power. If you had her heart, then you could reach your full potential."

"And now we come to the real reason you want me. I already know I'm the only one who can retrieve her heart, and no, I won't get it for you." She turned to walk away, but before she could get more than a few steps, Hisato grabbed her wrist and spun her around to face him.

He was taller than her by a few inches and she had to tilt her head back to look at him. He was handsome, all sharp angles and dark eyes. Suzume wrenched her hand away.

"I am not doing this for myself, Suzume." When he said her name again, it made her shiver.

"Really now?" He had let her go, but he still stood close to her, too close really. She should take a step back, but she didn't.

"With power like Kazue's, you could return your life to the way it was. You could go back to the palace, marry the general, flirt with the young men. You would never have to worry about the world of immortals ever again. You would be free of it."

"What, does Kazue's heart grant wishes?"

He chuckled, a dark, husky sound. "Not quite, but Kazue was one of the most powerful priestesses to ever live. With her staff and her heart, you would be unstoppable. You could do whatever you wanted. You could even be the empress."

A flood of images filled Suzume's mind. She remembered her life as it had been. The silk robes, servants who fell over themselves to attend to her every whim, hundreds of suitors who showered her in gifts, and most of all, she had never been hungry, scared or dirty. *I would be more powerful than my father. I could exile him to some remote shrine in the middle of the sea.* She smiled thinking of it.

"I can see this pleases you," Hisato purred.

She looked up at him with eyes narrowed. It was a pretty picture, but she couldn't help but think there were strings attached to this offer. "This seems too good to be true. How do I know you won't try to take the heart from me the moment I get it."

He laughed again and took another step closer to Suzume. He reached out and brushed her cheek with the back of his hand. His skin was soft. His fingers were long and tapered. It also occurred to her that sparks never flew when they touched.

"Why can you touch me without my body reacting?" she asked.

He leaned in, his breath mingling with hers. She knew she should step away—he was most likely using her, but she liked to imagine she was using him. He gave her information and she got all the benefit. At least that's how it played out in her mind.

"Haven't you realized it yet, Suzume?" He ran his thumb across her lips, which parted beneath his touch. "You were meant for me. We are destined. Get Kazue's heart, gain the power, and when you have everything you wished for, you will be able to return to the life you deserve." Hisato stepped away suddenly and Suzume felt a chill sweep over her. She wrapped her arms around her torso. "It's up to you, Suzume. Whom do you want to trust? The ones who have deceived you from the moment you met or me?"

"You attacked me on multiple occasions." Even when she said it, it lacked conviction. She felt strangely conflicted. Kaito had threatened her life more times than she could count. She was positive Akira and Tsuki were up to something—more than what they had disclosed. The world had turned upside down and she did not know who to trust.

He laughed. "I never meant to hurt you. I wanted you to see the truth, to see what they really wanted from you. Get Kazue's heart and you'll see I am right."

She swallowed past a lump in her throat. She hated to go back and face the others after storming off, so she kept talking instead. "You told me when you attacked you only intended to maim me."

"It was a joke. You will find our kind have a dark sense of humor."

"What do you mean, our kind? I seriously doubt you're human."

He laughed. "Do you really think you're human? Don't be naive."

Before she could form another retort, the orb of light had blinked out and she was plunged into darkness. Along with it was the sound of Tsuki, Kaito and Rin calling her name. Kaito was closest and she could hear him the clearest.

"Come back here before you're eaten. I will not save you from another Oni today."

"Technically that was me," Tsuki replied.

Suzume stared into the dark where Hisato had disappeared. She did not know who to trust, but she knew one thing for certain —the only person she could rely on was herself.

# 45

They continued their climb the next day. Other than a few playful jibes, there was no talk of Suzume's disappearance. Suzume was withdrawn most of the day, but no one seemed to notice, or care, for that matter. Her sullen silences were nothing new.

The climb was difficult and even the immortals struggled over boulders and slippery slopes. They reached a steep portion of the mountain, the incline almost vertical. Suzume tilted her head up—nothing but the gray and bleak sky reeling overhead; it made her head spin. She knew the others were watching, waiting for her to give up. She gritted her teeth and committed to climbing. She found a foothold and tested her weight. The others were almost halfway up and she had not even started her climb.

*How badly do I really want this heart? Hisato could be using me like all the rest.*

Kaito looked down at her from above. "Need help?" he called.

"No," she snarled and proceeded to climb the rock face. The stones were jagged and they cut her palms. It did not take long until they were covered in blood and sweat. Tsuki and Kaito had reached the top and Tsuki gave Rin a hand over the last boulder that protruded from the edge.

Suzume's legs shook and her hands were cramping. *I have to keep moving. I'm almost to the top.* If she looked down, she would regret it. She was within arm's reach of the precipice. Just another couple inches forward. She placed her foot on a toehold, but the rock crumbled beneath it. She slipped down a few inches, her face racked against the sharp side of the mountain, and rocks went cascading down the side, tinkling on their way down. She was lucky she had not fallen with them. She looked down and saw the ground too far away and her stomach flopped. She was unable to move.

"Suzume, what happened?" Tsuki called.

Her tongue was glued to the roof of her mouth. Her fingers trembled and her muscles would not obey her.

"I'm coming to get you," Kaito said. She could not even argue.

He climbed down the side of the rock face and stopped next to her. She was too busy hugging the rock.

"Give me your hand."

Heart hammering in her chest, she looked at him from the corner of her eye. There was not a hint of mocking in his expression. With shaking hands she reached out for him. He pulled her closer and wrapped her arm around his neck. Inch by inch, she slid onto his back and then, arms wrapped around his neck and legs dangling, they climbed the rest of the way.

When they reached the top, Suzume fell onto the ground in an exhausted heap. Rin came over and handed Suzume some water, which she gulped down greedily. She hated having to have Kaito save her, but she decided to keep the complaining to a minimum, because she could never really stop complaining altogether. They decided to stop there for a rest, mostly for Suzume's benefit. She sat on an oblong boulder, which made for a convenient seat, and took another swig of water.

Kaito paced back and forth restlessly. The muscles beneath his clothes rippled with tension. When Tsuki saw Suzume watching Kaito, he smirked at her. She looked away at the last moment, but the damage was done. She was going to hear about this later, she was sure of it. *That is, if there is a later. If I get Kazue's heart and harness her power, then I'll be back at the White Palace this time tomorrow.* Just the thought brought a smile to her face.

"If you have enough energy to smile, then I think we best head out again," Kaito announced. The tension in his body had transformed his normally smiling face. White lines circled his mouth from his clenched jaw.

Suzume scowled at him. She knew Kaito was on edge, but she could not help but argue. "What? Are you trying to kill me? How much further is this place? If we go any higher, we'll be in the kingdom of the Eight." It was an exaggeration, of course, the Eight's holy kingdom was only reachable in the afterlife.

Rin snickered at Suzume's joke, and when Kaito shot her a look, the smile wiped away from her face.

"I would not want Your Highness to grow tired. Should I carry you on my back?" Kaito turned his back to her as he squatted down, as if he were offering up a piggyback ride.

She scoffed. "I would rather not. I'd probably erupt into flames again."

"We wouldn't want that, now would we?" Tsuki said with a smirk.

She glared at him as well.

"It's just a bit further. Come, Suzume, I'll carry you if you like. And I promise you won't burst into flames if you touch me, at least not any visible part of you." He did not wait for her answer and instead swooped Suzume off her feet. She screeched as her feet left the ground and she kicked and swung at Tsuki, who laughed uproariously.

"Put me dow—" She could not even finish her sentence before Kaito grabbed her by the armpits and planted her back on her own two feet.

"You're capable of walking," he said, his tone tense. All trace of humor from before was wiped away.

Suzume opened her mouth to explain but clamped it down again. *I don't owe him an apology just because he thinks I belong to him. I am no man's property.* Suzume brushed off her robes and said to the ground, "I'm ready to go if everyone is done horsing around."

She looked up as Kaito walked away.

"He's a bit dense," Tsuki said.

Suzume looked at him from the corner of her eye. "What do you mean?"

Tsuki laughed. "Nothing, really." He swung his arms behind his head and clasped his fingers against his neck. He whistled as he followed after Kaito.

Rin had hung back, but when Suzume looked to her for an explanation, Rin only shrugged and joined the boys. *Damn their secrets.*

It turned out there was not much distance left to travel. They found a winding set of stairs carved into the stones themselves. The wind blew hard enough to pull the unwary off a cliff just feet away. Suzume's hair swirled around her. She pushed the strands away from her face and tilted her neck back to try to catch a glimpse of the top of the stairs. The steps disappeared into the clouds, obscuring their destination. *Kazue really did not want her remains to be found.*

"Do not tell me we have to climb that." Suzume said, pointing at the narrow stairs. On one side was the stone smooth and ancient. On the other side was a drop that led to the foot of the mountain.

Rin stood on the edge of the precipice. Her auburn hair flew around her head like a bright banner against the gray sky behind her. She did not seem afraid of the height, just curious. Kaito's gaze was fixed on the stairs. *He cannot wait to get there. I wonder if he's hoping Kazue is waiting for him at the end of this quest.* This thought filled her with bitterness. *What do I care? All I want is my old life back. Once I get that, none of this matters.*

"We're almost there, are you ready?" Tsuki said to Suzume. He grinned from ear to ear.

"You could at least try to hide your eagerness," she replied.

He tilted his head as he regarded her. "What would be the purpose of that? Now that we're all being *honest* with one another."

Suzume felt like there were cold fingers grasping the back of her neck. She rubbed it but did not look away from Tsuki. *There's no way he could know what Hisato told me. I am just being paranoid.*

"Are you trying to say there's more you're not telling me? Like is there something up there waiting for us?"

He shook his head. "We've told you all we know. Most of our information has been gleaned from the priests of the temple. This is the first time since we were cursed that we've left the temple."

Suzume's skin tingled. Small sparks burst along her skin, creating a red glow. Something was waiting for them at the top of these stairs, she could feel it. Either Tsuki was lying or he really didn't know, she could not be sure. *I cannot believe Kazue would go to all this trouble and not put extra protection around this place.*

"Let's get going while it's still light," Kaito said. He looked ready to pop from the anticipation. He shuffled from one foot to the other, his gaze ever upward.

They headed up the stairs. It was even more perilous than Suzume imagined. The steps were cramped together and worn smooth by the elements. They walked single file, and in a few spots, they had crumbled away and they had to jump over massive gaps. It was at this point that Suzume took a grudging ride on Tsuki's back across the chasm.

Halfway up she made the mistake of looking over the edge. Thick white clouds obscured most of the forest floor but for patches of green that peaked through breaks in the clouds. She clutched at the rough wall, her fingers finding no purchase. She felt like she would tilt over the side and fall forever. Suzume closed her eyes and leaned against the stone wall for a moment. She felt a hand in the small of her back, and when she opened her eyes, Akira was standing beside her.

"Just take it one step at a time, and try not to look down," Akira said.

Suzume nodded mutely before they continued their climb. She managed to climb the rest of the stairs without looking over the edge. Once she slipped on some loose rocks and fell down a few steps. Rin came to her rescue and kept her from tumbling all the way back down to the bottom or, worse, going over the edge. Suzume gave Rin a begrudging thank you. *They're all being so helpful today. Probably because they need me to retrieve Kazue's heart.*

---

Kaito had thought it a trick when Tsuki and Akira had told them to climb to the top of Mount Iwaki. None had tread here but the Eight; the palace of the Eight could not be reached by any other than the first children. It had been a long time since Kaito had been here, and just that they had reached the top unchallenged meant things had really changed.

The stairs ended at a torii arch similar to the ones that led into a temple. This one was faded and the wood scored with horizontal marks, like giant claws had slashed at them. Charms dangled from the beam and twirled in the wind. A bell chimed somewhere nearby. Beyond the torii arch lay a courtyard area ringed in more arches. Polished onyx made up the floor. He hesitated outside the arch. Kazue was here; he could feel her energy mixed with another power, something ancient and powerful that he had only glimpsed once. The entire area hummed with Kazue's energy, hidden in every stone, arch and charm as if she had poured herself into it.

"Hello?" Suzume said, and her voice echoed back at her, amplified by the mountains, which bounced it back towards her.

Akira glided into the courtyard first. She moved slowly, her gaze moving across the empty space, searching for life. "He should be here," she said in a hushed voice.

Rin walked along the edge of the courtyard, examining the other arches. Unlike the main one at the steps, these led onto nothing but gray-blue sky. Clouds drifted lazily past and skimmed across the courtyard covering half the space. *All my searching has led me here.*

Kaito stood in the center of the courtyard, his shoulders taut and his hands balled into fists at his sides. He looked straight forward into the mist, still as a statue. Somewhere in the mist, he felt Kazue's energy centered. Unlike with Suzume, this felt familiar, the woman he had known. *Why did you do it, Kazue?*

Then from the mist, a silhouette appeared. They strolled out toward Kaito. The clouds rolled away and revealed a young man. He had long black hair tied into a topknot. At his hip he wore two swords, their hilts frayed. He had a square jaw and a severe mouth. And on his forehead was a painted marking in an ancient forgotten language. But Kaito knew it, this was the mark of one of eight legendary swords sworn to protect the Eight. *Why are you here? I wonder.*

"Who dares enter this holy place?" he said in a gravelly voice.

"I do, the Dragon, ruler of Akatsuki," Kaito said in a rumbling voice that echoed off the mountains and surrounded them.

The man looked Kaito up and down. "Have you come to challenge me?"

Kaito smiled, his teeth had already begun to elongate and his hands were half claws. "I have come for Kazue's remains."

"Wait!" Akira shouted and ran between Kaito and the man. "Don't hurt him. That's our father."

Kaito growled. The man had not moved. His hand rested on

the hilt of one of his swords. He did not deny or refute Akira's statement.

"He looks like he's the same age as you," Suzume said in disbelief. "I was expecting an old man."

Akira looked at her father, her expression was a mix of emotions, fear and relief.

"We've all been cursed to stay the same. We do not age, which means he has stayed the same as well."

"Are you going to challenge me, then?" he said to Akira.

Akira's expression fell; she had expected him to recognize her, most like. Kazue's spell was strong if it broke the ties of family. *What have you done, Kazue?*

"Father, do you not recognize your daughter?"

He answered with the screech of metal against the scabbard. He pulled out one of the blades and pointed it at Akira. "Choose your weapon. If you wish to enter the inner sanctum, you must get past me."

Akira reached out to her father, but her hand jerked back at the last moment. "He is not himself, Akira," Tsuki said, using his sister's face. "We have to get through to him, let me fight."

Akira looked to her father and then dropped her head. "You're right."

They switched in a seamless motion. Akira's soft mouth and rounded cheeks melted into Tsuki's high cheekbones.

"I'll need a weapon," Tsuki said. His voice had lost all of its usual humor.

His father removed the second blade and tossed it to Tsuki. He caught it in midair. He removed the blade from its sheath and then he tossed the scabbard aside. Tsuki's father, the guardian, took a defensive stance, his legs spread apart and the blade pointed at his son. Tsuki took on a similar pose, and they bowed to one another—a half smirk slipped across Tsuki's face.

*They are the children of a legendary sword. No wonder he is a capable fighter.* Kaito stepped back to let them fight, curious to see

Tsuki in action. They moved around in circles before the first attack. Tsuki moved first. He rushed his father with a low swipe, which his father dodged and rolled away. The guardian's robes rippled like water. Kaito had encountered this particular legendary sword, though never had the pleasure of seeing him fight. He moved gracefully as if it were part of a dance.

Tsuki stumbled, having expected to land a blow, and the guardian swung back around with a thrust to Tsuki's shoulder, but Tsuki spun and blocked with his blade. Metal screeched against metal, echoing around the audience. They broke apart and Tsuki jumped backwards as his father rushed him once more, slashing and cutting into Tsuki's shoulder. Tsuki did not even acknowledge his wound. He thrust forward for another attack. Tsuki tried to parry only to have his blade torn from his hand. It landed a few feet away at Kaito's feet. Tsuki knelt on the ground, panting, his father's blade pointed at his throat.

"You are not worthy." The guardian pulled the sword back, ready to strike, when another sword blocked his swing.

The guardian looked up. "You challenge me?"

"I do," Kaito said with a grin. "I have been waiting five hundred years to see Kazue, and I will not let you stop me. I let the child play, now it is time I get some answers."

The guardian smiled, a faint echo of his son's smile. Rin helped Tsuki to his feet and the two of them returned to the edge of the battlefield while Kaito's battle ensued. Though he preferred to use his claws and teeth, he was no stranger to a blade. Kaito blocked all of the guardian's thrusts and moved about in circles, matching the guardian blow for blow.

The guardian, meanwhile, gave no inch. He harried Kaito around the courtyard, metal clanked against metal, and the battle continued. The battle lasted much longer than Tsuki's. Time lost all meaning as he lunged and dodged, all the while at the back of his mind he knew he had to win, to get a chance to find Kazue.

Then his energy flagged. He was not at full strength, and the guardian had lifetimes to wait. Kaito started to slip.

At first it was just a small mistake, the guardian got within his defense and slashed Kaito's thigh. Then Kaito stumbled, falling to his knees. The guardian lifted his blade high, ready for a final blow. Time slowed down. From the corner of his eye, he saw Suzume inching closer. He reached for his blade, ignoring the priestess, she would only distract him. But his moment's hesitation could have been his death; he moved too slowly to block the oncoming attack.

Suzume rushed forward and put herself between him and the coming blade.

"Stop!" she shouted.

And then the sword fell.

# 46

A rush of wind blew her hair away from her face. The blade grazed the side of her hand, but did not break the skin. The cold steel did not touch her aside from that but went past her and drove into the ground. Kaito knelt beside her, panting. She did not look at him, but she felt him staring at the back of her head, probably wondering why she had jumped to his rescue. The truth was she was wondering the same thing. The guardian had his hands held in front of him, palms up. He looked down at his large calloused hands and then slowly raised his wide dark eyes to Suzume's face.

"You are... Kazue?" His voice cracked as he fell into a deep bow.

Suzume looked around to Rin and Tsuki. Rin seemed to be just as baffled as Suzume. Tsuki was back on his feet and he looked prepared to leap forward and embrace his father, but something held him back.

"No, my name is Suzume. I am... I guess I'm Kazue's reincarnation." She shrugged. *This has taken a strange turn. A few seconds ago he was ready to kill us all, now he's bowing?*

The guardian looked up at Suzume and his expression shifted.

Gone was the blank stare of a mindless puppet, and the expression that replaced it was one of unadulterated fury. Something had snapped inside of him, it seemed. He yanked his sword from the ground and swung it at her.

Kaito grabbed her around the waist and pulled her back in time to save her from being sliced in half.

"What was that for?" Suzume shouted at him. "I thought we were calling a truce?"

"I have been chained to this desolate place for nearly five hundred years! What do you have to say for yourself, Kazue?" He did not seem to hear Suzume; he was blinded by his anger.

Suzume took a step back, her hands up. "Hey, I'm not here to fight you. Just show me to Kazue's remains and I'll be on my way."

The guardian pointed the blade at Suzume. "You will not be going anywhere until you prove you are worthy of the prize."

Suzume swallowed past a lump in her throat. If Kaito couldn't beat him, how could she expect to?

"You see, I'm more of a pacifist, really." She took a few more small steps backwards, Kaito at her side, but he did not transform and his sword lay at the feet of the guardian.

She tried to catch his eye to silently signal him to defend her, but he was staring at the guardian with a fixed expression. She looked to Rin and Tsuki.

Tsuki clutched at the wound on his shoulder. He did not move either. Rin's hand was frozen in midair as if she was going to yell out. *He froze them somehow. I guess I am on my own.* Just the prospect sent nervous tingles racing up and down her spine. Her power coalesced around her in a maelstrom of fire. It was not the same inferno as back in the forest, more like a controlled blaze.

Suzume drew the staff and for once it came out smoothly and flawlessly. For a half second, she felt powerful. The energy coursed through her veins. But the moment was short lived as the guardian swung at her. She shrieked and threw up the staff on impulse to block his attack. His blade sliced through the flames and, unlike when Akira tried to touch her, the flames did not try to burn him.

"Did you think the holy fire would harm me? You are mistaken, I was formed by holy fire. You cannot harm me with it," he said, then swung at Suzume.

She held up the staff to take his blows. The force of it rattled her arms down to the sockets and her footing slipped. He hit her again and again. The guardian came at her, his expression grim as he pushed her backwards, closer and closer to the edge of the courtyard, towards the archways that opened up onto the sky. It took all the minimal skill she had just to block his attacks and even that seemed like an impossible feat. She tried to stay away from the edge, but he kept pushing her back. Her arms trembled from the effort of keeping the staff in front of her and the force of the guardian's blows.

"If any of you want to step in and help at any time, that would be great," Suzume said, knowing full well the others could do nothing to help her. It helped her feel less alone to talk to them. *I think this is it, this is how I am going to die. I was so close to going back, it's not fair.*

"They cannot help you now, Kazue. They will only awaken when one of our blood is spilled, and I intend for it to be yours."

"Yeah, here's the thing. I share a soul with Kazue, but I do not really have the same goals as her," Suzume said to the guardian between strikes of his sword.

He did not respond to her but kept hacking at her with his blade. If she had a moment to concentrate, she might be able to erect a barrier, but it was taking all her concentration to not lose her head, literally.

The edge was getting ever closer and Suzume's body could only take so much of a beating. When she had a brilliant plan.

"I can understand why you would hate Kazue. Believe me, I have a few bones to pick with her myself, but maybe we can come to some sort of agreement."

The guardian had his blade held up, but he lowered it half an inch now. "What sort of agreement."

"I can tell just being near me has brought you out of whatever zombie trance you were in."

He nodded his head and his brow was furrowed. "Yes, when I saw you, it was like waking from a very long sleep, one full of nightmares."

His tone was haunted and Suzume wondered how many people had tried and failed to retrieve Kazue's remains. "Well, that guy over there is your son, and he is trapped in the same body as your daughter."

The guardian turned his head to look at Tsuki, who stood frozen in place, clutching the injury his father had given him.

"That cannot be possible... I sired no children."

"If you don't believe me, release your spell and ask him yourself," Suzume said.

The guardian glowered at her. "How do I know this is not a trick?"

"You don't. But I know you're curious; just release him and ask. I promise I won't attack."

The guardian looked over to his son, his expression full of longing. He debated silently for a moment before he drew his blade and slashed it against his palm. Blood welled there and he strode over to Tsuki and dropped a few droplets at Tsuki's feet.

Tsuki lowered his arm from his wound, looking from his father to Suzume. "What happened? The last thing I remember you were about to cut into Suzume."

"He sealed you and the others to stop you from helping me," Suzume said. She waved her arm, which was still flickering with flame.

Tsuki nodded. "Ah."

While Tsuki and Suzume bantered, the guardian studied Tsuki. He tilted his head from one side to the other as if he were taking in a painting.

"I can see it now, you are my son."

If Suzume had been hoping for a heartfelt reunion, she was not going to get it. The guardian still held his weapon at his side as he regarded his son.

Tsuki smiled. "I am. We have been looking for you for a long time, Father."

"We?" the guardian asked.

"My sister and I, we share this body."

The guardian was not fazed, he only stared at his son a moment longer without speaking. "How did this happen?" he said at last.

*Uh-oh, this talking thing might not have been my best idea.*

"It was Kazue," Tsuki said in a matter-of-fact tone.

The guardian turned back to Suzume. "What game are you playing at? Are you trying to enrage me, Kazue?"

"Stop calling me that, I'm Suzume," she corrected with a huff.

The guardian gripped his sword tighter and Suzume amended her statement. "We are seeking Kazue's remains to save your children from their curse and you as well," Suzume lied.

Tsuki did not move to correct her. None of them knew about her real motives. She felt filthy lying in front of them. When before she would have done anything to get her way, now she felt guilty for tricking them.

The guardian lowered his head and contemplated her words. He never took his eyes off her. From the corner of her eye, Suzume spotted Kaito creeping closer. While she had been fighting the guardian, he had been making tiny steps towards the sword on the ground. He knelt down behind the guardian and picked it up.

"Do not move, or I will kill Kazue." The guardian pulled a dagger out and had it trained to throw at Suzume.

Kaito growled in his throat and Suzume was not sure if she should be scared or flattered that Kaito was trying to protect her. *Why didn't he move to protect me sooner?*

374

She glanced over at Kaito and the expression she caught made her stomach twist in knots. There was real concern on his face. *He's getting sentimental because the guardian keeps calling me Kazue. He's not really seeing me.*

She turned back to the guardian. "Show me to Kazue's remains and I will use the power to save you all."

The guardian lowered the dagger. She felt a wave of relief until he said, "I'll let you pass if you tell me what happened to Satsuki. Where is she? If you have my children, then you must have her as well."

Suzume's eyes grew large. She had no idea what Kazue had done with his wife, if she had done anything at all. She could be dead for all she knew. How could she? Everything she knew came from what the others told her. She looked to Kaito; he shrugged. He knew less than her, having been sealed for so long. She looked to Tsuki, who only shook his head. It was Rin who stepped up. When the guardian spilled his blood, it had broken the spell on all of them.

"She was sealed away," Rin said, addressing the guardian.

"Why?" the guardian asked Suzume. She had no idea how to answer, so she made something up.

"Kazue was trying to save her. There's a dark power that is gathering and she wanted to save them. She knew that she wouldn't be able to save everyone in her lifetime, so she sealed you, your children and your wife to prepare for my arrival. I am the hope for the future, but only if you can get me to Kazue's remains."

No one spoke against her, they were all set on getting to Kazue's remains. They were willing to go along with her ruse.

"Is this true?" The guardian looked to his son.

Tsuki met Suzume's gaze. She nodded her head infinitesimally. "It's true, Father. Will you help us?"

The guardian sighed before sheathing his sword. "I will show you, but only Kazue may enter the holy shrine."

Kaito looked prepared to argue, but Suzume spoke before he could. "Good, it would not be proper for anyone else to go." *I am so close to freedom, I can taste it. The others will scramble to explain to the guardian once I am gone, but I am sure he'll forgive Tsuki and Akira.*

He turned on his heel and walked towards the clouds that covered the other half of the courtyard. Now that the threat of a fight was over, the fire died and she was back to normal. Despite what the guardian had said, Kaito joined her. He walked beside her, not touching but close enough to do so. The guardian walked ahead of them, his arms swinging. Kaito leaned into Suzume and whispered, "Nice cover back there."

His breath was warm against her neck, and though she wanted to push him away, she couldn't help but enjoy the feel of his walking next to her. When it was just the two of them, it felt normal and natural to walk together and even his compliments felt genuine. *But it's all an illusion. He is just reliving his life with Kazue through me, but I'm not her, not really.*

The clouds were so thick she could barely see the guardian but for the impression of his body moving through the clouds. She did not realize it at first, but there was a maze of arches and pathways hidden behind the cloud cover.

"Stay close, one wrong step could be your last. This area is heavily warded," the guardian said from a few feet away.

Suzume skirted around a hole that fizzled and sparked when she got too close. Kaito grabbed her hand and pulled her close to him. She thought about protesting, but for once her body did not light up at his touch. Instead his hand felt warm against hers, large and enveloping. She was glad she could not see his face or she might have had second thoughts about what she planned to do. This was just an indulgence, a short trip into a land of fantasy where Kaito was a normal decent man, the type a princess could marry, not a maniac dragon who would most likely get her killed. After this she would never see him again. She was surprised by how sad that thought made her.

They wandered down the twisting pathway, following after the guardian. Eventually they came to a halt. A red arch loomed in the mist and Suzume let go of Kaito's hand. It felt cold when he stepped away from her and crossed his arms over his chest.

"This is as far as I can take you; from here, you journey alone."

Suzume looked past the arch into a cave that was dark and bottomless. She was tempted to turn back around. But she had come this far, what was one more step? She went through the archway. There were no explosions or dangers lurking within. The tunnel was dark at first, but her eyes adjusted enough that she could navigate through it. It seemed to go on forever, dipping down, twisting and turning. Eventually it emptied out into a large chamber. Her footsteps echoed as she entered.

Light came from a hole in the ceiling and in the center of the room sat a pedestal wrapped in charms. Suzume took a step towards it and then waited. Part of her thought her impure intentions would set off some magical defense or that the actual artifact would be warded so no one could touch it. When nothing happened, she took a few more steps.

The pedestal held a single object, a ruby stone that glimmered in the single shaft of light. She hovered over it, staring down at the blood-red stone. It was nothing special, really. It was even hard to believe this had once been a human heart. It looked an ordinary stone.

Suzume's hand trembled as she reached out and closed her fingers around it, and then a bright light erupted from between her fingers. Suzume used her free hand to shield her eyes. She closed her eyes against the rush of air and light that was pelting her. When she opened them, she was no longer in the dark chamber but in a field of wildflowers. A woman stood nearby looking out across the mountain scape. She had ebony hair that fell to her waist.

She turned to look at Suzume. It was Kazue.

## 47

Suzume stood in mute shock. Kazue turned, but she did not seem to see Suzume. Kazue walked down the hill and past Suzume before Suzume realized what she was seeing was not the living Kazue but a vision of the past.

The field they stood in was strewn with crimson flowers, which swayed in the breeze on long leafless stalks. The bright petals curled inward and were surrounded by thin tendrils, which flickered like flames as Kazue swept through them. Pollen clung to Kazue's red pants and sprinkled them with golden dust. Kazue, attired as a priestess with her white tunic top and red pants, stopped to pick a flower and rolled the long stem between her fingers. She looked up at the sky, as if waiting for something.

Then Suzume heard a rumble like the crash of thunder. Kazue smiled at the sky and Suzume followed her gaze. Kaito, in his dragon form, weaved through the clouds, his serpentine body disappearing behind clouds and reappearing moments later. He twisted through the sky before tilting down towards the ground at an incredible speed. Kazue laughed.

"Enough drama, come down here. I have something exciting to tell you!" Kazue rested her hand against the flat of her stomach.

Kaito came down at a sharp angle towards Kazue. Had it been Suzume, she would have turned the other way and ran. Before he could collide with Kazue, though, he transformed in midair and hit the ground. He rolled head over heels then popped up in front of Kazue. He threw his hands up in the air with a flourish.

Kazue clapped. "Very nice," she said with a roll of her eyes, but she was smiling all the while.

"I will not stand you rolling your eyes at me, Priestess."

She shrieked in reply and ran away from him. He ran after her and caught her easily enough. He gathered Kazue up in his arms by her waist. He swung her around as she giggled. Just seeing them together made Suzume's stomach twist with jealousy. She knew it was the past, but it might as well have been the Kaito she knew flaunting his love for Suzume's past life in front of her. *Is Kazue trying to torture me? Why do I have to watch this sappy scene?* When they were done kissing, Kaito set Kazue down on her feet.

"Now will you let me tell you my news?" Kazue said, eyes dancing. Her hair was a tangled halo around her head and a few crushed red petals clung to the strands.

"In a moment," Kaito said as he plucked a petal from her hair. "I want to drink in your body a bit longer." He nuzzled her neck and kissed it. Suzume had to resist the urge to roll her eyes. *How much longer is this going to go on?*

Kazue pushed him away gently. "First let me tell you what I was going to say."

Kaito nodded, but there was a smirk playing at the corner of his lips. Suzume knew that look, he was going to try something any moment. Kazue continued onward, ignoring Kaito's mischievous smirk. "You know we've been talking about the future—what we will do once I die..."

Kaito's smile faded and he frowned instead. "Kazue, we've talked about this a hundred times. I cannot make you immortal." He took a step away from Kazue. His shoulders were tense and

Kazue's posture changed, she was tight and alert. *I get the feeling this is an old argument—they're both ready to fight.*

Kazue crossed her arms over her chest. For Suzume, it was like looking in the mirror. She herself had done that same thing hundreds of times, seeing Kazue do it was familiar, like déjà vu or a half-remembered song where the lyrics were lost but you still had the impression of the melody. *Maybe we are more alike than I thought.* Suzume took a moment to study Kazue. They did not look alike. Kazue's face was more round, with a bow-shaped mouth and petite nose. Her eyes were larger than Suzume's as well. *We don't look much alike. At least I am prettier,* Suzume thought with mild satisfaction.

"How can you stand to watch me wither away and die while you stay the same? Today I am young and beautiful, but what about ten years, twenty and thirty years from now? I will change and you will stay forever the same, unchanging... What then, will you love me when I am old and ugly?"

Kaito reached out to brush his hand against her cheek, but Kazue slapped his hand away and scowled at him.

Kaito was visibly angered. His brow creased and his mouth had white lines surrounding it. "Kazue, I love you, and I still will when you look like a pickled plum." He attempted a smile to coax her out of her sullen mood.

Kazue lowered her lashes. Her hand hovered over her stomach, but she did not rest it there. Instead she let her hands fall to her sides. "What about children? I always dreamed of becoming a mother."

He sighed. "It is forbidden, such a child could never live."

Tears gathered along Kazue's lashes. "Is that why you forced me to become a priestess? So you could have your way with me and never fear siring a child? I was married. I had a life prepared for me that I gave up for you, Kaito!"

He threw his hands up and Suzume involuntarily flinched, even though his anger was not directed at her. Kazue, however, held her ground. She looked at Kaito with a defiant lift of her chin. Once more echoing Suzume's own mannerisms.

Kaito huffed and then said, "Do you think I have not made sacrifices for you? I am laughed at by my equals and even my inferiors. They call me weak because a human woman has captured my heart. They say the great Dragon has been brought to his knees by a mortal! I risk losing my domain because I want to be with you." He tossed his hand in her direction.

"But if I were immortal..." she pleaded.

"No, Kazue." He spoke her name and thunderclouds rolled and shook the sky. She did not cower, which Suzume had to admit was admirable. She had been on the receiving end of Kaito's temper plenty of times. He sighed again. The clouds cleared away, revealing once more a bright day. He reached for Kazue again and this time she fell into his embrace. He buried his head in her hair as she clutched the fabric on his chest. "Can we not enjoy this time as we have it now? I do not want to think of a future without you, but if I must, I will find you in the next life and the next. We are meant for one another."

"You're right. I'm sorry, I will not mention it again," Kazue said. Suzume could see Kazue's expression. Suzmume had made that same face many times in her life. Kazue had made up her mind and she would not be dissuaded.


The field melted away and in its place, Suzume stood along the craggy surface of a mountain. The center of the mountain was cracked open like an egg and molten rock bubbled and hissed within. Someone walked along a narrow pathway between jagged rocks, a cloak pulled up over their head. Suzume knew her just from the way she walked, full of intent and power.

Suzume followed Kazue to her destination, which was a hut carved out of the volcanic rock. The door was painted bright red, and outside were scattered chunks of ore and metal. Kazue knocked on the door in a deliberate rhythm. The door swung open and revealed an old bent woman. The old woman lifted her head and revealed sockets devoid of eyes, with the lids sewn shut. Her long white hair dragged on the ground. Her large knobbly hands clutched at a hammer with an enormous iron head that was bigger than the old woman's head. She held it with ease.

"Who is it?" the old woman said. Her voice was reedy and high pitched.

"My name is Kazue. Please let me in, I was told you could help me."

The old woman sniffed noisily in Kazue's direction. "Very well, come in, Priestess." The old woman stepped aside to let Kazue in.

Suzume followed, slipping in just before the door closed. Inside, more bits of half-formed metal gathered in the corners of the room. Steam hung about the ceiling like a cloud, and at one end a large fireplace dominated a wall. Inside, Suzume could see red-hot coals burning and bubbling. *Is she using the volcano to make weapons?* Blacksmith tools were laid next to the bellows, an anvil, and metal forms where the swords were poured.

Kazue stood in the center of the room, looking out of place. The old woman moved some things around, shifting hunks of ore about. She would lift them up, sniff them, and either toss them back down or throw them into the flames of her forge.

"You've come looking for a weapon, I assume."

"Yes," Kazue said. Her breath exhaled and with it was all the tension she had been holding in.

"Well, you've come to the right place. What sort of weapon, perhaps a sword? Or a bow and arrow? I have an arrow that is sure to hit the mark every time."

Kazue shook her head. "No, I am looking for a weapon that can channel my spiritual energy."

The old woman, who had been hobbling around the room, stopped. "Are you now?" She turned her sightless face to Kazue once more and took a deep breath.

"You're a human, but you've the stink of dragon on you. What does a priestess want with such a weapon?"

"There is something I must do. I need the weapon to do that."

The old woman tutted. "It will not be easy to make."

"Name your price. Whatever it is, I am willing to give it."

"I want a dragon scale."

Kazue sucked in a breath.

"Your dragon doesn't know you're here, does he?" the old woman said. She grinned and revealed rows of sharpened teeth.

Kazue looked at her hands, which she balled into fists. "No, he would disapprove if he knew."

The old woman cackled. "Mortals, I will never understand you. Well, that's my price, dearie. Bring me the scale and we can conclude our business."

"I will bring it to you. I will return within the week for my weapon; have it ready."

The old woman cackled as the vision faded.


Now Kazue paced back and forth in the same meadow as before. The flowers had withered and left behind only long leaves, which brushed against the hem of Kazue's robe. In her hand Kazue held the staff. It glimmered with gold markings worked along the shaft and near the handle. Suzume reached for the staff, but in this dream world she was unarmed. *I wonder what the markings mean. Perhaps Kazue can tell me? If only I could reach her.*

Kazue stopped pacing and looked to the sky. There was no more joyful anticipation. The sky overhead was a bleak gray. The rumble of Kaito's approach rippled through the meadow and the leaves trembled. Kazue set down the staff among the leaves and went back to the crest of the hill to wait for Kaito.

This time when Kaito landed there was no playful greeting. He was angry. His blue eyes sparked and the clouds overhead grew thicker and stronger. Thunder rumbled above as Kaito marched over to Kazue.

"Kazue, what have you done?" Kaito said with a snarl. "Did you not think I would find out about the scale, about the iron woman's deal? The moment you left, she sent word to me. How could you betray me like this?"

"Kaito, listen, I can explain—"

"No!" he shouted. His voice shook the sky and the ground trembled beneath his feet. Lightning flashed across the gray sky.

"I was a fool to trust you. The others were right, humans and immortals were never meant to mix. I should have known you would use me from the start."

She reached for him, but he slapped her hand away. She recoiled and pressed her injured hand to her mouth.

"Kaito, I was going to tell you about the scale once I finished. I found a way to solve all our problems."

He shook his head. "That's what you do not understand. There is no us any longer. You cannot deceive me and expect forgiveness."

"Kaito—"

"Silence!"

She took a step back. Though she looked ready to cry, she did not. She closed her eyes, took a deep breath, and took a few steps back towards where the staff was concealed.

Kaito saw her and took a few steps to stop her. "Kazue, I do not want to hurt you, but if you raise that weapon to me—"

"I'm sorry, I did not want to have to do this, but you leave me no choice." Kazue's voice cracked.

Kazue picked up the staff and twirled it in front of her. It blurred into a circle of brown and gold. She sang a high and clear note. As she sang, lights burst to life in a circle at Kaito's feet. The leaves of the flowers had hidden it from him until then. He looked down at his feet and noticed too late the circle drawn into the earth. He looked up at Kazue, his expression fierce.

"Kazue, how could you?"

Tears streamed down her face, but she continued to sing. The sound was melancholy and so beautiful that it hurt Suzume to listen. She felt Kazue's emotions, her fear for her unborn child growing in her womb. Her love for the man she was trapping with her spell, and most of all her guilt.

The lights spun around Kaito, slowly at first but gradually gaining speed and closing in on him little by little. He pressed against them, but touching them burned him. He howled like a wounded animal and cursed Kazue's name as the circle enveloped him, and when the spinning stopped, all that remained was a small round stone. Kazue fell to her knees. Rain burst from the clouds overhead and soaked Kazue to the skin.

"I promise you. I will release you as soon as I am immortal. Then you will understand and we will be together again."

The image faded and Suzume stood back in the cave, the stone in her hand. She stared at it for a moment. *Now I see why Kaito was so angry when he woke up. I would be angry too.*

"Now that you have seen what I have done, are you willing to listen, Suzume?"

Suzume turned slowly, uncertain at first, but then she saw her standing there. Kazue, not as she had seen her in her visions, but a statue made of red stone. Suzume's mouth was dry, and speaking proved difficult for a moment. At last she managed to reply. "I don't suppose I have much of a choice, do I?'

The apparition that was Kazue smiled. "No, not really."

# 48

"So," Suzume said. She was not sure where to begin. "I guess you're me in a past life?"

Kazue smiled; it looked strange coming from someone that was a bright hue of red. Even her teeth were red; it was like looking through colored glass. "I suppose you want an explanation as to why I showed you what I did," Kazue said in response.

Suzume looked down at the stone in her hand. It was warm. The inside flickered like a flame. It seemed to throb in her hand, as if she were holding a tiny heart. *What I really want is to return to the life I had. I want to be revered and cared for, not tossed around and nearly killed at every turn.* For some reason, it was difficult to get those words out. She was face to face with Kazue, who was the real-life embodiment of Suzume's past life, and after seeing what Kazue had gone through just to spend eternity with Kaito, even if her methods were a bit strange, it made her own wants look selfish and petty.

"I know you want to return to your former life, but that stone will not do that for you," Kazue said, seemingly reading Suzume's mind.

Suzume looked up in shock. "How do you know that?" she

asked. *I should have known Hisato would lie to me. He just wanted me to retrieve this stone.*

"Because I am a part of you, Suzume. Or more accurately, you are a part of me," Kazue explained. She tilted her head as she regarded Suzume, her hands folded in front of her, resting on her stomach.

"Does that mean I can read your thoughts, or I can see your memories because I lived them in a past life?" Suzume stared at Kazue, trying to summon the memories of the past, just to prove she could. When nothing happened, she frowned.

Kazue chuckled. It was a delicate sound like the tinkling of bells. "No, you cannot summon the past, just as I cannot divine the future. We are two parts of one greater whole, but we are separate."

Suzume held up her hand. "Please spare me the poetry. I've had enough to last me a lifetime. What are you trying to say?"

"That you are not my reincarnation, but a broken piece of my soul is lodged inside yours."

"What?"

Kazue glided over to Suzume. Her footfalls made no sound. In fact, her feet did not even seem to touch the ground. Kazue placed her ruby hand over Suzume's chest. Suzume's heart raced. When Kazue touched her, she was not so much solid but more like vapor. She was warm like flames, but they did not burn Suzume.

"Inside you is a part of my soul, broken in my attempt to make myself immortal."

Suzume felt like a part of her was trying to break free; it was reaching for Kazue. She took a step back away from Suzume. The feeling lessened, but it remained. There was an ache in her that she had never felt before, like there was a hole inside her that needed to be filled.

Suzume put her hand over her beating heart. It felt just the same as always, a reliable rhythm that told her she was alive. "Are you saying I am you? Not just your reincarnation but you-you?"

"No." Kazue shook her head. "You are Suzume. But a piece of my soul resides in you, more specifically, the flame of my soul."

"So you're possessing me?"

Kazue laughed genuinely, and it bounced off the walls and surrounded them. Suzume just glowered at her, feeling more confused than ever.

"Perhaps it would be easier if I started at the beginning. As you saw in the vision, I wanted more than anything to be immortal so that I could spend an eternity with Kaito. He was content to live our lives as they were, but as you have seen, immortals do not live their lives as we do. They have eternity, and brief human lives are beyond their comprehension. Twenty years to us is but a summer to them. So I feared, in my own vanity, that Kaito would leave me once time ravaged me and left me old and twisted. I assumed he would just tire of me one day and I had resolved myself to my fate, until I conceived our child. As you can imagine, the immortals forbid the offspring of these unions; they are considered an abomination and oftentimes they are killed in the crib. I refused to let that same fate fall upon our child. And so I resumed my search for a way to gain immortality."

"And did you find it?" Suzume asked. She was curious. She had never thought about what it would be like to live forever. But the idea of never dying or aging had its appeal.

"I did. There is an old spell that could make a human immortal, but it took much power to do it. More than any mortal could hope to have on their own."

"So you tried to convince Kaito to help you?"

Kazue looked away as if she were looking through time and remembering the things she had seen and done. "I did. We argued about it many times, and each time he was adamant that I would not become an immortal. He was convinced he would stay with me no matter what." She sighed. It seemed strange for an apparition to do since she had no breath to breathe. *Maybe she does it out of habit.*

"Is that why you sealed him away?" Suzume asked.

Kazue turned to look at Suzume and her expression was pained. "In part, yes. I am ashamed to admit this, but I needed his power to perform the ceremony."

"And it wasn't enough." It was obvious because Kazue was dead, or at least Suzume thought her current state qualified as dead.

"No. Kaito was powerful, but he did not have the energy I needed. So I went in search of more power. I fought many immortals. I sealed them away and gathered power from them, but still it was not enough. When my pregnancy was well advanced, I stayed at a shrine, where I learned as much as I could about immortals until my son was born. Once he was born, I gave him to a priest to watch over him. My quest was not finished and I dared not risk his life during my fight. When I left, I also left the stone that had Kaito trapped inside. I felt his hate for me swirling inside it and I could not bear to keep it with me any longer. I swore to come back for both of them when the time was right.

"I traveled for many years and met many people, both mortal and immortal, and still the answer eluded me. Until finally I met one of the eight gods by chance. She was beautiful and dangerous. Our battle lasted for days. By this time I had fought and sealed hundreds of Yokai, my power had grown beyond imagining. I tricked her into a sealing circle and trapped her inside a stone, like I had done Kaito."

Kazue looked at her hands, turning them over. "Finally, finally, I had the power to do what I wanted. However, along the way I lost a part of my self. I forgot about my child and I forgot about Kaito, who I had sealed away. Drunk on power, all I could think about was getting more. I told myself that if I could defeat the rest of the Eight, then I would be prepared, then I would be ready to be immortal. So I went on a quest to seal them all. The Eight fell to me one by one. By then I did not just want to be immortal, I wanted to be a god."

Kazue looked up Suzume, and her eyes were haunted. Suzume could see images playing in Kazue's eyes, her opponents falling one by one. Kazue still remembered them all, Suzume could see that. "I was too greedy, and the gods would punish me for my avarice. I went to the top of this mountain, brought with me all the elements that represented the soul: fire, water, earth, air and the void. I mixed them together and—"

Kazue paused. Suzume could see it now, the images playing before her like in her earlier vision. There were on the mountaintop, in the courtyard where they had battled the guardian. The bleak and desolate wind howled as it pulled at Kazue's hair and clothes. Kazue knelt down; a circle had been drawn on the ground in white chalk. This place where Kazue performed the ceremony was a holy place, where the eight gods had gathered before Kazue had sealed them. How Suzume knew that, she was not certain, she just did.

Kazue arranged the eight stones in a circle around an inner circle of five stones each a different color: red, blue, green, gold, and black. Kazue lifted the staff above her head and sang the incantation. Her voice deeper than before, it resonated through Suzume as it echoed off the surrounding mountains. The ground shifted and shook. Kazue sang the final notes, which faded away into the mountains.

As the last notes escaped, Kazue fell to her knees and she cried out. Suzume felt it too. Her body was being ripped apart thread by thread. Everything burned, like fire, like ice, like she was a stone being ground to powder and then tossed out the window. The spell broke Kazue down to her most basic elements, fracturing her soul to the point of shattering.

Then one piece broke out from the rest. A lumped bulged in Kazue's stomach. She pressed her hands to it, groaning in pain. She rolled over onto her side as the mass grew. It pushed outward and a black blob burst from Kazue's stomach and plopped on the ground. It twitched and coalesced as it grew. Kazue watched in horror as the mass transformed and became a man. He uncurled like a butterfly. He spread out his long pale arms and then got to his feet. His naked body stood out against the gray sky overhead. Kazue knelt in front of him, panting and shaking.

"Hello, Mother," Hisato said.

Kazue looked up at him. "What are you?" she gasped.

He laughed. "I am your child, a piece of your soul born of the darkness within you."

"You are not my son!" she shouted. She had hardly the strength to kneel and she swayed back and forth.

Hisato stepped over to Kazue. He grabbed her chin and tilted her head back. "Oh yes, I am. Did you think that there would not be a price for immortality? I am that price. You blackened your heart to gain immortality. An immortal can have no darkness, they are not like humans, so you had to cast out the darkness in you, but the universe must maintain balance. I am that balance, Mother. I am the darkness in you. Human incarnate."

"No. This is not what I wanted. Go back! I did not want this!" Kazue panted. There was blood at the corner of her mouth as if she had been bleeding internally.

"It's too late. You are immortal now; it cannot be undone."

Weak and trembling, Kazue reached for her staff. Suzume despaired for Kazue. She had gone to such lengths to become immortal. Now when it was too late she learned the cost. She had lost the man she loved, her child, and now she had unleashed darkness unto the world.

"I may not be able to change what I have done, but I can stop you. I will seal you away. I will not unleash you on the world." She raised her staff and sang a song that was high pitched and desperate. Hisato looked about, his eyes wide, but the music rippled over him. He shrank down as he cried out. When Kazue's song ended, nothing remained but a black stone, which clanked as it fell to the ground. It fell into the center of the eight stones.

"I need to seal him," Kazue said. Suzume did not know who she was talking to until she saw the guardian approach. "I have ripped my soul apart; it is the only way to stop this evil from being unleashed upon the world."

She turned to the guardian, leaning heavily on her staff. "I leave you in charge of my protection. I am sorry, I promised to release you and your family, but this is for the greater good. She raised her staff and brought it down with a crash. The spheres rose up into the air and shot out in all directions in bright-colored streaks of light. All that remained was a round red stone. The guardian picked it up and looked to a cave nearby.

The vision cleared and Suzume stood once more in the cave with the apparition of Kazue. "I broke my soul to seal away my mistake. But someone has broken that seal. And the darkness of my soul has been unleashed. I believe whoever put my piece of soul in you has done so with others. You must retrieve the others and bring back the pieces of my soul together, only then can the darkness be destroyed for good."

Suzume trembled. It was almost too much to take in. "What am I supposed to do? I never wanted any of this. I'm not brave, I'm selfish, and honestly, I would rather be curled up in a ball when the fighting comes."

Kazue smiled. "I know, but he will not leave you be. He wants your portion of my soul, and he will do whatever it takes to get you. He needs you to complete his transformation."

"What transformation is that?" Suzume's mouth felt dry.

"He is the evil that was in my soul and now he wants to become a god. He is searching for the eight Kami that I hid when I sealed him. Once he has them and all the fragments of my soul, he will be able to transcend. He will be unstoppable."

Suzume chewed her lip. She did not want to be a hero. She kept trying to convince herself that she wanted the life she had before. But was that really the case after everything that had happened? She had fought Yokai, been under the spell of a spider, and lived more in a couple of weeks than she had in her entire life up until now. She had even passed up a chance to return to the palace when Daiki offered it. *What do I really want? Hisato wants my piece of Kazue's soul, which means I will be in danger no matter what.* It was something she had gotten used to. *I knew deep down he was no good. What if I could be a hero for once?*

"Fine. I'll stop him. Where do I go from here?"

"First you'll need to find the remaining pieces of my soul. Once you do that, you'll need the eight trapped gods."

"Great. Nothing too hard, then," Suzume said sarcastically.

"Well, they're all hidden. Even I do not know where they are."

Suzume resisted the urge to roll her eyes. Apparently Kazue did not understand sarcasm. "And they're probably warded and guarded by horrible beasts, huh?"

Kazue grinned. "Most definitely." *Okay, maybe she does get sarcasm.*

Suzume sighed. "I suppose I should get to work."

"I will help you as much as I can, but my power grows faint." Kazue's image flickered and disappeared. The stone was warm in Suzume's hand. The light continued to flicker as if Kazue watched her from inside. She turned to leave and continued the twisted trek out of the tunnels. At the top, the thick clouds blocked the entrance and everything was eerily quiet. She had expected the guardian and Kaito to be waiting for her, but there was no one there. *I don't like the looks of this.* The hairs on the back of Suzume's neck began to prickle.

*Something's wrong.* Kazue's voice spoke in Suzume's head. She was so surprised she nearly dropped the stone. "I didn't know you could talk in my head," Suzume said aloud.

*I forgot to mention that. Well, I can. There is something dangerous nearby; proceed with caution.*

"How do I get out of here? The guardian said this place is full of traps."

*I will guide you, just listen to my instructions.*

And so Kazue navigated Suzume through the maze in the

clouds. As they neared the end of the maze, the sound of fighting met her ears. Suzume hurried her pace and grabbed for her staff, which was strapped to her back.

When she broke through the cloud cover, she saw Kaito fighting off a dark humanoid creature without a face. The thing swung two blades in circles as it crept towards him. The guardian, Tsuki and Rin fought similar figures.

*This is the darkness' work. I can tell,* Kazue said.

Suzume only needed a signal to enter the fray.

"Why, Suzume, how nice of you to join the party," Hisato said as he reached around Suzume and grabbed a hold of her waist.

# 49

*Follow my lead*, Kazue whispered in Suzume's ear. Or at least that's how she imagined it since it was all in her head.

*Okay*, Suzume replied, though she was not certain Kazue could hear her thoughts.

*Hisato is a part of me, so he can anticipate your moves before you make them. You have to think outside your normal patterns. I want you to go along with whatever he says.*

*You make it sound so easy*, Suzume said, trying to infuse sarcasm into her mind's voice, but she was not certain the point came across.

"Did you get what you were searching for?" Hisato asked. He pulled her close, and she could feel all the planes of his muscles tensing as he tightened his grip. His breath, hot against her neck, sent ripples of goose bumps along her skin. He pressed his hand flat against her stomach. She tried to keep her muscles relaxed so as not to give away her discomfort.

"I did," she replied. Her voice shook somewhat. "I see you haven't been idle." Suzume's gaze swept across the courtyard. In total there were a dozen of the faceless figures. Empty sockets and smooth skin replaced what should have been their faces.

395

Rin had transformed into her fox form and she loomed above the creatures and swiped at them with a massive red paw. She knocked over three with one swipe and they burst apart into black clouds. Black sludge rained down and six more emerged from the pools of goop, this time with weapons in hand. They rushed Rin with spears. She bared her teeth at the creatures as they jabbed at her.

Shards of ice rained down from the gray clouds overhead, impaling several of the creatures. Suzume looked up to see Kaito in dragon form, flying overhead. But the impaled creatures only split into thirds, creating three new creatures, these ones with swords.

"No, I have not. Do you like my pets? I brought them for you," Hisato purred into Suzume's ear.

Suzume closed her eyes, just thinking that she had almost made a deal with this creep made her want to punch him. Her hand itched to reach for her staff, but Kazue's warning still rang through her head. That's what Hisato was expecting, he knew she would try to fight him, and if she did—she would lose.

Hisato spun Suzume around in his arms so they were standing face to face. He tilted her head back by grabbing her chin between his thumb and forefinger. She had wondered why when they touched he did not set off her defensive mechanisms, and now she knew it was because they came from the same source. At one point they had both been part of Kazue. Or at least the fragment of Kazue's soul attached to Suzume had.

"You're very kind, but I did not need you to kill them. I am planning on returning to the palace now. I should be going, actually…" She tried to unlock herself from his embrace, but he jerked her head back. Suzume gasped and bit down on an expletive. There were a few choice words she wanted to say, but she held them back.

"I'm not ready to let you go, Suzume. I told you before we are meant for one another—destined as you and the Dragon never could be."

A shiver of premonition rippled down her spine. "You knew the whole time. Why have me go into that cave if you knew..."

He smiled. "As I said, everything must maintain its balance. I cannot tell you a story that is not mine to tell. Just as I cannot force you to choose me."

"If you're not forcing me, then let me go." She wrenched her arm, but his grip only tightened. The fighting continued on around them, but it felt muted and distant, as all her attention was focused on Hisato.

"I cannot force you, but I can persuade." He leaned in close enough that his lips hovered over hers, but they did not touch. Her stomach tightened and she yanked her head back. Just the idea of kissing him made her feel like she would be kissing a sibling—never an enticing prospect.

"You're going to try to persuade me just like you tried to convince me to kill Kaito. Maybe the reason you cannot kill Kaito is because you are a part of Kazue and you love him too."

He threw his head back as he laughed. "No, I have no love for the Dragon. His power will help me grow, but I have no desire for male flesh. Yours, however..." He trailed a hand up her side and brushed against the side of her breast. It was the last straw. The power came with little effort; it was burning hot and fast. She imagined it in her hands, focusing on the palms. She placed her hands on Hisato's chest and forced the power into him.

He yelped and dropped Suzume. Two scorch marks in the shape of Suzume's hands were burned onto his chest. Suzume's chest burned as well. She touched her robe and the skin beneath was inflamed.

Hisato grinned. "Haven't you figured it out yet? We are of one flesh, Suzume. Anything that harms me will harm you."

*Would it have killed you to mention that detail?* Suzume thought to Kazue.

*I told you to play along with him,* Kazue replied. *I didn't think you would try to attack him.*

"But you attacked me back at the shrine, why weren't you hurt then?"

Hisato smiled in a disjointed way. "I never said it didn't hurt me."

"Just because we cannot harm one another does not mean I'm going to play along," Suzume said to Hisato.

"Would you change fate, Suzume? Would you give up your life for the Dragon's?"

"What are you talking about now?" Suzume said. She reached for the staff, she may not be able to attack, but it gave her some comfort.

*Just wait a moment longer,* Kazue said.

*I hope you have an idea because I'm running short of patience.*

Kazue did not answer.

Nearby Kaito growled as he was pulled to the ground by the strange black creatures. There were hundreds of them now. They pinned Kaito to the ground and one straddled his back and pulled on his whiskers. Rin lay still on the ground, her tails flopped over. The guardian and Tsuki fought back to back as more and more of the creatures circled around them.

"You see," Hisato said, "there is no use fighting. Join me, Suzume, and together we will rule. Apart we will fall. Our birth created an imbalance in the world, one that the Dragon will seek to correct. It is not you he wants but Kazue. If it means killing you to save her soul, he will not hesitate to do it. "

She knew he expected her to consider his offer, at least, but it was difficult to even pretend. A part of her wanted to agree with what he was saying. She knew Kaito loved Kazue, and once he learned she was not really Kazue but a fragment of her soul was attached to hers, his feelings would change. *Would he kill me, really?* She had been deceived by Hisato before. The others needed her help. Whatever their faults, they had fought alongside her and

398

come to her aid when she needed it. *I betrayed them once; I won't do it again. I have to save them.*

Before Suzume could be proud of her own growth, Hisato yanked on her arm and brought her over to Kaito. The black creatures had chained him to the ground. Whatever had bound him was searing his flesh, and the air smelled of burning skin and hair. Hisato forced Suzume onto her knees in front of Kaito.

"The time has come, Suzume. Prove to me how much you want to be free of him. Seal him away and use the power to return your life to the way it was."

She looked down at Kaito. Still in dragon form, he looked up at her with large blue eyes covered by bushy brows. He looked sad, damaged, betrayed. She could not look away. He had looked the same way when Kazue sealed him away, and it broke something inside her. *I can't do this. How much longer can I pretend?*

A few feet away the guardian roared for his son. Everything moved too fast. The creatures became a black undulating mass around her. Hisato faded away; all her attention focused on Kaito. Suzume reached for the staff, drew it, and pointed it at Kaito. She could feel Hisato's triumphant smile. She closed her eyes, took a deep breath, and then a song came to her from somewhere deep and primal. Perhaps it was Kazue that provided the words, Suzume could not be certain, but the power coursed through her veins, the dams broke and were shattered. She was living, breathing power. Energy rippled over her skin and lifted her hair off of her head.

She swung the staff in a circle, singing all the while. The sound of her voice echoed off the walls and surrounded them, wrapping together and making it sound as if there were a hundred of her singing the same song all at once. Kaito closed his eyes, prepared to have Suzume unleash the power upon him. Hisato laughed, gloating in his triumph, and then at the last moment Suzume turned towards Hisato. He stopped laughing and looked at

Suzume, his expression confused at first, then reality dawned on him.

*Now!* Kazue shouted inside Suzume's head. And the power burst from her in a torrent. She was emptied down to the last drop and she fell to her knees. Then standing in front of her was Kazue in the flesh. She looked powerful and beautiful. She took the staff from Suzume's fumbling hands.

Hisato looked amused, arms crossed over his chest and a smirk on his lips. Then Kazue attacked Hisato. To Suzume's and Hisato's surprise, the attacks did not affect Suzume. Though he was shocked at first, Hisato fought back once he realized the blows did not impact Suzume. He had a blade that was black as pitch and he swung it at Kazue as she thrust and dodged with the staff in hand.

Suzume watched it all in a haze as the glowing Kazue harried Hisato around the courtyard. The black creatures attacked her as well, but one swing of the staff sliced them in half and they disappeared into puffs of smoke.

When none were left but Hisato and Kazue, he put up his hands and said with a smile, "Well played, Mother. I shall cede the day to you, but I will return for my bride soon." With a wave of his hand, he opened a portal behind him and stepped through it. The rip in space closed, leaving behind gray sky as if he had never been there at all.

Kazue stood very still, staff lowered. Kaito rose to his feet. He walked at first and then ran to Kazue, who stood at the edge of the courtyard. While she had been fighting Hisato, she had been glowing and powerful, but even now she had begun to fade. Kaito grabbed onto her translucent shoulder and Kazue turned around to face him. He cupped her cheek and Suzume could see his fingers through Kazue's skin.

"You returned to me," Kaito said.

She turned her face into his hand. "I am sorry, my love. This was never how I intended this to happen."

"Shh. Don't speak like that."

She shook her head. She was nearly gone now, just a wisp of smoke. "This was all I had left, but I am glad I had this last chance to see your face." She reached up and kissed Kaito. Her lips brushed against his before she burst into sparkling red lights that faded and dimmed. It was the last thing Suzume saw before darkness crept over her and she lost consciousness.

# 50

Suzume hurt all over. She felt like an old rag that had been wrung out one too many times. Her eyes dragged open and she stared at the roof of an unfamiliar room. She tried to turn her head to look around, but it seemed to take too much energy. She closed her eyes again when she heard voices.

"What is wrong with her?" Kaito said. There was an edge to his voice that if she hadn't been so delusional with exhaustion, she would have thought it sounded like he was concerned for her.

Akira answered, "She unleashed Kazue's full power and it emptied her completely. It's going to take time for her to recover. I promise I will call you the moment she wakes."

He huffed. "Fine, I'm going out to look for Hisato again; I'll be back."

Suzume slipped under once more. She dreamed of the ocean. She had never seen it before, but it was clear in her mind. It was dark blue and green. It moved, rolling and rocking. Suzume floated along the surface, and her hair fanned out around her like seaweed drifting on the tide. The sky overhead was bright blue, and puffy white clouds floated lazily over her. *I could stay here forever, never worry, just float along.*

The waves pushed her along and she landed at the shore of an island. It was not much more than black rock. There was a small stone pathway that led upward and twisted around a jagged stone pyre. Before Suzume could take a few steps towards it, she woke in a dark room.

She was not sure how long she had been asleep, but judging from the white candles with wax burned down and pooling on the floor in puddles, it must be the middle of the night. She had just enough energy to roll her head to the side. She was surprised to see Rin kneeling down next to her cot. Suzume blinked a few times.

"What are you doing here?" Suzume's voice came out scratchy and thick. Her tongue felt too big for her mouth and her throat was dry.

Rin picked up a cup and offered it to Suzume. Suzume shook her head, though the liquid sounded divine, she did not even have the energy to hold a cup. Whatever Kazue had done, it had torn Suzume apart. *I wonder if I will ever be able to move again. Kazue?* Silence met her question. It would seem Kazue was gone.

"You need to drink," Rin said.

"I can't—" Suzume rasped.

Rin caught onto her meaning and dribbled the water into Suzume's mouth. It was the most refreshing thing she'd ever tasted. Suzume licked her cracked and dried lips. She closed her eyes, and the exhaustion attempted to pull her under into sweet oblivion once more.

Once Suzume had a few swallows, Rin set aside the cup and said, "For a moment, I thought you were going to try to seal him. I never thought you would come to his defense."

Suzume did not bother to open her eyes as she said in a halting raspy voice, "You are too kind."

Rin laughed. "That's not what I meant, I knew you were a decent person from the beginning, well, good enough for a human. I just thought history was going to repeat itself."

Suzume considered telling Rin that she had planned on doing just that. For a moment she had considered trying to seal Kaito to save him. If it hadn't been for Kazue's intervention, then Kaito would be back inside the stone.

"I wasn't sure myself," Suzume replied. She suddenly felt very tired again and it was more than physically tired. She was emotionally drained. So much had changed in such a short period of time. She felt like she did not even know herself anymore.

Rin stood up. "I'll let you rest."

Suzume did not bother responding. She slipped into the oblivion of sleep once more. She did not dream, or at least she did not remember her dreams upon her next waking.

The next time she opened her eyes, she woke with daylight coming through a window high in the wall. Some of her strength had started to return and she was able to sit up. Someone had left a bowl of soup. She picked it up and drank it down. The broth dribbled down her chin, and she wiped the liquid away with her sleeve. She was starving—she felt as if she had not eaten in days and perhaps she hadn't. She set down the empty bowl, and with shaking legs and leaning heavily on the wall, she left her room.

Outside the sliding door to her chamber, she was surprised to find a long hall, with flooring made of polished wood and several sliding doors on one side. The opposite side opened onto an ornamental garden complete with trimmed hedges and a koi pond. A maple tree stood to one end of the garden and red leaves drifted from it and landed on the surface of the water. She looked around and found more of the same. *Where am I?*

She took a few wobbling steps down the hall in search of the others. Using the wall for balance, she followed the sound of voices, which led her to a common area.

Akira and her father sat together, speaking in low tones. The room they occupied was big enough to host hundreds. Sliding doors surrounded it on all sides, but one had been left open, which faced the garden. From beyond the door, Suzume could see the mountain ranges. Suzume stood up straight as she cleared her throat.

They both looked up at her and Akira smiled. "Well, look who's awake."

Suzume inched into the room, and before she could collapse and make a fool of herself, she sat down hard on the ground. "I'm starving, is there anything to eat?" she said without preamble.

"I'm sure I can find something for you," Akira said. She stood up and left Suzume and the guardian alone.

Suzume watched Akira go, wishing she had not been left with someone she was pretty sure despised her.

She looked around the room, searching for a topic of conversation to cut through the tension. "Where is this place?" Suzume settled on a question at last.

"This has been my home for the past five hundred years."

She cast about the room. The floors were high-quality bamboo and the doors were well made, framed in wood, and well cared for. "It's a nice place."

"Even if you drape the prison in gold, a prison is still a prison," he said.

Suzume clamped her mouth shut and decided small talk was not necessary. Akira returned at just the right moment and brought with her a bowl of rice and several dishes with lids. She set them down in front of Suzume.

Suzume pulled the lids off the dishes, revealing blackened fish, dumplings and more soup. She dug in with gusto, hardly taking a moment to breathe between bites. She did not even ask where the food had come from. Were there servants here? She did not really care. She could not remember the last time she had been this hungry.

When she was finished, she stacked her dishes on the tray and looked to Akira. "Where is everyone?"

"Kaito has been gone for a couple of days, he's trying to find

Hisato, and Rin is out in the garden, I believe. She feels more comfortable outdoors."

Suzume nodded. She was relieved Kaito was away.

"We found Kazue's heart after you collapsed. I don't know if it will be of much use now," Akira said.

Suzume startled as she looked up at Akira. "What do you mean it won't be of much use?"

"It cracked in half." Akira removed the object from her pocket and tipped it into Suzume's hand.

Suzume stared at the jagged patterns in the red stone, which had dulled to a pale pink. The flickering light was gone and with it the power she had felt from it; Kazue was gone, for now. There still remained her shattered soul fragments that Suzume had to collect. She thought of Hisato's hand on the back of her neck, urging her to kill Kaito, and his threat to return for her. *How can I defeat someone who I cannot injure? But Kazue could attack him and I didn't get hurt. I wish I could ask her why.*

"We're not sure what to do now. We hoped my father would know what Kazue was after, but he was left in the dark. We've studied the staff, but it has yielded no answers."

Suzume closed her hand around the fragments of Kazue's heart. "There are things I need to tell you, but it might be best to wait until we are all together."

"Tell us what?" Rin said as she came in from outside, wearing a green robe with a pattern of maple leaves on it, and her auburn hair was tied up on the top of her head. *I guess now is as good a time as any. It will be easier telling them the truth without Kaito here. I don't want to face his wrath when he finds out I wanted to seal him.*

Suzume took a deep breath and then proceeded to tell the three of them the entire story. She left out the part about using the stone to return to the palace—they didn't really need to know that—but she did tell them about Hisato's offer and what she had learned from him. She told them about Kazue's revelation and her sacrifice to save Kaito, and when she finished, there was a deafening silence as the others contemplated her words.

"Does this mean you will not be able to free us?" Tsuki said with Akira's face.

Suzume held up her hand and twisted it over. "I don't think so, I don't feel any different than I did before. I think we'll have to gather all the pieces of Kazue's soul before we can do that."

The guardian sat with his arms folded over his chest. He had not said anything for a long time. Suzume kept glancing at him from time to time, expecting him to accuse her of lying or attack her because he thought she was Kazue.

"Father, what do you think we should do?" Akira said gently.

It was strange to think this man was her father, because he looked no more than five years older than Akira. But Suzume knew from the visions that he had served Kazue for a very long time.

"As I see it, I have no choice. I am bound to guard Kazue's heart, and while she possesses it, I am bound to her."

It wasn't quite a pledge of fealty, but it would have to do.

"Well, if you're going to join us on this hapless quest, maybe you could at least tell me your name. I can't call you the guardian forever."

He scowled at her, and she thought he was going to make her do just that when he said, "It's Naoki."

And thus their ragtag party gained another member.

---

It took time for Suzume to recover from her fight, and she spent much of her time sleeping or wandering the halls of the palace. Which she found rivaled the size of many a grand estate that she had visited. She wondered who had lived here before and why Kazue had chosen this place to seal her remains.

She discovered rooms full of strange objects, swords with

407

ancient inscriptions that she could not decipher, and carvings of people who did not look quite human. One sculpture had a man with antlers; another woman had a bird beak. She asked Rin and she told Suzume in a hushed tone that this had been the home of the Kami before Kazue sealed him away.

They had searched the place from top to bottom and had found no sign of the Kami. Kazue had hidden him somewhere and even Naoki did not remember. His time serving Kazue, as he put it, was like a hazy dream, and each day he forgot more of his time chained to Kazue's remains.

Kaito had been missing for days. No one seemed worried about him, so Suzume did not mention his absence to the others, but more than once she caught herself looking to the sky, awaiting his return. She both feared and anticipated their reunion. She had to tell him she was not Kazue's reincarnation but a piece of her soul lived inside her. She did not want to think about how that would change their dynamic. All the memories, the visions, and most likely even her powers came from that fragment.

One day while she was walking through the garden, she found Tsuki sitting in the crook of a cherry tree. It overlooked a pond that had been drained of water and now remained a barren crater. When he saw Suzume, he jumped down.

"Suzume, I've been looking for you."

"Oh?" She kept her distance, as of late Tsuki had been a little too friendly for her comfort.

"Yes, there's something I've been wanting to show you, will you come?" He held out his hand. She had no reason to say no, not really, and she was bored beyond belief.

She did not take his hand, but she did let him show her out of the garden and down a path that twisted and turned through rocks and at times was obscured by clouds. They emerged on a cliff that overlooked the valley. Mountains capped with snow burst from the clouds and the sky overhead was a brilliant blue.

"Hello!" Tsuki shouted and his voice echoed back at him. He turned to her with a grin.

"Did you bring me out here just to show me the echo?"

His smile widened. "Something like that."

She took a step back. "I don't know if you got the wrong impression, but I am not really interested in you as anything other than a friend."

He laughed and the sound of it surrounded them and made it feel like there were a hundred Tsukis standing with her on that cliff top. He reached out and grasped a strand of Suzume's hair between his fingers.

"Has it ever occurred to you that I might not be interested in you, but in doing what is best for you?"

She frowned. "Is that supposed to make me fall into your arms and your bed?"

"Not into my arms..." He grinned and leaned in close.

She clenched up, preparing to push him away if he tried to kiss her.

"I'm making the Dragon jealous so he'll return. He's been wandering around the mountain for days, and he won't come back." He planted a kiss on Suzume's cheek.

Then the sky filled with dark gray clouds, thunder rolled across the valley, and Suzume looked up to see the serpentine shape of the Dragon headed straight for them. Tsuki took a few steps back.

Suzume watched as Kaito came and landed on the cliff edge. His transformation from beast to man was seamless. She gasped when she saw him. His hair was down and falling over his shoulders. She remembered the first time they had met; she had thought him handsome then. *That was before he opened his mouth and I realized how obnoxious he is.*

"Tsuki!" Kaito growled.

"She's all yours, Great Dragon. Don't say I never did anything for you." He waved to them and scurried away before either of them could stop him.

Kaito watched him go, but eventually he turned to face Suzume. Her stomach clenched and she wished she could be anywhere but here. She had hoped she would not have to face him. But it was time she did; they had to clear the air at last.

She opened her mouth to say something, but Kaito interrupted her. "I have been flying around for days. At first I was looking for Hisato, and when it became apparent he cannot be found, I came back here. But I kept putting off landing."

She seemed to have lost the capability of speech. Her mouth felt incredibly dry all of a sudden. The tender moments they shared recently buzzed through her brain, but the one thought came to the forefront, *He thinks I am Kazue.*

Suzume opened and closed her mouth a few times like a fish out of water. She wanted to shout at him, hit, kick, punch, anything other than acknowledge what they were both dancing around.

"This is the part where you ask me what kept me away," he said. He took a step closer and she took a step back. "Suzume?" he said, but even if his mouth was saying her name, that was not what he meant.

*He thinks I am Kazue.* The words kept replaying in her mind. *That's the only reason he's saying these things. It's not me he loves, but the echo of the woman who once was. The piece of her soul that has invaded me.* She clutched her chest, wishing she could rip it out. "It's not me who you love," she blurted at last.

Kaito inhaled sharply, and his throat bobbed as he swallowed. "What are you talking about? No one said anything about..." He bit down on the word though she knew he was dying to say it. A small part of her wished he would. But that was the Suzume she had been. Before all of this happened, she would have delighted in his affection, no matter how disingenuous, but now she realized she wanted more. She wanted someone to love her for her, not her title or her power, just for who she was.

Suzume shook her head to rid herself of these melancholy thoughts. "Listen to me, you idiot. I'm not Kazue! So stop with the melodrama."

He frowned. "What are you talking about? I saw you, I saw you fight back Hisato for me."

Suzume's hands were balled into fists at her sides. *Why is this so difficult to get through his thick head?* "That wasn't me, that was Kazue. I'm not her reincarnation, she never really died. She was trying to become immortal so she could be with you, and instead she broke apart her soul and Hisato was born—or made, I suppose."

He took a step away from her. Confusion wrinkled his features. "She did it. She actually became immortal?" He looked around as if he expected to see Kazue standing there, waiting to throw herself into his arms.

And that was what hurt the most. Suzume felt as if he had jabbed a knife into her gut. He would never love Suzume, not really. A love like that was eternal. One way or another they would find each other. There was no place for Suzume in his heart. Once Suzume resurrected Kazue, Kaito and Kazue would be together again. *And what do I care? He's an arrogant jerk.* That same old argument rang hollow now.

"She's gone—or mostly. I have a fragment of her soul inside me, but the rest of it has been scattered. We have to find the pieces of her soul and resurrect her so she can stop Hisato from becoming a god."

Kaito swiveled his head back to Suzume as if he had just remembered she was there. "What do you mean before he becomes a god? You cannot become a god without having at least people to worship you. Even then, you would have to be an immortal with incredible power."

"That's what he's been doing this whole time, collecting power,

411

preparing to become a god. The eight gods were sealed by Kazue; there's no one that can stop him."

Kaito grinned. "Let me guess, except for you."

She answered his grin with a raised brow though she would have rather not looked into his eyes right then. She did not want him to realize how she really felt. Her stomach felt like it was tied in knots. "Yeah. I guess it's up to me to stop him."

"I'm assuming you'll need help, then?"

She scowled at him. "Why exactly would I need help? Don't you think I can do this on my own?"

He laughed a barking laugh. "Do you really think you could do something so important by yourself?"

She placed her hands on her hips. "Maybe I do."

"Well, you don't have a choice. Whether you want it or not, I'm coming with you."

She had to fight the smile that was threatening to bloom on her face. "Why? What about your revenge?"

His smile slipped. "Revenge won't change the past. No matter how much I want to hate her, I can't."

He may as well have twisted the knife in her gut. "I see."

"You may not be Kazue, but you're still my bride, Suzume. You were promised to me and I am not done with you yet."

A blush burned the back of her neck and crept over her cheeks. She knew it was a joke, but it hit a little too close to home in this instance. She crossed her arms and looked away from him, pretending to pout to hide her embarrassment. "I am not your bride. If anything, we are partners."

She could see his smile from the corner of her eye and it was difficult not to smile right along with him. A part of her had feared that they would be parting ways. She was relieved to realize they were not separating. *I can only imagine what danger awaits us. And most likely my life will be threatened, but as crazy as it sounds, I cannot wait for the journey to begin.*

# EXCERPT THE SEA STONE

A ball of fire zoomed through the air. When it collided with the torii arch, it burst apart in a shower of sparks. The paint on the arch bubbled and peeled, revealing scorched wood beneath.

Tsuki looked over his shoulder, raising an eyebrow as he whistled. "Well, at least you can make a ball of fire. But I think your aim needs some work." He plucked the paper target off the archway just to the left of the smoldering arch. "Do that again, and this time focus on the target."

Suzume huffed as her shoulders sagged, as if that breath was keeping her upright. "Again? But that took forever!" She couldn't keep the whine from her tone.

"With practice, it will come easier," Akira said using her brother's face, not bothering to shift into view. Since the siblings shared a body, they often took turns on who was visible. Whose face you saw correlated to what they were doing usually. Akira handled Suzume's spiritual training, Tsuki her combat training.

"How much practice exactly?" She put her hands on her hips. Just imagining another week or more of staring at her hands, willing flames to appear, made her want to throw herself on the ground and have a proper tantrum. When they first started her training, she thought mastering her powers would be easy, a couple days tops. It had been over a week and today was the first time she had managed to create a fireball. *Making fire is easy, leave me alone with Kaito for five minutes.* Focusing it and harnessing it to attack, that was the not so easy part.

"If you want we can practice with the staff instead." Tsuki grinned with a mischievous glint in his eye. She rubbed the bruise on her shoulder, one of a growing collection given to her by Tsuki during their sparring sessions. *He wants me to admit I'm tired, but I won't give him the satisfaction.*

Suzume glared at him while her arms twitched with the memory of exertion. Even propping them on her hips took a monumental effort. This body wasn't meant for this sort of abuse. It was accustomed to sitting around on cushions and writing poetry about nature while being admired from a far. Up until just recently, she had never even dressed herself. Now she was learning how to defend herself with a weapon, and how to stop fire from shooting out all over her body.

"Look who's here," Tsuki nodded his head in their newcomer's direction.

There was no point in turning to look, she knew by the sparks dancing along her arms who was joining them. As if keeping up the pretense in front of the conjoined siblings wasn't bad enough, Kaito the dragon, her greatest tormentor, strode into the court-yard. He inserted himself between Tsuki and Suzume, that infernal smirk upon his face.

"Training hard?" Kaito asked as his gazed skimmed over her to the rising tendrils of smoke coming off the burned torii arch, the only evidence of hours of practice. A weeks worth of practice, really.

"Yes, now leave, you're distracting," Suzume snapped at him at the same moment her arms gave up and fell like limp noodles at her side.

The hope was the dragon would leave her to gracefully weasel out of any more training today. She was not born lucky however.

"Suzume and I were just about to spar, care to watch?" Tsuki said to Kaito with a sly smile in her direction.

Suzume cursed him internally as she shot him a look that said 'you'll pay for this.'

He only grinned back at her with a look that said, 'you should admit when your beat.'

Two could play this game. "Tsuki was going to let me practice an emergency maneuver." Suzume fluttered her eyelashes in Tsuki's direction, while making a kicking motion in the direction of Tsuki's crotch. He reflexively covered his genitals with both hands

Akira's husky laughter spilled out of her brother's lips.

"Don't know why you insisted I teach her that," Tsuki mumbled.

Suzume laughed as Tsuki turned his lower body away from her. With narrowed eyes Kaito regarded the pair of them, a hint of ice in his stare. A touch of chill grasped at the back of her neck, eliciting sparks in reaction to his spiritual energy. Whenever Kaito got mad, Suzume was the first to feel it.

"I hope you're behaving." Kaito eyed Tsuki up and down. "I would hate to have to take over Suzume's training. It would really be a bother."

"You wouldn't teach me, you'd just throw me at the nearest yokai and expect me to figure it out," Suzume said.

"That method has worked in the past." Kaito smirked at her.

"If by 'worked' you mean it almost got me killed."

"Well, if you think Tsuki's method is more effective, prove it." Kaito gestured towards Tsuki before plopping down on the ground at the foot of a nearby torii arch. He leaned back and slung his arm over a bended knee. A casual observer would think he was disinterested as his gaze was not focused on her but skimming over the surrounding courtyard, but Suzume knew better. Nothing Kaito did was without motive.

Well there was no getting out of it now.

Tsuki's grin reached from ear to ear. Kaito might take the most pleasure from her discomfort but Tsuki was a close second. In a lot of ways he reminded her of one of her younger brothers, the ones who liked to leave creepy crawly things in her bed.

"Since you're tired, I'll take it easy on you," Tsuki said.

"I'm not tired, I could go for hours more." The lies just kept pouring out of her. *Would you stop already?*

Tsuki covered his mouth with his hand to disguise his smile. "I won't hold back then."

Suzume turned her head away from the others as she silently berated herself for not keeping her mouth shut. A single deep breath helped her regain her composure. But getting into position was harder than she anticipated. Just the mere effort of holding the staff up left her muscles trembling in protest.

Chin cupped in his hand, Tsuki looked her up and down. "Your arms are drooping, bring them up and closer to your chest."

With some difficulty, she did as Tsuki had instructed. But that made her muscles cramp. Pain rippled up her arms as her muscles clenched and spasmed. Suzume had to grit her teeth to keep from crying out. Shaking his head, Tsuki went behind Suzume. From there, he bent her elbows into the angle of his choosing. When she'd first started training with Tsuki being this close to him made her uncomfortable, but she was growing accustomed to it by now. Besides he was one of the few people who didn't bring out the fire in her.

His arms enveloped her, hands moving down her arms, his breath fanned against her skin as he said, "Do you see the dragon's scowl? He's so transparent."

Suzume refused to look in Kaito's direction, mostly because she feared if she stopped focusing on keeping her arms outright they'd betray her, but also because she could feel his displeasure. Her lungs burned from the pressure of his spiritual energy unfurled by his temper. Whenever he was angry the temperature dropped. If Tsuki kept this up she'd have icicles dangling from her nose. Many of her training sessions had been interrupted by the dragon under some pretense or another. But the end result was always him inserting himself between the two of them. Tsuki lingered a moment longer, his hands gliding to her hips pivoting her into the right stance.

"Can we get on with it," Suzume ground out.

Tsuki made one final adjustment to Suzume's legs, his hands sliding down to turn her foot. On stupid impulse, she chanced a glance in the dragon's direction. Kaito looked ready to burst from his skin. Tsuki had taken twice as long as normal to correct her positioning and she wasn't sure when the practice actually began she'd be able to perform. Tsuki took his place opposite her, his own staff in hand.

Even knowing what was coming she couldn't make her muscles obey. Her entire body felt as if she was trapped in mud, her legs and arms were glued in place. She could do nothing but watch helpless as Tsuki swung at her. The staff came towards her in slow motion. After an over-long delay, she thrust forward to block, and their staffs met with a clack. The force of his blow knocked her off balance and sent her skidding backwards. Tsuki gave her a second to recover before rushing towards her again. Her parry was too low, missing him and his staff entirely, and sent her forward and into Tsuki. He caught her, blocking her fall with his staff, their weapons slammed together and the impact jarred her arms forcing them to seize. Her muscles clenched and she couldn't prepare herself in time for the next swing, which sent her stumbling backwards. Suzume lost her balance, or her legs gave out, and she fell to the ground.

She landed on her rear and cursed aloud this time.

Tsuki wasn't even out of breath when he offered her a hand up, "Ready to admit you're tired?"

This was her chance to give up. All she had to do was admit she was tired, she was only human after all.

"If you can't keep up, maybe it's time to quit," Kaito said to her, but there was no mockery in his tone, which only made her angrier.

Kaito held out his hand to help her to her feet, but she knocked it aside, instead using her staff for leverage to hoist herself up. On her feet again she swayed for a moment as the world spun for a brief second.

Ignoring Kaito she said to Tsuki, "Let's go again."

"You can barely stand, let alone fight. You've done enough," Kaito said, this time irritation crept into his tone as he grabbed her bicep. Where his hand circled around her arms sparks erupted, clashing against the ice which encased his hand.

She shrugged off his grip, and a flurry of sparks danced between them as she turned her back on him. "I think I know my limits better than you," she spat. Then to Tsuki she said, "Let's go."

Tsuki watched their exchange with a frown across his brow. They squared off once more, and the results were not much different than the first time. But this time when she fell to the ground, Kaito practically flew through the air to help her up. Before he could try to help her however, she climbed onto shaking feet.

"I think you've done enough," Kaito said. He was really getting angry now.

Each breath was an uneven wheeze. The combination of Kaito's spiritual pressure and her own fatigue were wearing her down.

"Again," she rasped.

Tsuki looked to Kaito, his expression cautious. He had not resumed his position and his staff remained limp at his side.

"Are you sure?" Tsuki asked her.

"I... said... lets go!" she said between panting breaths. Suzume's form was sloppy, she couldn't hold the staff up all the way, and sweat rolled into her eyes and blurred her vision.

The dragon hovered nearby as Tsuki continued to hesitate,

and the two of them shared a look. Since Tsuki was wasting time, Suzume took the offensive and rushed towards Tsuki, her body fueled by her own stubborn will.

Tsuki blocked her half-hearted attacked with ease, knocking her backwards as easily as knocking down a blade of grass. For a moment she thought she was going to collapse until she found her balance once more and rushed towards Tsuki again. Though it was more of a half staggering and fumbled attack. Blinded by pride, and fueled by some reserve of adrenaline, Suzume attacked like a cornered animal. She swung at his head, his shoulder, his abdomen, anywhere she might land a blow was fine. Because her movements were so erratic and uncoordinated, Tsuki had to over-compensate, and accidentally struck her across the cheek with the end of his staff as he attempted to block. Flames erupted from where his blow landed, and she spun backwards as flickers of flame trailed behind her.

That was the final blow. Her knees buckled beneath her and Suzume crumpled to the ground. Kaito rushed over towards her where she lay on the ground with her eyes closed, feeling like a colossal fool. *You idiot, what were you hoping to prove?*

"You idiot," Kaito snarled.

Suzume's eyes flew open as she prepared a retort. Only she could call herself an that.

"Don't blame this one me," Tsuki snapped back. "When you're around, she's reckless."

"And you should stop her before she hurts herself."

"Are you really going to talk about me like I am not here?" Suzume interjected.

"You want her to learn, but you don't want her to get hurt. You can't have both." Tsuki crossed his arms over his chest.

"You said you knew how to teach her," Kaito growled.

"How can we teach her to harness her powers with you around? Your spiritual energy overwhelms hers," Akira said, coming to her brother's defense.

"Not to mention you're distracting her," Tsuki added.

"I am not distracted by him," Suzume shouted, trying to cut through the argument.

It worked a little too well because the pair of them swiveled to look at her, as if just remembering she was there. Tsuki, who had maintained control of the body he shared with his sister, had a sly smirk on his face as if this had been his plan all along. Kaito's lips were pulled back in a snarl.

"Then why didn't you stop?" ~~Kaito snapped at her~~.

With a huff, she crossed her arms over her chest. "Why are you even here? Don't you have better things to do?"

"I can't get to more important things until I can be sure you can defend yourself. You're a liability."

"I'm never going to learn if you keep distracting me."

"I thought you said I wasn't distracting you." A slow smirk spread across his face.

From beside Kaito, Tsuki chuckled. At least someone saw the humor in this. Suzume ignored him. Suzume had moved beyond pride and straight into anger.

"Fight me," she said. Drawing on some well of stupid pride, she puffed her chest out as she glared at him. This had to be the stupidest idea she'd ever had. Kaito had just watched Tsuki wipe the floor with her.

The dragon laughed, long and hard, enough where Suzume thought he might run out of air if he didn't stop soon. He wiped a tear from his eye. "You cannot be serious. Why would I do that?"

"You think you can teach me better than Tsuki, well prove it. But when I win you're forbidden from watching me practice."

He crossed his arms over his chest. "And if I win, you have to spend a night with me."

Suzume's stomach flopped. "What sort of request is that?" She stuttered and had to hide a blush that burned across her face.

"You'll find out when I win."

Want more? Get the Sea Stone here.

420

# ALSO BY NICOLETTE ANDREWS

## World of Akatsuki

**The Dragon Saga:**

The Priestess and the Dragon

The Sea Stone

The Song of the Wind

The Fractured Soul

The Immortal Vow

**Tales of Akatsuki**

Kitsune: A Little Mermaid Retelling

Yuki: A Snow White Retelling

Okami: A Little Red Ridinghood Retelling

## Diviner's World

Duchess

Diviner's Prophecy

Diviner's Curse

Diviner's Fate

Princess

## Thornwood Series

Heart of Thorns

Tangled in Thorns

Daughter of Thorns

Queen of Thorns

# ABOUT THE AUTHOR

Nicolette is a native San Diegan with a passion for the world of make believe. From a young age, Nicolette was telling stories whether it be writing plays for her friends to act out or making a series of children's books that her mother still likes drag out to embarrass her with in front of company. She still lives in her imagination but in reality she resides in San Diego with her husband, children and a couple cats. She loves reading, attempting arts and crafts, and cooking.

Manufactured by Amazon.ca
Bolton, ON